PROMETHEUS'S CHILD

Also by Harold Coyle

HAROLD COYLE'S STRATEGIC SOLUTIONS, INC.

PROMETHEUS'S CHILD

HAROLD COYLE
and
BARRETT TILLMAN

A Tom Doherty Associates Book
New York

This is a work of fiction. All of the characters, organizations, and events portrayed in this novel are either products of the author's imagination or are used fictitiously.

PROMETHEUS'S CHILD: HAROLD COYLE'S STRATEGIC SOLUTIONS, INC.

A Forge Book
Published by Tom Doherty Associates, LLC
175 Fifth Avenue
New York, NY 10010

www.tor-forge.com

Forge® is a registered trademark of Tom Doherty Associates, LLC.

Library of Congress Cataloging-in-Publication Data

Coyle, Harold, 1952–
    Prometheus's child : Harold Coyle's Strategic Solutions, Inc. / Harold Coyle
and Barrett Tillman. — 1st hardcover ed.
        p.   cm.
    "A Tom Doherty Associates book."
    ISBN-13: 978-0-7653-1372-0
    ISBN-10: 0-7653-1372-3
    1. Paramilitary, forces—Fiction.   2. Illegal arms transfers—Fiction.   3. Weapons
of mass destruction—Fiction.   4. Nuclear warfare—Prevention—Fiction.   I. Tillman,
Barrett.   II. Title.
    PS3553.O948P76   2007
    813'.54—dc22   2007018786

First Edition: October 2007

Printed in the United States of America

0 9 8 7 6 5 4 3 2 1

ACKNOWLEDGMENTS

Thanks to Marty Greenberg and John Helfers; Officer Bill Green; Peter Lindsay; John L. Tillman

PART I

ARLINGTON

MASSENYA, CHAD

"Bugger me, they're at it again!"

Gunfire erupted fifty meters away as Warrant Officer Derrick Martin wiped his hands on his "spotty dots" camouflage trousers and unslung his Steyr F88C assault rifle. Peering 'round the corner of the bullet-pocked market front, he was glad not for the first time that he had violated orders in carrying his personal weapon in the "blood box" armored ambulance. "Presence" was fine and good when all you wanted to do was impress the locals. It was downright stupid when those same people wanted to nail your hide to the wall like a plaster duck.

The American-made M113 "Bucket" continued burning a block and a half down the littered street, drawing a crowd of African celebrants. Few in the mob were armed, but some realized that the white soldiers who escaped from the light armored vehicle must be on foot. One Australian had not. His body was dragged away from the APC and some teenagers began stripping the corpse.

"They nailed Joji all right," Martin called to his wounded driver, two meters behind him.

Lance Corporal James Frasier looked up from his sitting position. "What about Dimitri?"

"Never bleeding got out, I reckon." Martin shook his head, pondering the geographic irony. What were the odds that a Fijian and a Russian would emigrate to Australia only to die in Chad?

It's Mogadishu all over, Martin thought. *Arsehole politicians keep sending Diggers as peacekeepers, then complain when we enforce the bloody peace.* He looked around, seeking a hiding spot. Besides his carbine, he was most grateful for the Wagtail radio that the wounded driver dragged in his left hand. The man's right hand was blistered and raw from detonation of the RPG, as was his right leg. Martin glanced down at his friend. "Jamie, how ya going?"

"I'm about buggered, Derro," Frasier croaked. He was hurt, winded, and scared. The fact that he addressed a superior by his nickname was an Aussie trait.

Martin ignored the response. "You got anybody yet?"

Frasier hefted the backpack radio. "Nothing yet. I've tried the allocated frequencies but this kit is only good for about eight kilometers. Only thing left is the high setting, but it'll use more juice."

"Well, give 'em a hoy. Every bleeding sot in this bleeding pesthole must know where we are by now."

As Frasier switched channels, Martin realized that the Australians had been seen. Several armed men motioned in their direction from up the street and began jogging toward the market. Martin looked around, confirming that he was out of the mob's line of sight. Sure enough, a woman waved a cloth from the second floor of a building behind him. She was saying something in Arabic, pointing to him and shouting to make herself heard.

Bloody bitch. Martin swung his Steyr to his shoulder, put the "death doughnut" aiming circle on the black woman's torso, and took up some of the slack in the single-stage trigger. She saw the 5.56 mm muzzle raising toward her and ducked inside, not knowing if the white man had intended to shoot.

Neither did Martin.

Frasier got his attention. "I can't get through, mate. It's jammed with calls. Apparently the army and a rebel faction are fighting all over the city."

Martin safed his F88, slung it again, and leaned down. He raised Frasier to standing and helped him limp down the dirty street, forcing his way through pedestrians with a wave of the Steyr. Along the way,

Martin's U.N. cap slid off his head but he was glad to be rid of the baby blue "target marker."

"In there!" Frasier called.

"What?"

Frasier did not reply. He just pointed inside an office with a sign "*Importons et Exportons*." Without asking why, Martin helped his friend through the door and shut it behind them.

Frasier reached for the telephone. "Please, Lord, let it work. I frigging *promise* I'll go see the damned God botherer on Sunday." He lifted the receiver and grinned through the smoke on his face. "I've got a dial tone! What number should I ring?"

"Hell's toes, I don't know. Try . . ."

A middle-aged Arab emerged from the rear of the office. He stopped dead in his tracks, assessed the uniformed strangers, and smiled. "Sir, I can help?" He spoke English with a French accent.

"Too bloody right, mate." Frasier extended the phone.

Martin responded more formally. "Yes, sir. We sure would appreciate any help. We need to contact our lot at the United Nations compound."

"Ah, *oui*." The dignified businessman bowed slightly, raising a hand to the tie he wore. He accepted the receiver from Frasier, dialed a number, and spoke alternately in French, Arabic, and English. Less than two minutes later he passed the phone back. "This is U.N., ah, house. Person talks not good English. Mostly French."

Bloody ethnics. Martin nodded his thanks. "Could you please tell him where we are? Ask if we can speak to anybody in the military advisory group." He tried to conjure the phrase: something like *Groupe advisory militaire*.

Mr. Haroun, as he introduced himself, was helpful and patient. Perhaps uncharitably, Martin was wondering what the businessman would expect in return for his assistance when a crowd of blacks rounded the corner half a block away. The composition was made for trouble: young, male, and angry.

Martin reached for Frasier and helped him toward the rear of the office. Mr. Haroun, apparently unflappable, remained standing at the desk, phone to his ear, awaiting more response from the functionary in N'Djamena.

Moments later the leading elements of the crowd reached the debris-littered street in front of the storefront. One of the young men leaned down and picked up an object. To Haroun it appeared as a colored rag. Apparently it meant something to the angry rioters.

Then he knew.

He slammed down the phone and paced to the rear of the store. Gesturing animatedly, he made shooing motions. "*Allez, allez!* You go! Now!"

Frasier looked up, confused. "What's he . . ."

"Oh, my God." It emerged as a low, fervent curse. Martin was peering around the hallway corner, fifteen meters to the front door. He turned back to his friend. "The bastards found my hat. We gotta be off like a bride's nightie."

Crashing glass and rising voices echoed through the building. The front rank of rioters reached the outer office, smashing furniture and fixtures. Martin turned his head. "Mr. Haroun, see to him, will you?"

"Derro! C'mon, mate!"

"Can't do it, Jamie. They'll catch us sure. You chuff off!"

With that, Martin turned back toward the hallway, already filling with men vocally intent on homicide. There were few firearms but several machetes. Martin looked over the top of his optical sight and began shooting.

SSI OFFICES
ARLINGTON, VIRGINIA

Peggy Springer buzzed the inner office.

"Mr. O'Connor is here, Admiral."

Michael Derringer punched the button on his console. "Thank you, Peggy. Please send him in."

The founder and CEO of Strategic Solutions, Incorporated, sat back and almost physically braced himself. Ryan O'Connor was not even on the third page of a single-spaced list of people the retired admiral wanted to see. It was not as if Derringer disliked the tweedy career bureaucrat; it was more that the ex-naval officer objected to the *concept* of most State Department dweebs.

Derringer knew the basics: Ryan O'Connor (Brown, class of '73; MA international relations) had joined State during the Carter administration and had climbed the GS ladder in pedestrian style. Considering that the earnest Bostonian had retained an Ivy League post-Vietnam view of America—aggressively imperialistic, hopelessly militaristic—Derringer occasionally marveled at O'Connor's advancement under three Republican administrations.

The door opened and Ryan Michael O'Connor entered in all his Foggy Bottomed glory: charcoal gray suit; power tie; $60 haircut; and $350 monogrammed attaché case.

Derringer pushed himself out of the padded chair and extended a hand. "Ryan, welcome back." He shook hands, remembering to grip extra hard, and was rewarded with the flicker of a grimace on O'Connor's face. "Please, sit down."

Beneath the cordial tone of his voice, Derringer cordially detested O'Connor's John Lennon glasses. It was a visceral reaction, not unlike the response the former naval officer had toward slouching, slack-jawed youths wearing ball caps backward. A sign of mindless conformity.

O'Connor took a seat and placed his black leather case on his knees. He did not bother to look around, as he knew the layout of the office, having dealt with SSI on occasion. The good admiral's walls were adorned with the sort of I-Love-Me esoterica common to retired military officers: lithographs depicting "glorious" historic events; signed photos bearing saccharine inscriptions from Very Important Republicans; and all manner of shield-shaped plaques denoting various assignments and commands. O'Connor almost sighed. *So little time, so many wars.*

He cleared his throat and began. "Admiral, as you know, I'm here on behalf of Undersecretary Quiller. He's expanding the role of Arms Control and International Security, and I'm his new deputy for human rights issues."

"How may we help you, Ryan?"

O'Connor bit his lip. He made a point of playing the Sir and Admiral game with the military types, and in turn they addressed him as if he were an adolescent nephew.

"Well . . . Mike . . . I know you're accustomed to working with DoD, but this time State has the ball. You've probably seen the coverage from Saharan Africa, especially Chad. Frankly, we're concerned about things getting even more out of control in the region, and the military doesn't have the resources or even the expertise to step in, as usual."

Derringer permitted himself a tight smile. "As usual." It wasn't entirely true, but he conceded that SSI and other private military contractors relied on DoD's perennial shortages.

O'Connor leaned forward, his vest bulging over the case on his lap. "You should treat this as close-hold for the present, but I can say that we are going to be a major player in that part of the world, both for diplomatic and humanitarian reasons."

"So the U.N.'s really pulling out."

The GS-14 sat back and blinked. Behind his rimless glasses, his wide-eyed gaze reminded Derringer of an astonished owl. "Well, I did not say that, Admiral. I certainly did not!"

Derringer shrugged. "Very well, then. Forget I mentioned it. But if we're getting more involved, obviously there's some sort of vacuum. With or without the blue berets, American interests are going to include PMCs." He raised a suggestive eyebrow. "Right?"

O'Connor retrieved the moment by nodding while looking down to unlock his attaché case. He withdrew a stapled document and placed it on the desk. "This is a summary of the situation as of last week, with predictions of near- and long-term requirements. Because SSI did such a fine job in Pakistan, Mr. Quiller wants to offer you first refusal on this training contract in Chad."

Derringer retrieved the paper, which had been left slightly beyond his reach, and idly thumbed through it. "Very well. I'll take a look and get back to you in a few days." He plopped the document on his desk pad and folded his hands. "Ryan, I know you're mainly concerned with human rights. What's your interest in Chad? I mean, it must have one of the worst reputations on the planet."

"Well . . . Mike . . . we're not so naïve as to think that we can convert the rest of the world to our kind of democracy merely by example. But neither can we affect events there without being involved. You know—directly engaged. When possible, State's position is to bring about change by helping from the inside rather than exerting force from the outside. As usual."

Gotcha, sonny. The tight little smile was back on Derringer's face. "You're certainly right there, Ryan. I can think of three examples right off the bat."

"Yes?"

"Germany, Italy, and Japan."

The elegant attaché case snapped closed. "Good day, Admiral."

"Good day, Mr. O'Connor."

SAHARA DESERT

If you wait long enough, you can see interesting things even in the most barren desert.

However, on the south side of the Chad–Libyan border, in the area known as the Aozou Strip, there is precious little to draw sightseers. The scenery is drab and the climate unattractive, often with a daytime low of ninety degrees Fahrenheit. Wildlife, though varied, is rare. Fortunate spotters might see antelope, gazelle, or ostrich.

The unfortunate might witness murder.

Early in the afternoon, amid swirling dust devils, a well-used Land Rover lurched to a stop in Chad's Borkou-Ennedi-Tibesti Prefecture. Three men and a woman stepped out; the men dragged two human forms from the rear, feet first. Each of the unfortunates was bound hand and foot and gagged. One had nearly suffocated during the long drive to the remote area.

The tallest of the three captors produced a stiletto and cut the straps securing each prisoner. Both raised themselves from the sand; one even bothered to dust himself off.

Both knew what was coming.

The driver leaned into the back of the vehicle and withdrew two shovels. He tossed them at the men's feet and merely said, "Dig."

The older of the doomed men folded his arms. "Why don't you just be done with it?"

"Because I don't dig."

"Well, then, *mon vieux*, we have something in common. Neither do I."

The leader of the captors resisted the urge to knife the insolent bastard where he stood. Instead, he rocked back on his heels and regarded the man. He had courage, and one had to admire courage wherever one found it.

Even in the Sahara. Maybe especially in the Sahara.

One of the captors picked up a shovel and swung it in an overhead arc, connecting with the defiant man's shoulders. The victim staggered, biting off a cry of pain, then sagged to one knee. "There are many uses for shovels," the assailant said evenly. He looked to his comrades for appreciation. Finding none, he raised the shovel again.

"Etienne!" The leader's bark stopped the offender in midswing.

The leader turned to the other victim, who stood trembling visibly. "You, dig for both of you."

The younger man looked to his partner, vainly seeking guidance. There was none—the older prisoner was still gasping for breath, rubbing his shoulder.

After an agonizingly long age—perhaps closer to an eon—the younger man found himself. "I won't dig, either." He spit into the dirt for emphasis, though his mouth was cotton-dry.

"Oh, I think you will." The leader turned to the senior prisoner and, with practiced ease, drew a 9 mm Makarov from his belt and fired into the kneeling man's cranium from four meters away. Eighty kilos of dead weight pitched face forward, twitched imperceptibly, and expired.

The executioner holstered and kicked the second shovel toward the survivor. No words were necessary.

I can see the hate and the fear in his eyes, the killer told himself. *It's always like this. At least one will always comply.*

The doomed survivor sucked in lungs full of arid Saharan air. He looked upward, saw cumulus clouds in the direction of the Atlas Mountains, and tried to control his bladder. Briefly, he thought of running. *But where?* Even if he escaped, he was literally in the middle of the desert.

With trembling hands, he picked up the shovel and began to dig.

"You see, Etienne? What did I tell you? Some men choose to die on their feet, but most will lick your boots for five more minutes of life."

It was longer than five minutes, for the spade man was neither strong nor eager to finish his task. But at length he reached a satisfactory depth. "Enough," the leader said. He drew the pistol again. "You wish to pray?" *They always do.*

The victim merely nodded, lowered his head, and cupped his hands. He mumbled the ancient words, dredged up from a far-off childhood.

The leader intended for the man to die before the prayer was over—as much a kindness as one could muster at such times. He motioned to the driver, who nodded compliance, raised his own pistol, and began to press the trigger.

"Let me." It was the woman.

The leader waved a hand. "My God, Gabrielle, you've seen men die before."

She leaned toward him, fists clenched before her. "But I've never *done* it, Marcel! Don't you understand? I want to know how it feels!"

Mentally he catalogued the progress of the situation. Her insistence on accompanying the killers; her pledge of silence on the drive, which had mostly been honored. Now, however, he recognized the signs: the little-girl petulance, complete with pouting lips.

With an eloquent shrug, the leader drew his Russian pistol and handed it to her. He was going to remind her about the safety but she was familiar with the weapon. She raised the pistol in both hands, flipped the lever, took two seconds to align the sights, and three more to press the double-action trigger.

The 9 mm round spat out, impacted the supplicant's left temple, and he collapsed into the hole he had dug.

She decocked the weapon and handed it back, butt first. The owner changed magazines and holstered it, faintly shaking his head.

"What?" she demanded.

He leveled his brown eyes at her baby blues. "Curiosity satisfied?"

"It's nothing." She shrugged as unconcernedly as possible and reached for a cigarette. She almost managed to suppress the tremor in her hand.

"Congratulations, my dear. Welcome to the club." He picked up both shovels and handed one to her. "Now you can help bury them."

———

Two hundred thirty meters away, partially concealed by a low-lying dune, two men watched the proceedings through precision optics. An observant bypasser would have pegged them in their thirties, though neither's face was visible. One had draped a sand-colored veil over his head to break up his outline and shield his Zeiss 8×25 binoculars. The other wore a white *kaffia* with a black diamond design while looking through a ten-power Hensoldt rifle scope.

Both had light-colored Saharan robes over French and Italian military fatigues, and both wore Israeli Army desert boots.

The observer carried a Romanian AKM with Egyptian ammunition. His partner had a British AWC sniper system with an integral suppressor on the barrel. It was loaded with match-grade 7.62×51 manufactured in America.

The mythical observer would have noted that both appeared accustomed to the desert.

When the executioners were finished with their chore, they climbed into their vintage Land Rover and drove off, leaving their handiwork buried in the lee of a dune. The distant witnesses watched them go, headed south across the Mourdi Depression toward Oasis Fada.

In their native tongue the two men discussed their options.

The sniper asked, "Should we check the bodies for papers?"

The leader thought for a moment. "No. No point. Any additional information probably isn't worth the risk of being seen. Besides, with the homer attached to the Land Rover we can track the Frenchmen wherever they go." He put his compact Zeiss in its case and consulted his map: Libya lay 165 kilometers to the north. "We'll walk back to the helicopter and have David call ahead for a jet. I want to be in N'Djamena before tomorrow morning."

SSI OFFICES

Frank Leopole was the last to arrive. He shut the door of the conference room and took the last vacant chair. The SSI brain trust seldom met in full session for other than monthly planning sessions, so the secure facility usually had room left over.

This time was different.

Seated at the head of the polished table, retired Rear Admiral Michael Derringer nodded to Lieutenant Colonel Leopole. The former Marine returned the gesture, taking in the audience. Besides Derringer and himself, Leopole counted five men and four women, including all the heavies. He saw that Derringer's personal secretary, Peggy Singer, was taking the minutes. That fact was not lost upon the head of SSI's operations division.

As chairman of the board, Derringer presided at the meeting. He glanced at his Rolex and saw the sweep hand tick through the twelve. The old radio call from his fleet days swam upward to surface in his consciousness: *Chocktaw, this is Jehovah. Stand by . . . execute!*

"Ladies and gentlemen, thank you for all being here on such short notice. The subject of this meeting is important enough to call a special session because we'll need a consensus to present to the board of directors next week."

Seated to Derringer's right was George Ferraro, SSI's vice president and chief financial officer. To Derringer's left was Marshall Wilmont, president and chief operating officer, looking haggard as ever. Leopole had no trouble reading the lay of the land: Wilmont occasionally attended planning meetings; Ferraro almost never. They were big-picture men, far more concerned with corporate policy and finances. In the argot of the trade they were bottom-line oriented.

Dominating the atmosphere in the room was the forbidding presence of Lieutenant General Thomas Jackson Varlowe, U.S. Army (Retired). Though retired nearly a decade, he still seemed to wear three stars on his starched collar. Leopole was barely acquainted with him but knew him as one of those generals who never quite adjusted to retirement—sometimes Varlowe even had to open doors for himself. However, he was astute and connected, and for those reasons Derringer had courted him as chairman of SSI's advisory board.

Leopole's reverie was broken as Derringer spoke again. "We have been approached by the State Department for a potentially lucrative contract. It involves training in Africa, which is why I've asked our training and foreign operations officers to attend." He inclined his head toward Leopole, who ran operations; former Lieutenant Colonel Sandra Carmichael of international operations; and Dr. Omar Mohammed, the Iranian-born director of training.

"The situation is this: over the past several months the government of Chad has received United Nations assistance with improving internal security against rebel factions that have caused widespread problems. As most of you know, the original U.N. mission there was peacekeeping, officially a neutral presence more intended to keep the warring factions apart than actually solving anything." Derringer allowed himself an ironic grin. No one in the room had the least difficulty interpreting his meaning. The United Nations was not one of Michael Derringer's favored causes.

"Well, over the past couple of weeks the peacekeepers took some hard knocks. Both the rebels and elements of the Chadian Army resented their presence, and there were several disputes leading to violence. Some peacekeepers were killed and others were surrounded and captured."

Ferraro, ever mindful of the cost-benefit ratio, asked the pending question. "Mike, are we thinking of getting involved in Chad?"

Derringer cleared his throat and nodded slightly. "I got a call from O'Connor at State. The secretary has authorized a PMC for a short-term contract to train a unit of the Chadian Army in counterinsurgency. We're the go-to company for projects that the State Department wants kept below the horizon. That especially applies to Chad."

"How's that?" Ferraro asked.

Derringer shifted in his seat, a sign of unusual nervousness. "Well, I did some checking. It turns out that a European watchdog group keeps track of corruption and human rights violations around the world. Chad and Ethiopia are tied for the dubious honor of the most corrupt government on earth."

Marshall Wilmont was visibly perplexed. "I don't understand something. Why would State, and presumably the entire U.S. Government, want to support Chad? Something doesn't fit."

"Well, you're right, Marsh. I haven't told the whole story yet." He paused for emphasis. Looking at each person in sequence, he said, "Everything said here, stays here. Is that absolutely clear?"

Heads bobbed to the accompanying litany, "Yes, sir."

"Very well. There's some high-level horse trading going on because the U.N. is anxious to save itself more embarrassment. The French have agreed to send a replacement peacekeeping force operating with the appearance of U.N. authority but in fact they'll answer to Paris, not New York. In exchange, our State Department will sign off on a PMC to conduct some of the training."

Ferraro began to interject. "Mike, I think . . ."

With a raised hand, Derringer interrupted him. "I know where you're going. Everybody just hold on until I've finished." He glanced down at his notes and continued. "You're wondering why France is interested in bailing out the U.N. Well, there's a couple of reasons. Chad is a former French possession and therefore is still regarded as within France's sphere of interest. There are also certain, ah, resources in the country that could prove valuable.

"Beyond that, Prime Minister LeBlanc is a Gaullist at heart. He and his cabinet want to increase French prestige, and by volunteering for an apparently humanitarian program, his government figures to score some points. My guess is, they plan to leverage the goodwill in Africa and the Third World generally. That's likely to translate to more influence, wider markets, and a counterbalance to other powers."

"Like us," Wilmont opined.

"Exactly," Derringer said.

Leopole raised a hand. "Admiral, if the French are going to replace the peacekeepers, why does the U.N. want an American firm involved?"

"Actually, the U.N. doesn't. At least that's what O'Connor said, and he's a big U.N. booster. But in exchange for American support on the Security Council, the administration requires a PMC to be involved. That's where the horse trading comes in. State wants an American presence in Chad, especially during the transition period while the French are taking over."

The former Marine nodded his crew-cut head. "Gotcha." He shrugged. "Well, I don't see any reason we can't do it." He looked at Omar Mohammed. "If it's going to be a training mission, how long will we plan for?"

"Well, let's not get ahead of ourselves. Certainly our operations and training departments will have to coordinate SSI activities, but the main reason I called this meeting is brainstorming. Before we start planning for Chad, I need to hear arguments pro and con. What do each of you want the board to consider?" He nodded at Leopole again.

"Yes, sir. As far as operations are concerned, we shouldn't have much problem. A training cadre would be fairly small, and we don't have any heavy commitments other than the Peruvian contract. I'll need to huddle with Matt Finch but finding enough personnel won't be much trouble, depending on specifics."

Derringer looked at Mohammed. "Omar? Any thoughts on training?"

"Yes, just a couple." Mohammed rubbed his manicured goatee, gathering his thoughts. Though he spoke almost unaccented English, he used such moments to give the impression he was considering his words. "The biggest consideration will be linguistic. Chad has two official languages: Arabic and French, and finding enough instructors competent in either may be difficult. It's possible to work through translators, but that is inefficient. And it limits the bonding between teachers and students."

"Okay, that makes sense," Derringer replied. "Anything else?"

"Yes, this matter of counterinsurgency. Certainly we can provide qualified instructors, but let us be frank. I suspect that the Chadian Army does not have anything resembling an elite unit. From what I know of the situation, the Army and police answer only to the president, who buys their loyalty with favors and by looking the other way when they abuse the population."

Derringer sat back in his chair, drumming his fingers on the table. "That's undoubtedly an accurate statement. But since State is pushing the program and offered it to us, I think we should consider it."

"Well, sir, I am merely saying that, assuming we take the contract, we need to say exactly what we can deliver. We cannot turn an armed mob into a competent counterguerrilla force in a few months." He turned a manicured hand palm upward. "If we are going to do a decent job, we may be there for a year or more."

Derringer gave an ironic smile. "I think that's what the secretary has in mind."

Mohammed's dark eyes widened in comprehension. "Ah, I see. The French connection, so to speak."

Derringer turned toward Sandra Carmichael. "Sandy, overseas operations are your department. Do you have anything beyond Frank's general ops comments?"

The honey blond retiree had scribbled a few notes during the discussion. "No, sir. As Frank and Omar said, the main concern is signing up the right people. I can think of two or three good men offhand. For the others, we'll have to dig around."

"Very well. Regina, most of our training contracts are pretty low budget. Any reason to think this would be any different?"

Regina Wells, Leopole's operations assistant, kept her professional hand on the department's financial pulse. "No, sir. It should be a cost-effective job. Especially if it lasts more than a year. I'm assuming we'd pass along the bonus fees to the client?"

Derringer raised an eyebrow and cocked his head toward Ferraro, the chief financial officer. "George?"

"Well, naturally I'd consult with Ms. Pilong, but SSI policy has always been to add long-term and hardship bonuses to the base fee. The only exceptions have been projects where we wanted to break into a particular market. Besides, I'd think that State would be glad to cover the extra fees. Otherwise we wouldn't have been offered the job."

In turn, Derringer swiveled his chair and looked at Corin Pilong, SSI's legal director. She was deceptively demure: a five-foot-three Filipina with a baby-doll face and a Harvard law degree.

She leaned forward on both elbows, a sure sign that an argument was coming. "Admiral, I am not concerned with contractual matters just now. Everything we have heard so far appears proper and aboveboard. But I must say, I am not in favor of this contract."

No surprise there, Derringer told himself. He knew Corin Pilong as a donor to humanitarian causes who sometimes considered herself a rare bird in a nest of knuckle-dragging trigger men. "Please elaborate," he said.

"We have already noted Chad's terrible human rights record. That bothers me. I would not want to be smeared by association with so corrupt a regime. Beyond that, what guarantees do we have that our training will not be turned against the civilians of Chad?"

Derringer shrugged. "No foolproof guarantees, of course. But if our training is limited to counterinsurgency . . ." He looked to Mohammed.

"Quite right," the training officer interjected. "The techniques we would provide are not very applicable to police or civil concerns." He looked across the table at Pilong. "Frankly, nobody needs any training to beat up political opponents or blackmail people into compliance. From what I've heard, the Chadians already have plenty of experience in those areas."

"Well, maybe so," Pilong responded. "I'll take your word for that, Doctor. But I'm also an advocate for this company. What about our reputation? Hasn't it occurred to anybody that the government wants a PMC to do its dirty work so the military doesn't get the blame?"

Derringer nodded vigorously. "That is exactly the reason I called this meeting. It's also why I invoked extreme secrecy at this point. I'd be remiss if I didn't consider all aspects, the potential benefits against the risks. So I think that Corin is asking the right questions—the same questions that our board will raise."

After a moment the CEO shoved back from the table. "Very well. I'll have your comments summarized for distribution at the board meeting. Thank you, everyone."

In the hall, Leopole and Carmichael stopped at the water fountain. "What d'you think?" he asked.

She winked. "It's a go, Frank. I understand Corin's viewpoint, but I'd bet next month's retirement check that the board will approve."

He nodded. "Concur. I could practically hear Ferraro's gears crunching the numbers. This is a low-cost, high-return project."

"There's just one thing," Carmichael said. "Through that whole meeting, General Varlowe didn't utter one syllable. Isn't that odd? I mean, he's head of the advisory board. The admiral didn't even ask him what he thought."

"Yeah, I know. That means they both want to take the contract."

5

SSI OFFICES

"The meeting will come to order."

Derringer convened the board of directors the morning after his meeting with SSI's department heads. Mrs. Springer noted the attendees and double-checked each item on the agenda. Thomas Varlowe represented the advisory board, though he was entered in the minutes as Lieutenant General Varlowe.

Strategic Solutions, Incorporated, was structured like many PMCs. The directors all had personal interest in the firm's success, and in fact most of them had been selected with finances in mind. Several were contributors to the start-up process; most were astute businessmen; all were connected militarily and/or politically. All were approximately patriotic; most fell somewhere between jaundiced and cynical. None would be described as naïve.

As president and senior vice president, Marsh Wilmont and George Ferraro already were familiar with the topic at hand. Derringer already had their support and had obtained the proxy of another director, retired Colonel Samuel A. Small, formerly of Air Force Systems Command.

"Let the record show that we have a quorum. Colonel Small is in Europe but he faxed me his proxy. Dr. Craven is attending a conference in Hawaii and could not be reached in time."

Derringer continued. "Gentlemen—and ladies—we will dispense with old business until a pressing matter is addressed. In fact, I would hope for a fast decision on an opportunity that has come our way. I refer you to the first information sheet in your meeting folders.

"As you see, the State Department has offered us first refusal on a training contract in Chad. The briefing paper describes the background to the situation: the U.N. peacekeeping force is being withdrawn after prolonged conflict among the government and warring factions. The French will send a sizable contingent independent of the U.N., which probably means a more effective presence in the country. Our role will be training selected units of the Chadian Army in counterinsurgency warfare."

He looked around the room. "Any comments or questions?"

Harrison E. Rowell was a retired brigadier general with excellent connections on the Hill. It was hardly surprising, considering his lengthy service in the Army's congressional affairs office. "Mike, the paper doesn't mention the duration of the contract, though the monthly fee looks good enough. How long are we talking here?"

"It's more or less open-ended, Harry. We didn't try to estimate the length of the project because State still doesn't have a handle on that. My guess is that it'll be at least as long as the French need to stabilize things. Several months, anyway. Likely over a year."

"Can we sustain enough instructors in a place like that, more or less indefinitely?"

Derringer nodded. "I discussed the salient details with operations and training yesterday. Frank and Omar believe we can recruit enough people with the military and language skills necessary. Matt Finch and his personnel office are already at work. They're coordinating with our DoD liaison officer as well."

Reuben J. Frisch, a Ph.D. in international relations, was a notable pragmatist in a crowd of pragmatists. "Admiral, I admit that this looks good on paper—low investment, potentially a nice yield. So I have to wonder: what's the down side? Other than the obvious, that is."

"I understand your concern, Doctor. That's one of the reasons I convened a premature department head meeting yesterday. Marsh and George and I thought that we needed to hear the views of the people who'll get their hands dirty over there. Colonel Leopole in operations and Dr. Mohammed in training, with some of their subordinates, all agree that we can provide the service requested. If necessary, we can ro- tate training teams in and out of the country so nobody has to stay for too long at a time."

Frisch nodded his balding head and adjusted his glasses. "But there are other aspects . . ."

"Yes, there are. Frankly, one or two of our senior people expressed doubt about being seen as supporting a corrupt, even brutal govern- ment. It's important enough to bring to a vote, which is why I bumped it to the top of today's agenda. But I'd point out that we're acting on behalf of the U.S. Government, and we can truthfully say that we're working with military forces, not the national police."

"Excuse me, gentlemen. I'd like to clarify something." Major Gen- eral Richard D. Jonas had made his reputation in the Air Force's elec- tronic warfare community. His post-retirement fortune had been made in defense electronics. "I admit that I don't know much about Chad or the situation there. Just how bad is it? For instance, would our training team likely be in danger?"

Derringer swiveled his chair toward Thomas Varlowe. "The head of our advisory committee is well informed on that situation."

Varlowe had the facts at the tips of his manicured fingers. "As far as the current situation, the U.N. peacekeeping force is pretty typical: a hodgepodge with a few troops from several countries with at least as many observers as active 'peacekeepers.'" With his fingers he etched quote marks around "peacekeepers."

"There's troops from Argentina, Australia, Bangladesh, Egypt, France, Ghana, Greece, Italy, Kenya, Nigeria, Pakistan, Poland, and Rus- sia. I'm told that some of those like Argentina, Greece, Italy, and Poland only have a few observers just to run up the numbers for PR purposes. The ones doing most of the patrolling and getting shot at are Muslims and other Africans: Egyptians, Kenyans, Nigerians, and Pakistanis. How- ever, Italy's and Poland's contingents have taken casualties and they're already pulling out." He shrugged. "And you heard about the Aus- tralians. They had a light armored outfit shot up pretty badly the other day.

"Now, the other player is the African Union, which draws on a lot of the same sources as the U.N. for peacekeepers. It's not terribly effec- tive, and probably will withdraw before the French move in. Conse- quently, there's a growing power vacuum. Some areas are more secure than others, and some are under control of various rebel factions.

"Dick, to answer your question more specifically: our teams should operate in fairly secure areas. After all, they can't do much training if they're being shot at very often."

"General Varlowe, does that mean the advisory committee recommends approving the contract?" Beverly Ann Shumard, who knew her way around a boardroom, also knew the value of consensus building. She had learned that as a four-term congresswoman from Pennsylvania.

Varlowe glanced at Derringer, who nodded. "Yes, ma'am," the general replied. "Of the members I polled, it was six to two."

"What were the objections, if I may ask?"

"One member was queasy about working with the Chad Government. The other was worried about the military situation, but that was before the U.N. announced its pullout in favor of the French."

Beverly Shumard immediately went on point. "Uh, when did you ask the board members, General? I mean, we only just learned of the situation this morning."

"Last week. We . . ."

"Beverly, that was my doing," Derringer interjected. "We got a heads-up from our liaison at State. I thought it advisable to start contingency planning in case the contract materialized, but I didn't expect it this soon."

Shumard leaned back, tapping her polished nails on the table. "All right." The tone of her voice was flat, noncommittal.

Rowell sensed a growing tension in the room and decided to deflate it. "If I may, I'd like to address a couple of other matters. First, what's the down side to this contract? I don't mean risk to our people, but potential harm to SSI."

Derringer was about to speak when Wilmont intervened. "That's a legitimate concern, Harry. We've already assessed the corporate prospects, and as you'll note in the briefing paper, we believe that the risk is minimal while the downstream benefits could be substantial. Worst case: something goes wrong while our team's over there and we're implicated in some wrongdoing by the Chad regime. Frankly, and I don't want this repeated, that would be worse than having some of our men killed. The State Department could fall over itself backpedaling away from having issued us the contract. Consequently, we might have trouble getting more work in Africa."

"But we're not doing much there right now," Derringer interjected. "That's one of the reasons for taking this job. Not only does it open the door for other work in the region, but it actually enhances our reputation at the same time. If we have to spin the contract to Congress or the public, we can always hang it on the antiterrorism hook. It wouldn't be hard to justify our work as fighting local terrorists, some of whom certainly have radical Islamic contacts."

"Okay," Rowell said. "Second question. What plans are there for extracting our people if things go south?"

"As a matter of course, we always have two contingencies for getting SSI personnel out of a trouble spot." Wilmont was warming to his subject, glad to have something substantive to discuss for a change. "The first is usually priority airline scheduling. With minimal notice, our teams can get aboard most government transportation, and that's especially so in this case because we're working for the State Department. The backup plan is having our own assets standing by elsewhere in the region. We don't have details yet but I'd guess in Egypt; possibly Niger. That's expensive, but it's always part of our planning." He looked around the room, making eye contact with each person. "We have never yet left anyone behind."

Sensing that the board was swinging his way, Derringer risked a question. "Very well. I think we're about finished. Any other points of discussion?" He looked at Shumard. "Beverly?"

Dr. Shumard bit her lip—she rarely wore lipstick—obviously unconvinced. "Well, I don't . . . no! There is one thing." Her hazel eyes locked on to Derringer's. "I'd like to see the contract written so we can withdraw over matters of ethics. I mean, if some of the troops we're training are involved in abusing people, we should pull out, with no penalty to us."

Derringer spread his hands, palms up. "I see no problem with that. But we'd have to specify who makes the decision. Presumably it would be this board, but realize that State will have a voice in the matter. After all, we're working for them. Do we need a vote on Beverly's motion? Any objections?"

No one spoke; clearly most were disinterested.

"Excuse me," Varlowe said.

"Yes, General."

"I don't want to seem cynical, but I think you should consider something. Let's face it: the U.S. Government is unlikely to invoke sanctions against a black nation because of the domestic political fallout." He paused for a moment, emphasizing his point. "Assuming that some of our clients get out of line, how is State going to adopt an ethical standard in Chad that it ignores in Zimbabwe or Sudan or Angola or several other places? They're also among the most corrupt on earth but they still receive millions in foreign aid, and who knows where the money really goes?"

Shumard was an intuitive counterpuncher, and she replied in kind. "General, no one has ever accused me of being naïve, but let's face facts. If we withheld aid from every corrupt government in Africa or anywhere else, we'd just about isolate ourselves from the human race."

Varlowe conceded the point with a graceful dip of his head. "Indeed we would, ma'am. Indeed we would." The tone in his voice said, *Not a bad idea, toots.* "I'm only suggesting that the board considers the problems inherent in a double standard before concluding this contract."

"Very well," Derringer said. "Mrs. Singer, please note Dr. Shumard's concern. We'll revisit the subject in our next meeting, before concluding the contract."

Hardly missing a beat, Derringer picked up the agenda. "Now, under old business, we have the proposal to expand our electronic warfare support program . . ."

WESTERN SAHARA

"This is the place." The Chadian guide waved a bony hand as if revealing a marvel.

The three "tourists"—two French, one Belgian—took in the Saharan vista. They were vastly unimpressed.

Felix Moungar sought to improve his guests' opinion of the region. "We have had two surveys conducted by geologists," the official explained. As a deputy of the Ministry of Mining, Energy, and Petroleum, he was well placed to know such things.

"You say the surveys were both positive?" The inquiry came from the obvious leader of the trio, a swarthy, heavyset native of Nice. He had a perennial two-day beard, partly in concession to a scar running along his left cheek. It was a souvenir of his time in *La Legion Étrangère*.

Moungar nodded eagerly, flashing his white smile. "*Oui, monsieur.* The last was only two months ago. This remains a worthwhile site."

The visitors took in the gaping pit, many meters deep and perhaps two-thirds of a kilometer wide. Some abandoned excavating machinery lay about, giving the facility a forlorn, idle appearance.

The Frenchman regarded his guide. "If this mine is still useful, why isn't it in operation?"

Deputy Minister Moungar raised his narrow shoulders in elegant resignation. "Alas, my friend. There is practically a glut on the world market. But the consortium's, ah, partners are willing to fund a small start-up because of the secrecy this place provides."

The explanation only drew a grunt from the former Legionnaire. No more response was necessary: he already knew the identities of the parties, including the silent partners beyond the borders of Chad and France. What they did with the product was no concern of his. He and his colleagues were merely interested in the lucrative contract they stood to conclude for protecting the short-term operation and ensuring the product's safe shipment.

He glanced at the nearest of his friends. "Etienne, what do you think?"

The tall Belgian glanced around. "Good approaches, no surprises. I suggest using only the main road in and out—better control of access and egress. And random patrols, of course."

"Of course." The older man winked at his friend. A covert smile passed between them. He turned to the third visitor. "Paul?"

The youngest of the trio idly toed the sand, musing again that he was far from the green hills of Gascony. "I'll take a closer look, but from here I see no reason it shouldn't work out. We should not stay too long, though."

"I was told there would be another security firm in the area."

Sideways glances flicked among the three Europeans. Only an unusually perceptive observer would have caught the import.

"We heard the same thing," said the older man.

Moungar felt the ephemeral awkwardness, then recovered. "Gentlemen, I shall drive you into the pit for your closer examination. But I agree with Monsieur Laroque. We should avoid prolonged exposure inside the pit—with all that uranium ore."

7

Colonel David Main turned left off Vass Road onto the two-forked Shaw Road and crossed Little River southbound. A bit farther on he came to Manchester, turned left and proceeded to the Cyclone gate. The sign said "Range 14."

It looked much like the rest of Fort Bragg: a pine forest redolent with moist soil after a rain. Main always enjoyed North Carolina: the scenery was pleasant, the aroma refreshing, and the sounds familiar.

Especially the sounds.

The sonic-metallic clatter came to him. *Blink-blink-blink*-bang-*blink*. A combination of Bang and Clink when the bullet hit the target. *Pulled the fourth one*, Main thought. *Good cadence, though.*

Somebody was shooting falling plates with a pistol. A delightful way to spend an afternoon, for those who cared about such things.

For an ephemeral moment, the pain returned to Main's consciousness. Almost six years had passed since Cindy's death. The frustration had been awful, the knowledge that he could do nothing to help her. Nobody could. The tumor that pressed against her brain had been untreatable, and all he could do was hold his son and daughter tight while Mommy died by inches.

Shooting helped. Someday he thought he might write an article about "ballistic therapy." On those occasions when he could get away, he crammed a stack of loaded magazines in his range bag and went to the local club to shoot plates with his custom Kimber .45. It was more fun than the issue Beretta: single-actions were preferable to double-actions with their heavier triggers.

It was odd: with his electronic timer Main noticed that in the two months before Cindy died, he consistently bested his times on five plates at ten yards. He knew the reason, of course: he was venting his anger and grief through the muzzle. In the three to five seconds when he was slaying dragons in the form of eight-inch steel plates, he was completely free of care. Just sight picture, sight alignment, and trigger control. *Pop-pop-pop-pop-pop.* Five up and five down. *I always shoot a little better when I'm pissed.*

Then the grief had eased and he was never so fast again.

Main parked the loaned Hummer and stepped out, feeling conspicuous in his dress greens. He could barely put into words how he loathed the black beret, the floppy legacy of a service politician's effort to declare the entire Army "elite." Some soldiers called it "the pet beret" because it actually required grooming to fit properly. *What an absurd concept: if everybody's "elite" then obviously nobody is elite.* The Ranger tab below his left shoulder testified to David Main's elite status.

"Hey, junior! You lost or somethin'?"

Main could not imagine who would possibly wear enough rank to address an O-6 as "junior," but then the voice carried its own answer. Turning toward the raspy baritone, Main saw a toothy grin approaching in ground-eating strides. The colonel smiled in spite of himself.

"Sergeant Major Alford, I believe." Main extended a hand.

"*Retired* sergeant major," replied the irreverent erstwhile noncom. "And damn glad of it, I'm here to tell you."

"How you doing, Red?"

"Just fine, Colonel. Just fine." Alford made a point of touching the silver eagle on Main's epaulette. "Nice to see they finally recognized a good man for a change. 'Bout time, too. Hell, it took me nearly four years to make a decent soldier out of you."

Main shook his head, trying to suppress a smile. He had long since lost track of the times that his onetime top sergeant had provided subtle advice or an emotional kick in the pants to Lieutenant—later Captain—Main. "Red, can we talk somewhere?"

"Sure, let's take a walk." Alford called over his shoulder. "Tyler! Stay with Sergeant Drago. You can shoot the Beretta until I get back."

As more pistol shots clattered on tempered steel, Main regarded his longtime friend. "You still keeping your shootin' eye?"

Alford ruefully shook his head. "Naw, not really. But I want my grandson to get a leg up on shooting and moving. He's gonna be Airborne all the way. Doesn't even want to attend college."

"How old is he?"

"Fourteen goin' on twenty-nine, if you know what I mean. I've talked to his mother a few times. She's dead set against him being a soldier like his dad and me, but she's smart enough to know she can't refuse him. So she goes along with me. This war on terror—it's gonna outlast us, isn't it?"

Main looked down at his mud-spattered shoes. "Yup."

Alford nodded. "Well, there you go. The boy's gonna be in it, and I want him to have the basics dialed in before he ever hits Basic." The former NCO eyed his friend. "How're your kids, Dave?"

"Jenny's doing pretty well. Smart as a whip, pretty as her mother. Starts college next year, can you believe that?"

"And the boy?"

"Oh, he's coming along. He's big on sports, especially basketball, but I sort of worry, you know? He doesn't seem to have much focus other than athletics. That's why I'm thinking of putting in my papers."

"What would you do?"

Main stopped pacing and turned to Alford. "You recall the PMC that I mentioned a while back?"

Alford stuffed his hands in his field jacket and nodded. "Strategic something?"

"Solutions. Strategic Solutions in Arlington. I've been liaison with them for a while, as well as some other contractors. It's a good outfit with top-notch leadership. Admiral Derringer says I can start work for him at noon tomorrow if I want."

"Doing what?"

"More of the same—for good money and damn little travel. It's just about perfect, especially with Brian still in school."

"Well, sir, how can I help?"

"Red, this is close hold for now. That's why I called to say I was coming in person." He allowed himself to smile. "Besides, it's good to get out of D.C."

"Hoo-ah that, sir."

"Strategic Solutions is likely to have a job with the State Department in Chad."

Alford rocked back on his heels as if struck on the jaw. "Oh . . . my . . . God!"

Main chuckled aloud. "All right, you see where I'm headed with this. It's a training mission: weapons, tactics, and counterinsurgency."

"And Third Special Forces Group just happens to have the African part of the world! No wonder you came down to Bragg. You're a damn headhunter, Colonel!"

Main shrugged. "If you want to hunt ducks, you gotta go where the ducks are. I remember somebody telling me that quite some time ago. Sergeant."

Alford looked around, as if concerned somebody might hear him. "Dave, if the green beanies knew why you're here, they'd ban you for life. Cripes a'mighty! You're looking for gold-plated people who speak Arabic and—what?—French?"

"*Oui, mon sergeant.*"

"You got *any* idea how tight the Army is about folks like that? I mean, holy shit! Somebody who can explain how to field strip a weapon in freakin' *Arabic?*"

"Which is exactly why I'm asking for some leads, Red. Oh, yeah, while I'm here I'll talk to Third Group's S-1, and a request is going through channels but that'll take weeks. Besides, they're not going to tell me everything they know, and I can't blame them. Meanwhile, the clock's running. But *you*, Sergeant Major Alford, you know who's who and, more important, who's getting out or thinking of getting out." Main raised his eyebrows suggestively.

Alford folded his arms and chewed his lip. "What's in it for me?"

Main was taken aback. He had never known Charles Ambrose Alford to barter with a friend. "Well, I don't know, Red. I'm not authorized to offer a bounty . . . or anything."

"How about a referral fee?"

"What's the difference?"

"Damned if I know," Alford replied. "How's a grand per head sound?"

Main opened his mouth, but nothing came out.

"Gotcha!" Alford swung a roundhouse right that connected with Main's left arm, knocking him off balance.

"You bastard." Main made a show of rubbing his bicep.

Alford led his former CO back to the firing line. "Hey, you oughta get up here more often. We've got a real nice club with matches most weekends." He grinned his toothy smile again. "We can shoot for beers. Hell, I'll even spot you, oh, three seconds per stage."

"I thought you said you don't shoot much anymore."

Alford grinned again. "I lied."

SSI OFFICES

The staff meeting included Frank Leopole as head of operations, Omar Mohammed as director of training, and Jack Peters as director of recruiting.

As DO, Leopole chaired the meeting, which was focused on selecting the Chad team. "Okay, people, listen up. Language skill is crucial to this contract: French and Arabic. We still don't have enough folks who are fluent in Arabic but we're recruiting some well-qualified guys from under SpecOps' noses. Fort Bragg and Hurlbert Field will scream bloody murder but hey, it's a dog-eat-dog business world, you know?"

With no response to the rhetorical question, Leopold proceeded. "All right, I think we all know the obvious choices. Let's start with J. J. Johnson. Jack, have you talked to him?"

"Yesterday morning. I reached him at his home town in Idaho. He saw the advantages but he's not real enthused about going to Chad."

Leopole smirked. "Who is? What'd he say about the bonus?"

"Said he'd think about it. If I don't hear back by Thursday I'll call again . . ."

"Yes?" Leopole sensed that Peters was not finished.

"Well, I really don't think that Johnson is going to be swayed by money. He's just not wired that way. I mean, nobody joins the Foreign Legion for the pay! Right now I think it's a matter of how well he's recovered from—"

Leopold interrupted. "Oh, I think he's recovered. I'm just not sure he'll want to go. Even before the Pakistan op he was talking about settling down, getting a real job, and finding Miss Right."

"Well, I guess I can understand it," Peters responded. "I mean, a hitch in the Foreign Legion and then the way the Pakistani terrorists whipped the skin off him." Peters shook his head. "Poor bastard was practically flayed."

"But you know what he did, don't you?" Leopold responded. "He killed a guard, captured another and took him with him, and won a shoot-out with three others. J. J. may seem a quiet, pleasant young man, but I've learned something. You gotta watch out for the quiet ones."

Mohammed interjected in his cultured French accent. "Mr. Peters is right. Men such as J. J. are not motivated by pay, but consider this: he joined the Legion as a young man in search of adventure and a chance to prove himself. He has done that, and more. Now, at age thirty or so, he wants to start building something for himself. I know for a fact that he would like to start a family." He shrugged eloquently. "Perhaps we should send someone to talk to him in person."

Peters accepted the training director's assessment. He knew Dr. Mohammed as a perceptive student of the human animal; astute enough to work as a psychologist if he wished. "All right, we'll do that. And I can sweeten the pot a bit by offering him a supervisory position. With his language ability and military background, he would have instant credibility with our clients."

Leopole interjected, "Okay, J. J.'s a possible. What about Dave Main's raid on Fort Bragg?"

Peters's brown eyes twinkled. "Well, as you can imagine, he wasn't exactly greeted with open arms. But he dropped a few nickels in the right slots and got some return. We have three prospects: Special Forces guys with French and/or Arabic ability. I'll know more in a couple of days."

"When are they available?" Sandy Carmichael was thinking ahead of the game, mentally juggling the increasingly tight schedule with known and possible assets.

"One just got out and sounds like a sure thing. The others have put their papers in. We may have the admiral pull some strings to expedite their release."

"I was hoping that Dave would turn up more than three." Carmichael had a lot of confidence in her West Point classmate but she was secretly disappointed that he had not called before his trip to North Carolina. Leopole was looking at her with his head cocked. She tried hard not to blush. *Frank knows, damn it.* Not quite an office romance, but the next thing to it.

Peters and Mohammed also noticed Sandra Carmichael's cheeks turn pink. Both inferred the correct meaning.

"Well, it's still a bit early," Peters offered. "Colonel Main has one or two other leads to follow."

Leopole glanced at his briefing list. "All right, then. We still need at least three other trainers. I'd like to have SF people because they make their money training the locals. But if we have to dip into our usual bag, I think we can count on Boscombe and Brezyinski."

Sandy Carmichael rolled her baby blues. Omar Mohammed permitted himself a smile through his goatee. "Bosco and Breezy. Good boys."

Peters was only vaguely acquainted with the former paratrooper and Ranger. "Something I should know?"

Leopole, who had worked with both more than once, chuckled aloud. "Some people consider them the Laurel and Hardy of SSI. But they're good, they're reliable, and they're available."

Sandy said, "I know they don't speak Arabic, but does either of them speak French?"

"Hell, they hardly speak English!" The former Marine rapped his knuckles in appreciation at his own humor.

Mohammed waved a placating hand. "What is important is their knowledge. They can demonstrate anything the Chadians need to know. With translators, they can manage just fine. Besides, if there's a problem, there is no one I would rather have along."

Leopole flipped a check mark on his paper.

"Okay. What about Martha?"

Carmichael sat back in her padded chair, trying to conjure a reason to decline the suggestion.

Martha Whitney: smart, sassy, and articulate. She read people well—a product of the Detroit streets. Because Carmichael and Whitney were influential women within SSI, many staffers assumed they were close. It was a reasonable conclusion: both were single mothers—Carmichael with two daughters, Whitney with college-age sons—who had been successful in a previously all-male environment.

Carmichael could not think of a valid reason for voicing opposition, other than the fact that she cordially disliked Martha Whitney. That made Carmichael a member of a big club. "Well, I suppose we can consider her."

Leopole spread his hands. "What's to consider, Sandy? My God, she's smart, she's capable, she's qualified. And she's black!"

"Yeah, I know," she said resignedly. "That would be an advantage in Chad."

"Well then?" Leopole allowed the question to dangle in midair.

"Well, for one thing she's a staffer without much field experience. I mean, she's very good at what she does but . . ."

"That sounds a lot like *you*," Leopole interjected. He gave Carmichael his patented gotcha grin. "Besides, she has field experience from the Agency. She just hasn't got her hands dirty in a few years."

"I'm just saying that in a heavily Muslim country a woman isn't going to be accepted as an authority figure."

"She doesn't have to be in authority, Sandy." Leopole was tiring of the sparring. He thought that he knew what lay behind Carmichael's aversion to Whitney. The forty-one-year-old Detroit native had proven her worth in CIA covert ops before joining SSI, where her Agency contacts were valuable. Lieutenant Colonel Carmichael envied Whitney's record as an agent—something Carmichael herself relished, but she knew that she would draw too much attention in the field. Her prom-queen good looks were a detriment in most situations.

Sensing his advantage, Leopole pressed ahead. "There's something else to consider. *Parlez-vous français?*"

"You know I don't." Carmichael was semifluent in Italian.

"Well, one of her grandparents was Haitian. She passed the government fluency test in French. Eighty-three percent, I think."

Peters, who had not run SSI recruiting until recently, was barely acquainted with Whitney. "How much of that sassy mouth of hers is legit and how much is insecurity?"

Leopole shrugged. "Damifiknow. But I tell you what: I've seen her at work. When things get reeeal tense, she's pretty damn cool. Jabbers like a blue jay when the smoke clears, but Martha can hack the program.

"There's another advantage, and for obvious reasons I wouldn't want it repeated. I mean, she's an overweight black woman who's not very attractive. Nobody's going to look at her and think she's a threat."

Carmichael shot Leopole a feminine dart. *I am Woman, hear me roar.* "That's pretty shallow, isn't it, Frank?"

"Tactical, babe. Tactical."

Omar Mohammed, who had grown to like Frank Leopole despite their initial coolness, decided to intervene on the former Marine's side. "As long as we are committed to Chad, a black woman would be advantageous. She could be especially helpful in surveillance."

Leopole nodded his crew-cut head. "Absolutely."

Peters merely said, "Concur."

Carmichael threw up her hands, literally and figuratively. "Okay." She tended to twitch her nose at such moments. Leopole wondered what it was about Sandys—he had never known one who wasn't downright cute.

Nobody had ever said that about Martha Whitney.

9

"Alex, they are moving again." The younger member of the surveillance team spoke into his lightweight headset. As the limousine pulled away from the Hotel D'Afrique, he let it go halfway down the block before he kicked his Vespa scooter into gear. He trailed it at a discreet distance, using some of the capital's traffic to screen his presence.

His earpiece crackled as the carrier wave was activated. "Maintain contact," the senior partner said.

The limo departed the hotel in the west side of town and took the street parallel to the Chari River, passing the U.S. Aid office just off Gouverneur Felix Eboue. It passed the federal buildings, town hall, and police headquarters along Rue du Colonel Moll, the avenue commemorating a notable French officer who died in 1908, fighting tribesmen near Djirbel.

The scooter tailed the limousine through a dogleg right through the Place de l'Etoile on General de Gaulle. From there it was nearly a straight run up Commandant Curlu, passing the National Assembly on the left en route to the airport on the north side of the capital.

Approaching the passenger terminal, the limo's brake lights came on. The Vespa driver checked his tail, swerved to the corner just ahead of an ancient Citroën, and stopped beside a taxi stand. He gave the attendant a ten-dollar bill worth about five thousand Chad francs and promised another if the Vespa was still there in an hour or so.

The chauffeur and passengers emerged from the limousine: four men and a woman whom the surveillance operative confirmed as his marks. He turned away from them as they struggled with their luggage, speaking discreetly into his handset. "Subjects arrived at departure. Proceeding normally."

"Continue observation" was the terse reply.

With the aid of the chauffeur, two passengers and a couple of porters, the luggage was taken to the Air France counter. Following check-in the three travelers exchanged farewells with their hosts, the older man and the woman, apparently his wife. She was fortyish, well coiffed, and gave each traveler a continental kiss: left cheek, right cheek, left.

The Vespa driver noticed that during the parting the older man spoke with one of the travelers with earnest brevity. A heartfelt hug and they parted. The older man and woman returned to the limousine.

The limo had diplomatic plates. Anybody with knowledge of the numbers would have identified it as belonging to the French embassy.

While the surveillance operative walked toward his scooter he made one more transmission. "Subjects departed for Paris."

As he reached in his pocket to pay the attendant, he was approached from behind. Strong, silent men grasped each arm, took him a few steps to the curb, and shoved him into a waiting van. The door slid shut as the Volkswagen drove away.

Leopole asked, "Jack, have you heard back from Main?"

Jack Peters felt a bit defensive; he had ceded some of his responsibility to Sandra Carmichael, head of foreign ops. "Not yet—it's only been a couple of days. But I told him that we need small-arms and tactics instructors qualified in French and Arabic. The most likely prospects are Special Forces guys since one of their missions is training local people." He almost said "indigenous personnel" but thought better of it. SSI was not big on Pentagonese.

Leopole twirled the pencil between his fingers. "Well, these days the French part shouldn't cause much fuss. But Arabic speakers are golden. We might have to call in some markers to get a couple of those guys." He looked back at Mohammed. "Unless . . ."

Seated across the room, Omar Mohammed read his colleague's mind. "Oh, no you don't. *Non. Laa.*" He waved a deprecatory hand.

Leopole got the drift, though he spoke neither French nor Arabic. However, Omar Mohammed spoke them fluently, and five other languages besides. Now he was nearing completion of a course in Indonesian.

"Hey, you did just fine in Pakistan on the Pandora Project," Leopole insisted.

Mohammed almost winced at the memory. "Only because I was the default for Pashto and Urdu." He shook his head. "Nope, no way, Jose." The latter phrase, incongruously crafted in Dr. Mohammed's cultivated tones, drew immediate grins and chuckles around the table. With his dignified manner and elegant Vandyke beard, Mohammed appeared the last person in Arlington, Virginia, who would employ colloquialisms.

Leopole spoke to Peters again. "Jack, I take it that our standby files don't have anybody with the language and technical skills just now."

"The people we have on file are qualified either in French or Arabic, or they're gun guys. Not both, other than J. J. But I'll see if Dave can get his personnel contacts to move faster."

Mohammed had a thought: "Where is Alex Cohen? After all, he speaks fluent Arabic."

Leopole and Carmichael exchanged glances. Without waiting for Leopole, she replied, "Ah, he's traveling. Besides, I don't think an Israeli-American would be too popular in a Muslim—"

"Sorry I'm late, everybody!"

Martha Whitney burst into the room. It was odd, Carmichael thought, how Martha inevitably "burst." Partly it was her joie de vivre; partly it seemed calculated. Martha was a thespian at heart—always "up," always "on."

Most of her colleagues thought it noteworthy that Whitney, who hailed from Detroit, usually affected a southern accent. It was as if she went through life doing a decent impersonation of Pearl Bailey. At forty-eight, she was heavier than a few years before, partly the result of bearing and rearing two sons.

"There was a three-car pile-up on 395 just before the Washington exit," she explained. "I tell you what, baby, it looked pretty bad when I drove past. There was this Subaru with the front end all . . ."

"Martha, thanks for the traffic report," Leopole interjected.

Whitney barely registered the mild rebuke. "Well, I was gonna stop on account of my CPR training, you know? But the ambulance just arrived so I kept on a-comin'."

Leopole made certain that everyone ways introduced, then nodded to Carmichael, the tacit message plain on his face. *You have the conn. Babe.*

"Ah, Martha, we're discussing a training mission in Chad. We think you could make a contribution so we'd like to discuss it with . . ."

Whitney arranged herself in the padded chair. "Well, I'm not much of an instructor, y'know. But I've worked in Africa before. In the field, that is."

Carmichael didn't know whether to take that last comment as a catty dig at her lack of covert ops experience. She decided to ignore it. For now.

"Well, there are other reasons for considering you for this mission. After all, you speak French, and that's . . ."

Whitney waved a bejeweled hand. "Oh, c'mon, honey. You think I don't know why I was hired? Same reason the Company hired me: I'm practically invisible. Baby, I be Stealth Woman. Despite thirty years of women's lib and sensitivity training, the plain fact is that most folks don't expect much from a black woman." She gave a conspiratorial grin. "That includes some black men." After a dramatic pause and a furrowed brow she added, "No, wait. That includes *most* black men."

Jack Peters had never met Martha Whitney. That was obvious to Leopole and Carmichael when he said, "Obviously it would help to have an African-American in Chad."

Whitney's cheery face abruptly wrinkled in disdain. She shook her head in one direction and a warning finger in the other. "Darlin'," she began. "Don't you be layin' that PC BS on me. When I hear 'African-American' or 'Eye-talian-American' or 'Mexican-American' that's like a red flag to the bull, you know? It's like you're sayin' I'm *half* American. Like maybe I don't quite measure up, you know?"

"Well, I was just . . ."

"Now I'm tellin' you for sure. If you figure you got to describe me racially, well, honey, I'm sorry for you. I'm a woman, and I'm black, so I'm a black female American. That's an adverb modifying an adjective modifying a noun, and the proper noun is American! But I ain't never an *African*-American. If you gotta hyphenate me, then you better remember that I'm an *All*-American!"

He gulped visibly. "Yes, ma'am!"

It was too late; Whitney was spooled up. "Just 'cause I can't show you my pedigree don't mean that I walk around like my oldest boy, wearin' his kinte cloth. I don't know what tribe sold my people into slavery, or even if they ever *was* slaves. But I figure anything that happened before my people learned to read and write is way beyond my poor ability to add or detract, so let's get past it, shall we?"

Leopole smiled in spite of himself. Martha Whitney had given an impromptu English lesson and, knowingly or otherwise, had quoted the Gettysburg Address.

Peters stuck out his hand. "Let's start over. Martha, I'm Jack."

She shook. "Glad to meet you, honey."

ANNANDALE, VIRGINIA

Sandy Carmichael walked into the lobby of the indoor shooting range, toting her concealed-carry purse with her custom Kimber .45. She was a regular at The Bullet Trap; at least monthly, sometimes more. There were better equipped ranges at Chantilly and Springfield but Annandale was closer to SSI, just off Route 495.

"Hi, Ed!" Sandy gave the co-owner her cheeriest cheerleader grin. She took care to pronounce her greeting as "Hah, Ay-ed." She had learned earlier than most females that a perky smile and a southern accent melted the testosterone in some males and pumped it in others.

Near as she could recall, she'd been about three and a half.

Ed Masterson liked to hint that he was related to the gunfighting Bat, but the frontiersman had carved his single notch three years before Ed's forebears disembarked at Norfolk in 1879. "Why, Colonel Carmichael. We haven't seen you around much, young lady."

"Oh, Ay-ed, y'all're u-shally workin' too early for me. I been in here at least twice-et since I last saw y'all." She waved a deprecating hand, adding, "Ah sway-yer, ya'll're avoidin' me." She batted her baby blues for effect. *No harm in keeping in practice*, she told herself.

Truth be told, sometimes it was so easy that it wasn't even fun any-more. A mid-fortyish single mom with no steady relationship had ample time to perfect her flirting technique—no head tilt or hair flip this time—and poor, lovable Ay-ed was *so* easy.

Masterson actually blushed, his ruddy complexion contrasting with his pale blue shirt with The Bullet Trap logo. He recovered enough to reply, "Colonel, honey, you surely know how to shine on an ol' southern boy."

"Well dip me in honeysuckle an' pour me full of mint juleps. The cornpone is getting hip deep in here."

Sandy turned at the familiar voice: the lilting tones, the slightly ex-aggerated accent.

Martha Whitney.

She stood there, a formidable mixture of Queen Latifah fashion and Aunt Jemima bonhomie. Carrying a combination-lock gun case, Whitney advanced to the counter and nodded to her colleague. "Evenin', Sandy."

"Hullo, Martha." Carmichael managed an ephemeral grin.

Behind the counter, Ed Masterson noted a perceptible drop in the ambient temperature. He knew Sandra Carmichael better than Martha Whitney, whom he had once introduced as "Martha Washington." He never did *that* again.

Shoving a registration sheet across the glass display case, he sought to retrieve the situation. "Just sign in, ladies. We're a little slow this af-ternoon so I can give you adjoining lanes if you . . ."

Sandy began, "Well, I was . . ."

"Why that'd be just precious, Sugar." Martha smiled hugely, pro-nouncing the endearment as "Sugah." She flashed her driver's license and signed the hold-harmless release without reading it. "Girls' night out, at the shooting range," she enthused.

At that moment Sandra Carmichael abandoned any thought of meaningful practice.

"Lanes four and five," Masterson said, accepting Sandy's registration slip.

"Thanks, Ed," she intoned. "Ay-ed" was long gone as she went all squinty-eyed in anticipation of the impending battle.

Watching the two women stride toward the glassed-in shooting bay, Ed mused that it was gonna be a combination gunfight and catfight and, if it strayed to the cafeteria next door, likely a food fight as well.

Taking their positions beside one another, the SSI operatives were separated by a Plexiglas barrier to stop flying brass. Neither spoke as they loaded magazines: Carmichael using Blazer .45; Whitney Wolf 9 mm.

With fewer rounds to load, Carmichael finished first. She activated her remote target console and picked up two targets. "Silhouette or bull's-eye?"

Whitney suggested, "Why not both, darlin'?"

"Why not?"

From two previous encounters, Sandy knew that she was more accurate but Martha shot faster. The tacit agreement seemed headed for a tie: Sandy would likely take the bull's-eye contest and Martha the "combat" segment.

They ran their targets out to fifteen meters, pulled on their glasses and ear protectors, and went to low ready. Sandy's Kimber and Martha's Glock touched the bench in front of them. "Ten rounds," Sandy said.

Martha nodded.

"Ready, go!"

Thirty-two seconds and a reload later, Sandy laid down her Kimber, the thumb safety engaged.

Martha finished four seconds later, the Glock 19's slide locked back.

"You usually shoot faster than that," Sandy ventured.

"Baby, I'm shootin' for score this time."

They reeled in their targets and counted scores. Sandy won, forty-two to thirty-nine. "You got bigger holes," Whitney observed. "Those .45s turn nines into tens."

Sandy beamed. "Sure do, Sugar."

"Well, honey, the first man I killed didn't know the difference 'cause I put six out of six in his sorry ass."

Sandy shrugged. "First man I killed only took two."

Martha ignored the retort, knowing that her rival had shot two armed intruders in SSI offices less than a year before. "Then the next time . . . well, the next time I done smoked two of 'em. I'd tell you 'bout it but it's still classified, don't you know."

"We gonna talk or shoot?" Sandy taped up her silhouette target and ran it out to ten meters. Martha did the same.

Sandy picked up the Pact timer and set it for delay start. "Five rounds, rapid fire." She pressed the button and three seconds later the beep went.

Whitney pushed the Glock's black snout straight out from her body, locked her arms in an isosceles triangle, and went to work on the trigger. Allowing the trigger to reset after each shot, she dumped five rounds into the torso in less than three seconds. The hits were scattered in a buckshot pattern, but they were all there.

Sandy brought the .45 to eye level in a Weaver stance, left elbow low, and took nearly five seconds to put five rounds into a melon-sized group in the target's solar plexus. "More recoil," she murmured unnecessarily.

In the lobby a small crowd was gathering, all fascinated, all male. The observers stepped close to the safety glass partition for a better look.

"What's with the women?" asked a revolver shooter.

"Catfight," explained Ay-ed.

"Who's winning?" queried a Sig advocate.

"Looks about even," the wheelgunner opined.

Sig turned to Masterson. "Well, who are they?"

"Oh, a coupla ladies who work for a Beltway outfit."

"Dang," Wheelgunner exclaimed. "I never saw a black gal shoot before."

"Not like that you didn't," Masterson said.

The conversation lagged while the women resumed firing. The next string was timed head shots.

The string after that was strong hand only, fifteen meters.

The string after that was support hand only, ten meters.

"Looks like they've done this before," Sig observed.

Wheelgunner nodded. "Looks like they're plumb serious."

Masterson knew something about Colonel Sandra Carmichael, U.S. Army, retired. "Serious as it gets, Earl."

When the range session ended the crowd parted as the women hung up their earmuffs. The parting words were Whitney's:

"Hey, girlfriend, your Kimber's dandy but my Glock is the ultimate in feminine protection!"

GOWEN FIELD, BOISE, IDAHO

The United 777 had barely begun debarking passengers when Bosco strode down the jetway. He overtook the first-class passengers, bumping a dignified woman old enough to be his mother and then some. Barely missing a beat, he barked, "Excusemema'am," took her valise from her without being asked, and solicitously carried it to the security gate.

"Bosco!"

"J. J. my man!"

The two mercenaries exchanged male-bonding hugs accompanied by considerable back slapping. As Johnson stepped back, he grinned conspiratorially. "Aren't you forgetting something?"

Bosco looked around. "Like what?" Then the light dawned. "Oh, hell, I ain't gonna say, like, '*I love ya, man.*'"

With an exaggerated motion, Johnson pointed over Bosco's left shoulder. The gray-haired lady stood with a bemused expression, her pale blue eyes sparkling at the boisterous pair.

Bosco blushed visibly—a rarity for him—and sheepishly handed back the valise. "Sorry, ma'am. I sorta forgot . . ."

She patted his muscled arm and leaned close. "It's quite all right, young man. I heard you say that you love your partner." She winked. "My godson is gay, too."

Bosco watched the sympathetic lady walk away, his jaw at half mast. "What'd she say?" Johnson asked.

"Uh . . . she . . . uh." He looked at the carpeted floor. "I couldn't understand her."

As they walked to the baggage claim Johnson enthused, "Hey, I'm goin' trout fishing in a couple days. I have a buddy from LaGrande—ex-Marine who says they're biting real well at Horsethief. I can fix you up with everything you'd need. I hear that Chironomid and Woolly Buggers are workin' real well."

Boscombe shook his head in wonderment. "What language is that?"

"Hell, man, it's fish talk. What do you think it is?"

Bosco shrugged his big shoulders. "Klingon?"

Johnson nudged his friend with an elbow. "C'mon, man. It's not far north of here. We could have a good time. You catch 'em and I'll clean 'em. *Laissez le bon roulement de périodes.*"

"There's that language thing again."

"It's, like, 'Let the good times roll.'"

SSI OFFICES

Frank Leopole rapped his bronzed knuckles on the polished table. The chatter in the room abated.

"Okay. This meeting is about filling out the training team." He nodded to SSI's director of training.

Dr. Omar Mohammed was the Iranian-born son of a shah's diplomat, valued for his versatility. In addition to supervising SSI training, he was an accomplished linguist, having grown up with Farsi, French, English, and Arabic. Now he spoke four other languages besides. He began, "Jack and I contacted David Main. He's still our DoD liaison, and now that he's a full colonel he can tap some assets that were less certain before."

Leopole beamed. "Doc, you're just determined to see your picture on the hostile targets at Benning, aren't you?"

The PhD leaned back, hands comfortably clasped behind his head. "It's all relative. After all, we recruit from the top of the milk bottle so we can skim the cream. Yes, Special Forces soldiers fluent in Arabic are high-value assets, as the saying goes. Which is precisely why we pay them what they're worth on the open market." He arched an eyebrow. "Once their obligations are fulfilled, of course."

Retired Gunnery Sergeant Daniel Foyte caught Leopole's eye. They were longtime friends and connoisseurs of Tennessee sippin' whiskey.

"Just a quick question. How good do we want the Chadians to be?"

"How do you mean?" Mohammed asked.

"I mean, considering what their government's like, do we really want to train these clients to the highest possible standard?"

Mohammed stared at the far wall, visualizing the stories he had heard about the *Savak*, the shah's secret police trained by America and Israel. All that had ended in 1979, of course, when Omar Mohammed was still attending Cambridge. Leopole interjected, "That's more a philosophical than an operational question, Gunny."

"I respectfully disagree, Colonel." As Mohammed defaulted to the more respectful term—he might have addressed Leopole by his given name. "I believe they are directly linked."

Privately, Leopole ceded his colleague's point. But he did not want to give SSI the impression that he ever held any qualms about accepting a contract. "I understand your concern, Omar. I really do. But let's be totally honest: it's more a matter of degree than substance. However long we work with the Chadians, they're not likely to come up to more than third-class military status. There's too much of a cultural gap, and if that appears racist, so be it."

"You seem to be saying, let our team develop these clients to their full potential, even though we know the end result will be inferior."

"Only by our standards, Omar. By their standards they'll be six-hundred-pound gorillas."

Mohammed nodded slowly. "Very well." As the meeting proceeded, he penned himself a note for discussion with Mike Derringer. *What do we owe our clients? Our best or their best? And how do we arrange the distinction?*

HORSETHIEF RESERVOIR, IDAHO

"Did you ever see *A River Runs Through It?*"

J. J. Johnson knew that he had just asked a rhetorical question. Jason Boscombe's taste in cinema ran in two directions: action and skin, not necessarily in that order. Fishing lay far, far down the former Ranger's list of interests.

"Yeah, I watched it on TV with my mom. She liked it because of the photography and stuff."

Johnson finished tying a fly to Bosco's line. The Parachute Adams dangled at the end of the tippet. "Well, I figured you being from Ellensburg, you'd have some fisherman's blood in you."

Bosco frowned perceptibly. "I was more into hunting than fishing. My old man liked to go after steelhead, but he and I . . ." His voice trailed off.

Johnson ignored the tacit message. He knew that Boscombe had seldom returned to eastern Washington after his mother's death. "Well, the reason I ask about the movie is that it showed fly casting as an accuracy game. That's the great thing about it: you don't have to get a strike to enjoy it."

"If you say so."

"I do say so." Johnson handed the spare rod to Bosco and unreeled a length of line from his own. Standing on the bank, he looked at the calm, gray water and found what he wanted. "Target. Eleven o'clock, fifteen meters."

Bosco searched in the direction indicated. "You mean that leaf?"

"That's it." Johnson whipped his graphite rod back and forth two or three times, then made his cast. The fly alit five inches from the target. "Damn."

"What do you mean, 'damn'? Looked like you almost hit it!"

"Naw, too short. I'll try again." Johnson made a longer cast next time, placing the fly three inches beyond the leaf.

"You got it bracketed, dude. Fire for effect!"

Johnson grinned. "Well, you don't actually want to hit your fish. You want to put the fly within a couple inches of his nose so he'll be able to grab it. But don't just let it float there. Real bugs don't act that way. They sort of skitter across the water, like this." The fisherman gave his rod a series of short, precise strokes that drew the Adams hopping across the surface.

A trout rose to the bait, snapped at the fly, and dived.

"Whoa!" Bosco exclaimed. "You got 'im, J. J.! Awesome!" He slapped his friend on the back. "How'd you know he was there?"

"Ah, you learn." He tugged on his rod, enjoying the small adrenaline spike and the tension of the fish fighting on the other end.

He did not admit that the trout had surprised him as much as it did Bosco.

Abruptly the line went slack. "He slipped the hook," Johnson said calmly. "Didn't sink it when he took the fly. But we'll stay with Parachutes for a while, since they're about the most versatile surface flies around. I'll change to Woolly Buggers later in the day."

Bosco hefted his rod and looked around. The reservoir was ringed with tall evergreens, their piney scent filling the morning air. "This is nice, J. J. Better than I thought. Where should I try?"

"Hey, I knew you'd like it here." He pointed to his right. "Step out on those flat rocks. That way you'll be clear of the trees when you cast. Remember, back to ten o'clock and forward to two."

"Gotcha."

Johnson watched his friend for the first few casts. Like most beginners, Bosco exaggerated the pause at the ten and two positions, but eventually the casts became more fluid and the range increased. During the morning he even got a couple of strikes.

At the lunch break, the discussion turned to shop talk.

Bosco began with more subtlety than usual. "Admiral Derringer's a fisherman, isn't he? Does he ever go fly fishing?"

"Don't think so. Far as I know he's into deep-sea fishing. He got a near record marlin last year."

"Yeah, I remember him talking about that," Bosco replied. He regarded the former Foreign Legionnaire. "Just before we went to Pakistan, wasn't it?"

Johnson shook his head. "I don't know for sure. I was still pretty new with the company at the time."

"Well, Breezy and I really like working for SSI. We're going to Chad, you know."

So that's it. Johnson turned toward Boscombe. "You're here to recruit me, aren't you?"

Bosco began to avert his eyes, then riveted them on Johnson's. "How am I doing?"

Johnson lifted his Coors, took a sip, then set the beer down. "You know, you missed your calling."

"Yeah? How's that?"

"Well, you're a shit-hot recruiter, that's all."

Bosco flicked his head as if avoiding a gnat. "J. J., what are you trying to say?"

"I'm trying to say, dude, that I'm in. I'll go to Chad."

Boscombe's eyes widened in realization. "You sumbitch! You already made up your mind!"

Johnson winked. "Gotcha." He thought for a moment, then said,

"There's something you should know. Frank Leopole and Sandy Carmichael, too."

"Yeah?"

"Well, I've had lots of time to think about this kind of work since . . . the last job."

Bosco knew enough when to keep quiet.

"I'm going to Chad because it's a training job," Johnson explained. "I don't plan to work in the field again. Ever."

Bosco set down his beer. "J. J., I think I know where you're coming from. But if you're still worried about what happened in Pak . . ."

"Damn straight it's about what happened over there. I compromised a mission and put good folks in the crosshairs because . . . because I . . ." He swallowed hard.

"Because the bastards tortured you. Is that it?"

Johnson took a pull at his bottle. He hardly noticed it was empty. Finally he managed to speak. "No, man. Not because they tortured me. *Because I broke!*"

"Well, hell, J. J.. Everybody breaks. Look at all those guys in the Hanoi Hilton. The gooks broke every one of 'em. It's not like you're the only one who ever had too much pain. C'mon, man."

"No, that's not quite right, Bosco. Some of them didn't break. They died before they'd give in."

Bosco leaned forward and punched his friend's arm. "Makes my case, J. J. If you hadn't talked, the ragheads would've killed you. You know that. Besides, nobody got hurt because you talked."

"That was just luck. So I don't ever want to be in that position again. There's just too . . ."

Boscombe was more perceptive than the hey-dude persona he showed the world. *Something else is goin' on here*, he told himself.

"J. J., I know you're prob'ly still having, well, trouble, with what happened there. Bad dreams? Things like that?"

The brief nod again. "Something like that." He stared into the empty long-necked bottle. He wondered how much he could tell Bosco and keep his self-respect. The scars on his back, buttocks, and upper thighs were physical reminders of the scalding he received at the hands of the Islamist cell in Pakistan, headed by the tormented genius determined to destroy the SSI team sent to find him and prevent the spread of the Marburg virus.

But the emotional scars went bone deep.

Almost without realizing it, Johnson found himself talking.

"I met a girl, Bosco. A really good woman. We knew each other before she got married but now she's divorced and we ran into each other not long ago. We're getting serious. I mean . . . really serious, you know?"

Bosco wondered how to respond when Johnson continued. "It's like, I keep visualizing what it's going to be like the first time we go to bed. She's going to see my scars and if I haven't told her about it, she'll wonder why. But if I tell her before, she'll know that I cracked and she . . ."

"You think she won't want to be with you?"

Johnson shrugged. "Maybe. I mean . . . hell, man, I just don't know."

Bosco let a feral grin escape his lips. "Shee-it, J. J., do I have to draw you a picture? Unless you want to spend the rest of your life holding hands with women, tell her the whole story. Maybe it won't matter. Hell, maybe she'll want to comfort you. But at least you'll be over the hump, you know? Either it'll work out with her or it won't. If not with her, then with another gal." He finished off his Coors and set it down. "Next subject." He belched and added, "Gimme another brew."

13

SSI OFFICES

Leopole and Mohammed had some news to share.

Addressing the staff, Leopole began, "I've heard from some embassy folks in Chad, and I think you all need to know what you might find over there.

"We learned that at least two French PMCs were operating in-country. The frontrunner is called Groupe FGN, which is named for the original three partners. Apparently only one of them is still alive—chap named Geurrier—but he's largely retired. His family runs the company but the hands-on guy is a hard case named Marcel Hurtubise, ex-Foreign Legion and jack of all mercenary trades. He'll literally work for anybody, and has, especially in Africa: Sudan, Libya, Algeria, and so on."

"I wonder how he stays legit with those clients," Carmichael said.

Leopole gave a sardonic grin. "Well, he also works for the French government. One of his recent jobs was UXB removal in Kosovo, and that sort of work lends respectability. It checks the Humanitarian box."

Sandy shook her head. "UXB?"

"Unexploded bombs, or ordnance generally. It's an old Brit term but today it usually means land mines. They're really un-PC in some circles."

"Oh, yes. I remember. That was one of Princess Di's big causes."

"Yeah. I guess she never heard of the DMZ."

"Which one?"

"The one along the thirty-eighth parallel. It sort of keeps North Korea out of South Korea."

Foyte fidgeted. "All right, so how does the French outfit affect us?"

"I don't know that it does for sure, but there's something going on. The two senior members of the other PMC disappeared several days ago. The others went home on Air France."

Foyte emitted a long, low whistle. "You think . . ."

"Yeah."

Carmichael leaned forward, her hands clasped. "Frank, I see where you're going. But there must be other explanations."

The crew-cut head bobbed. "Sure, lots of 'em in that area. But we can't overlook the possibility that there's been some corporate feuding."

"Man, talk about cutthroat competition!" Foyte almost smiled. "Are we likely to rub noses with these guys?"

Leopold arched an eyebrow. Dan Foyte's idea of rubbing noses had nothing in common with Eskimo greetings. "Don't know, Gunny. But it's something to keep in mind."

Foyte accepted that advice and shifted gears. "All right, what can we expect in Chad right now? Who will we work with before the French take over?" The team leader needed to know for planning purposes.

"Well, evidently the blue beanies will leave some folks in place for transition, though the U.N. generally isn't real happy with the situation. But there's not much choice. Either they help hand over to us and the French or they leave the place totally on its own, which simply isn't realistic."

Leopole looked around the table. "All right, people. It's crunch time. We need to select a training team leader and his deputy." He circled something on his briefing paper. His choice had already been made.

Sandy Carmichael saw the motion, knew its meaning, and tacitly concurred. "How about Gunny?"

"That's what I was thinking," Leopole replied.

Foyte was genuinely surprised. "Hey, I don't speak French, let alone Arabic."

Leople chuckled to himself. *Hell, the sumbitch hardly speaks English!*

Carmichael conceded, "No way around that. But you'll have our translators as well as whatever the Chadians have over there. And J. J. Johnson's fluent in French. You've worked together before. You two should make a good team."

"So he's going?" Foyte asked.

"Yup." Carmichael gave a sly grin. "Seems that he took Bosco fishing—and Bosco landed him!"

"That's not how I heard it," Leopole replied.

"What do you mean?"

"I called J. J. last evening. He admitted that he already decided to go. Just wanted to have some company so he lured Bosco in. Played him like—well, like a trout!"

N'DJAMENA, CHAD

The kidnapped Vespa driver stirred at the sound of a key in the lock. He had lost track of time, and suspected that was not coincidental. Judging by the fading light through the narrow window, it was evening. Probably the third day.

He rose from the floor where he had been trying to sleep. But his captors kept a bare bulb illuminated in the high ceiling—too high to reach. He was sore, tired, hungry—and frightened.

Two men opened the door and motioned him out. One carried a truncheon and appeared capable of using it. The prisoner accepted the tacit invitation and stepped into the adjoining room. He had been blindfolded when he arrived, and welcomed the view of his immediate surroundings.

Directed to a chair, the man sat and was immediately grasped from behind. Two other thugs secured him with cargo straps around the chest and abdomen, pinning his arms.

The older man turned from a companion and regarded the prisoner. In French-accented English, he said, "Your passport says that you are David Scourby, an Englishman. We know that you are David Olmert, and you are Israeli. You are working with at least two other Jewish agents, and you have been watching us. You are going to tell us why."

Olmert's mind raced. *They didn't know who I was before. That's why it took three days. But they still don't know about Alex and the others.*

I have to tell them something.

"We were interested in the French security company."

The inquisitor smiled grimly. His right hand snapped out, striking Olmert's left cheek. "We know that! We caught you reporting their take-off!"

Strapped into the chair, Olmert could only glare at his tormentor.

"Who did you report to?"

"To my superior, of course." *And so the game goes, each step leading to the next.*

The Frenchman's left fist struck the bridge of Olmert's nose.

An ambidextrous bastard.

"Well?" The interrogator spat it out.

Olmert shook off the blow. "Nathan. That's the name he uses."

"Your accomplice is known to you by an alias?" Left, right, left. Hard, full-force punches, expertly delivered. This time they drew blood. Olmert tasted the salty tang on his tongue. He knew that his nose was broken.

Forcing himself to focus, he realized that he had seen the thug before. Through a rifle scope—the day the two competing contractors had been murdered along the Aozou Strip.

That knowledge settled over David Olmert like a shroud.

N'DJAMENA

It was time.

"Etienne, call Gabrielle in here." Marcel's voice was irritated, petulant.

Etienne Stevin recognized the signs.

Olmert was again strapped to his chair. He looked the worse for wear following a full day of threats, cajolery, and beatings. Not even cigarettes to the soles of his feet elicited full disclosure.

Marcel Hurtubise tolerated Gabrielle Tixier for any number of reasons, not least of which was her sadomasochistic streak. She specialized in humiliation.

Entering the room, the young woman wielded a pair of scissors that she snipped playfully around her face. She wore a sleeveless blouse, tied at the midriff, with a pair of green shorts.

She strode slowly to Olmert, fixing his eyes with hers. She made a point of smiling and saw the fear cross his face. *He knows what's coming,* she thought. *C'est bon.*

She traced the curve of his cheek with the point of the scissors, lingering around the eyes. Then she began cutting his shirt away. Marcel watched impassively; Etienne was less detached. He shifted on his feet and licked his lips.

Gabrielle gave the little-girl pout that she had mastered as a child. It had worked on Papa, up to the point that he became aroused by it. She had fled at thirteen and met Marcel six years later. Yes, he was cunning, violent, and amoral, but he was generally good to her. Sometimes she wondered why; childhood abuse often left victims doubting their own worth.

This was not one of those times.

She waved a manicured finger in the captive's face. The sheen on his skin told her all she needed to know. Gabrielle Tixier had long since been able to sense the presence of fear.

"You are not very talkative, *mon cher*. Don't you like to make conversation with your hosts?" She gave an exaggerated roll of her blue eyes. "Oh! Now I understand. All this male atmosphere. It is *so* dull, isn't it?"

She stepped close and placed her hands behind Olmert's head. She stroked his matted hair with her left hand, cooing at him.

Then, with her right hand, she snipped his left earlobe. He screamed in pain and surprise. "Bitch!"

"There, you see?" She caressed his cheek with her free hand. "It is so much nicer to talk to little Gabrielle. Actually, I am doing us all a favor. I have shown you that we make no idle threats, and perhaps that will save you much pain. Also, it may save us some time. It depends on you, *mon petit*."

She held his jaw and snipped the right earlobe as well. Blood trickled down his neck. "Let that be a lesson to you, *chéri*."

The pout again. "Now, won't you tell me what Marcel and Etienne want to know? Please?"

Olmert's face was reddened with fear and rage. He glared at her with hateful eyes. "Why should I talk? You're going to kill me anyway."

"Did I say such a thing? No, of course not. But as I said, you can save yourself much pain." She curled the ends of her mouth. "Oh, yes. A great deal of pain."

Slowly, as if choreographed, Gabrielle turned to the two men and nodded. They walked away without looking back. Olmert felt a shudder, a liquid tremor in his bowels.

Gabrielle clicked the scissors again. Without speaking, she began cutting away the rest of his shirt. It was awkward, as he was tied to the chair, but she proceeded with enthusiasm, humming to herself.

When the shirt was gone, she cut a slice from each pectoral. Then she turned to his trousers.

She pulled the tattered remains of Olmert's pants from beneath him and flung them across the room. Then she leaned over him, allowing her breasts to press against his chest, and carefully snipped through his briefs. First the left side, then the right. The shorts fell away.

Still grasping the scissors, she clasped his head in her hands. Stroking his face, she gave him the little-girl pout. "Won't you talk to Gabrielle, David? Before I have to cut you . . ." She glanced downward.

He turned his face away, choking down a sob.

Three minutes later Gabrielle emerged from the room. "He broke, poor boy. They always do, you know. But there is not much to tell. Most of what he said, you already guessed. He is working for a cutout, a private contractor with ties to Israeli intelligence. His field partner is an American. They were at the airport to confirm that the other contractor had left after . . . well, after their team disappeared."

Marcel leaned forward. "What does he know about *that?*"

She shrugged. "I did not ask. You said you wanted to know why they were observing the other firm and who pays them."

The former Legionnaire rubbed his stubbled chin. "All right. I will ask him myself, but he will not talk about that. He's not stupid. He knows it would mean a bullet for him."

"Then . . ."

"Then he gets a bullet anyway. Whatever he says."

15

BEALETON, VIRGINIA

Sandra Carmichael turned off Route 17, taking 644 eastward. Following the signs, she soon came to a private air park. She drove past the sign advertising orientation flights on weekends, May through October.

Terry Keegan was waiting for her. There wasn't much activity on a Friday morning in April.

Sandy found him where he said he would be: with his head in the accessory section of an odd-looking, cherry red airplane. It had a racy, pugnacious appearance, from its chrome spinner to its round tail. She approached him from behind but he sensed her presence.

"Isn't it great?" Keegan enthused. "I'm a one-third partner in this beauty. Beech built 781 of them and even though there's a few hundred still flying, they're real spendy."

Carmichael was mildly curious. "Why's that?"

"Well, this is the Beech Model 17, better known as the Staggerwing because of the negative stagger of the top wing. It's a classic from the golden age of aviation. It dates from 1932, so it's an antique. You can fly to any air show in the country and automatically park with the exhibitors so you get to see all the other planes up close. Then you can fly home faster than most current light planes."

"How fast is it?"

Keegan patted the propeller. "She'll do an honest two hundred miles per hour straight and level, and she'll outcruise some Bonanzas. In fact, Staggerwings won a lot of races in the 1930s. But she lands at about forty-five, so there's not many places you can't get into."

Carmichael thought she should feign interest. "How old is this one?"

"It's one of the last twenty, built in 1947."

Carmichael looked into the cabin and emitted a low whistle. "Boy, it smells like a new car!"

"Yeah, we had the seats reupholstered last year. Mohair and leather were factory standard, so that's what we got. Carries five people and all the luggage you can stuff into it."

"Terry, are we going to fly or what?"

The former submarine hunter could not suppress a smile. "Hey, Colonel, why do you think I asked you to meet me here?"

Having already performed the preflight inspection, Keegan helped Sandy into the right seat, then settled in the left. After priming the Pratt and Whitney R985, he turned on the fuel pump, checked left and right, switched the magnetos to Both, and called out, "Clear prop!" The Wasp Junior settled into a throaty rumble. He waited a few minutes, allowing the engine to reach operating temperature.

The pilot closed his door and, satisfied with the pressure and temperature gauges, eased on some throttle. The Beech rolled toward the downwind end of the grass runway, ess-turning so Keegan could see around the nose.

After a final check, Keegan smoothly advanced the throttle. The tail came up and he tracked straight ahead, nudging right rudder to keep the Beech in the center of the strip. Lift quickly overcame gravity as thrust defeated drag and the Staggerwing galloped off the earth behind 450 horses.

The landing gear retracted into the well with a *thump-thump* as Keegan adjusted power for cruise climb. Headed northeast, he pointed out Warrenton broad on the port beam with Calverton at ten o'clock. He turned to the Alabaman. "Hey, you're a military pro. There's Manassas ahead of us and Fredericksburg down there to the right." He grinned slyly. "Here there be rebels, Colonel."

Sandy squirmed in her seat and adjusted the earphones. She appreciated Virginia's verdant vista, but she had other things on her mind. "Terry, you know we're sending a training team to Chad."

"Yeah, I heard something about it. I'm glad I'm not going there!"

She turned her head toward him, removed her sunglasses, and looked into his eyes.

He grimaced. "Oooh no . . ."

"Now wait a minute," she interjected. "You wouldn't have to be there all the time. In fact, you wouldn't have to be there much at all. We just need somebody in the area who could, you know, help out if need be."

Keegan laughed, then lapsed into his Irish brogue. "Colonel darling, sure and you're talkin' about a dustoff on a hot LZ!"

She conceded, "Well, yeah, something like that. It's not that we actually think anything will happen, Terry. But you know the admiral's policy. We never leave any SSI people in a position where we can't get them out, even if we have to do it ourselves." *Terry can't refuse the admiral*, she reminded herself. She knew that Mike Derringer lived by the creed: loyalty down breeds loyalty up.

Terry nodded, scanning the instruments. "Roger that. Remember me? Last Chance Keegan they call me. As in, Guatemala. As in, Pakistan."

Sandy thought better of pressing the matter so she changed the subject. "You know, my youngest daughter thinks she wants to fly. But she can't decide if she would rather go with the Air Force or Navy."

Keegan recalled the naval aviation axiom. *Air Force: flare to land, squat to pee*. He decided against expressing his service preference. Instead, he observed, "And you an Army family? What's the matter with that girl?"

Carmichael curled her lips. "Oh, Emily wants to fly jets. Then she wants to pilot the space shuttle."

"Ah-ha." Keegan let it go at that. Privately, he disdained females who only saw the military as a way into NASA. He had never known a woman aviator who wanted to bomb and strafe more than she wanted to fly the damned shuttle.

Finally he turned and looked at his passenger. "Tell me more about Chad."

16

SSI OFFICES

"Admiral, Colonel Main to see you."

Derringer waved from his desk, beckoning the Army officer into the office. Derringer raised from his chair, extending a hand across the desk. "Good to see you, David. I didn't expect you today."

Main crumpled his beret—he wanted to strangle the poofter garment—and slid into a chair. "I'm sorry for the unexpected visit, Admiral. But something's come up that I need to discuss with you in person."

"Sure thing. Fire when ready."

"Well, sir, I've just had a call from my back-channel contact at Bragg. Master Sergeant Alford is wired into the SF community like nobody else I know, and he thinks we should reconsider one of the guys we interviewed."

"Why's that?"

Main cleared his throat—an unusual sign of nervousness. "Apparently Staff Sergeant Gayler is under investigation for misappropriating funds and equipment. Alford thinks that's why the Army cut him loose so quickly." Main shook his head, silently berating himself. "I should've caught it, Admiral. I mean, the Army just doesn't release an Arabic speaker that easily."

Derringer braced his chin on a bridge of clasped hands. He surveyed Main's face, sensing as much as seeing the embarrassment there. "David, it's not your fault. In fact, I'm not certain this Segreant . . ."

"Gayler. Fred Gayler."

"We don't know if he's guilty of anything. You said he's under investigation."

"That's true, sir. But . . . well, Alford says that Gayler also has a temper. He barely got away with spousal abuse because his former CO covered for him."

"And you accept Alford's word implicitly."

A decisive nod. "I've trusted my life with him. He deals in facts, not gossip."

"Okay, then. Gayler's out. You'd better talk to Jack Peters so his recruiting records are updated."

"I'll do that, sir." He turned to go. "Oh, I saw Steve Lee in the hall. Is he involved in the Chad mission?"

Derringer perked up. "No, at least not yet. I didn't know he was back from vacation but he must've stopped in to check with my niece. He and Sallie seem to enjoy each other's company."

"Shall I send him in, Admiral?"

Derringer unconsciously reverted to his percussion habit. His fingers drummed the desk top: *paradiddle-paradiddle-tap-tap-tap.* He said, "Yes, please. I'd like to talk to him."

Moments later Lee appeared at the office door. "Hello, Admiral."

Derringer rose and extended a hand across the desk. "Come in, Steve, come in!" As they shook, he said, "I lost track of the time. Didn't expect to see you for a week or so."

"Oh, you know me, sir. I can only stand so much sun, surf, and bikinis."

"Maui?"

Lee gave a self-conscious grin. "Actually, I was out in Marana, getting some jump practice. It'd been a while."

"A parachuting vacation? Well, why not. I hear there's sunshine in Arizona, too."

"Yes, sir. Six or eight jumps a day."

Derringer folded his hands on the desk and looked more closely at Major Steven Lee, U.S. Army, prematurely retired. The admiral saw a fit, self-composed alpha male who looked younger than forty-two. Only the military-issue spectacles hinted at his age.

"Steve, let me ask you a personal question. What do you want to do with your life?"

Lee took three heartbeats to answer the unexpected inquiry. "Just what I'm doing, Admiral. Jumping, shooting, kicking in the occasional door." The levity in his voice was genuine enough, even if the statement was incomplete. He leaned forward in his chair. "I'll tell you, sir. Not a day passes that I don't regret leaving the Army as an O-4. But I had a choice to make and I made it. I tried to save my marriage at the expense of my career. That's why I like working for SSI. It still lets me do what I was meant to do."

"Well, I've said it before but it bears repeating. You did a fine job in Pakistan. Would you be interested in another contract?"

"Ah, yes, sir. Depending on what it involves. I'm not much interested in security work, you know."

"No, we're putting together a training package in Africa. Several months, probably. If you're interested, ask Peggy to give you the briefing sheet on Chad."

"Chad! My God." He laughed. "I haven't left anything there, Admiral!"

Derringer chuckled in appreciation of the sentiment. "Neither have I, Steve. But you know the State Department pays us pretty well these days."

"All right, sir. I'll take a look."

———

It was a three-ring briefing, rare even for a fairly small organization such as SSI.

As director of operations Frank Leopold sat at the head of the room, flanked by Sandra Carmichael, foreign ops, and Omar Mohammed, training. The team selected for Chad occupied the first two rows of chairs. Leopold scanned the faces, mostly familiar: Gunny Foyte, J. J. Johnson, Bosco, Breezy, Martha Whitney, and two newbies from Bragg: newly retired NCOs Christopher Nissen and Joshua Wallender.

Michael Derringer slipped into the back of the room. Few noticed, and those who did see him knew his intent. He was there to observe and learn rather than command.

Leopole stood to make the introductions. "This is the first time the Chad team has been fully assembled, though most of you are well acquainted. I want to introduce our two newest members, Staff Sergeants Chris Nissen and Josh Wallender. They're fresh out of Fort Bragg, both experienced Special Forces operators. Gentlemen, welcome to SSI."

Martha Whitney turned in her seat and pointedly looked Nissen up and down. Clearly she liked what she saw. "Hey, bro," she beamed.

Nissen fidgeted slightly. His wife, Shawna, could have given Halle Berry a run for her money, and he was not looking to round out his romantic résumé.

Leopole added, "Chris is a weapons instructor and medic who speaks pretty good Arabic. Josh is rated in French and specializes in communications. They're both well qualified for this mission, and we're glad to have them aboard."

He turned to the rest of the audience. "Very well. This meeting will familiarize you with most of the background information on the contract. As you know, it's a training mission, administered by the State Department, to assist Chadian government forces in developing a greater counterinsurgency capability. Since it's an overseas training operation it comes under Lieutenant Colonel Carmichael and Dr. Mohammed, and I'll turn it over to them."

Sandy rose to her feet. "What do we know about Chad?" she asked rhetorically. "Well, I went to the CIA World Factbook site, which is more current than any almanac. Here's the short version." She activated her PowerPoint display, beginning with a map of northern Africa.

"Geography: Chad is bounded by six countries: Libya, Niger, Nigeria, Central African Republic, Cameroon, and Sudan. The area is almost 500,000 square miles, nearly twice the size of Texas. There's mostly desert in the north, mountains in the northwest, arid plains in the middle, and lowlands in the south.

"Chad was a French possession until 1960 but the next thirty years involved civil war and border feuds with Libya. There was a general settlement in 1990 with a constitution and elections in '96 and '97. But the next year another internal dispute broke out and continued until 2002. The government and the rebels signed agreements that year and the next but there's still unrest.

"The government's controlled by one of the minority factions, but it has enough support to stay in power. There's been widespread reports of human rights abuses including murder, kidnapping, torture, and extortion. Some military and security forces have been named in specific complaints."

Bosco raised a hand. "Then why are we helping those people?"

Carmichael blinked. Then she blinked again. "Why, Mr. Boscombe, I do believe you are naïve."

Bosco gave an exaggerated flinch. "Uh, yessma'am. Gotcha."

Carmichael grinned. "Check. It's the same old story with PMCs. Deniability. The U.S. Government does not want to appear too cozy with an oppressive regime, so DoD and State call us. Since we're not wearing the uniform of the day, we're 'clean.'"

Bosco persisted. "But like, what're we really doing? There must be something more than teaching border guards how to intercept bad guys. I mean, they don't need us to do that."

Carmichael squinted behind her glasses. Sometimes Bosco actually showed signs of latent intelligence. "Well, we'd have to discuss it eventually so we might as well explain it now." She paused, looked at Leopold and Mohammed, and received nods in return. She activated her laser pointer.

"The crucial area is here in the north, along the Libyan border. There are uranium deposits there, and nobody wants that material getting to the wrong hands—including the U.N. So our job is actually more than counterinsurgency. It's interdiction of illicit strategic materials. Which is why our clients need to be more capable than the regular army. They're likely to run up against some aggressive, capable opponents." *Like ex-Foreign Legion troops who'll work for anybody.*

"Anyway, you'll receive more briefings as you get closer to deploying. Meanwhile, here's the background.

"Demographics: the capital is N'Djamena, over here in the far west just beneath the lake, population at least six hundred thousand. The official languages are Arabic and French. There's no state religion but the population is over half Muslim and one-third Christian, mostly Catholic. Life expectancy runs forty-seven years.

"Chadian rebels have used Libya as a base for cross-border raids, and there's a long-standing dispute with three other countries over demarcation lines on Lake Chad. More importantly, huge numbers of refugees have entered Chad from Sudan, where there's an ongoing famine. The region has what I'd call biblical problems: droughts and locust plagues.

"Population is now pushing ten million. There's a couple hundred ethnic groups with the Saras the biggest, over twenty-five percent. Most of the population is in the southern half or less, since the north is part of the Sahara Desert. There's about 120 languages and dialects but less than half the people are literate.

"Health concerns: malaria, meningitis, hepatitis, and typhoid, among others. About five percent of the population has HIV or AIDS.

"In short, it's a mess.

"Government: officially Chad has a bicameral legislature but only the National Assembly is seated. The Senate hasn't been formed. Anyway, there's half a dozen political parties. In '05 they passed a referendum allowing the president to run for a third term."

Bosco wrinkled his forehead. "What's bicameral?"

Johnson gaped. "Geez, man, didn't you take civics in high school?"

"Hey, I studied football and basketball and cheerleaders. Not necessarily in that order."

Johnson suspected that Boscombe was playing dumb again, for reasons personal and obscure. "Bicameral, as in *bi*, as in two, you know? Two houses in the legislature, like Congress and the Senate."

"Oh. Gotcha."

Carmichael regained control of the discussion. "The president is basically a strongman, the latest in a long line. The military is more or less loyal to him, as are the police forces as long as they get paid regularly. In turn, the government doesn't look too closely at how some soldiers and policemen make extra income. In dealing with government officials, always remember that Chad is one of the two most corrupt places on earth.

"Economy: Chad exports cotton to Europe and Asia but only about three percent of the land is under cultivation. So far the greatest export potential is oil, and that's a growth industry but the country doesn't have much infrastructure to exploit it. The exchange rate is around 550 francs per dollar.

"Infrastructure: only 267 kilometers of paved highway—that's, what? Maybe 150 miles. There's fifty airports or at least landing fields, seven with paved runways. Fortunately, cell phones and Internet access are pretty reliable.

"Military concerns: the longest border is with Libya, up here in the north." She tapped the map, indicating the east-west line. "The Aozou Strip was a disputed area for years, mainly because Colonel Qadhafi wanted the natural resources in the area. That includes the uranium deposits I mentioned. Anyway, Libya occupied the strip in 1972 and there was off and on combat for about fifteen years. In the mid eighties we gave Chad enough help to drive the Libyans out, but they still claimed the strip. Finally, both sides agreed to arbitration and an international court declared that the Aozou belonged to Chad."

Foyte asked, "What kind of help did we provide, Colonel?"

Carmichael consulted her notes. "Mostly basic stuff: small arms, antitank weapons, medical supplies, even uniforms. I'm told that we put a Hawk antiaircraft battery in the capital but evidently it wasn't there very long. The biggest thing apparently was training and contract maintenance."

Bosco nodded. "Some things don't change."

"*Plus ça change*," Johnson interjected.

Breezy wrinkled his brow. "Say what?"

"*Plus ça change, c'est la même chose*." Mohammed nodded toward Johnson. "It means, the more things change, the more they remain the same."

———

Huddled in the corner, some of the worker bees commiserated after monitoring the meeting. "Hey," asked Breezy, "are we gonna have to learn French or something?"

J. J. Johnson tried to imagine Mark Brezyinski getting his tongue around a European language. It just did not compute. He replied, "Well, besides me, our French-speaking liaison used to be with the Agency. She's a . . ."

"She?"

"Yeah, she. As in, female. As in, *La Belle Dame Sans Merci*."

"Hey, I never read much Tennyson," quipped Breezy.

Johnson tried to keep a straight face. "Keats would be glad to hear that."

"Why's that, dude?"

"Like, he wrote it, dude."

Bosco went on point. "What's she look like? I mean . . ."

Johnson nudged his colleague. "You mean, does she look single?"

Breezy snorted. "Hell, man, he means, like, does she look female!"

Johnson, who had met Martha Whitney, allowed himself a conspiratorial smile. "Affirmative on both counts."

"Well, when you gonna introduce us?" Bosco demanded.

"*Tous en temps utile*." Noting the vacant stares of the two commandos, Johnson added, "At the right time. Dudes."

SSI OFFICES

Daniel Foyte convened the next briefing with Omar Mohammed alongside as SSI's chief training officer. They sat at the apex of a semicircle of folding chairs.

"Okay," Foyte began in his gravelly baritone. "This briefing will focus on specific mission objectives so it's more detailed than the overall brief that Colonel Carmichael gave us."

He referred to his notes, once neatly typed but now littered with pen and ink hieroglyphics. He felt odd sitting; he was accustomed to standing or kneeling from twenty years of addressing Marines in classrooms, tents, oases, triple-canopy jungle, and other venues.

"First a little more about Chad's military structure." He turned to Mohammed. "Doctor?"

The urbane Iranian-American required few notes. He began, "The armed forces consist of the army, air force, and gendarmerie, plus more specialized units such as National and Nomadic Guard, which is a border force, the Rapid Intervention Force, and regular police. Presumably the most 'elite' unit"—he etched quote marks in the air—"is the presidential guard."

Chris Nissen raised a hand. Though brand-new to SSI, he was not shy. "Excuse me, Doctor. Does the intervention force deploy outside Chad?"

"Not that I know of," Mohammed replied. "I infer that it's an internal unit. For what it's worth, it was originally formed as the Republican Guard." After an ironic response from the audience, he added, "Any similarity to the Iraqi organization of the same name is probably intentional.

"Current military spending runs a little over one hundred million dollars. To put that in perspective, it would not buy much over half of an F-22 stealth fighter.

"The military has a draft for twenty-year-olds for three years," he continued. "Officially, enlistments are accepted at eighteen, but in truth there's no minimum with parental consent. You will be dealing with men at least in their second tour.

"The Air Force has no combat aircraft: mostly C-130s, An-126s, and even some C-47s. Helicopters are Alouette IIIs."

Mohammed shifted his weight, speaking extemporaneously. "Now, here's some background. There's been speculation over the years why the Reagan administration was so eager to help Chad against Libya. Aside from Qadhafi's blatant aggression, there didn't seem much reason for our intervention, even though we were allied with the French. Far as I know, neither of us needed much African uranium, and that caused some raised eyebrows. But I think that the critics overlooked something pretty obvious: if we didn't need the stuff, other places did."

Nissen said, "So it was in our mutual interest to keep the Strip out of Libyan hands."

"Just so."

Foyte resumed the briefing, turning to his bread and butter: hardware.

"The Chad Army is pretty much a hodgepodge as far as small arms. There's no standard infantry rifle: depending on the branch and unit there's M16s, AKs, FALs, Sigs, and G3s. Squad automatics are RPDs, RPKs, and even some old M24/29s."

Breezy asked, "What're those, Gunny?"

"They look like the British Bren Gun: a 7.5 mm with top-feed magazine. They replaced the Chauchaut after World War I.

"For the units we'll train, I'm recommending standardization on the Heckler-Koch system. That means G3s and HK-21s, with obvious advantages: same 7.62 mm ammo and the same operating system. That roller-locking action can be hard for low-dedication troopies to maintain but the guns are reliable as tax time. They'll keep working with minimum maintenance."

"Why not M16s?" asked Joshua Wallender. "I mean, we know them inside out and they're easier to shoot than the .30 calibers."

"Concur, as far as you go. If we could ever use decent 5.56 ammo, something designed to kill people rather than meet some pussy standard in Sweden—which hasn't fought a war in about two hundred years—I might consider M16s. However, in this case we're contractors to the U.S. Government, so we gotta abide by its regs.

"But the big problem is that we're working in Chad. As in, desert. As in, sand. As in, major malfunction. M16s just aren't reliable enough."

Wallender ventured another query. "Well, why not AKs? They work everywhere."

Foyte was slightly disappointed in the new man. A veteran NCO should know the reason. "Because the opposition likely uses them. No point giving the guerrillas more guns and ammo that they can use."

Wallender seemed to blush slightly. Foyte predicted that he would shut up for a while.

"Now, personally, I trust AKs and I like FALs," Foyte enthused. "And I *really* like Sigs. Good sights, good trigger. But FALs aren't a lot better than '16s in the desert and I've never used Sigs in that area, so I don't want to be the one who's experimenting. So we'll use G3s and related systems. We'll get up to speed on those before we leave."

Mohammed interjected. "If I may add something."

Foyte nodded.

"Because of the language situation, we should review the course material even if the Chadians will not see it. I can work with the French and Arabic speakers to standardize phraseology." He glanced at Johnson, Nissen, and Wallender.

Breezy leaned toward Bosco and muttered, "Ignorance is bliss, dude."

Foyte speared the former paratrooper with a Parris Island glare. "Something to add, Brezyinski?"

Breezy sat upright. "Ah, nosir. Gunny."

Foyte walked in front of the rostrum and leaned forward, hands akimbo. "Oh, come now, my boy. You would not interrupt Dr. Mohammed unless you had something significant to contribute."

Bosco smirked behind one hand, enjoying his pal's discomfiture.

"Ah, I was just remarking to my esteemed Ranger colleague here that I consider myself fortunate not to be bilingual. Sir."

Foyte squinted as through a rifle sight. "How many times do I gotta say it? Don't call me 'sir' . . ."

"I WORK FOR A LIVING," the audience chimed in.

Mohammed enjoyed the exchange as much as anyone, but decided to make a point. "Gentlemen, regardless of the language, we need to be consistent in our instruction. For example, what is the difference between covering fire and suppressing fire?"

Bosco and Breezy exchanged looks. "Damn'fiknow," Breezy responded.

Bosco shrugged. "I'm not sure there is any difference. Just terminology."

Foyte was primed. "Well, for our purposes there *is* a difference. Covering fire is basically suppressive fire for a specific purpose—getting a squad close enough to engage a defended position, for instance. Suppressing fire is just a straight-up shoot-out. We lay down a heavier, more accurate volume of fire than the bad guys so they stop shooting at us."

"Fire superiority, in other words," Breezy offered.

Foyte grunted. The audience took that as an affirmative.

Johnson raised a hand. "Gunny, I don't mean to seem superior or anything, but are the Chadians going to understand the distinction?"

Foyte's grimace said that the un-PC question had struck home. "Well, let's just say that it's our damn job to make sure they do. By the way, Johnson, how do you say 'covering and suppressing fire' in French?"

"Covering fire would be *Le feu de bache.* Suppressing fire would be *Suppression de feu.*" Johnson paused a moment. "When you think about it, that makes a lot of sense. The literal translation would be 'the fire that covers' and 'suppression of fire.' "

"Go to the head of the class, Johnson." Foyte actually smiled at the former Legionnaire. "Now then, we have a lot of other ground to cover. If you'll refer to your briefing papers . . ."

SSI OFFICES

Strategic Solutions took little for granted. Predeployment planning was thorough for any client, but especially so for overseas business. Aside from contract negotiations—the meat in the corporate sandwich— Michael Derringer kept close contact with his subordinates, none moreso than those charged with operations.

Sometimes his supervisory duties trod the thin line between too much oversight and too little. After all, Marshall Wilmont was the chief operating officer, but he had multiple pies in the oven. Never a micromanager, the retired admiral nonetheless kept his fingers on his baby's pulse. And SSI was definitely his baby.

At the end of a staff meeting, Derringer took Leopold aside. "Frank, I've been thinking about leadership of the Chad team. Don't misunderstand me: I have every confidence in Gunny Foyte. But I wonder how our clients will relate to a former NCO. They may pay more attention to a retired officer."

Leopole rubbed his square jaw. Derringer knew the sign: Lieutenant Colonel Leopole was an objective professional. The former Marine was playing mental tug of war between Loyalty and The Mission.

Derringer interrupted Leopole's reverie. "I'm thinking that some-body like Steve Lee could run interference for our team, leaving Foyte to do the hands-on work."

Leopole had worked with Major Lee and respected him, though they were not close. West Pointer, Ranger, sniper instructor, HALO parachuting instructor, all the bells and whistles. His Been-There-Done-That sheet contained operations in five countries. Despite the glasses, he had command presence that went over especially well in the third world.

"All right, sir. Lee would do a good job. But I don't know if he's avail-able."

Derringer smiled imperceptibly. He had checked before raising the matter. "I believe he is, actually." Derringer knew that Steve Lee, twice divorced with no children, was marking time. Derringer thought, *He's like Martin Sheen in* Apocalypse Now. *Waiting for another mission.*

"I'll call him," Derringer continued. "He works all right with Gunny Foyte, doesn't he?"

Leopold gave an eloquent shrug. "They're both pros, Admiral."

Derringer appeared content with that assessment. It was what he bought and sold: professionalism. "One thing, though, Lee doesn't speak French, let alone Arabic. German, if I remember correctly. So we'll have to rely on Johnson, Nissen, and Wallender in that regard."

Leopole grinned hugely. "Don't forget Martha."

The admiral returned the sentiment, rolling his eyes. "How could I? She wouldn't let me even if I could!"

"Speak of the devil. There she is." Leopold motioned over his shoulder.

Martha Whitney announced her presence with a contralto greeting to Josh Wallender. *"Bon après midi, mon sergeant."*

The erstwhile Green Beret returned the salutation with a continen-tal kiss of the hand. *"Et à vous, madame. Enchanté."*

Breezy Brezyinski took in the arcane ritual and shook his head. "Man, oh, man. Looks like we can't take a contract without a female anymore."

Bosco Boscombe knew what he meant. Dr. Carolyn Padgett-Smith, a medical researcher, had been invaluable on the Pandora Project, hunt-ing down an Islamic cell that spread the Marburg virus in the west. "By the way, any word on CPS?"

Breezy replied, "Last I heard, she was back at work. Don't suppose she's doing much rock climbing, though. Not after the exposure she had to that bug in Pakistan."

With a skeptical glance, Bosco made a mental comparison between the bejeweled, garrulous Ms. Whitney and the athletic, attractive British immunologist. "I tell you what: this lady has a looong way to go in Doc Smith's league."

"Well, I don't reckon there's gonna be many mountains to climb or Taliban to shoot where we're going. Besides, Whitney's gig is language and intel, not operations."

"Thank God!" Bosco exclaimed. "Queen Latifah meets G.I. Jane!"

Breezy nearly choked while suppressing a laugh. "Sandy Carmichael says Martha's supposed to blend into the crowd. Like, mingle with the locals when she's not coordinating with Steve Lee and the Chad liaison officers."

"Major Lee is welcome to that chore. Big time."

"Fershure, dude."

N'DJAMENA, CHAD

The operator called Alexander was resigned to his loss. David Olmert clearly was not coming back. It was as if he had vanished off the face of the earth.

Alexander knew why.

The reason or reasons would likely remain unknown for years; perhaps forever. David had been careless, unobservant, or committed some error of tradecraft. In any case, he was gone.

At a café off the Place de l'Etoile, Alex slipped into a chair beside a distinguished-looking Arab gentleman. Which is to say, the well-groomed diner appeared to be an Arab. They spoke Arabic, keeping their voices beneath the background chatter.

"*Etfadel echrab kahwa.*" The older man poured some coffee from the pot on his table. "No word?" he asked. He sipped from his own small cup, then absentmindedly brushed his gray goatee. Anyone glancing at him would mark him for a sixtyish businessman; likely a Saudi. In truth he had been born in Jerusalem nearly seventy years ago.

Alexander shook his head. "*Wala hayoh.*"

Mustafah—for such was his name these days—placed his cup on

the saucer. He did not wish to seem callous, but he and his accomplice both knew the lay of the land. One had to expect losses in their profession, and it did not do to take them too personally.

"Permit me to summarize," Mustafah said. "We know that the preferred French contractor ran afoul of Groupe FGN, which eliminated the competition."

"Of course! David and I saw it ourselves."

"And David confirmed that the surviving members of Agents d'Alsace Incorpore's team left for Paris the day he disappeared."

"That was the last thing I heard from him. It would be easy to check their arrival at Orly."

"*Maalish*," Mustafah replied. "Never mind." He toyed with his miniature cup. At length he looked at his colleague. "I have my own theory as to why Groupe FGN is behaving so brazenly. I have not heard yours."

Alex leaned forward, moving his cup and saucer aside. "My friend, I have not been in the trade nearly as long as you, but I have learned one or two things. For example, I know the danger of drawing the obvious conclusion."

"Which is?"

"Hurtubise and his killers want to remove any competition for the government contract to guard the uranium mine near the Libyan border."

Mustafah's eyes narrowed in concentration. "Obviously they have done so. But to what purpose?"

"Well, apparently not just for the contract. It would be profitable, yes, but they could have underbid AAI without much difficulty."

"Go on, Alex."

"It seems clear that FGN has another motive. Maybe I can understand such drastic measures within the mercenary business. But taking David, who was only observing both companies, raises the stakes. I mean, it exposes Hurtubise to Israeli scrutiny. Surely he knows the risk that carries."

"You mean retaliation."

Alexander's eyes glinted gunmetal gray. "I should hope so."

Mustafah absorbed the sentiment, catalogued it, and continued. "You assume he knows that David works for us."

The younger man rubbed a bronzed hand through his dark, curly hair. "It strains credulity that he does not. Especially after . . ."

"After extended interrogation."

Alexander merely nodded. He did not trust his voice just then.

"Very well," Mustafah concluded. "Your assessment largely matches mine. With a few exceptions."

"Yes?"

The Middle Eastern "businessman" leaned back, folding his hands over his ample stomach. "There are always extensions and permutations, Alex. What is known in the West as unintended consequences.

"We can assume for the moment that Groupe FGN considers the risk it has brought upon itself worth the effort. The ultimate reason may be inferred, considering that uranium ore is involved. That makes Hurtubise and company exceedingly dangerous."

"Sir, with respect. That is nothing new."

Mustafah inclined his head in acknowledgment. "Remember, my friend. FGN now has the support of this government and likely another."

Alex furrowed his brow. "Another?"

"Certainly. Chad has no need of uranium ore. There is no way to process it in this backward country. No, the end user is certainly a more developed nation—one hostile to Israel."

The agent relaxed despite the implications. "Well, the list is long and undistinguished."

"But don't you see, Alex? It can only be a country with the ability to use uranium. That narrows your undistinguished list considerably, don't you think?"

Alexander bit his lip. Looking over his superior's shoulder, he said, "Two or three. Especially . . ."

"There is one more thing."

"Please?"

"Whatever our opponents have in mind—they do not fear us."

SSI OFFICES

Terry Keegan rapped his knuckles on Daniel Foyte's cubicle. "You wanted to see me, Gunny?"

The erstwhile Force Recon NCO swiveled in his chair, turning away from his computer screen. The miniature office was much like its occupant: austere, uncluttered, utilitarian. The only décor was a Marine Corps logo and a poster of John Wayne as Sergeant John M. Stryker in *The Sands of Iwo Jima*. "Oh, yeah. Terry." Foyte habitually referred to people by their surname. He had almost forgotten Keegan's, though they had worked together twice.

The pilot eased into Foyte's "guest chair," a folding metal fixture calculated to keep guests uncomfortable and visits short. "You want to talk about contingencies for Chad." It was a statement, not a question.

"Affirm." After a four-count, Keegan realized that Foyte expected him to carry the conversation. If the ex-Navy man had learned anything about Marines, it was the futility of trying to be one of them. The Corps was like the IRA of Keegan's ancestors: "Once in, never out."

"Well," Keegan began, "the admiral always wants a backup in case local exits are blocked. So I've been looking at a couple of ways to extract you guys."

"Fixed wing or helo?"

"Both, depending on conditions. The Chadians have Alouettes, which is a plus. It's one of my three go-to choppers like the Huey and the Hip because you find it everywhere. Something like fifty countries use Alouettes. Anyway, I try to stay current in them because you never know when you might have to steal one." He did not smile when he said it.

"Uh, have you ever had to?"

Keegan finally grinned. "I don't understand the question."

"Gotcha."

"Thing is, if we have to extract the whole team, we'll need at least two choppers, maybe three. I'd rather use a twin-engine plane: something that can get in and out of a small field in just one trip. Also, something with enough range to get us out of Dodge on one tank of gas."

"Like how far?"

Keegan unfolded a map of Saharan Africa. "Well, of course it depends on where we start from. I mean, Chad's a pretty big place: about a thousand miles north to south, and Libya's the only northern exit." He fingered the capital. "For starters, let's assume we're near N'Djamena. That's down here, right on the border with Cameroon. With enough warning, we could easily drive into Cameroon or fly straight across the northern part into Nigeria. That might be advisable, depending on the political situation in those countries. I think Nigeria is pretty friendly."

"What kind of fighters operate in those countries?" Foyte asked.

"Niger just has some military transports. That's the good news. The bad news is that the nearest airfield is over here at Zinder, about four hundred miles west of N'Djamena. But Zinder has a six-thousand-foot runway. They speak French but that's probably the best bet for a friendly reception. The capital is Niamey, and I have a contact there."

Foyte scanned the map, gauging the distances and geometry. "What do they fly in Nigeria?"

Keegan smirked. "They had Jaguars and MiG-21s but those have been down for a long time. The government wanted to sell them to help finance newer equipment but apparently it didn't happen. Anyway, Maiduguri is only 150 miles from Chad, and has a nine-thousand-foot runway. Also, they speak English there. Apparently Sandy Carmichael served with the current defense attaché, who's another West Point gal."

Foyte merely nodded. After two divorces he had a decidedly unromantic attitude toward females. "Any problems with Cameroon?"

"Well, their Air Force has a few Alpha Jets and Magisters. Not much, really, but they could cause a helo a big-time hurt. However, we're on pretty good terms with the place right now. The nearest city to N'Djamena is Maroua, less than 150 miles south. It's a good field: 6,800 feet paved. Garoua is even better: 11,000 feet but maybe 250 miles from N'Djamena."

The former noncom leaned back, hands behind his head. "Okay. Sounds like you've got the threats all doped out. But what about nav aids in that part of the world? It looks like a lot of open space."

"Well, there's a saying: the desert is an ocean in which no oar is dipped."

"Who said that?"

"I think it was T. E. Lawrence. Or maybe Peter O'Toole."

"Who?"

Keegan should have known that Dan Foyte was not a movie fan. "Ah, he played Lawrence of Arabia. In *Lawrence of Arabia*."

Foyte shook his balding head. "Okay. What's it mean?"

"Just that navigating over featureless terrain is no different than over water. You're back to time and distance, which is something naval aviators know about. If the nav aids go down, we still have GPS. If that goes down, we fall back on dead reckoning."

Foyte rubbed his chin, playing the perennial game of What If. "Okay, let's say we get away from Chad with no big problems. If we're in a hurry, and haven't filed a flight plan or anything, how do we know where to land?"

Keegan's eyes twinkled. "Hey, my attitude about unauthorized landings is that it's easier to ask forgiveness than permission."

The former Marine gave a grunt that seemed to imply approval. Finally he asked, "Is the admiral going to spring for renting some choppers or a charter jet?"

"Too soon to say, Gunny. But I'll have at least two prospects lined up before you guys hit Chad. After that it's a matter of monitoring the situation."

In truth, Terrence Keegan knew empirically that a pistol barrel in someone's ear could cut a great deal of red tape when "renting" an aircraft. "Anyway, we have four possible airports from 150 to 400 miles from N'Djamena. All are paved with long runways. Depending on what shakes out, I'll plan on cross-border hops by helo into Cameroon or longer flights to Cameroon and Niger with Nigeria as second alternate."

Foyte beamed. "Nice to have options, ain't it?"

"Freakin' right, Gunny. Freakin' right."

SSI OFFICES

"Look at this," Breezy exclaimed. He straightened the pages from a week-old *London Gazette* that Derringer had left in the lounge.

"What?" Bosco was barely interested in the news; he was engrossed in his sci-fi thriller.

"Well, it says here that an Aussie just got the Victoria Cross. First time in about forty years." Breezy paused for effect. "In Chad."

Bosco turned from voluptuous Carmogian females wielding phased-array plasma weapons in the Second Virgo Galaxy War. "You mean, the guys we're replacing?"

"Guess so." Breezy read aloud. "'The queen has been graciously pleased on the advice of her Australian ministers to approve the posthumous award of the Victoria Cross to the undermentioned:

"'Warrant Officer Class Two Derrick Jasper Martin, the 138th Signals Squadron.

"'Warrant Officer Martin carried out an act of great heroism by which he saved the life of a comrade. The act was in direct face of hostile forces, under intense fire, at great personal risk leading to his death. His valour is worthy of the highest recognition.

" 'While engaged in peacekeeping operations near Massenya, Chad, on fourth September, Martin's vehicle was destroyed by hostile fire that killed two crew members. Nevertheless, Martin pulled his badly wounded driver from the burning vehicle and, exhibiting selfless courage, carried him to temporary safety while employing his personal weapon to suppress close-range fire from local gunmen. Upon reaching temporary shelter in a nearby building, Martin defended his comrade with the greatest determination, accounting for a large number of hostile rioters. Without succor from security forces, with whom he could not communicate, Martin passed his driver to friendly civilians and continued covering their withdrawal until his ammunition was exhausted. When last seen he was retrieving an enemy weapon to continue his extraordinarily gallant fight against overwhelming odds.' "

When Breezy finished reading, Bosco made no comment, flippant or otherwise. It was unusual for the mountaineering ex-Ranger, SSI's rappelling expert. His friend asked, "What do you think, man?"

Jason Boscombe seemed to be focused somewhere beyond the wall. Finally he turned to the onetime paratrooper and said, "I think that the Silver Star they pinned on me in Iraq doesn't amount to that dude's shoelaces. That's what I think."

Neither operator had ever wanted to dissect their stock in trade: courage under lethal stress. It was not what door-kickers talked about, certainly not as much as guns and gear or babes and baseball.

Breezy looked over his shoulder. Nobody was within earshot so he ventured an opinion. "Hell, dude, you'd do the same as that Aussie. So would any of the guys."

Bosco leveled his gaze at his partner. "Tell me somethin', Breeze. What's the most you were ever scared?"

Breyzinski was tempted to toss off a reply about Charlotte Bernstein's parents returning unexpectedly early one evening, but he checked himself. *Bosco really wants to talk.* He thought for a moment. "Oh, I dunno, man. There's been several, you know?" He catalogued the first few that came to mind. "Prob'ly on my fourth qualifying jump at Bragg. I got a streamer and had to cut away from the main. I popped my reserve just in time. Swung twice and hit the ground like a sack of potatoes." He grinned self-consciously. "Wasn't pretty."

"But you did what you had to do," Bosco prompted.

"Well, sure, dude! I mean, it's not like I had a choice." He raised both hands palms up, as if measuring two weights. "Live. Die. Live. Die." He laughed nervously this time. "Some choice!"

Breezy straightened in his chair, facing Bosco. "Well, that's what I'm saying, man. You, me, the other guys. We're here because we reacted like we were trained. It's like Uncle Sugar programmed the last setting into our brain housing unit, and when the computer was about to crash, we defaulted to our survival program. Right?"

Bosco bit his lip in concentration. He nodded. "Affirm. That's right. But what's your point?"

"My point is, man, that what we're talking about was this much time." He held up a thumb and forefinger, not quite touching. "We really didn't have time to think, whether it was a bad chute or a skid on an icy road or a gomer swinging his AK on you. We just reacted. But that WO2, he had time to *think* about it. I mean, he had *this* much time." The thumb extended two inches from the trigger finger. "He could think about what he was going to do before he had to do it."

"I see what you mean," Bosco said. "But I still don't think it makes a lot of difference. Like I said, dude. You or me or anybody we know— we'd all have done what that Aussie guy did. I mean, can you imagine yourself walking away from a bud in deep serious?" He shook his head emphatically. "No way, man. Just no way."

"So you'd rather die than look bad. That what you're saying?"

"No, damn it, that's not what I'm saying. I'd just stick with a friend and try to help him out, you know?"

Breezy pushed the point. "Even if you know you'd die."

Bosco had heard enough. "Damn it, Breeze, what's got into you?"

Brezyinski crumpled the newspaper and set it aside. "I dunno. All of a sudden I just got a bad feeling about this Chad thing." He stood up and stretched. "You wanna get a burger or something for dinner?"

Bosco felt a tiny shiver between his shoulder blades. "After your cheerful conversation, I think I want some brewskis."

"Well, okay. C'mon to my place. We'll make some poppa-charlie and pop some lids."

"Sounds like a date, dude." Bosco was always up for popcorn. None of that diet variety; the more salt and butter the better.

"Sure, dinner and a movie." Breezy felt better at the light banter.

Bosco perked up. "What's the movie?"

"*Black Hawk Down.*"

"Oh, good," Bosco replied. "I like happy endings."

PART

II

CHAD

HASSAN DJAMOUS AIRPORT
N'DJAMENA, CHAD

The door opened and Chadian wind blew Saharan dust into the Airbus A-320.

Breezy recoiled. "Geez, you can smell it in here already."

Bosco's attention was focused elsewhere. He had been playing visual patty-cake with one of the Air France flight attendants for the last 650 kilometers.

"What'd you say?"

"Never mind," Breezy replied. He opened the overhead compartment and grasped his valise.

The rest of the SSI team exited in orderly fashion but Breezy had to retrieve his errant partner by the collar.

"Hey, dude," Bosco protested. "I was just makin' progress. Her name is Nadine. She used to be a figure skater. Get that? *Figure* skater. Not ice skater."

"Like there's a difference?"

Bosco lowered his Oakley shades from atop his head and flashed a white smile. "Well, sure. I mean, she speaks fluent English, you know? She emphasized it: *fig-ure* skater. As in, girls with figures."

"I'd say she came to the wrong part of the world, dude. Not much ice around here."

With a fond look over his shoulder, Bosco allowed himself to be steered toward the Airbus's forward door. Nadine waved bye-bye with a coquettish smile.

Breezy wasn't sure, but he thought the brown-eyed blond winked at him.

———

Daniel Foyte assembled the SSI crew inside the passenger terminal while Steve Lee searched for the reception he had been told to expect. Bosco was still craning his neck for another glimpse of Nadine when the assistant attaché appeared.

A tall, black U.S. Army officer strode down the corridor. "Gentlemen, you must be the training team." The voice carried Georgia tones mixed with Barry White resonance.

"Yessir," Foyte replied. He kept his tone respectfully noncommittal. Tardiness was not a military virtue—certainly not a Marine virtue, anyway.

The officer extended his hand. "I'm Major Roosevelt. Matt Roosevelt, defense attaché. Colonel Posen of the military advisory group expected to meet you but he got a last-minute call from the ambassador. I hope you haven't been waiting too long."

"Dan Foyte," the gunny said, giving the Army man an ooh-rah handshake, extra crispy with mustard on top. He quickly introduced the others, taking care to dwell on Martha Whitney. "She and Major Lee are going to be our liaison with the Chad ministries."

Whitney had already gone on point. She noticed that Major Roosevelt's left hand was unencumbered by any rings.

The attaché, being a well brought up young man, did not offer his hand to a lady. Martha, being polite by her neighborhood standards, slapped him on the forearm. "Pleased to meet you, Major baby. We're gonna see a lot of each other, I can tell." She beamed at him. "I bet they call you Rosey."

Roosevelt did not see her wink at Foyte. The former Marine tried to keep a straight face, wondering when Whitney would treat the major to her African-American speech.

If Roosevelt sensed something passing between the two SSI delegates, he decided to ignore it. Instead he explained, "Most travelers are required to register with the *Sûreté Nationale*, the National Police, within seventy-two hours. But because you're officially with State, you can skip that. I'll escort you through Customs and then we'll drive to your compound."

"Thank you Major," Foyte replied. "But we need to wait for Major Lee."

"Oh, is he still aboard the plane?"

Foyte was formulating a diplomatic reply when Whitney interjected, "Oh, no, darlin'. He's runnin' around lookin' for our reception committee!" Leaning close, she whispered just loud enough to be overheard. "West Pointer. You know how tight those academy boys are wrapped."

Roosevelt shook his head imperceptibly, as if avoiding a persistent insect. When he found his voice he said, "Yes, ma'am. I surely do. Class of '93." He flashed the ring on his right hand.

Without missing a beat, Whitney batted her big brown eyes and touched his arm again. "Oh, I think that's *so* stylish. May I see it?"

Major Matthew Roosevelt had just learned the first thing about Martha Whitney: she could not be embarrassed or flustered.

At that moment Lee arrived, momentarily wondering why Whitney was holding hands with a stranger. As he approached, Lee realized that she was examining the man's USMA jewelry.

Foyte made the introductions. As the two West Pointers shook hands, Whitney reluctantly released her grip on the attaché.

"Welcome to Chad," Roosevelt exclaimed.

"Thanks," Lee replied. Trying to minimize Whitney's representation as an SSI member, he sought to talk shop. "Ah, you know, I was surprised to see we have an attaché office here. Is that new?"

Roosevelt nodded. "Affirmative. Usually we just maintain an advisory group, but the way things are going in the region, it was decided to upgrade the staff. We also have an Air Force rep out of Cairo who rotates between here and Niger."

As the group gathered its luggage, Whitney was distracted long enough for Roosevelt to give Lee the visual equivalent of the West Point secret handshake. "Tell me something," the attaché muttered. "Is she always like this?"

Lee grimaced. "Yeah, pretty much. Martha would flirt with the Pope and call him 'honey.' "

Roosevelt's eyes widened. "Hey, I think I'll invite her to the next diplomatic reception!"

N'DJAMENA
MINISTRY OF INTERIOR AND SECURITY

François Kadabi was a tall, slender bureaucrat with an easy command of French, English, Arabic, and several Chadian dialectcs. He extended a long, bony hand and purred, "Ah, Major Lee. So good to meet you." The deputy secretary motioned with his other hand. "Shall we have some tea?"

Lee disliked the man immediately, so he smiled broadly. "My pleasure, sir. And thank you. I would enjoy that."

Settled at the marble-topped table, the two officials regarded one another as a servant poured. Kadabi dismissed the man with a flick of the hand, as if shooing away a bothersome pest.

Once they were alone, the Chadian immediately set down his cup and leaned forward. "Major, I shall do you the honor of speaking plainly." He gave an ingratiating smile. "That is, if you do not object to candor so soon in our . . . relationship."

The American nodded slowly. "Certainly, sir." He paused. "After all, honesty *is* the best policy." His tone dripped with irony.

Kadabi seemed to relax. He leaned back, grinning whitely, his head rearward. "Ah-ha! I thought so!" The bureaucrat actually slapped a knee. "You Americans and your sense of humor! You say one thing but your voice and your face speaks the opposite."

Before Lee could respond, Kadabi was leaning forward again, all angular urgency. "Major, I believe that we both know the ways of politics and politicians." He shrugged eloquently. "For myself, I live in the world of politicians, of course, but I am merely a facilitator. My country, poor as she is, badly needs the services that your firm can provide. But I wanted this opportunity to explain something to you."

Lee felt his initial frostiness receding. He thought: *I've been wrong before. Just can't remember when.*

François Kadabi was rubbing his elegant hands together, apparently unconsciously. "Much as we need you, I believe that you should hear the truth. There are, I fear, people in this nation and in the government who do not wish you to succeed. Their motives are plain—jealousy and money. Always money."

Lee turned his head as if studying the specimen more closely. Which in fact was the case. "Sir, I had a pretty thorough briefing before I left Washington and I've met with our attaché here. He explained the, ah, rivalry that exists between the army and the security forces. But if there's more to it, I'd be grateful for your views."

Kadabi folded his hands beneath his chin. "Major Lee, this after all is Africa. On top of the political rivalries that exist everywhere, there is our own set of complications. Some are historic, some are tribal. But you are charged with forming an elite unit—a *truly* elite unit—and that makes certain persons nervous. Yes, quite nervous."

Lee did not want to assume too much of Mr. Kadabi's education, nor too little. He ventured an historic comparison. "The praetorian guard syndrome?"

"No, not exactly." Kadabi abruptly rose, turned to his desk, and produced a folder. "A praetorian guard owes its allegiance to the head of state, keeping that head upon its throne." He grinned archly. "Or, more precisely, upon its shoulders."

Steve Lee seldom changed his mind quickly. He was aware that his opinion of François Kadabi represented an exception.

"This country has two or three praetorian guards. Maybe more. But your unit is undoubtedly going to be technically competent and capably led. That means it could be seen as a threat." His eyebrows arched. "You see the implications, of course."

Lee stood to face his new ally. "Sir, I am most appreciative of your candor. But let me ask: how can our counterinsurgency force be a threat to the power structure? For one thing, we're not political—we're operational. For another, we're probably going to be operating well away from the capital."

Kadabi gave another ingratiating smile, this time with some warmth. "Major, you are correct. But please indulge me if I say that you are taking the military man's perspective. I must account for other factors." He paused, gathering his thoughts. "Consider this: when your contract is completed, you will return to America. But your force will remain, and it may be seen as a virus that could multiply and spread. For that reason, I share my concerns with you."

Immediately, Lee knew that the African was right. "Then we have a lot more to discuss, sir. I mean, I'd like to know who we can trust to . . ."

"Trust!" Kadabi raised his eyes to the paneled ceiling. "Major Lee, you and I may trust one another, I believe. Outside this room . . . I would be far more cautious. Yes, far more cautious."

Lee sat down again, demonstrating his willingness for further discussion. "Well, as long as there's enough tea to keep my throat wet, I'll be glad to talk, Mr. Karabi."

The minister unleashed his slippery grin again. Pointedly glancing at his Swiss watch, he said, "It is still rather early in the day, my friend. But, ah, shall we change to something more . . . convivial?"

Before Lee could answer, Karabi pressed the buzzer on his desktop. The servant reappeared, bearing a bottle of iced champagne.

The American's expression opened visibly. "Ah, Mr. Kar . . ."

Karabi raised his slim right hand again. "Please. From now on I am François."

"All right . . . François. I'm Steve."

"Now then, Steve, this is a decent '89. That is, if you do not object."

Lee shook his head slightly. "Not hardly, sir. Er, François. Usually I'm partial to single-malt scotch."

"Very well, Steve. I shall remember. For next time."

23

N'DJAMENA

Major Matthew Roosevelt wasted no time in the orientation briefing. "There's a lot of crime in the city," he began. "We do not recommend going anywhere alone, especially after dark."

Breezy raised a hand. "What about packing?"

Roosevelt's eyes widened. "You mean, carrying a concealed weapon?"

"Well, sure. Most of us have pistols."

Roosevelt rubbed his jaw. "I'm not sure. I mean, I understand your desire to defend yourself. But—"

Lee interrupted. "Major, I think we can claim diplomatic status. I mean, we're contracted to the State Department and we have ID to that effect."

Lee's intent was clear: if any SSI people had to shoot for blood, they would invoke immunity.

Roosevelt walked to the door and made a point of closing it. When he returned to the head of the room he inhaled, held his breath, and let it out. "All right, look. You did not hear this from me. I'll deny it if anybody quotes me, okay?"

Lee nodded. Foyte uttered an "Ooh-rah."

"I hardly go anywhere without my Hi-Power. But if I ever had to use it, I'd probably be out of the Army by noon the next day, if I wasn't in jail. What I'm saying is, I'd go a loooong way around the block to avoid having to shoot somebody."

"Certainly," Lee replied. "We've been in that situation before."

The assistant attaché surveyed the audience. "What do you guys carry?"

Foyte responded. "We settled on nine millimeters, Sigs and Glocks. We brought a couple cases of Romanian ammo so any brass we leave behind will be untraceable. If we need more, nine mil's easy to get."

Roosevelt grinned despite himself. "Gunny, you are one sneaky son of a . . . gun."

"Roger that, sir." Foyte managed a deadpan expression.

"Any nonlethal stuff?"

"Like what?" Bosco asked.

"Pepper spray, Tasers, that sort of thing."

Foyte and Lee glanced at Martha Whitney. She almost blushed. "Maje, honey, I got both. I also got two knives including a switchblade." She flashed her Aunt Jemima grin. "And, Sugah, Ah knows how to use *all* of 'em."

Roosevelt ignored the endearment and nodded gravely. "Well, if you can disable an assailant without killing him, there'll be a lot less paperwork."

U.S. EMBASSY

Steve Lee and Dan Foyte entered the American embassy on the south side of Avenue du Gouverneur Felix Eboue, about four hundred meters west of Rue Victor Schoelcher. They were close enough to the embankment to smell the ambience of the Chari River.

Matt Roosevelt and Colonel Brian Posen were waiting for them.

Posen showed the SSI men to a secure meeting room and wasted little time with formalities. Taking the chair at the head of the table, the chief of the advisory group looked at Lee. "I understand your meeting with Kadabi went pretty well."

Lee glanced at Foyte, who realized that a mere NCO counted for little. It was not the first time.

The erstwhile West Pointer squirmed slightly and, with a sideways glance, said, "Well, Colonel, as I was telling Gunny Foyte, I found Mr. Kadabi both friendly and forthcoming."

Posen nodded, hands folded before him. "That's fine, Major. Fine. As far as it goes." He chewed his lip for a moment. "Let me warn you, though. If François Kadabi is acting friendly, it's because he wants something. Oh, he's not entirely disingenuous. He can be genuinely helpful, but in our experience it's only when he sees an advantage for himself."

Lee nodded. "Very well, sir. What's that mean where we're concerned?"

Posen nodded to Roosevelt, who swiveled in his chair. "Steve, I was taken by your mention that Kadabi warned you about jealousies within the Army and security forces. Ordinarily that'd just be common sense in a place like this. But we know that Kadabi pulled strings to get the liaison job with SSI. Apparently he called in one or two markers."

Beneath his breath, Foyte began whistling "The Marines' Hymn" when Lee kicked him beneath the table. In a rare gesture of interservice harmony, Foyte shifted to "The Caisson Song."

"All right," Lee replied. "What's the significance?"

Roosevelt flipped his notebook. "He went over his department head to make sure he worked with you. It took a little pull because of the diplomatic connection on our end, but he got it done. He's working with an upper-level manager in the natural resources ministry."

Lee shrugged. "So?"

"So," Posen interjected, "that gentleman is a cousin of Kadabi's. He deals with Chad's uranium exports."

Lee and Foyte exchanged raised eyebrows. Lee asked, "Then why weren't we told about that before?"

"Steve, I just found out about it myself," Roosevelt replied. "Apparently it was worked out a couple of months ago but they're keeping it quiet. For obvious reasons."

Foyte decided that he had endured enough of being ignored. Looking at Roosevelt, he asked, "Sir, I'm just a retired jarhead noncom. What's obvious about it?"

Roosevelt fielded the question before Posen could visibly take offense. "Ah, excuse me, Gunny. I was speaking about the connection between the counterinsurgency force you'll be training and the country's uranium deposits. One of our main Co-In concerns is keeping those assets out of rebel hands. In other words—"

"In words a Marine can understand," Foyte interrupted, "you don't want this Kadabi character making deals with his cousin while SSI's clients provide his muscle for him."

A question occurred to Lee. "Who's the cousin?"

Posen shook his head. "Excuse me?"

"Kadabi's cousin. Who is he?"

Roosevelt consulted his notebook again. "Moungar. Felix Moungar."

"Does he have authority in security matters?"

Roosevelt thought for a moment. "He might. But if he doesn't, Kadabi sure does. Their main advantage is a lot of information and mutual back scratching."

Foyte whistled aloud. "Then it's like we discussed with Frank Leopole before we left. We damn well better decide just how well we're gonna train these boys."

Roosevelt grimaced. "Ah, Gunny, I would caution you against describing black men as 'boys.' "

Foyte opened his mouth, then pressed his lips together. Political correctness and racial sensitivity ranked in his esteem somewhere between women's lib and communism. He merely nodded, staring into the assistant attaché's brown eyes.

Lee retrieved the situation, deftly saying, "Your point is well taken, Matt, but Gunny's question still stands. We discussed it before leaving, but of course it's not an SSI decision. So . . . just how well is this new outfit to be trained? For that matter, how much training can it really absorb?"

Roosevelt and Posen exchanged glances. The senior officer took up the subject. "The background is in your briefing packet," Posen began, "but I'll summarize." He paused, gathering his thoughts. "Most of the men you'll deal with have field experience within the past couple of years. Many of them have combat experience. All of them speak French, many Arabic as well. They come from units that have received training from U.S. or French instructors, and that combined with what you'll teach them is expected to result in a two-tiered mission: greater operational capability and providing a cadre for domestic training as well."

Lee replied, "Yes, sir. That's my understanding. We were told that we're going to build up to battalion strength."

Roosevelt made a politely skeptical sound, not quite a snort. "Well, yes, officially. But actually the unit is going to look more like a reinforced company: about 240 men at first. It's commanded by a lieutenant colonel because that's commensurate with a battalion."

Foyte ventured another opinion. "Then we'll be operating in platoon strength most likely."

"Well," Roosevelt responded, "we don't expect you guys to operate with them, but you might provide, ah, advice on occasion. But essentially yes, they'll probably deploy with thirty to forty men most of the time."

Lee smiled to himself but Roosevelt caught the look. "Something on your mind, Steve?"

The West Pointer leaned back, drumming his fingers on the desk. "Oh, I was just thinking—that's how we got involved in Vietnam."

SSI COMPOUND

J. J. Johnson was the lead briefer, but he did not relish the task. He much preferred instructing to lecturing, but his fluency in French military terminology made him the hands-down favorite for delivering the SSI Counterinsurgency Brief. It was essentially boilerplate, distilling the conventional wisdom of Co-In philosophy for use almost anywhere the company might operate.

Facing a room full of Chadian Army officers, Johnson introduced himself, minimizing his Legion background by referring the audience to the SSI personnel sheets in their packets.

In his Parisian accent, the American began by apologizing for duplication of any subject matter that the Chadians might already have studied. Privately, he felt that probably few had ever given ten minutes' thought to counterinsurgency doctrine, but he did not want to alienate potential allies. It was dogma with SSI to avoid the appearance of condescension toward any clients.

Johnson had practiced the presentation with PowerPoint and a flip chart, depending on local facilities. He was pleased to see that the electronic option was preferred, at least in the elevated ambience of the security offices. He inhaled, focused, and began to summarize the six points.

"*Premier: Identifiez qu'il n'y a aucune solution purement militaire.* Recognize that there is no purely military solution. Nearly all insurgencies are caused by dissatisfaction with the status quo, for whatever reason. Therefore, while military methods might gain a temporary advantage, political and economic measures must go hand in hand.

"*Deuxième: Obtenez l'intelligence fiable.* Obtain reliable intelligence.

That's often easier said than done, gentlemen. There are many sources of information on rebellious factions, including disaffected members of those groups. But you should beware of relying too heavily on prisoner interrogations. Torture seldom provides reliable intel, especially for long-term plans. Instead, consider infiltrating the groups, paying informants for accurate information, and bribing marginally committed rebels.

"*Troisième: Établissez une politique coordonnée de gouvernement à tous les niveaux.* Establish a coordinated government policy at all levels. This of course is beyond the military's control, unless the army runs the government. But it is essential to have all agencies and organizations working toward the same goals with a consistent approach. If insurgents see the agriculture department as being lax while the health agency is hardcore, they will only want to deal with agriculture.

"*Quatrième: Séparez les insurgés de leur appui.* Separate the insurgents from their support. In some cases physical separation can prove successful, as the British did in Malaya in the 1950s. In Vietnam the so-called strategic hamlet concept was employed with less success, partly because the locals still needed to return to their villages and farms. A better method is political and economic separation: make it in the interest of the population to support the government rather than the insurgents, especially where the rebels are not of the same ethnicity.

"*Cinquième: Neutralisez ou détruisez l'organisation insurgée.* Neutralize or destroy the insurgent organization. That requires a closer look at the second principle: intelligence. Once you know where to find the rebels, you can make plans for military action. Or you can employ financial or other methods, such as making it difficult or impossible for insurgents to move about.

"*Sixième: Prévoyez une stratégie continue soulignant la stabilité politique.* Provide for a continuing strategy emphasizing political stability. This principle is related to the first. Once you have gained the upper hand militarily, keep up the pressure on the insurgents by continuing successful policies and expanding others, such as food, medical, and financial aid. In time the combination of these factors will drive the insurgents away."

With that brief preview, the American turned to his audience. A Chadian lieutenant colonel raised his hand. "Mr. Johnson, I wish to ask about specifics in our current crisis."

Johnson nodded. "Certainly, sir."

The officer, who bore a nasty scar on his chin and left cheek, clearly had seen combat. "Our concern is not so much with local dissidents as with outsiders. They make little pretense of caring for the Chadian people. Mainly they wish only to cause us problems, to spread our troops too thin and expend money on more security forces." He arched an eyebrow. "When the enemy lives in Libya and Sudan, which of your principles apply?"

It was an unexpectedly astute question, and Johnson glanced toward Steve Lee, sitting in the third row. A slight nod of the head. *Your call, J. J.*

"Well, in that case, sir, it depends on the specifics, as you say. If the insurgents are operating on their own, obviously the local population is far less a factor. In that case, it's no longer really an insurgency."

Johnson stopped speaking French and turned to Lee. "Major, is it safe to say that State and our attaché would have to approve if we became involved in repelling cross-border attacks?"

Lee stood briefly, knowing that some of the Chadians understood English. "Mr. Johnson is correct. Our team is limited to a training and advisory capacity. Any operations beyond those positions would require approval of U.S. Government agencies and probably renegotiation of our contract."

Johnson summarized the team leader's response. "*Toutes les opérations au delà de ces positions exigeraient l'approbation des organismes gouvernementaux des États Unis et probablement de la renégociation de notre contrat.*"

<hr>

After the briefing, Johnson sidled up to Lee, both pretending to appreciate the local tea and wafers. "Boss, what do you make of the colonel's question? Are they asking us for help beyond the Co-In contract?"

Lee squinted behind his glasses. "I don't know, J. J., but we damn well need to find out."

"Hey, I'm just a multilingual grunt. Want me to ask him one to one?"

Lee nodded. "See if you can steer him over here. Maybe we can get some straight answers if nobody else is listening." He tipped his cup to his lips, barely feeling the hot liquid, staring straight ahead.

"Something else?" Johnson asked.

"Oh. Well, I was just thinking. This coming after my meeting at the security ministry the other day. I'll tell you what, J. J.: I think we've stepped into something more than we expected over here."

N'DJAMENA

"There is another team. American this time."

Etienne Stevin delivered the news dispassionately, as was his wont. It was one reason that Marcel Hurtubise valued the man: he was immune to panic. Whenever his time came, he would die with a far lower pulse than most men, that seemed certain.

It also meant that Stevin lacked a certain amount of imagination, excepting a sentimental romanticism about dying as befitted a Legionnaire. But such men were valuable nonetheless.

Hurtubise swiveled in his padded chair and laid down *La Chanson de Roland*. The mercenary seldom tired of reading the ancient account of the Battle of Roncevaux. "Tell me."

Stevin detoured to the refrigerator, extracted a beer, and slid into a straight-backed chair. He twisted off the cap in one swift motion. His hands were large, powerful, experienced.

"I do not know the full number yet, but at least six. Paul and I saw that many get off the bus at the training compound. He stayed to watch them but others stayed aboard. I followed the bus awhile, but it didn't stop before I lost it in a traffic jam." He drained one-quarter of the beer and wiped his mouth. "You know how these niggers drive."

"What about Paul?"

"He can take a taxi or maybe Gabrielle . . ."

"No!" Hurtubise regretted the sharp tone. Not because of concern for Stevin's feelings—the man hardly possessed any—but because it was not wise to indicate any undue concern for the young woman. He thought quickly, a well-developed habit. "She needs the Renault for an errand this afternoon."

Stevin's face remained impassive. If he suspected any worry about "Gabby's" relationship with the attractive, cheerful Gascon, he did not betray it. Besides, what anyone else did was of no interest, as long as it did not affect his health or his income.

Hurtubise asked, "What do you think about the new team? How do you know they're Americans?"

Another long draught from the bottle and it was nearly empty. Stevin smacked his lips and thought for a moment. "They came from the American embassy. You remember the woman you hired a few weeks ago? I checked the letter drop in the park and found this." He pulled a crumpled paper from his pocket and passed it to his boss. "She's a good investment, that one."

Hurtubise read the note and set it aside. He would burn it when he was through. "Well, since she's a translator she sees most of the things that would interest us. And she's been reliable before."

The leader of Groupe FGN's team rubbed his stubbled chin. "Obviously this is a training team, but it could be involved in security operations as well. The question is, who are they training, and for what purpose?"

"Paul might have something when he gets back."

"Probably not much if he has to wait outside the compound. I'll wait to see what he says. Then if necessary I'll see some of my Legion comrades."

"You think they will be working with the Americans?"

"Possibly. But at least they're another set of ears." Hurtubise almost smiled. "A wonderful thing about *La Legion*, my friend. You're never really out of it."

25

Foyte held sway during the planning session.

"Okay, people. Listen up."

The gossip and horseplay quickly abated as the operators turned toward the senior delegate. "Major Lee and Ms. Whitney are at the embassy again," Foyte began, "but here's what we're gonna talk about today." He turned to the white board propped on an easel at the head of the room.

"The course Steve and I laid out has been approved by the Chadian CO, Lieutenant Colonel Malloum. We're going to start with individual skills, which the good colonel assures me won't take long." Foyte cocked an eyebrow by way of tacit comment. "After that we'll start working at the squad level, which I think is where we'll devote most of our attention. Fire and movement stuff. You guys can do that in your sleep but that's why I want to focus on it a bit later. What we take for granted, our clients might have to work at. Anyway, at the upper end we'll hope to bring it all together with platoon exercises."

Johnson ventured a question from the front row. "Gunny, I've talked to a few of the troops already. I don't get much of a fuzzy feeling about their interest in mundane stuff like commo or supply. What's your take on that?"

"Odd you should ask," Foyte said. "Malloum understands the need for those things, and others besides. For instance, there's a serious shortage of medics. Not enough for each platoon yet. Oh, some of these boy . . . guys . . . have some practical experience, but not much book learning. The Chadians are going to select some candidates and maybe transfer in some others who haven't 'volunteered' yet for an elite unit." He looked at the recently retired Staff Sergeant Nissen. "Chris is our resident corpsman and he's working up a syllabus for that class."

Nissen raised in his seat. "Ah, Gunny, in the Army we're called medics."

Foyte deadpanned a response. "Right. As I was saying, Chris will start training some corpsmen. He speaks Arabic so that's a big plus." The former Marine unzipped an evil grin. "Staff Sergeant Nissen, how do you say 'sucking chest wound' in Arabic?"

Nissen feigned concentration for a long moment. "*Inshallah.*"

"Isn't that like 'the will of God' or something?"

"It certainly is, Gunnery Sergeant. It certainly is."

CO-IN BATTALION COMPOUND

Foyte and Johnson coordinated initial weapons training with the battalion sergeant major. He was a short, stocky man of indeterminate age and a sober disposition.

Sergeant Major Hissen Alingue Bawoyeu told Johnson, "Some of these men have little practice with their rifles. Perhaps they should begin by lying down to steady their aim."

Foyte thought for a moment. "I'd rather have them shoot off a bench or table. There's less recoil that way. When they're prone, they feel the recoil more and are likely to flinch."

Johnson translated for Bawoyeu, who seemed unconvinced. At length the Chadian asked, "*A quelle gamme devrions-nous enregistrer nous fusils?*"

Johnson said, "He wants to know what distance you recommend for zeroing."

"Oh, two hundred yards. Er, meters."

After more back and forthing, Johnson announced, "They don't have a two hundred-meter range. At least not anywhere nearby. The most they have with a decent backstop is about sixty-seventy meters."

Foyte pondered for a few seconds. "Tell him that should be okay. We can zero at twenty-five yards and that'll be close on at two hundred."

"He wants to know how that's possible. He says some of his men may not understand that a bullet can shoot to point of aim at two distances."

The gunny silently ground his emotional teeth. "Jeez, an infantryman doesn't know the difference between minimum and maximum ordinate?"

Johnson gave a smirk. "In words of one syllable, yup."

Foyte gnawed on that information for a long moment, then decided that he had seen worse. "Well, I've known military trained snipers who don't know how to use a shooting sling. Hell, my cousin—the one our family doesn't talk about—joined the Army. He said he met soldierettes who thought magazines came loaded at the factory." Foyte gave a down-home kind of grin. "Prob'ly the same kinda kids who think milk comes from cartons."

Sergeant Major Bawoyeu tried to return the advisors to his own problems. Gaining Johnson's attention, the NCO asked what Foyte perceived as a complex question. Finally Johnson nodded and turned back to Foyte.

"Our colleague here wants our recommendation for squad automatic weapons. I told him we'd have to check with the front office. What do you think, Gunny?"

"Well, as I see it, we have two choices: HK-21s and maybe the new .308 caliber PKMs."

Johnson agreed. "That makes sense. Both use the same cartridge as the G3 rifle."

"Yeah, I wouldn't want to have different ammo for our rifles and SAWs. The HK burns a lot of ammo, though. I think the cyclic is over 800 rpm, but it's semi, three-round, and full auto. Anyway, it takes some technique to shoot well. As I recall, it pulls high and right so you need a seven o'clock or seven-thirty hold. In fact, if you're not solidly behind the gun, it pushes you back."

Johnson replied, "We can confirm that with some range tests. But I like the idea of the same trigger group and bolt for the rifle and MG." He translated for Bawoyeu's benefit, and the Chadian asked a question in turn.

"He asks, 'What about the PKM?' I think he has a point. Obviously it's reliable, based on the AK-47."

"We'll have to see what links they use," Foyte replied. "The PKM extracts the round from the links rather than pushes them because the original Russian cartridge has a rimmed case. But it's more controllable than the HK; runs around 650 to 700 rpm." He made a point of looking Bawoyeu in the eyes. *"Très bien,"* Foyte managed.

For the first time in the Americans' experience, Sergeant Major Hissen Alingue Bawoyeu actually smiled.

N'DJAMENA

"What did you learn?"

Paul Deladier slumped into a padded chair that, unlike the vintage wine he sipped, had not improved with age. He regarded his boss, then replied, "There is more to the American team than we thought."

"Well?" Hurtubise was never known for his tolerance.

"I managed a chance meeting with the black woman. I tailed her from the American embassy and talked to her for a few minutes. She said she's a temporary stenographer, but I don't believe her."

"Why not?"

Deladier mussed his dark blond hair and swirled the wine in its glass. "Well, for one thing, Etienne and I have seen her with the training team. There is no reason for her to associate with them unless it's social, which is unlikely."

Hurtubise swung his legs away from the kitchen table. He was becoming more interested in his young colleague's opinions. "Go on."

A Gallic shrug. "Just a sense of her. She's confident, looks you in the eye. Not at all like some prissy little clerk." Deladier paused for a moment, recalling the woman's face; her expression. "I think she might be an operator."

Marcel Hurtubise sat back, rubbing his trademark stubble. "Now that is an interesting observation. She's what? Forties? Overweight, not very attractive."

Deladier smiled. "You are no gentleman, *monsieur*."

Hurtubise ignored the backward compliment. "Nobody would expect a fat black American female to be very capable, would they?"

"No, I suppose not. Which is why . . ."

". . . she would be an excellent undercover agent."

Deladier drained the glass and smacked his lips. "Should I talk to her again?"

Hurtubise shook his head. "No, that would be too much of a coincidence. I have another idea."

"Yes?"

"My young friend, you don't always send a fox to catch a chicken. Sometimes you send another hen."

27

COUNTERINSURGENCY COMPOUND

Daniel Foyte, being a retired gunnery sergeant, knew a great deal about marksmanship and precious little about diplomacy. At the moment he was caught with one foot in each world, attempting to convince Sergeant Major Bawoyeu of the institutional wisdom of the United States Marine Corps. He assessed a couple of the Chadians' targets and collected his thoughts. Turning to his African colleague, he said, "I'm not worried about where they're hitting right now. We can move the group to point of aim by adjusting the sights. I'd rather see better groups before we start worrying about that. After all, trigger control is a lot more important than sights."

The sergeant major seemed unconvinced. "It is not necessary to aim so carefully when a rifle fires automatically."

Foyte ground his molars in silent frustration. When he finally spoke, he managed a civil tone. "*Mon adjutant*, that is the difference between probability theory and marksmanship." He picked up a G3 and hefted it for emphasis. "Even with a fairly heavy rifle, controlling the recoil on full auto is almost impossible. It wastes ammunition. I recommend that we have a policy of semiautomatic fire only. In fact, I would suggest having the armorers insert a pin through the receiver making full auto impossible."

Bawoyeu shrugged eloquently. Clearly he did not care to dispute with so senior an advisor, but equally clearly the close-cropped American was more concerned with theories than reality.

Foyte turned away, stalking the firing line and stopping occasionally to assess his team's instruction technique. He listened as Boscombe and Johnson tackled a problem shooter.

"Keep the stock firm against your shoulder," Bosco said to the soldier. "Don't grab the fore end with your left hand; just let it rest there. Otherwise you'll get lateral dispersion."

He looked at Johnson. "How do you say that?"

J. J. grinned at his partner. "*Vous obtiendrez la dispersion latérale.*"

Breezy furrowed his brow. "Really? It's a lot like English."

"*Mon ami*, English is about forty percent French."

"G'won. Is not."

"Is too."

"Is not!"

Johnson slowly shook his head in bemusement. "Dude, you are *so* behind. Haven't you ever heard of the Norman Conquest?"

"Norman who?"

J. J. threw up his hands in frustration. He wondered if he weren't being sandbagged but decided to press on.

"Look, it's like this. About . . . oh, 950 years ago there were these guys, the Normans. Okay? Their leader was a dude named William. He was like the Duke of Normandy. You *have* heard of Normandy?"

Bosco nodded gravely. "Damn straight. Omaha Beach and The Big Red One."

"Right! Except, well, not exactly. The Conquest was like D-Day in reverse. From France to England instead of the other way around. Anyway, William decided that he should rule England, so he took his guys and whupped up on the Anglo-Saxons. Their leader was named Harold, and he checked into an arrow at a place called Hastings."

Bosco scratched his head. "When did you say this was?"

"Man, aren't you listening? I said, like 1066."

"Oh. Right. Nine hunnerd an' fifty years ago." He frowned in concentration. "So what's that got to do with forty percent French?"

"Bosco, the Normans *were* French. They spoke a kind of French, which is Latin based, instead of the Germanic lingo like Harold. They, you know, took their language with them to England."

"So why'd this Harold dude and his guys start talking French?"

Somewhere far back in the recesses of his cranium, J. J. Johnson badly wanted to scream.

"Because they were frigging *conquered*, that's why! Besides, like I said, Harold was KIA. So William turned England into a Norman kind of government. Over a few centuries a lot of French words became English."

"Well that's pretty gnarly."

Jeremy Johnson had no response to that observation.

N'DJAMENA

To say that the home team won decisively would have been gross understatement. Chad: eleven. America: three.

The SSI clients had laid out a soccer field one hundred meters long by fifty meters wide, with markings scratched in the packed dirt. The Americans had trouble getting their brains around the game's extreme flexibility, with teams composed anything from seven to eleven players. Since SSI could only field six willing warriors—they steadfastly refused to allow Martha Whitney on the team—the locals convinced two Foreign Legionnaires into an ad-hoc alliance. The Americans and "French," actually an Algerian and a Spaniard, elected J. J. Johnson team captain on the basis of his previous Legion service.

Johnson had his linguistic hands full, shouting directions alternately in English and French. At one point, with the score at four-zip, he had to deliver an earnest lecture to Bosco who in frustration had picked up the ball and drop-kicked it into the Chadian net from inside the penalty line.

The Spaniard was drafted as SSI goalie, and *Caporal* Moratinos did tolerably well considering that four of the opposition goals were scored on free kicks or penalties.

That concluded the first forty-five-minute period. Since it was painfully obvious that the Western Allies were not going to narrow the gap, a near unanimous decision was reached: cancel the second half and get on with the barbecue.

Johnson shook hands with Sergeant Kawlabi, captain of the Specialty Battalion team. They were briefly joined by Sergeant Major Bawoyeu who had served as head referee aided by two Legionnaires. Any concern about his impartiality had dissipated within minutes of the starting whistle—clearly the Chadians required no such assistance in achieving a decisive victory.

Bawoyeu was all toothy bonhomie. "Your team did well, considering how little the men have played," he offered graciously.

"Thank you, *Adjutant*," Johnson replied. "But I doubt that many of them are ready for a rematch."

Johnson turned toward the sidelines and saw Brezyinski sitting on the ground. Chris Nissen was tending a serious bruise on the paratrooper's left knee. "What do you think, Doc? He gonna live?"

Nissen glanced up at Johnson. "Well, like we say at Bragg. I may not be the best doctor around, but I reckon I'm the best practicing without a license. It's going to swell if I don't pack some ice on it right away."

"What happened, Breeze?"

Brezyinski waved a hand dismissively. "Ah, that big ape tripped me." He indicated a husky six-foot soldier who glanced in their direction and failed utterly to conceal a smile.

"I'd think you Eighty-second guys would know all about falling down. What do you call it? The parachute landing roll?"

Breezy grunted. "Fall. But you ever try to do a PLF with six goons crowding all around you?"

"Well, consider the big picture. It's in a good cause. After all, we've been lording it over these guys, basically showing them how little they know. It's only fair that they get to show us something."

Breezy gave an exaggerated grimace. "Easy for you to say, dude. Your picture—my knee!"

While Nissen helped the ambulatory casualty to the sidelines, Johnson was approached by his newfound Legion friends, all of whom understood the significance of the obscure date 27 April 1832. They found that they had heard of some of the same people, which was not surprising. Though *La Legion* contained troops from seventeen nations, with only eight thousand men, there was bound to be some overlap.

Standing nearby, Bosco observed the Legionnaires—current and past—bonding with one another. They recounted the training and the only way out: climbing the rock, ringing the bell to announce they had enough, but not before spending twenty-four hours in jail before release.

"Unwavering solidarity—leave no one behind!" chanted *Caporal* Moratinos.

Johnson seemed almost sentimental. "I remember what *Caporal Chef* Calmy said, '*Les épreuves et les tribulations sont normaux dans la*

*vie—la douleur est facultative. Pour éviter de souffrir, vous apprenez sim-
plement à vous conformer.'* "

"Which means?" Bosco spoke nothing but English.

"Trials and tribulations are normal in life—suffering is optional. To avoid suffering, you merely learn to conform."

"It's still the same," the Spaniard offered. "Hours and hours of absurd detail: cleaning and ironing; pleats within a millimeter of specifications."

Once they had satisfied one another with arcane gestures and slogans, the men fell into an easy comradeship cemented by off-key rendering of the patient, almost ponderous marching song:

*Tiens, voilà du boudin, voilà du boudin, voilà du boudin
Pour les Alsaciens, les Suisses, et les Lorrains,
Pour les Belges, y en a plus . . .*

"What's that?" Bosco asked.

Johnson interrupted the songfest just long enough to explain. "It's the Legion's most famous song, *"Le Boudin."* It means 'blood sausage' and says something about almost everybody: Alsatians, Swiss, Lorraines, even Belgians." He thought a moment. "Especially Belgians. Not very complimentary, actually."

Bosco munched a sandwich that he assumed was pork, never considering that he was the guest of a passel of Muslims. Johnson reckoned it was lamb or goat, but decided not to educate his benighted friend. "Sounds way too slow for a march," Bosco declared.

"Well, in the Legion we take our time with those things."

Bosco espied Martha Whitney approaching and decided to make himself scarce. His departure allowed him to resume his *Pro Patria* discussion.

Corporal Moratinos regarded the other Americans. "You probably do not have the kind of morale like *La Legion*," he ventured. "That is, the sense of unity."

"Oh, we have good morale," Johnson replied. "Our company's president is a really fine man, a retired admiral. He really takes care of his people."

The Spaniard absorbed that sentiment, then asked, "What do you make of the French firm? It has several ex-Legionnaires."

Johnson cocked his head. "What firm is that?"

Moratinos seemed surprised. "You have not heard of Groupe FGN? It's probably the biggest security contractor in the country."

"No, not a word. What do they do?"

The Legionnaire rolled his eyes in exaggeration. "What don't they do?" He looked left and right, as if confirming the need for secrecy. "Come let's take a short walk, *mon ami*. You should know about a man named Marcel Hurtubise."

SSI COMPOUND

Steve Lee turned from his IBM ThinkPad and greeted his visitors. "Hi, guys. C'mon in."

Dan Foyte, Jeremy Johnson, and Martha Whitney shoe-horned themselves into the small office that the Chadians had provided for SSI's administrative use. Johnson gallantly offered the vacant chair to Whitney, who steadfastly refused the gesture. "No thanks, J. J. honey. I may be fat but I can still stand up." She gave him a nudge in the ribs.

Lee exchanged male-bonding glances with Johnson and Foyte, then got down to business. "After J. J. mentioned the Foreign Legion's information on Groupe FGN, I checked back with headquarters in Arlington. We had a heads-up that a couple of French outfits were working here but we didn't know what they were doing. Well, it appears that this Hurtubise character got rid of the competition by one means or another. Marsh Wilmont and Frank Leopold think we should regard him as hostile."

"How's he a threat to us?" asked Foyte. "I mean, he's not competing for our contract."

"No, but there's some interesting background info on him. I e-mailed

David Dare and his spooks to look into him and they found some interesting stuff. He's a pro, all right. National service 1982–84, Foreign Legion 1986–91, freelance for a while, then joined FGN. Evidently he was going to be excommunicated at one point but he beat the wrap. That puts him in pretty exclusive company because the research guys only found about fifteen people who were dumped by the Catholic Church in the twentieth century, including Castro and Juan Péron."

Whitney gasped aloud. "My God, what'd he do?"

"It's not clear, but apparently he took some hostages in a church or monastery in Burundi when he was freelancing several years ago. Some of them, including monks or nuns, were killed in the fighting and he was held responsible. My guess is that he wasn't declared anathema because nobody could prove that he gave the order."

"All right," Foyte replied. "He's a gold-plated bastard. But like I said, what's our interest in him?"

Lee nodded to Johnson, who took the hint. "The Legionnaires I talked to all said pretty much the same thing. Hurtubise is all about results. He just doesn't care who gets trampled as long as he gets what he wants. It can't be proven, but it's the next thing to certain that he or his people got rid of the other French PMC guys." Johnson paused for emphasis. "If this FGN outfit starts to regard us as competition in any way, it could mean big trouble."

"What's FGN doing here, anyway?" Whitney asked.

Lee shot her a grin. "Bingo—the sixty-four-franc question. As Gunny says, we're not doing the same thing—at least it looks as if Hurtubise and company aren't involved in training. The most we can find out right now is some sort of security work. Not just here in the capital but up along the border as well."

Foyte asked, "Where are they based?"

"They have an address near the French embassy but apparently that's just a room with a phone and a mail drop. Near as I can tell so far, they move around a lot, in and out of the city. I've asked Roosevelt to see what he can find, but he's pretty high-profile, being an attaché." Lee turned back to Whitney. "Martha, I'd like you to snoop around, ask some discreet questions and see what you can learn. Don't risk drawing attention to yourself, but maybe develop some contacts in our embassy and theirs."

"Will do, Maje. I done already got a cover as a stenographer."

Johnson looked at her. "I didn't know you can take dictation."

She waved a bejeweled hand at him. "Honey, I can't write a word in that chicken-scratchy text. But I remember conversations for quite a while afterward. I can write 'em down or use a recorder." She winked broadly. "Mind like a platinum trap."

"Uh, I think that's steel trap," Johnson replied.

"Well, sweet cheeks, some folks got steel minds and some of us got platinum."

She waved bye-bye and strode out of the room, humming "Hello, Dolly!"

29

AOZOU STRIP

The metallic cacophony was grating to refined ears. Grinding gears, scraping noises, and diesel engines were not the ambience either of the observers ordinarily preferred. But they both acknowledged that occasionally one had to endure unpleasant surroundings in order to reap the potential benefit.

Overlooking the open pit, Felix Moungar and Marcel Hurtubise took in the machinery and surveyed the surroundings. Other than the dilapidated huts that once housed the workforce, they were satisfied with what they saw.

"There has been much progress since our last inspection," the government man offered. "I trust that your team will be able to maintain security for the time required."

Hurtubise nodded. "My men are already moving in. Some of them may grumble about living in tents, but they understand the need for secrecy." His meaning was easily grasped: the less attention drawn to the once abandoned mine, the better. Construction of even temporary quarters would tell any observers that something beyond routine maintenance was under way.

Moungar shrugged in indifference. The discomfort of a dozen foreign mercenaries was of little concern to him as long as they maintained order and secrecy for the duration of the renewed mining. Still, conditions in the Sahara were strenuous at the best of times: sand that found its way into every orifice, beastly heat, and furious winds.

But Hurtubise had greater concerns. He suspected that one or two people at the embassy in N'Djamena might have grown leery of his true allegiance—an entity that had little to do with the current crop of Paris politicians—but if he acted fast enough, his goal would be achieved and he could finally retire. Somewhere suitable both to Gabrielle and himself. Switzerland was nice . . .

Hurtubise forced his attention back to the job at hand. He asked, "What of the yellow cake processing?"

Moungar unzipped a wry grin. "It goes slowly but steadily, my friend. We should have enough for a shipment in a week or so. After that, as much as your . . . customers . . . can manage."

"Well, as you know, they do not require a great deal. Just as long as the shipments get sent by the deadline, we will both be wealthy."

The African grinned again. "*Mon ami*, I am already wealthy by my country's standards. I intend to be wealthy by *your* standards."

As they walked around the periphery of the mine, the unlikely partners exchanged concerns. Since Groupe FGN was hired to provide security, Hurtubise looked inward as well as outward. "Felix, tell me again about the workers you have hired. How reliable are they? Some of them are bound to talk about their time here."

The African waved a dismissive hand. "Naturally, my associates and I would prefer that none of them discuss their work. But we are going to keep them busy with minor chores after the shipment. Nobody will be permitted to leave until I know that the yellow cake has reached its trans-shipment point."

The Frenchman regarded his colleague with renewed confidence. In his experience, most Africans were so nearsighted that they seldom thought beyond the next paycheck, or even the next meal. But knowing who was funding the project made a difference as well. Deep pockets combined with astute planning formed a powerful inducement. "What do you propose if some workers get too eager to spend their pay and want to leave prematurely?"

Moungar gave the ghost of a smile. "Why, I propose to let your men handle that problem."

Marcel Hurtubise's own smile came to life, far more than a ghost. "*C'est bien, mon ami.*"

N'DJAMENA

Paul Deladier nudged his partner. "There she is."

Gabrielle ran a quick assessment of her target. A black American woman, mid to late forties, on the heavy side. But she seemed aware of her surroundings. Gabrielle's brain defaulted to her years on the street before Marcel found her. This woman would not be an easy mark: alert, large, and probably strong. An experienced mugger or strong-arm bandit would look elsewhere.

Gabrielle Tixier was not looking for a snatch and grab purse theft. She was after something more difficult—information.

It had been a long wait outside the American compound, but not entirely unpleasant. Gabrielle and Paul had played the role of flirtatious young Europeans visiting an exotic land, and despite his absence of deodorant on occasion, Gabrielle found the well-built Gascon a tolerable companion. She knew that Marcel would understand the tactical reason for her arms around Deladier's neck.

She *hoped* he would understand.

Gabrielle gave Deladier a not so quick kiss on the cheek and waved as he turned to go. In truth, he would duck into a vendor's stall about twenty meters away.

After all, the American might have a partner, too.

Feigning interest in some fruit, Deladier watched the young woman walk toward her intercept point. Not quite thirty, Gabrielle always looked good from behind, especially wearing tight jeans. He suspected that her saucy walk was more calculated than natural, but the effect was pleasing to males on at least two continents.

Deladier purchased some dates and leaned back to enjoy them without looking directly at Martha Whitney. She was approaching him on the opposite side of the street, making her way through pedestrian traffic, but he did not want to be recognized as the young man who had bummed a cigarette a few days before.

Gabrielle suddenly turned right, sprinted in front of an ancient Citroën taxi, and feigned frustration at the seeming near miss. The driver laid on the horn, prompting a Gallic snit expressed in blunt Parisian French unsuited for a well brought up young lady.

Stepping to the sidewalk, purposefully looking behind her, Gabrielle Tixier collided with Martha Whitney.

From his stall, Deladier admired the tradecraft. Even to his experienced eyes, the incident appeared accidental, and he could almost read the young woman's lips, profusely apologizing to the older lady.

In less than four minutes by his imitation Rolex, Deladier catalogued Tixier's progress: from collision to apology to discussion to an interval in a tea shop.

She's quite good, Deladier acknowledged.

He waited long enough to confirm there was no tail for the American, then began the long walk to the apartment.

Most of the way back he visualized Gabrielle's derriere just beyond arm's reach.

30

"So who are they working for?" Lee asked.

Roosevelt consulted his notes. "Well, part of their operation is legit. At least it looks that way. They have several people doing extracurricular security work for the French embassy and some other agencies. VIP escort, that sort of thing."

"Okay," Lee replied. "That makes sense. Genuine work to cover the covert stuff."

"You got it. Thing is, though, from what our people can tell, FGN's other clients are not related to the French embassy or even the French government. They seem to have business connections all over the Middle East."

"Like who?"

The attaché flipped through his pad. "Like this guy, for instance. Mohammed al Fasari. Big import-export guy with outlets from here to there: Rome, Cyprus, Cairo, Beirut, Damascus, Baghdad. Even Tehran."

Lee went on point. "Tehran?"

"Uh-huh. Exotic stuff. Pricey things like rugs and ancient artifacts."

Lee removed his glasses and polished the lenses. "Could that be a cover for smuggling other things?"

"I suppose so. Why?"

Lee replaced his military-issue frames. "Just speculating, Matt. I mean, if this Fasari character is shipping things out of Iran, he could be sneaking things in as well. Know what I mean?"

Roosevelt laid down his notepad and leaned forward. "I think so. And it makes me nervous."

"Me, too." Lee scrawled a note to himself for passing along to David Dare's mysterious intel shop back in Arlington. "All right, who else might interest us?"

"Let's see . . . several prospects. Oh, there's quite a bit of activity with a mid-level Chad government official. In fact, you might recognize the name: Felix Moungar."

Lee recognized the name. "Moungar! Hey, isn't he related to Kadabi, the defense ministry representative?"

"Affirmative. François Kadabi. I think you've met him."

"Sure have. Two or three times."

Roosevelt leaned back, biting his lip in concentration. "Moungar is with the natural resources ministry. I think he deals with mining contracts and things like that."

"What would he have to do with Hurtubise?"

"Well, it's no secret that FGN has provided security consultants to the ministry. In fact, I think it's on the company's Web site. But that might be a forest and trees situation."

"How's that?" Lee asked.

"As you know, there's something hinky going on along the northern strip. Since the logistics are serious—it's about six hundred miles up there—it's not really possible to keep the lid on. Somebody would notice the traffic in and out of the area. So I think it's possible . . ."

"Hiding out in the open."

"You got it."

Lee asked a rhetorical question. "Now, what's the most interesting commodity that's mined up there?"

Roosevelt's eyes widened. "Uranium!"

"And our friend Hurtubise has contacts with the mining ministry and with one of the major exporters in the region. A legitimate businessman who has ties to Iran."

"Ho-lee sh . . ."

"You said it." Lee extended a hand. "Go Army!"

Roosevelt grinned hugely. "Beat Navy!"

SSI COMPOUND

Steve Lee closed the door to his small office and poured Martha Whitney two fingers of bourbon. She applied a token amount of water, swirled twice, and took an educated sip.

"Aaah," she enthused. "At times like this I'm sho' 'nuff glad I'm a Baptist and not a Muslim."

Lee's eyes gleamed in response. "And here I thought that Baptists were mostly teetotalers."

"Honey, they's Baptists and then they's *Baptists*! Besides, I'm more spiritual than religious. Ya'll know what I mean?"

He touched Styrofoam cups with her. "And how."

"*Here's* how," she replied. Another sip, this time with closed eyes, the better to appreciate the warmth trickling southward.

Lee set his cup down. "Okay, tell me."

Whitney reclined as much as possible in the straight-backed chair. "Well, I gotta give the girl credit. She done real good. For a minute there I wasn't sure."

"You're saying she's a pro."

Another long, slow sip. "Uh-huh. She's been 'round the block a time or two. Even at her age, poor thing."

"But . . ."

Martha gave the Aunt Jemima grin again. "But . . . Maje honey, I done been around the world an' Dee-troit twice. No, she's had some experience; maybe even some training. But I made her early on."

"How's that?"

"Well, for one thing, she didn't maintain eye contact like a person would've done in that situation. Oh, she handled bumping into me real well, but she was lookin' over my shoulder as much as lookin' me eye to eye. And she wasn't nearly as flustered as somebody would be after presumably dodging a car."

Lee played devil's advocate. "Martha, you know people are different."

She waved a bejeweled hand. "Oh, course I know that. But like they taught us at Langley: pay attention to your instincts. Usually they're right."

"Okay. For the moment let's say you're right. She's working you. But why?"

"Well, honey, it sure ain't because she wants to practice her English with me. She speaks it well enough, and in fact I suspect she speaks better than she lets on. But that's what she said. Insisted on buying me tea so we could talk *en anglais* for a while."

"What *did* you talk about?"

"Chitchat at first. Background, work, that sort of thing. I kept with my embassy story—temporary steno help out of Cairo. She said she's touring with her boyfriend. When I said that not many tourists come to Chad, she hesitated just a little. Said he's a photographer working up a portfolio."

Lee finished his one finger of bourbon. "That shouldn't be hard to confirm. What's his name? I'll run a Google search on him."

"She just said Paul. I didn't push it at that point. We're gonna get together again in a couple of days."

"Well, okay. I'll make sure that your name is on the embassy list so the phone operators don't ask 'Martha who?' if she calls."

"Oh . . . I was gonna tell you. I'm not Martha Whitney. I'm Martha White."

Lee made a point of reaching back in his lower drawer. "I think I need a drink!"

CO-IN COMPOUND

Bosco slumped into a folding chair to the side of the training compound. He watched *Adjutant* Bawoyeu dismiss the second platoon of the day and anticipated a long bath in his quarters. If Breezy didn't beat him to it—the sumbitch would hog the tub if he got there first.

Bosco accepted a bottle of water from Chris Nissen and hoisted the plastic container in tacit salute. They were working together better than before, partly because Mr. Boscombe was beginning to recognize certain useful phrases. Apart from *fusil automatique* and other technical terms, he had just mastered the phrase "Keep your elbow under the weapon." "*Gardez votre coude sous l'arme.*"

Nissen did not bother to explain that Bosco's pronunciation left worlds to be desired.

"So whatchathink, Sarge?"

Nissen shot a glance at the budding commandos departing the arena.

"Well, they're making progress. We have to remember that some of these guys have never had any foreign training. Believe it or not, I've seen worse."

Bosco took a pull at his bottle and regarded his new colleague. "Would you trust them in combat?"

"That depends. Against who?"

"Well, let me rephrase it. Would you trust them not to run off and leave you high and dry?"

Nissen looked around, confirming that nobody else was within earshot. "Within limits, yeah. I would. But it depends on who's leading them. I mean, doesn't it seem odd to you that we hardly ever see any officers?"

Bosco was ready for that one. He dipped into his stash of patented responses and brought one to the surface. "Why let rank lead when ability does better?"

Nissen's face was serious in the slanting evening light. "Lieutenant Colonel Malloum shows up once in a while, and I guess he's busy with admin jobs. But we've only seen a couple of company-grade officers. It's like they're just passing through."

A bulb flicked on in Boscombe's cranium. He sat up straight. "Wait a minute. Are you saying that *we* are gonna have to hand-hold these dudes through their first few ops?"

Nissen shrugged. "I don't know. I mean, that's not in our contract. And I know for sure that J. J. doesn't plan to do any fieldwork. But still . . ."

"Damn!" Bosco threw the half-empty bottle at a trash can and missed. He ignored it. "We need to talk to Lee. *Muy pronto.*"

"That's *Major* Lee, maggot."

Bosco turned at the sound of Foyte's voice. "Hey, how 'bout it, Gunny. Are we expected to fill in for the junior officers?"

Foyte took a DI's stance: hands behind his back, feet spread, slightly inclined forward. "In words of one syllable—what an Army puke would understand—there's no pukin' way."

Nissen grinned despite himself. "Hey, Boscombe. You know how Marines count?"

Bosco rose to the occasion. "No, Staff Sergeant Nissen. How do Marines count?"

"Hup, two, three, many! Hup, two, three, many!"

Foyte ignored the jibe—he had heard it dozens of times. He knelt before the two Army veterans. "I been talkin' to Johnson and a couple of the others. These guys seem to understand fire team and squad tactics: fire and movement stuff. That's good. It's the basic building blocks. We'll keep reinforcing those maneuvers, but we're also gonna bear down on marksmanship. Too many of these boys think that ammo capacity equals firepower. And I'm here to tell you . . ."

"Firepower is hits on the target!" Boscombe replied. Nissen did not answer: he was pondering Foyte's use of "boys" again.

Foyte removed his cover and rubbed the stubble on his head. "Well, I'm glad that *somebody* understands that. Now look here." He pulled his ever-present notebook from a pocket. "I have a list of the twenty best shooters in the battalion. I'm gonna suggest that we reassign them throughout the platoons so there's some depth in each unit. Then I think we should put about half of 'em on the belt-fed guns."

Nissen frowned in concentration. "Wouldn't they be better used as precision riflemen?"

"Maybe later. But for now we don't have any precision rifles, and won't for at least a few weeks. Meanwhile, I keep thinking of what a very great man once said."

Bosco nudged Nissen. "What great Marine was that?"

Foyte was serious. "Well, since you ask, I'll tell you. His name was Merritt Edson, and he was a Distinguished Rifleman who got a Medal of Honor at Guadalcanal. Maybe you heard of it."

"Is that anything like the Erie Canal?" Bosco was enjoying the banter, but knew he could only push Foyte so far.

Foyte turned to Nissen. "Red Mike Edson wrote that only accurate firepower is effective, which is why he put expert riflemen on his BARs. I think that makes a lot of sense, especially since not many of our guys are very proficient shooters."

Nissen nodded. "Concur, Gunnery Sergeant."

Foyte stood up, giving the black NCO a comradely tap on the arm. "Like I always said: people are smart when they agree with me!"

31

N'DJAMENA

Steve Lee and Chris Nissen leaned over Martha Whitney, whom they had poured onto the couch. She failed in her effort to suppress a loud belch. Regaining her breath, she inhaled deeply and accepted the cold cloth that the medic offered.

"Martha, what did she say?" Lee did not want to seem too insistent but he was eager to learn the results of Whitney's latest meeting with the Frenchwoman.

"Oooh, my goodness," Whitney exhaled. She forced herself to focus. "That girl can drink but she can't hold it."

"You mean you drank her under the table?"

Whitney waved feebly. "I mean, she couldn' hol' it. Puked all over her shoes *an' mine*!"

"But what did she say? What are they up to?"

"Oooh my." Whitney pressed the cloth closer to her eyes. "Not so loud, Maje."

Lee and Nissen exchanged empathetic looks. Both men were trying not to smile. Neither objected to seeing the self-confident Ms. Whitney brought down two or three pegs.

Lee moderated his voice. "All right, Martha. Try to concentrate. Did you get anything out of her?"

"Oh, 'bout three quarts I'd say. My shoes . . ."

Chris Nissen turned away, clasping a hand to his mouth. Lee saw the sergeant's shoulders shaking in silent laughter.

Steve Lee pried the wet cloth from Whitney's stubby fingers. She blinked in the light. "Martha, listen to me. What . . . did . . . she . . . say?"

The former spook smacked her lips loud enough to be heard, then tasted the taste. "Oooh my." Finally she gestured toward her purse. "Wrote it down in th' taxi."

Nissen went through her bag and fetched a notebook. He flipped through the first few pages with assorted notes unrelated to the meeting with Gabrielle Tixier. Then he held the notebook out at arm's length. A few seconds later he looked at Lee. "I can't make out anything. Just a couple of words."

Lee took the pad and squinted. Finally he shook his head. "Martha, we can't read your handwriting. You'll have to read it for us." He held it before her, knowing she lacked the strength to sit up.

Whitney blinked in concentration, trying hard to focus. She raised her head, put a hand on Lee's, and adjusted the focal length. After a valiant effort she slumped back. "Nobody can read that. Not even me."

"My God, what'd you drink?" Nissen asked.

"Oooh my, what didn't we drink? She was ready for me, tha's fershure, honey. Started with wine, then whiskey. Then somethin' else. I was doin' okay. Then she brought out the cognac . . ." Whitney burped again.

"Brandy?" Nissen frowned. "If you can handle whiskey, why not . . ."

"Eighty proof," Whitney ventured. "Seven years old."

Lee stood up, his hands wide in exasperation. "Chris, we have to sober her up. Time's important."

The tall, black NCO shook his head, smiling at the victim. "Major, I can deal with penetrating wounds, fractures, blunt trauma. Even childbirth. But I cannot cure a major hangover. Nature's gotta take its course."

Lee slumped into a chair. "So we let her sleep?"

"Look at her!" In the short interval, Martha Whitney had finally succumbed. When they turned out the light and left the room she was snoring like a rhinoceros.

32

AOZOU STRIP

"How much longer?"

Marcel Hurtubise was a past master at controlling his emotions, let alone his voice, but he also heeded his instincts. The mining seemed to be progressing well, but he sensed a need for greater urgency.

The site manager was an elderly French engineer—a piece of colonial driftwood remaining above the high tide mark when the colonial surf had receded. His name was Adolphe something or other, and he had tried returning to metropolitan France two or three times since the 1960s. It never lasted long; Africa kept fetching him back.

Adolphe gave a Gallic shrug—an eloquent gesture communicating infinite wisdom if not immediate knowledge. Four decades in *l'Afrique* could not exorcize his parents' chromosomes. "A few days. Maybe less. The equipment, it is . . . vintage. *Vous savez?*"

Hurtubise knew. He had to admit that Adolphe knew his business, both technical and managerial. How he kept the black laggards working on anything resembling a schedule was the next thing to miraculous. "Well, *mon vieux*, once the ore is processed and the yellow cake packaged, your work will be done. Then you can . . ." His voice trailed off. For a shred of an instant, Hurtubise was almost embarrassed. He realized that he could not finish the sentence. Adolphe can . . . what? Probably return to a desultory life of cheap booze and cheaper accommodations.

"You can . . . rest." He even managed a smile for the old man.

Adolphe seemed not to hear. He glared at a machinery operator and began cursing him with equal fluency in French and Arabic, not managing to raise his mask over his face.

Hurtubise turned away, seeking Etienne. He found the Belgian supervising the guard change at the top of the hour. Four on, six off, seemed optimum for the limited crew of mercenaries available.

"How goes it?" Hurtubise asked. It was a rhetorical question. Etienne was as reliable as gravity—always there, whether needed or not.

"Well enough," the husky man replied. Marcel noticed that the Belgian had his sleeves rolled down, either from concern over sunburn or the less likely risk of contamination through a cut or abrasion. But since the guards seldom went near the machinery, and the open-air mine had ample ventilation, there was little cause for concern. Briefly Hurtubise wondered if his colleague—not quite a friend—actually had plans for longevity.

"All right," Hurtubise replied. "I'm flying back to N'Djamena tonight to put in an appearance at the embassy."

"So soon?" Etienne realized that his boss had been back and forth twice in the past week—more travel than usual.

"I need to make sure the ministry is coordinating the arrangements here and with the shippers. There's too much at stake to rely on . . . a couple of Africans. I'll be back in two or three days. If you need me . . ."

Etienne raised a pudgy hand, then tapped the cell phone on his belt. It was there all the time, opposite his Browning Hi-Power. "Say hello to Gabby for me." He gave a crooked grin; he knew how much she disliked that name—and him.

"I'll give her more than that," Hurtubise replied. For a change, he was smiling when he walked away.

SSI COMPOUND

Steve Lee paced to the front of the briefing room, about-faced, and looked at his team.

"We've just received a warning order."

The SSI operators exchanged querulous glances. Then everybody was speaking at once.

"But we're a training team!"

"Whose orders?"

"Holy shit!"

The latter sentiment predominated.

Lee raised both hands, urging quiet. When the noise abated he glanced at J. J., who was particularly vocal against going operational again.

Bosco interjected, "Gunny Foyte said just the . . ."

"Yeah, where is he?" Nissen asked.

Lee was growing petulant. "As I was saying . . ." He allowed the sentiment to drag out, hanging suspended in the seemingly frigid air.

"As I was saying, we're advised to start planning for an op. Gunny Foyte is on the horn to Arlington, though he may not get anybody with the time difference. Meanwhile, I'm going to meet with the embassy staff. But before any of you decide to go spastic, maybe you'd like to hear the details."

The tone of Lee's voice said as much as his words. After a pause he continued. "By 'we' I mean the Co-In battalion. Not necessarily us in this room."

Johnson raised a hand. "Major, we were just discussing this sort of thing the other day. There's hardly any junior officers up to speed as near as I can tell. So who's going . . ."

"Nobody with SSI is required to do anything. Okay? Get that straight." Lee lasered the room with his glare, obviously displeased with the response. "But Johnson is right. There's not enough officers qualified to lead more than a couple of platoons right now. Evidently that's partly due to some infighting to get assigned to an elite unit. But on the other hand, some experienced Chadians don't want to join the Co-In force just because it's considered elite. They're worried it'll draw attention from the president's office and mark them as a potential threat."

Breezy raised an eyebrow. "Man, talk about damned if you do . . ."

"Now listen up," Lee resumed. "We've been asked to contribute a couple of French speakers to help out. Officially they'd be liaison. Unofficially, they'll probably be acting platoon leaders. Otherwise we'll hope for a couple of you to work with Chadian translators."

Eyes turned toward Johnson and Joshua Wallender, the most competent French linguists. Chris Nissen was fluent in Arabic and conversant in French.

Sensing the mood in the room, Lee pushed ahead. "First, I'll emphasize that if anybody volunteers for this op, they'll be advising more than leading. Second, there's a hefty combat bonus. That's already been confirmed by the company. Third . . . well, we need you."

"What's the mission, Steve?" Bosco intentionally used Lee's given name to inject a note of immediacy.

Lee turned to a map pinned to the wall behind him. "Up here along the Libyan border there's some activity that interests this government and ours as well. It has to do with mining—that's about all I can say right now, but more intel is coming. That's been a hot area for years, going back to the seventies and eighties when Chad and Qadhafi were feuding."

Wallender, who hardly ever spoke in meetings, leaned forward in his chair. "Major, let me ask something: why us? Why not a regular Army unit?"

"I was just coming to that, Josh. The reason is security. I'm given to understand that the Army units can't be trusted because the rebels, or whomever, can buy almost any information they want. With corruption like it is in this country, that's a real concern."

Wallender sat back, clearly unsatisfied. "Well, what's to say that none of our guys will sell out?"

"Nothing's guaranteed," Lee replied. "But think about it. Our battalion is separated here. There's almost no outside contact, and we'll lock down everything as soon as we know what's up. Additionally, it'll be a no-notice deployment as far as the troops are concerned. We'll have at least a couple days to get ready, but they won't know it. Far as they're concerned, we're doing inventory and training for rapid deployment."

Nissen eyed the distance between N'Djamena and the border. "That's a fur piece up there, Major. How do we get there?"

"We pre-position some trucks and vehicles, probably here, at Bardai." He jabbed a finger on the map. "We fly there in two C-130s and we have some helos on standby. In fact, I've alerted Terry Keegan and a couple of his rotorheads. They'll be ready to insert or extract on short notice."

Wielding a pointer, Lee said, "There's two possible fields west of the op area, both unpaved. Bardai is six thousand feet long, about a hundred miles from our objective, and Zouar is forty-seven hundred, even farther away. Another option is Ouinianga Kebir, down here a couple of hundred miles southeast of the area of interest."

Wallender was clearly unhappy with the situation. "Either way, that's a long haul to the target with much hope of surprise. Especially if we're using Chadian aircraft."

Lee grinned wolfishly. "We're not. Uncle Sugar is sending three Hercs just for this mission. That includes a spare."

"Major, I don't know about the other guys but I'd sure like to know what's up there that's so important."

Lee laid down his pointer and said one word. "Uranium."

SSI OFFICES

Leopole found Derringer's door ajar and recognized the "come in" signal. Nonetheless, SSI's foreign operations chief politely rapped twice with his knuckles.

"Admiral, we got trouble."

Derringer looked up from his keyboard. "Well, that's our middle name when it isn't 'Solutions.' What is it, Frank?"

Leopole strode to the desk and laid an e-mail printout before Derringer. "Sandy just got this. She's checking with State right now, but it looks as if our Chad team has been drafted into a clandestine op."

Derringer adjusted his military-frame glasses and scanned the short message. Then he looked up. "Why didn't we get a heads-up? Wasn't there time to consult?"

"There was a phone recording from Gunny last night, saying to look for an e-mail. Ordinarily this would come from DoD or State via Marsh as chief operating officer, but he's hobnobbing with a couple of undersecretaries at Rock Creek." Leopole glanced at his watch. "By now I reckon they're on the back nine."

The CEO visualized the verdant lushness: narrow fairways flanked by dense trees. It called for serious risk assessment of a kind that Frank Leopole would never appreciate. To the former Marine officer, golf was a silly pastime lacking loud noise, recoil, and supersonic objects. Still, more serious business was conducted on manicured lawns—or in the clubhouse—than most D.C. denizens would ever admit.

Derringer swiveled in his chair, mulling over the prospects. "All right, Sandy's next in line as foreign operations officer and she'd have to deal with this development anyway. But getting our people involved in a Chadian government contract didn't just drop out of the sky. What's behind it?"

Leopole slid into a chair, elbows on the desk. "I think I can read between the lines. You remember a few days ago that Steve sent us a summary of his discussion with the defense attaché? Major Roosevelt?"

"Yes, I saw it. But I didn't follow the way they connected the dots. I mean, how'd they tumble to this French character's likely involvement with uranium smuggling? Apparently nobody in the intel business saw the forest for the trees."

"Admiral, I guess they just G-2'd it. Plain old good headwork with some help from Martha Whitney. After all, they're right there with their boots on the ground. But they didn't expect to have to act on it. Roosevelt apparently sent a memo up the food chain and somebody went Oscar Sierra. Like, 'We gotta do something, *now!*'"

Derringer nodded, sorting out the prospects. "That makes sense, Frank. But wouldn't it be logical to expect a query from Steve Lee? After all, he's not going to act without consulting us."

"We don't even know if he's been approached yet. In fact . . ."

Sandra Carmichael strode into the room, not bothering to knock. Derringer looked up. "Sandy, what've you got?"

Without formality, she replied, "Whole lotta shakin' goin' on, sir. I hardly replied to State's liaison office when this e-mail arrived from Steve. He confirms that his team has been asked by the embassy to participate in what he calls 'an important but acceptably low-risk tactical operation.' He's already done some contingency planning and has alerted Terry Keegan, who's inbound to take over a couple of helos. Steve expects to launch the op up on the Libyan border within seventy-two hours or so. That is, assuming we agree."

Derringer rubbed his chin. "Very well. Tell Steve that I'll call an emergency meeting of the board, NLT tomorrow morning. Meanwhile, he can continue his planning."

Leopole stood up. "Sandy, I don't understand something. Why do our guys and their partly trained outfit have to do this? There must be other units available."

Carmichael's blue eyes gleamed. "Go with your strength, Colonel." She liked talking to the former leatherneck as one O-5 to another. "Actually, Steve alluded to OpSec concerns. I'm sure he'll elaborate, but I suspect that operational security is a big factor, considering how corrupt things are in Chad."

"Very well." Derringer brought up his contacts file and scrolled toward the bottom. Under "Wilmont" he selected his associate's cell and clicked on "call." Looking up, he confided, "I just hope I can reach Marsh before they get to the clubhouse. He likes to stay late."

34

CAIRO

Between them, Terry Keegan and Eddie Marsh possessed nearly all the professional airman ratings available to Americans. As Keegan liked to joke, "Everything but multi-engine jet seaplane." But in truth, their forte was not flying: it was improvisation.

It was time to improvise.

Keegan hung up the phone and turned to his partner. "Okay, things are rolling. We're going to N'Djamena on a commercial flight and meet the air attaché, or whatever they call him. He'll give us the info on whatever choppers are available. After that, we're pretty much on our own."

"Sounds like a real purple operation," Marsh enthused. Keegan, a former naval aviator, smiled in appreciation of the joint ops sentiment. Marsh was an ex-Army warrant officer and they would be dealing with the Air Force.

Keegan sat down on his bed while Marsh lazed in his. "The big thing is going to be comm. We're supposed to get hi-freq radios from the embassy and presumably everybody will be able to talk to everybody else: us, the Herc crews, and our guys on the ground."

Marsh stretched his lanky frame and stifled a yawn. "You know it won't work, Terry. It never does."

Keegan, who shared the sentiment, wanted to appear more optimistic. "No reason it shouldn't. I mean, it's a pretty straightforward situation. We need standardized comm and can't rely on the radios in the helos because everybody in Chad has those freqs. As long as the HF radios work, it should be no sweat. And we'll test them before we launch."

The Army veteran shrugged. "We'll see. Hey, not that it matters, but what're we going after?"

"There's some sort of mining operation up along the Libyan border. Our instructors have orders to secure the place with some of the counterinsurgency people they're training. Steve Lee says it has to be done fast with minimal warning. He's not even telling his Chadians about it until they board the 130s."

"Well, how much info will we have for route planning and timing?"

"Oh, we'll have enough. But not much more. It's a State and DoD operation so . . ."

Marsh chuckled. "So like I said. It's not gonna work like it's planned."

"Never does, pal. Never does."

35

SSI COMPOUND

"How's Ms. Congeniality today?"

Chris Nissen knew the question was rhetorical. He grinned at Lee who entered the hostel at the stroke of 0830. The medic thought, *They can keep that clock!*

"Walking wounded." Nissen thumbed a gesture over his shoulder, toward the bathroom. Lee heard stirrings therein, and assumed that the patient was ambulatory.

Lee sat down. "Chris, I need her awake and lucid. We have to know . . ."

"I know." Nissen raised both hands. "I know. And she's a lot better. But I didn't try to debrief her about her outing with the French chick. Figured you'd want to handle that in person."

"Well, can she remember anything?"

"Major, all she said was something about her brow chakra trying to pull her solar chakra out through her crown chakra. Whatever *that* means."

Lee laughed aloud: a long, genuine cackle. When he gulped in some air, he explained. "Martha's a spiritualist. Oh, she talks about being Baptist, but she's a big believer in the Hindu power points of the body.

What she's saying is that her headache is so bad that it wants to lift her stomach out through the top of her cranium." He chuckled again. "I never heard it explained better!"

Nissen gave a slight shake of his head. "Never figured you for a Hindu."

"Oh, I'm not. If anything I'm a lapsed Congregationalist. But I studied eastern and oriental philosophy in graduate school. Actually, there's something to the chakras. There's an internal logic to the wheel of life . . ."

"Maje, I'm just a fugitive from the Elm Street boys' choir. That's as far as my religion went."

"Okay," Lee said with a grin. "Enough philosophy for now."

"Honey, we're just getting started!" Whitney appeared at the bathroom door, fresh scrubbed and dressed in a striped garment that Lee could only describe as a mumu.

"My God, Martha. You look . . . great!"

She rubbed her hands together in exaggerated fashion. "And I feel great, too. Sergeant Nissen, what's for breakfast, bro?"

The medic turned chef rose from his chair. "I'll get started. But this is no short order house. You get what I fix."

She placed her arms akimbo and gave Nissen a stern look. "And you're likely to get it back on your shoes if'n I don't like it!"

"Uh, that chakra thing?"

"Solar chakra, honey. As in, from the bottom of my stomach."

"How 'bout a nice omelette? With black coffee."

"Now you're cookin', sugar." She pronounced it "sugah."

Whitney slid into the vacant chair and leaned toward Lee. "Now, Major honey. What do y'all want to know?"

Lee produced a notebook and sat back. "Everything."

She told him.

SSI OFFICES

"Gentlemen—ladies—we don't have much time."

Derringer scanned the eight people seated around the polished table. He would have preferred a late night meeting or even a phone poll, but most of SSI's directors had other obligations, and 0800 was the best he could manage.

"Here's the short version," he began. "Our team in Chad has made good progress with the counterinsurgency unit it's training. But they're not up to speed and aren't expected to complete the first cycle for a couple of months. Meanwhile, a potentially critical development has occurred in-country that requires a quick response. There's a French PMC operating legitimately with the French government but apparently it's doing some moonlighting as well. Steve Lee, Martha Whitney, and the military attaché in N'Djamena have discovered that a clandestine mining operation is under way along the northern border with Libya. We don't know for sure but it looks as if our counterparts from Paris are planning on smuggling uranium ore, and possibly processed yellow cake, out of the country."

"What's the destination?" asked George Ferraro. The former naval systems analyst already thought he had a good idea.

"Well, one of the PMC's usual suspects is an Iranian."

"But we don't know for certain that's the end user."

"We do not," Derringer replied. "But State, DoD, and the embassy folks are worried enough to put our team on the operation."

Marshall Wilmont spoke up. "I'd like to hear Matt's appraisal of the personnel aspects." Matthew Finch of the administrative support division seldom attended board meetings but Wilmont wanted his perspective.

Finch was a button-down Marylander whom Leopole insisted had been born in a vest. "Well, our contract has a clause saying that SSI training personnel can be activated for operations provided there's adequate consultation, approval, and so forth. Evidently some of the team is willing to go and others . . . well, they're not so eager. In any case, there's precedent for such action if that's a concern to anyone. Obviously it doesn't bother State or DoD. Beyond that, we have an escalating fee scale based on a pretty subjective set of risk factors. Of course, if any casualties occur, the coverage automatically kicks in, regardless of the cause."

Ferraro asked, "Has Ms. Pilong been consulted?"

Finch nodded. "I talked to Corin on the phone just before we convened. She's taking care of a sick child, but she said there's no contractual barriers."

Derringer leaned back. "There you have it. Our people are in place, some willing to participate in a clandestine operation, and their assistance is wanted by State and Defense. We won't make a lot of extra money off it, but I think we should take it. The risk seems fully acceptable, and the operation will gain SSI additional goodwill with our main client. The United States Government."

Sam Small, a retired Air Force colonel and sometime SR-71 pilot, was first to respond. "Looks like a no-brainer to me. Minimal risk, possible big benefit. I don't even know if we need to discuss it."

Wilmont interjected, "Sammy, I understand your attitude, and I share your opinion. But anytime we're faced with altering a contract, and this involves possible combat, Mike and I think the board needs to consider it."

Small gave a shrug. "Okay, let's go."

Beverly Shumard's icy blue eyes betrayed no emotion. "Ordinarily I would agree that this proposal, coming from two agencies, is worthwhile. But I wonder if we're overlooking something."

"Yes?" Derringer prompted.

"Unintended consequences, Admiral. If, as seems possible, we end up chasing uranium all the way to Iran, we might find ourselves in over our collective heads."

"Beverly, there's always the possibility of events spinning out of control. We all accept that fact when we sign on, whether in the military or with SSI. But as I've noted, this is a low-risk operation, limited in time and place." Derringer looked around the room again. "Anybody else?"

No one responded so Derringer called for a voice vote.

"Dr. Craven?"

"Go."

"General Rowell?"

"Affirm."

"General Jonas?"

"You bet."

"Dr. Frisch?"

"Yes."

"We've already heard from Colonel Small. Bev, what do you think?"

Shumard managed a slight grin that dimpled her cheeks. "You know what I think, Admiral. But since we already have a clear majority, I'll go along."

Derringer glanced at Mrs. Springer, who was keeping notes. "Then it's unanimous." He turned to Wilmont and Carmichael. "Marsh, you can inform State that we're proceeding. Sandy, tell Steve Lee that it's a go."

N'DJAMENA

Hurtubise was in the apartment less than one minute before he sensed trouble.

Gabrielle gave him a perfunctory kiss that set bells ringing—the farthest kind from romantic bells.

Alarm bells.

"What is it?" he asked.

She looked up at him—he was four inches taller—and bit her lip. He mistook it for a pout, and Gabrielle Tixier could pout with the best of them. A sensual, little-girl pout perfected over years. She used it to manipulate men.

When she turned away, he grasped her arm and spun her around. "I asked, what is it?"

"I feel terrible," she replied.

"Yes, I can see that, Gabrielle." He modulated his voice, allowing just enough flat tone to imply something pending. Something probably unpleasant.

"I did what you wanted," she said, immediately regretting the defensive whine building at the end of the phrase. "I met the American woman again and we . . . talked."

"You did more than talk. You drank. A lot." It was a statement of fact; a certainty like magnetism or taxes.

She touched her forehead and flicked the light brown bangs. "Yes. All right. We drank. A lot. We learned about each other. That's what you wanted, wasn't it?"

He folded his arms—a sure sign of irritation—and leaned forward. "Don't play games, Gabrielle! I set a hen to catch a hen, and now I am beginning to think that the American hen was a chicken hawk." He stared her down; she never could meet his eyes for more than several seconds.

She plopped into the only comfortable chair and looked at him again. "I . . ." Her voice trailed off.

"What did you tell her?"

Her mouth opened. Nothing followed. Finally she swallowed and croaked, "I . . . I don't know. Not everything."

He sprang at her, raising a hand, and she flinched from long experience.

Hurtubise stopped in midstride. He realized that if he struck her again, this time she probably would leave. Personal considerations aside, she would also take any useful information with her.

He knelt before her, balanced on one knee. "Gabrielle. I'm sorry. I told you four years ago that I would never do that again. And I keep my word."

She was crying now, tears tracking down both cheeks. "Marcel . . . I'm so sorry. I thought I could handle her. Honestly I did. But . . ."

The emotional dam burst and the sobs came. She leaned forward on her elbows, her slender torso visibly shaking with each painful exhalation.

He reached out, touched an arm, and squeezed. Harder than he intended, but a calming gesture nonetheless.

Inside, his mind was raging.

Marcel Hurtubise was nothing if not composed. He was aware of the American phrase "control freak." *Commandez le phénomène* was as close as he could come. But however you said it, he had it. "Come here, my darling." He wrapped his muscular arms around her and pulled her to him. Over her shoulder, he glanced at his watch and estimated that she would tell him what he needed to know in three minutes.

It was more like five.

When she had confessed all she could—everything she could remember or thought she could remember—she allowed herself to relax a bit. By now she was feeling more certain of herself. It had happened before—a long period of good to excellent behavior followed by an inevitable lapse leading to confession, contrition, and forgiveness. Sometimes Gabrielle wondered if Marcel had been a priest in a previous incarnation.

But there was always the penance. In this instance, it came on an icy wind.

"Good, Gabrielle. Very good. It is always best to tell the truth. I cannot make things better without knowing everything. You understand?"

She nodded briskly, not trusting her voice.

"Very well." He stroked her hair, tracing the line of her cheek with the knuckles of one hand. "We must assume that she knows about the mine, so there is only one thing to do."

"Yes?"

"Kill her."

37

"Okay: here's what we know," Lee began. He pointed to a map of Chad propped on an easel. "The mine is here in the Aozou Strip up near the Libyan border. It's been relatively inactive for a few years but apparently some of the equipment has been maintained, maybe with this time in mind. At any rate, our colleagues with Groupe FGN have been using their legitimate work through the French embassy to provide security for the clandestine operation that's under way at the mine. We do not know the ultimate destination of the yellow cake, but it could be Iran." He allowed that sentiment to linger in midair for a moment.

"Anyway, that really doesn't matter. The important thing is, our people here and in D.C. do not want that product to leave the country. That's why it's such a hurry-up operation. We don't know exactly when the yellow cake will be ready for export, but indications are that it's imminent."

Lee turned back to his audience and took three steps forward. "Gentlemen, I'll repeat what I said before. This is strictly a volunteer basis. If you don't want to go, you don't have to. Personally, I'm convinced that it's a low-risk operation, but there could be some shooting. Since you've all signed training contracts, you're at liberty to stay here. But we need experienced leadership on the ground up there, and that's why our team got the nod." He looked at each man in turn. "Any questions?"

There were none so Lee nodded to Foyte. "Gunny will conduct the briefing since he's been working on the op order."

Foyte walked to the head of the room. "Thank you, Major." He flipped his notebook open and ran through the standard headings.

"Mission: well, you know that. Secure the mine and prevent any yellow cake from getting out. After we're done, a joint U.S., Chad, and IAEA team will move in."

Bosco raised a hand. "Uh, what's IAEA?"

"International Atomic Energy Agency. It's a multinational inspection organization."

"U.N.?" asked Bosco.

"It's based in Vienna but is chartered by the U.N. Why?"

"Ah, I never trust anybody who wears baby blue berets," Bosco replied. Some chuckles skittered through the room. Foyte ignored them.

"Enemy forces: probably twelve to twenty French or European mercs from Groupe FGN. That does not include the mine workers. Expect small arms and automatic weapons, and watch for imbedded explosives.

"Friendly forces: well, that's us, of course. We're taking two platoons: one to assault and one to secure the perimeter and provide backup.

"Execution: fly to the op area in C-130s and take pre-positioned transport to the mine. We'll have two choppers in support for contingencies and med-evac. We plan to hit the place at dawn. You'll get specific assignments the night before.

"Command and control: this is gonna be the kicker. Almost none of our clients speak English so there's a premium on French and Arabic speakers. We'll have a couple of translators from the embassy as backup." He looked at Chris Nissen and J. J. Johnson. Nissen was in—he could use the combat bonus for his daughter's college fund. Johnson still had not committed.

"We'll have at least two common frequencies on radios. I'm told that our rotor heads also are getting UHF sets from the blue suits so the helos can talk to us on the ground.

"Security. Well, that's the reason we're doing this job. The locals would gladly sell any information to anybody, which is why SSI and our Co-In team has been tasked. We're administratively and physically separate from the rest of the Chadian armed forces, and nobody's left the training area for two days. Additionally, we're using our own transportation and USAF 130s. Now, I'm not saying there couldn't be some word to the frogs, but it looks pretty tight.

"ROE: fire discipline is important here, more for our platoons than ourselves. Yeah, I know—a lot of the Chadians we're training have been shot at before, but if somebody caps off a round by accident, you know damn well what'll happen. Firing contagion. With all the civilians in the area, that could be really bad news. So we're gonna stress that our troops don't shoot at anybody who isn't pointing a weapon at them.

"POWs, if that's the term. We will have to disarm the Frenchies and put them under detention. Major Lee and I hope that a superior show of force will convince them to stand down. In that case, we'll treat them well and hold them until the suits arrive. If not—well, it's their funeral. So to speak."

Foyte looked up. "Questions?"

Breezy stirred in his seat. "Gunny, wouldn't it be better to go in before dawn? Take 'em more by surprise?"

The Marine nodded. "Of course. But do you want to take the boys we're training and have them running around in the dark with loaded weapons?" He did not await a response. "Next."

Josh Wallender gave the high sign. "What's the risk of radiation?"

Lee stood up again. "Very slight. You're going to hear from an expert that the big problem with uranium ore is underground, where there's poor ventilation. This mine is a big pit in the open. You'll have respirators for the time you're actually in the pit but avoid cuts and you'll be okay. We're not going to be there very long, anyway."

Lee asked, "Anything else?" When no one responded, he gestured to a man in the back of the room.

"Gentlemen, this is Mr. Langevin. He's with the IAEA and has been briefed on our mission. Now, before anybody gets excited, I can say that he's on our side. He's a former Air Force nuke who works in the arms control field. He will fill us in on uranium ore."

Langevin had not reached the front of the room before Breezy leaned to Bosco and said in a loud whisper, "Funny. He doesn't look like an Air Force puke."

Boscombe took the hint. He swatted his partner, exclaiming, "You dummy. That's *nuke*, not puke!"

Langevin, a short, slightly built man with receding dark hair, turned to the Army men. "What's the atomic number of uranium?"

Bosco and Breezy exchanged glances. "Uh, 235," essayed Breezy.

"*Beeeep!* Wrong!" Langevin imitated a quiz-show buzzer. "It's ninety-two, because the uranium atom has ninety-two protons and electrons. Now, I don't expect you snake eaters to understand about earth elements, let alone lanthanide or actinide series. So there's no way you're going to understand 92, let alone 235!"

While the grunts in the room tried to absorb the fact that a skinny techno-nerd could take their guff and toss it back, Langevin launched into his briefing.

"A bit of background, gentlemen. Uranium is a naturally occurring element found at low levels in nearly all rocks, soils, and water. It is considered more common than gold, silver, or tungsten, and nearly as much as arsenic or molybdenum. It is found in many minerals such as lignite, and monazite sands in uranium-rich ores. It is mined from those sources.

"Now, as you heard from Major Lee, uranium ore produces radon gas that needs ventilation unless it's mined in an open pit. Fortunately, that's the case where we're concerned . . ."

Breezy interrupted. "Ah, we? As in, you're going with us? Sir?"

"You got it, son. And I'm packing. If I have to double-tap somebody, I'll do it, too."

The former paratrooper raised an eyebrow and regarded the dweeb with new respect. "Ah, yessir."

"Good." Langevin shot a glance at Lee and winked. Then he continued.

"Now, it doesn't really bear on our mission but you might benefit from some background. The U.S. hasn't had to import uranium for many years, at least not for military purposes. Most people don't realize that Australia has nearly thirty percent of the world's known supply, but only exports it for nonmilitary use. However, Canada probably exports more total product though the worldwide demand has dropped. Uranium hit an all-time low of seven dollars a pound in 2001 but has bounced back to about thirty."

Wallender interjected. "Sir, I don't understand something. If uranium is widely available, why the concern about deposits in a remote place like Chad? I mean, it's got to be harder and more expensive to get there than almost anywhere."

"That's a good question," Langevin responded. "The reason is, Chad and much of Africa have ample supplies, but the mines and transportation systems are not monitored very well. Remember, Chad has been named one of the two most corrupt governments on earth. With enough money and minimal resources, almost anyone could obtain enough ore to produce yellow cake and ship it anywhere. Say, like North Korea. Or Iran."

"Gulp."

"You said it."

Langevin began pacing, turning to keep his audience in view. "What we're concerned with isn't the ore, it's uranic oxide, better known as yellow cake, that's used for processing. It's roughly seventy-five percent uranate, produced by milling uranium ore. It's a radioactive powder with a high melting temperature—nearly three thousand degrees Centigrade. It's insoluble in water."

"How's it produced?" asked Foyte.

"Well, the ore is crushed to produce what's called pulp. That's dipped in sulfuric acid to leach out the product. What's left after drying and filtering is the yellow cake."

"So we're looking for, like, a yellow powder, right?"

"Well, no. The stuff is actually dark brown or even black. The yellow name is left over from early processes that weren't as efficient as today."

Johnson, still uncertain whether he would participate, was intrigued. "Sir, how much yellow cake is needed for a bomb?"

"Actually, none," the scientist replied. "Yellow cake is unenriched uranium so it's no use in a weapon. It's mostly used to obtain purified uranium oxide in fuel rods. That in turn can be part of weapons grade production, especially plutonium."

"Then, if I understand it right, producing yellow cake really isn't very hard," the former Legionnaire said.

"No, it's a relatively straightforward process. But in most parts of the world the procedure is closely guarded through international accords. That's where I come in, with IAEA. But in Chad and other places, that's not always so. Consequently, the extra cost of mining relatively small quantities is not a real concern. The people who want uranium without anybody knowing it are well funded, and to a large extent they don't care what it costs." He shrugged. "When you sell billions of barrels of oil a year, several million dollars for yellow cake is no big deal."

"Like Iran?" Breezy suggested.

"Certainly. Iran consistently ranks in the top five oil exporters, between three and four million barrels a day."

Langevin saw Bosco and Breezy exchange whispered comments. "Ah, something you want to discuss, gentlemen?"

Breezy sat upright. "We were, uh, just saying that you seem really well informed. Sir."

Bernard Langevin beamed. The former Air Force short colonel was unaccustomed to compliments from knuckle-dragging door-kickers. "Just doing my job, son. Just doing my job."

38

N'DJAMENA

Whitney knocked on the apartment's weathered door. It had "safe house" written all over it: not too fancy, a plain, white-washed exterior with a good view front and back and access to two streets. She resisted the urge to look over her shoulder, knowing that Johnson and Wallender would be watching her from a rented panel truck.

Gabrielle answered the door and greeted her guest in English. "Martha! So good to see you. Please come in." She stepped back to allow the American to enter.

Whitney took three steps inside, facing her host. As she did so, she took in the setting with the mindset of an alumna of the CIA Directorate of Operations. *Curtains partly drawn to limit the view from outside. Too suspicious if they were closed. Large rug on the floor: good footing but she won't try anything here in case there's bloodstains.*

Tixier smiled. "After last time I think we should have some tea!" She managed a credible giggle. So did Whitney. *Female bonding, nice touch, honey.* "I have a pot warming in the kitchen," Tixier explained with a gesture toward the back of the house.

Whitney nodded politely. *"Après vous."* She thought: *No way am I letting you behind me, sweet cheeks.*

Tixier accepted the fact that she had been outmaneuvered and led the way to the kitchen. Whitney recognized the signs of a setup: venetian blinds mostly closed, tile floor for easy cleanup of messy fluids.

Gabrielle made a point of turning to the stove to retrieve the teapot while Martha remained standing, holding her purse. The sound-activated mike inside was tuned to the frequency that J. J. Johnson was monitoring in case the conversation was conducted in French. He and Wallender could be inside in about thirty seconds, which was the best compromise. Any closer and they would surely be spotted.

While Tixier was adjusting the burner, Whitney did a complete scan. She was comfortable that nobody else was nearby. Not yet, anyway. She turned back to Tixier. *Just you and me, babe.*

The Frenchwoman carried the pot to the table where cups and saucers were set. She looked a little surprised. "Oh, please, sit down, Martha." She patted a chair to the left of her own.

Whitney took the chair opposite Tixier rather than the one indicated, keeping the table between them. Apparently in frustration, Tixier dropped the smiling pretense. She took two quick steps to the side of the table, dropped the teapot's lid, and flung the contents at Whitney's face.

Martha reacted instinctively. She sidestepped most of the scalding brew, ignoring the liquid pain on her left arm and shoulder. As Tixier grabbed for a towel on the ledge, Whitney stepped in, connected with a swift overhand karate chop to the base of the neck, immediately following with a backhand blow to the larynx. Tixier gasped, slumped against the counter, and grabbed for the towel. As she fell to both knees, a 9 mm Makarov clattered to the floor.

Whitney kicked the pistol away and drew her Glock. "She's down, J. J.!" Whitney wanted backup available soonest. "I'm unlocking the back door."

Before turning away from an assailant, Whitney wanted some insurance. She set down her bag, brought up a can of pepper spray, and gave Tixier a four-second dose to the face. The Frenchwoman reeled away, fell on her back, and rolled in pain, hands at her eyes.

Johnson and Wallender entered with pistols drawn. Without a word, they obeyed Whitney's head gesture to clear the apartment. They disappeared through the door, "slicing the pie" to search progressively around each corner.

Whitney knew it would take at least a couple of minutes to complete the search. She locked the door and closed the blinds all the way. Then she turned to Gabrielle Tixier.

The fight was gone from her. She had managed to raise herself to a semi-reclining position, back against a kitchen cabinet. She inhaled slowly, watching the American woman with awe in one eye, fear in the other; streaming tears in both.

Whitney picked up the Makarov, dropped the magazine, and ejected the chambered round into the sink. She ran some water in a glass and examined her assailant. "That's right, honey. Slow breaths. Breathe through the mouth; your sinuses are messed up."

Wetting one end of the towel, Whitney poured water over Tixier's face and gently wiped away some of the OC spray. Nasty stuff. Great stuff. She allowed the younger woman to rinse her mouth with some water and spit it onto the floor. Tixier needed both hands to steady the glass, allowing Whitney to search her. There was a switchblade in one vest pocket. "You expecting trouble, sweetie?" Whitney grinned as she tossed the shiv over her shoulder.

In a moment Tixier was able to focus. Then she said, "*Tuez moi.*"

Whitney gave a forced laugh. "Kill you? Why would I do that?"

Tixier spat out some mucus. "If you don't, Marcel will. That's why I had to kill you." She spat again. "I am finished."

Martha made a point of sitting on the floor, appearing less threatening. "Sweetie, don't you think you're premature? You can come with me. We'll take you away and you never need to see him again."

Tixier's blue eyes were still watery. She rubbed them with the back of one hand, an endearing little-girl gesture. She sniffed loudly, then shook her head. "No, it's no good. I know something of the intelligence world. I would be useful for a while, then . . ." She shrugged. "Believe me, if it took the rest of his life, Marcel would find me. I would never have any peace. I would rather be dead."

Whitney placed a hand on Tixier's arm. "Gabrielle . . ." She sought the right words. "You know, in America we have a saying. Never kid a kidder. Well, honey, we've been trying to kid each other. You know what I mean? We been playing this damn game trying to get each other to talk. The other night you talked more than I did, and now your friend Marcel wants me dead. But you know what? It don't matter. He must know that, too. My friends already have the information, sweetie."

Tixier nodded gravely, staring at the far wall. "Yes, I know."

"Well then?"

"It is as you say, Martha. It doesn't matter. Marcel knows that I betrayed him even if I didn't mean to. There's no going back." She turned her head to spit up again.

"But . . ."

Tixier raised her left hand. It trembled as if from Parkinson's. "You don't know him. A few years ago he thought a man had betrayed him. A friend from *La Legion*. Marcel spent eight months tracking him down. Then he killed him most . . . painfully."

"Well, I see what you're saying . . ."

"No you don't, Martha. A few weeks later Marcel learned that the man had not betrayed him. Somebody else did and blamed the Legionnaire. You know what Marcel said?" Before Whitney could respond, Tixier added, "He said, '*Mauvaise chance.*' "

"Bad luck?"

"That's all. Just that. Then he spent more time looking for the one who really turned on him. But that man had burned too many others and he turned up dead in Marseilles. So Marcel never got his revenge. He was furious about that. Which is why I know he will never stop until he finds me."

Johnson stepped into the kitchen, holstering his Sig. "All clear. Martha, we'd better get her out of here."

Whitney stood up, rubbing her arm. "Gonna have to get some ointment," she said.

"Yeah, but what about . . ."

"No. She's made up her mind."

"Well, I don't know, Martha. She's a good source."

Whitney leaned down to touch Tixier's cheek. "She's already told us everything we need, J. J." She looked at her younger colleague with moisture in her brown eyes. "And she just told me what she needs."

Tixier mouthed the words. *Thank you.*

Martha Whitney almost smiled. *"Adieu, ma chérie."*

39

KOSSEO AIR BASE, N'DJAMENA

Terry Keegan had seen worse maintained helicopters, but not recently.

Standing on the ramp with Eddie Marsh and their contract mechanic, Keegan waited for the Air Force advisor to conclude his arcane business with the Chadian officer. Keegan knew that at one point the commander of the *Force Aerienne Tchadienne* held the exalted rank of lieutenant.

At length the advisor shook hands with the African officer and walked toward Keegan and Marsh. "Come on, we're going over there," the major said, pointing beyond the security perimeter.

"What's the deal, sir? Aren't we using these birds?"

Major Allen "Jigger" Lowe kept a straight face. "What's the matter, Mr. Keegan? Do you *like* flying old, leaky helos or something?"

"Well, it's just that . . ."

Lowe stopped so abruptly that his charges went two steps beyond him. He motioned over his shoulder. "You see that Chadian officer back there? Well, he told me that *he* wouldn't fly very high in one of the Alouettes you just saw."

Eddie Marsh ventured an opinion. "Sort of like the hang glider's motto?"

Lowe grinned in appreciation. "You got it. 'Don't fly any higher than you're willing to fall.' Which is why we're going the long way 'round to check out the other helos."

Keegan gave a tight-lipped grin. "I see, said the blind man. We're gonna borrow some of the French birds."

"I can neither confirm nor deny." Lowe began walking again. "But it's all been arranged back-channel; I just had to settle with our, ah, colleague over there."

Keegan regarded the blue-suiter with growing admiration. The former Navy man suspected that his Air Force host had just greased somebody's sweaty palm.

Moments later, Keegan and Marsh were looking at newer, obviously better maintained Alouette IIIs. No visible leaks; no pitted Plexiglas; not much chipped paint. A couple of them even had Chad's red-yellow-blue cockade over the red-white-blue emblem of France.

Keegan consulted with his mechanic, a burly, monosyllabic individual between thirty-five and fifty years of age, who spoke fluent French and aviation English with a Canadian accent. The Americans knew him as Charles Haegelin; heaven knew what his passport said, let alone his birth certificate. Keegan only knew him slightly; they had partnered with SSI once before.

Lowe opened the door of the nearest Alouette and withdrew a canvas satchel. "Mr. Haegelin, here's the airframe and engine logs. I believe this is the low-time bird of the bunch. I'll stick around while you gentlemen decide which ones you want to use, but you'll have to sign for them before you leave."

While Haegelin and Marsh checked fuel and fluids on the first helo, Marsh and Lowe examined another. Far enough from inquiring ears, Marsh leaned close. "Jigger, how'd you swing the loan of some of the French birds?"

The advisor was deadpan. "I don't understand the question."

Keegan thought he detected a wink, but perhaps it was an ordinary blink. "Okay, I won't ask embarrassing questions."

"Works for me," Lowe said. "Now, how much Alouette time do you have?"

"Oh, maybe two hundred hours."

"Current?"

"Yeah, I flew a few days before we left home."

Lowe nodded. "Good 'nuf for government work!"

40

N'DJAMENA

Paul Deladier glanced up from his paper as Marcel entered. "I've been waiting for you," the younger man said. "I thought you'd be back by now."

"It always takes longer at the embassy," Hurtubise replied evenly. He loosened his tie and looked around. "Where's Gabrielle?"

Paul shrugged. "I haven't seen her today."

Hurtubise glanced at the clock on the stove. "She should be back by now."

Deladier turned a page. "Maybe she's out shopping with her nigger friends. I don't know what she sees in them."

"No, she was . . ."

Four sharp raps came from the door. One, pause, three. "That's Raoul," Hurtubise said. He opened the door.

Raoul Clary's face told the story. "She's dead."

Deladier gasped audibly. "My God! Gabby . . ."

Hurtubise pulled the operative inside, then closed and locked the door. "Tell me." His voice was emotionless, flat.

"I followed her as you said, making sure she didn't try to run. But she kept the appointment all right. She met the fat American at the other apartment like you suggested. Gerard and I had the van with a body bag and cleaning supplies and the medical kit. All we had to do was look for her signal." He spread his hands. "Marcel, why didn't you let us do it? There would have been no trouble. The black woman would just disappear."

"I have my reasons," Hurtubise snapped. "Go on."

"Well, after twenty minutes we saw the American arrive. She left not long after that. There was no sign of Gabrielle so we waited a little more, then entered through the bedroom window. She was dead in the kitchen."

"How?"

"Shot in the head."

"Executed?" Hurtubise asked.

"No, not if you mean from behind. But . . ."

"Yes?"

"Well, now that I think of it, the entry was in the left temple. Her Makarov was on the floor beside her."

"Had it been fired?"

Clary nodded. "Once."

Hurtubise felt a chill. Gabrielle had been left-handed. "No other ballistics? Any sign of a fight?"

"No. Oh, it looked like she had been sprayed with Mace. We could smell it a bit, too."

"Where is she?"

"Gabrielle?"

"Yes, Gabrielle, you idiot!"

"Well, I thought you might mean the American. Gabrielle's body is still in the van. Gerard is parked outside. We thought it best to come here rather than risk calling."

Hurtubise began pacing, biting his lip in concentration. Deladier and Clary watched him closely. They thought they knew what Gabrielle Tixier meant to him, but they also knew his ruthless quality. It was at once a strength and a fault.

Abruptly he turned on a heel. "Raoul, you and Gerard get rid of the body. Remove all identification, everything. In fact, bring the clothes. I'll burn them myself." He turned to Deladier. "Paul, call the charter pilot."

"Where are we going?"

"We're flying up to the mine tonight. Something's going to happen there. I feel it. Let Etienne know we're coming."

Deladier merely nodded. Then he asked, "What are you going to do, Marcel?"

Hurtubise regarded his colleague with a shark's flat eyes. "I'm going for a walk."

41

SSI COMPOUND

Steve Lee hung up the phone and turned to Daniel Foyte. "Gunny, we're set. That was Roosevelt. He says the 130s are landing tomorrow and we'll have the final briefing two days later. That allows for some slack in the schedule, mainly for deploying the helos up north."

Foyte was helping himself to a pinch of Redman, an old habit. He only used smokeless tobacco, as it gave little indication of his presence whenever the urge hit on an ambush site. He settled the wad in his cheek, then said, "Very well, sir. I'll tell the guys. Uh, when do you want to spring it on the two action platoons?"

"Not until we're ready to board the Hercs. Far as the troops will know, we're just conducting a mobilization drill. Colonel Maloum might go along but he understands it'd just be for show."

The former Marine went to work on the chaw, nodding his approval. "Yessir. Uh, what about the choppers?"

Lee suppressed a yawn; he had been up much of the night, finalizing arrangements for the operation. "Keegan and Marsh are checking out two Alouettes today. The attaché will help them test fly two birds and get them headed for the border tomorrow afternoon at the latest."

"What about maintenance?"

"Already handled, Gunny. Our pilots brought a guy who knows Alouettes inside out, and one or two Chadian mechs are going along with some spare parts."

Foyte was working on his wad now, savoring the juice. "Well, all right, Major. But I'd be damn nervous riding in a machine that wants to tear itself apart on a good day, let alone one maintained by some of the boys in this neck of the woods."

Lee sat upright, looking Foyte full in the face. "Gunnery Sergeant, this has come up before, and I need you to tune your command set to 'receive.' Are you reading me?"

Foyte knew what was coming. "Yessir. I read you five by five. No more talk about 'boys.'"

"You got it."

N'DJAMENA

Marcel Hurtubise walked rapidly, covering ground in a purposeful stride that led nowhere. Hands in his pockets, uncharacteristically looking at the ground rather than 360 degrees around him, he realized with a start that he had circled a city block for the second time. He looked at the sky. *Late afternoon. Gabrielle has been dead at least six hours.*

He resumed walking.

In his lonely, violent forty-four years, Marcel Jules Marie Hurtubise had learned to rely upon himself. Oh, there had been the comradely nature of the Legion—*Legio pro patria* and all that—but it was not strong enough to hold him. He had wanted something else, something more.

Gabrielle.

He saw her again in his memory for the first time: the defiant, skinny teenager who could use a good meal and a hot bath. He had seen many like her: frightened, angry runaways seeking temporary shelter, both physical and emotional. Somehow, it had worked with her. Most of the time, anyway. It had not been easy, getting her off drugs and off the street. But in months rather than years, his attention and his patience had won her. He remembered the first time she had given herself to him. And with something approaching remorse, he recalled the only time he had forced her—the result of a simple job that had gone terribly bad and there was no one else to take his wrath. She swore that if he ever did that again, she would kill him, herself, or both of them.

He believed her.

After that, the years had been more good than bad. She grew to mental maturity, if not emotional, and occasionally shared in his work. She was a natural in some ways—coy, manipulative, astute about people. Especially men. But eventually he had seen the edge return, something hard and bitter behind the big blue eyes. When she had wanted to execute the Israeli, he knew she had turned a corner that offered little chance of return.

Raoul's question forced its way to Marcel's consciousness again. *Why not let us do it?*

He had answered, "I have my reasons."

True, Clary and any of the others could have handled the intrusive American female, but Marcel wanted Gabrielle to do the killing. She had arrogantly asserted that she could handle the con job, and when she failed, it became her responsibility to put things right. If she did it, maybe there was a chance she could recover. If not . . . well . . .

Mauvaise chance.

Hurtubise bit his lip until it hurt. He thought he tasted the salty tang of blood. *We came so close, Gabby. After this job, we could go anywhere, settle down, enjoy life.* He even had a spot picked out, a semi-secluded property in Switzerland. Wonderful scenery, skiing in the winter, not too many neighbors.

Now that was gone. It was partly her fault, partly his, and partly theirs.

By God, the Americans were going to pay.

He turned around and strode back to the apartment.

42

SSI COMPOUND

Steve Lee was a professional pessimist. He spent much of his life contemplating what might go wrong, and shared that philosophy with the SSI team's final briefing for the raid.

"As I see it, the biggest problem we might have is the people north of the border." He indicated the boundary with Libya, barely forty kilometers from the uranium mine. "Now, there's no reason to think that they'll get involved, but in my experience that's reason to think they might." He gave an ironic grin that prompted polite chuckles from his audience.

"If we take them by surprise, there shouldn't be much trouble. But if they 'make' us inbound, if they have much warning at all, they could have some yellow cake on a couple of trucks hightailing it for Colonel Qadhafi. From there, the load could go anywhere. Like Iran."

Bernard Langevin, monitoring the briefing from the back row, raised a hand. "Steve, I agree that's a concern. But I just don't think the Libyans are going to pick a fight with the U.S., not even in Chad."

Lee laid down his pointer and turned to the scientist. "Look at it from their boots, Bernie. They won't know we're Americans. Hell, officially we're not even involved in this op. That's the whole idea behind SSI: deniability."

Before Langevin could respond, Brezyinski posed a question. "Sir, doesn't Iran have uranium? I mean, why go to all the trouble to smuggle the stuff from Chad or someplace?"

Langevin nodded. "Reasonable question. But you've just had a hint of the answer from Major Lee: deniability."

Breezy wrinkled a brow. "How's that, Doc?"

"Almost every uranium ore has its own identification, like a finger-print. If there's anyplace on earth that hasn't been fingerprinted, so to speak, I don't know where it is. So if the Iranians want to nuke some-place, they're not going to use material from their own backyard. They have at least three mines but they'll want to use refined ore from some-place else, the farther away the better. They'd use it from Colorado if they could get enough of it."

Bosco, whose scientific interest generally was limited to pulp fiction and *Star Wars* movies, now took a closer interest. "Excuse me, sir. But how much uranium do you need for a bomb?"

Langevin grinned hugely. His smile said, *Low, slow one over the mid-dle of the plate.* Finally he replied, "Well, I could tell you but then I'd have to kill you."

When the laughter abated, the scientist raised a hand. "Sorry, I couldn't help myself. But it's a fair question. I can't talk about current weapons, but for the Little Boy that flattened Hiroshima, about sixty-five kilos. Less than 150 pounds." Warming to his subject, he continued. "But that's not a very efficient use of a valuable product. Now, take Fat Man, the Nagasaki bomb. That only used six kilos of plutonium, but of course you need a lot of uranium to process plutonium. There's an in-termediate step called a composite, with a core using both uranium and plutonium. A little over three kilos of plutonium and six and a half of U-235." He shrugged. "Actually, it doesn't make a lot of difference. An exact duplicate of Little Boy is still about twelve to fifteen KT yield, and we know what that did to Hiroshima."

"I have a question." It was Josh Wallender, who rarely spoke in meet-ings. "Libya has been awfully quiet for several years, like maybe they learned a lesson. Why would they risk another setback on behalf of Iran?"

Langevin shifted in his seat to face the Green Beret. "Good ques-tion, Sergeant. For some years there was cooperation between Libya and Iran on weapons research, even though Qadhafi's regime is pretty secular. But there was a Libyan group of Islamic extremists that attacked government facilities inside Libya so Qadhafi had them expelled. They went to Afghanistan, then settled in Iran with some other al Qaeda groups. Along the way, some of their recent knowledge about Iran's nuclear program got back to Libya, and that had something to do with Qadhafi renouncing WMDs in 2004. So it looks like there's a connection: Tehran doesn't want Libya spilling what it knows about the Iranian bomb program, and threatens to return the radicals to Libya if that happens."

Wallender emitted a long, low whistle.

Langevin smiled in appreciation. "Yeah. Welcome to the Middle East."

Regaining control of the session, Lee said, "That's the long way 'round the block to say that we should be prepared for a Libyan reaction. It's entirely possible that some yellow cake can be moved to Libya with or without the government's knowledge, and shipped elsewhere. That means we want to do this as slick and quick as possible."

He scanned the room, unblinking behind his Army issue glasses. "Anything else for discussion?" He glanced at Foyte, who shook his head.

"Very well then." Lee shot a look at his watch. "Let's get our people moving. Equipment check before the briefing and nobody leaves the compound. We're wheels in the well in four plus thirty."

43

AOZOU STRIP

The Cessna 421 braked to a halt on the hard-packed runway and shut down the left engine first. Before the three-bladed propeller had stopped spinning, the door opened and two men immediately debarked. Marcel Hurtubise and Paul Deladier carried overnight bags that contained few clothes. Anyone hefting the satchels would have commented upon the weight.

Cruising at 190 knots, the trip had taken over three hours. Deladier would have preferred to try to sleep during the trip but his superior had other priorities. In one way, however, Deladier welcomed the diversion. He did not want to dwell upon Gabrielle Tixier.

Etienne Stevin was waiting. Anticipating the question, he met Hurtubise and said, "We're almost ready."

The three mercenaries climbed into the Land Rover and talked en route to the mine. "Tell me," Hurtubise commanded.

Stevin's stubby fingers grasped the wheel, navigating the unpaved road from the landing strip. "After we got Paul's message, we reinforced the guard and changed the schedule. We're now at fifty percent alert during the night, thirty-three percent during the day. Moungar's assistant is practically using a whip on the blacks; they're pushing hard to get two full loads ready for loading."

"How soon?"

"The first one—maybe day after tomorrow. No later than Tuesday. The second load maybe later that day."

Hurtubise chewed his lip and rubbed his stubbled chin, measuring the time-distance equation. It was going to be tight. He could feel it. He looked at Stevin. "Who is the assistant?"

"Name's Jean Djimasta. I thought you met him before."

"I did. I just don't remember the name. Medium-sized, really black, balding. Bit of an attitude for a nigger."

"That's him."

Hurtubise glanced over his shoulder to Deladier in the rear seat. "Well, seeing that he's getting the job done, we can tolerate some attitude. But not too much, eh?" He almost laughed.

Deladier leaned forward between the front seats. "What about Moungar? Will he be here?"

"No," Hurtubise replied. "I'd like to have him here because he represents the government. But he's making arrangements with our friends across the border."

Downshifting to cross a narrow defile, Stevin said, "Boss, I'd like to hear more. What do we really know about the Americans? And how good is the information?"

Hurtubise dropped the impending grin. "The information is about as good as we can expect, but it's the usual situation. You never have everything you want. I got suspicious when Gabrielle came back from her second meeting with the American woman." He shook his head in self reproach. "That was my fault, really. I thought she could handle it. The little shrew was pretty good at getting people to talk but . . ."

Deladier felt a small, electric prickling between the shoulders at Tixier's name. He sat back, grasping a door handle to steady himself as the Land Rover jounced over the graded road.

"Anyway, she spilled more than she learned," Hurtubise continued. "When I realized what had happened, I sent her to deal with the American broad but she didn't come back."

Stevin did not know what to say. Deladier had already described the basics so the burly Belgian merely nodded.

"The rest I filled in with contacts at the embassy, and intuition. The American firm is training a counterinsurgency unit in N'Djamena but we have to assume they can get up here pretty fast if they want. That's why I want to get at least two loads out as soon as possible. After that, we've met our contract. Anything else is a bonus."

Stevin turned toward his boss and unzipped a tobacco-stained grin. "I like bonuses."

Hurtubise scowled in reply. "You just blow it on gambling and booze and whores. In a couple of weeks or months you're broke again."

The Belgian nodded gravely, looking at the road again. Then he perked up. "But there's always another job. Thanks to you."

The Frenchman regarded his colleague with a sideways glance. "Not after this one, Etienne. Not after this one."

BORKOU-ENNEDI-TIBESTI PREFECTURE

Terry Keegan had a good opinion of his dead-reckoning ability, but he was glad of the GPS set in the borrowed Alouette III. Flying with Charles the mechanic in the seat beside him, the former naval aviator led his two helicopters in a descent to Bardai airfield in the rugged terrain of northern Chad.

From studying aeronautical charts and Web sites, Keegan knew that only seven of the nation's fifty-one airports had paved runways. Bardai, at thirty-five hundred feet elevation, was unpaved but its fifty-nine-hundred-foot runway would accommodate the C-130s inbound behind him.

Major Lowe, flying with Eddie Marsh, handled air-ground communications, such as they were. Though Bardai was a military field, it impressed the Americans as an extraordinarily low-key operation. They air-taxied to the area indicated by the controller, alit side by side, and shut down. The Turbomeca engines wheezed to a stop and the four men debarked. They were mildly surprised when no one met them.

"Not a bad thing," Lowe observed. "As long as we can get refueled and arrange security, I'd just as soon be ignored until we're finished here."

While the Air Force officer arranged for fuel, Keegan, Marsh, and Haegelin conducted post-flight inspections on both choppers. "I'm using a little more oil than the manual lists, but I guess it's okay," Marsh said.

"What do you mean, you *guess* it's okay?" Keegan never took anything for granted: it was part of the reason he had survived four western Pacific deployments as a sub hunter, operating in big waves off some small decks.

"Charles says it's in limits," Marsh replied. "And he sure knows more about these machines than I do." The former Army flier quipped, "Hey, I'm an H-47 kinda guy."

Keegan tried to suppress a smile, and failed. "Chinooks—they're like women. You can't live with 'em and you can't live without 'em."

"No lie, GI. The '47 was in the inventory twelve years before I was born!"

A low, insistent pulsing thrummed through the atmosphere, coming from the southwest. The helo pilots turned in that direction, shading their eyes against the slanting westerly rays of the sun. Several moments later Marsh exclaimed, "There! Just above the horizon."

The tall-tailed silhouettes of two C-130Hs hove into view at 290 knots, slanting toward the field. They flew a straight-in approach, taking landing interval but not bothering with the traffic pattern. "They probably don't want to draw any more attention than they need to," Keegan surmised.

Charles Haegelin ventured a rare sentiment, as he had not been asked a question. "With that kind of noise, they cannot keep hidden so well."

He had a point. Each Hercules's four Allison turboprops conspired to produce a pulsing resonance that could not be ignored. The lead transport touched down in the first quarter of the hard-packed runway and the pilot reversed the propellers, visibly slowing the big Lockheed, which turned off before the end of the strip. The second plane loitered momentarily in its approach, allowing the dust to disperse. In a few minutes both planes were parked, their engines whining a descending dirge as propellers windmilled into stillness.

"Hey look," Keegan exclaimed. "New paint job."

Marsh squinted at the 130s. Finally he saw the Navy man's meaning. Chad's tricolor cockade was painted over the tactical black-on-gray American insignia on fuselage and wings. There was also a fin flash on the vertical stabilizer. "That's not going to fool anybody," Marsh ventured. "Besides, it's probably not legal."

Terry Keegan nudged him. "Like Teddy Roosevelt said, Why spoil the beauty of the thing with legality?"

AOZOU STRIP

The mine was a welter of noise and activity. As the mercenaries alit from their Land Rover, they were approached by the foreman.

"Jean Djimesta," Etienne reintroduced the African to Hurtubise.

"Mr. Djimesta." Hurtubise slung his FA-MAS rifle from his right shoulder, muzzle down. He had already chambered the first round of 5.56 mm ammunition from the twenty-five-round magazine. Deladier did likewise; both had carried the compact bullpup design in the Legion.

The Chadian raised a hand and gestured behind him. "We are proceeding as fast as possible, *monsieur*." He anticipated the Frenchman's concern, adding, "We should be able to load the first truck before sunrise. The second perhaps two hours later."

Hurtubise nodded; it was better than he expected. "We can expect uninvited guests before dawn. Keep the men working."

Before Djimesta could reply, Hurtubise turned away and strode toward the perimeter. His colleagues followed.

"Paul, I want you to go with the first truck. Stay with it until it's ready to leave. You know the procedure at the border?"

"Yes," Deladier said. "Moungar already gave us the details."

"All right." He turned to Stevin. "Etienne, you will remain in command of perimeter defense. But I need you sober, you understand?"

The Belgian ignored the implication, unflappable as usual. "What do you think they'll hit us with, Boss?"

Hurtubise rubbed his chin. He needed a shave but hardly registered that fact. "I'm not sure they'll come in shooting. I think they'll make a show of force to make us back down without a fight. I wish we had more heavy weapons, but there's no time to bring them up here. Anyway, I'll talk to the men in a little while, but be sure they all understand: no shooting unless we're attacked. If we need to slow them down so the trucks can get away, I'll give that word. After that it's up to you again." He gave Stevin an unaccustomed pat on the arm.

Good of you to die for me, mon ami. *That's what you seem to want.*

Deladier asked, "What are they likely to bring?"

"I don't think they'll have APCs or anything like that. Probably they'll arrive in trucks. Maybe a few helicopters. But they won't pursue us into Libya, that's for sure."

Stevin chuckled aloud. "We can handle a chopper or two."

45

BARDAI AIRPORT

Steve Lee found himself functioning as a company commander again. It had been several years, but he relished the challenge.

In a large tent erected well clear of the flight line, he described the plan to his unit: the first platoon plus the SSI team and some support personnel. He spoke slowly and clearly, allowing J. J. Johnson to translate for the Chadians.

"First platoon is the assault element. Second platoon will provide the blocking force and perimeter security." He described a semicircle around the entrance to the mine and a roadblock to the north. "We will use both helos: one to lift a squad to overtake any vehicle that gets past the roadblock, the other to insert a second squad as a reaction force, wherever it might be needed."

In the orange-yellow glow of the suspended lights, he indicated where he wanted the Alouettes positioned at the moment of the assault. He glanced at Terry Keegan and Eddie Marsh; both seemed attentive and composed.

"Now this is important," Lee stressed. He paused longer than necessary after Johnson said, "*C'est important.*"

"No one will open fire, even if we are fired upon, unless we take casualties." Lee awaited the expected murmur of protest from the Chadians. "I repeat: this is important. We want to secure the mine as quickly as possible. If we have to shoot our way in, that gives the smugglers time to get away, possibly with some yellow cake. That's why we want a blocking force in position, but we cannot assume it will stop everybody trying to escape."

When Johnson finished elaborating, Lee continued. "We want to intimidate the guards into surrendering. Therefore, we will not return fire if they merely shoot in our direction. When we close with them, if they're still shooting, either I or Mr. Johnson will give the order. Is that clear?"

"*Est-ce clairement?*"

Resentful nods and assents came from the audience.

"Now," Lee continued. "Once we've secured the facility, Mr. Langevin will be in charge. You will take orders from him, especially in regard to any uranium ore, yellow cake, or equipment. If everything goes well, we can pack up and return to the capital day after tomorrow."

Keegan and Marsh exchanged knowing glances. *Never freakin' happen.*

Marsh raised a hand. "Sir, how do we know the yellow cake won't be taken out tonight?"

Lee assumed a relaxed posture. "We don't, Mr. Marsh. That's why Sergeant Nissen and three troopies are watching the roads in and out of there. They left right after we landed. If they see suspicious activity, they'll call us and both you gentlemen will hustle up there with five Chadians apiece." He grinned ironically. "Sorry, but you may not get much sleep tonight."

Keegan appreciated the plan if not the specifics. "What will the rest of you do in that case, sir?"

"We'll man up the trucks and be there in about three-zero mikes." He looked around. "Yes, Sergeant Bawoyeu."

The Chadian NCO asked, "*Qu'est connu au sujet des gardes? Sont-elles les combattants expérimentés?*"

Johnson translated: "What do we know about the guards? Are they experienced fighters?"

Lee responded, "That's a fair question. We don't know exactly how many are up there—maybe twelve to twenty. Since they presumably work for Groupe FGN, we can assume they know what they're doing. Probably several of them are ex-Foreign Legion. But we outnumber them and we'll have some degree of surprise."

Lee consulted his briefing notes, checking off each item. "Oh, yes: prisoner handling. Everybody there will be disarmed and searched. But it should be done professionally, with a minimum of force. Actually, they're not prisoners, just detainees. If they don't resist us, they're not liable to prosecution. So we'll keep them in a secure area until things settle down.

"Lastly: casualty treatment. We have a Green Beret medic with us as well as two Chadian corpsmen. The Air Force has part of a combat control team and some PJs on one of the Hercs, and those folks will establish an aid station on board the airplane. If we have to, we can use one of the choppers for a med-evac."

He looked around again. "Anything else?"

When no one responded, Lee gave a brisk nod. "Very well, gentlemen. Unless something pops tonight, we arrive at the mine ten minutes past daybreak."

46

BORKOU-ENNEDI-TIBESTI PREFECTURE

"Trucks are coming from the south. Maybe three kilometers out, moving fast." Etienne Stevin's voice was urgent, slightly slurred.

Marcel Hurtubise rolled off his cot and scooped up his FA-MAS. He glanced at his watch: about two hours' sleep. "Paul?"

Stevin shook his head. "What?"

Hurtubise gritted his teeth in frustration. The realization struck him: Stevin had been drinking last night. *Of all times!* He modulated his voice. "I asked about Paul, you oaf! Where is he?"

"Oh. I think he's still with the first truck. You wanted him to stick with it, didn't you?"

"All right. You meet our guests. Don't shoot if you don't have to, but give us time to get going." He held Stevin's gaze to emphasize the importance. "You understand?"

Stevin nodded, dropped the tent flap, and disappeared. Hurtubise was angry: with his deputy, with the workers, with the equpment, with himself. *Just thirty more minutes and we would have been away from here!*

He stepped outside, seeing the gray hues of dawn stretching across the barren landscape. He stopped for a moment, reviewing his dispositions. Full alert: sixteen men awake and fully armed. Five at the front gate with Etienne, four more a hundred meters back to provide fire support. Three positioned at the north gate to defend the exit, two each with the trucks. He would have liked another section at the exit gate, since the Americans were likely to attempt an end-around, but he needed most of his force to slow the attack along the main axis of advance.

Hurtubise took the spare Range Rover, cranked the engine, and coaxed its 2.4 liters into life. With his rifle and kit bag beside him, he stepped on the gas and sped for the quarry.

In the back of the lead truck, two SSI operators accompanied Bernard Langevin and eight Chadian troopers. As the Renault sped toward the mine, Langevin looked at his nearest companion, the man known as Breezy. He had his eyes shut as he seemed to inhale deeply, hold his breath, and expel it.

On the opposite side, Bosco caught the scientist's eye. He gave a knowing grin.

"What's he doing?" Lanvegin asked.

"It's called the count of four. You inhale on a four count, hold it for four, and exhale for four. Do that four times. It's, like, a relaxation technique."

"Does it work?"

Breezy opened his eyes. "It's my pre-combat routine, Doc. Lowers the heart rate, gets more oxygen into the blood." He regarded the nuclear specialist. "Give it a try."

"Well, I . . ."

Lee opened the flap separating the bed from the cab. "Line of departure, gentlemen! Lock and load!"

Terry Keegan knew something would go wrong; it always did. He did not expect it to be communications.

Inbound at two hundred feet, he banked his Alouette to clear the uranium mine, lest the operators assume he was a threat. He intended to hover nearby while the truck convoy confronted the gate guards, leaving Eddie Marsh to handle contingencies. But moments before the first truck squealed to a stop, Keegan lost contact with Marsh.

Beside him, Charles Haegelin played with the unfamiliar radio set. After twisting the knobs for volume and gain without avail, he shifted frequencies—still no success. "It is no good," the French Canadian mechanic conceded. "I can do nothing in the air. Maybe if we landed . . ."

Keegan shook his head. "We can't do that, Charles. Not until I know how things are going down there. Otherwise our troopies might be out of position if we need 'em." He nodded over his shoulder, indicating the five Chadian soldiers behind him.

"Can you still talk to Major Lee?"

"Yeah. I ran a comm check on the way in. But I can't talk directly to Eddie." He thought for a moment. "If I have to, I could relay a message to him via the ground team."

Haegelin shrugged. "Well, he knows what to do."

——— ———

Paul Deladier heard the warning shouts, saw Hurtubise's Range Rover speeding toward him, and discerned helicopters in the distance. He did not need to await more information. He nudged his driver, a former *caballero legionario* of the Spanish Legion. "*Allez, allez!*" The mercenary, who had grown up in the Pyrenees, was fluent in French and Spanish. He put the Mercedes-Benz Axor in gear and, pulling a semi van, headed for the northern exit.

———

Etienne Stevin's experienced eyes were bleary but they took in the rapidly developing situation. Three trucks deployed within fifty meters of the entrance, disgorging two trucks worth of troops. He realized that whoever commanded the operation was an experienced soldier.

Three men advanced toward the gate: a white and two Africans. Two carried rifles, muzzles down; the white man bore no visible weapons.

"*Bonjour,*" the apparent leader greeted Stevin. The man introduced himself as Dr. Bernard Langevin, producing identification from the International Atomic Energy Agency. "We wish to inspect this facility," the American said. He added something about authority of the United Nations and the Chadian government, indicating his nearest black colleague who in fact was Sergeant Major Bawoyeu. However, the introductions were drowned out by the passage of a second helicopter orbiting overhead.

From the center truck Steve Lee looked up, growing impatient with the flier's antics. He approved Keegan's cautious approach, hovering menacingly in the distance, but Eddie Marsh seemed to be pushing his orders. Lee keyed his microphone. "Beanie Two from Grunt One."

"Beanie here. Go." Marsh's voice was light and chipper on the UHF frequency.

"Back off, Beanie. You're bothering the locals. Over."

Marsh responded with two mike clicks, lowered his nose, and moved off to the northeast.

Langevin took advantage of the momentary interruption while Stevin watched the Alouette depart. Though not trained as an operator, the scientist recognized a well-planned position: two machine guns placed for mutual support with riflemen on the flanks. But he was certain that the defenders had not shown him everything.

Addressing the senior guard again, Langevin repeated his demand. "We are here to inspect the facility. May we enter?"

The Belgian mercenary remained calm. "I have no objection, *monsieur*, but I shall have to check with my commandant. Please wait."

Langevin watched the burly guard walk past the gate, taking his time en route wherever he was going. "He's stalling," the American said to Bawoyeu.

As if in confirmation, Marsh was back on the radio. "Be advised, there's a truck and trailer headed for the north gate!"

Lee was monitoring the channel. "Beanie Two, are there any other vehicles?"

After a short interval, Marsh replied, "Affirmative. Another truck and semi and a couple of SUVs. One is headed for the parked truck. Over."

Lee visualized the developing situation. Time mattered now more than ever. "Beanie Two, keep an eye on the mover. Break break. Grunt Four, copy?"

Chris Nissen's baritone snapped back. "Copy, One. We're in position, over."

"Ah, roger, Four. Do what you have to but stop that truck."

"Affirm. Out."

Satisfied that Nissen's squad would handle the northern roadblock, Lee set down the microphone on his command set. Then he checked his portable radio and leaned out of the door. He made a circular motion with one hand, signaling the deployed squads to advance on the perimeter. J. J. Johnson caught the sign and directed the maneuver element. With that, Lee nodded for his driver to head for the gate.

Above and behind him, Breezy pushed the canvas tarp aside to deploy a bipoded HK-21, leaning into the 7.62 machine gun and trying to steady it on the roof of the cab.

———————

Marcel Hurtubise grasped the emerging confrontation. Ruefully he sped past the second Mercedes, not quite half full of yellow cake. Briefly he considered driving the truck himself to salvage more of his end user's product, but he dismissed the option. *Paul will need some support.* He braked to a stop, urged two of his reaction squad to jump in, and resumed his northward dash.

———————

Etienne Stevin labored under many human frailties. Some would say most of them, but he was nothing if not loyal. That sense of camaraderie mixed with the cognac he had consumed now conspired to produce a mental binary. Deep in the recesses of his memory he heard the measured strains of *"Le Boudin"* and grasped the essential rightness of it all. Outnumbered, beset by desert enemies beyond the gate, surrounded by his fellows: *this* was how a Legionnaire died!

Sensing the helicopter threat to Deladier's truck, the Belgian tossed aside a tarp and picked up a Mistral missile launcher. It was one of three stashed within the compound.

Stevin had not fired a man-portable SAM in several years, but he knew the drill.

Hefting its nineteen kilograms, Steven settled the loaded launcher on his right shoulder. He tracked the Alouette in his sight, pressed the enabling switch to activate the homer, and held his breath. In seconds he was rewarded with the light confirming that the missile's seeker head was tracking a heat source within range.

He pressed the firing button.

Inside the launcher, the booster motor ejected the missile with an impulse lasting less than half a second. Fifty feet downrange, the sustainer motor burst into life, accelerating with eye-watering velocity. At more than twice the speed of sound, the Mistral ate up the distance to the target.

Sevin knew that the Mistral was rated effective against helicopters at four kilometers. His target was barely half that far.

Three kilometers up the road, Chris Nissen saw the missile's telltale wake. He pressed his mike button, hardly knowing what to say.

Had Nissen or Stevin or anyone else had a heartbeat to ponder the situation, they might have been struck by the irony. A French missile—named for a cold north wind that blows along the Riviera—dashed with demonic obsession toward a French helicopter, fired by a Belgian employed by a French firm. But most missiles are like bullets, conceived without a conscience, pursuing their embedded purposes depending upon the preference of their human masters.

Since Stevin's Mistral lacked a logic board, and Marsh's Alouette lacked IFF or even chaff or flares, the result of the firing was nearly certain. Stevin did not recall the precise figure, but he had read that Mistrals could be ninety percent effective when launched within parameters.

Before Nissen could shout a warning, the missile exploded. Its laser proximity fuse sensed the overtake on the heat source and detonated the three-kilogram warhead.

Scores of tungsten balls erupted outward from the blast pattern, ruining the helo's airframe. The boom was nearly severed from the cabin, sending the Alouette spiraling crazily to earth.

BORKOU-ENNEDI-TIBESTI PREFECTURE

"Look at that!"

Racing to catch Deladier's semi truck and trailer, Hurtubise shot a glance to his right. Following his companion's extended trigger finger, Marcel glimpsed a missile plume and a receding midair explosion in the gray Saharan sky. "Damn it to hell! I said no unnecessary shooting!" Things were turning to hash. He put his foot on the floor.

———

Everybody was talking at once. The air and ground radios were jammed with shouts, questions, and exclamations.

Lee sought to make sense of the babble. He knew he would have to wait a few moments for the talkers to get a grip on themselves. *Bad show*, he told himself. *No radio discipline.*

Terry Keegan was the first to break through the noise. He dispensed with call signs. "Steve, Terry. Eddie's down! Repeat, Eddie's down. A missile got him."

"Where'd it come from? Over."

"Inside the perimeter. I think more to the south side."

Looking outside his truck, Lee saw the remaining Alouette lower its nose and accelerate to the north. "Terry, Steve. Do not proceed north. Repeat, do not go north."

"Ah . . . Steve, I can reach him faster than Nissen."

"I know, Terry, I know. But we can't risk you and the reaction force. Please stay back here 'til we get sorted out. Over."

The helo continued almost to the perimeter before slowing. Then Keegan executed a pedal turn and pivoted right, heading easterly. "Acknowledged, out."

Steve Lee's mind raced, sorting priorities and options. Likely Marsh and his Chadian troops were dead. In any case, they could not be helped just now. He keyed his mike. "Grunt Four from Grunt One, over."

Several heartbeats later Nissen's voice was on the air. "Grunt Four. Steve, I see it. I'm going to check for survivors."

"Ah, negative, Chris. Not yet. We need to keep the back door closed. There's a truck and trailer headed your way."

More seconds ticked away before Nissen responded. "Steve, I'm already on the way to the crash, about two klicks away. It's starting to burn and we might save some guys . . ." His voice trailed off before the carrier wave went dead. Lee could read Nissen's mind. *He's a good NCO, looking out for his fellow soldiers but the mission should come first.*

"Okay, Chris. Keep me informed.

"Break-break. Beanie One, copy?"

"One is up." Keegan's voice rasped over the air-ground freq; eager, alert. Maybe a little tense.

"Terry, I need you to back up Grunt Four. He's headed for the crash but we have to intercept the truck. Do an end-around to cut him off. Put your team on the road far enough ahead so you're out of the SAM envelope. I'll send our reserve force ASAP. Copy?"

"Will do, Steve." Lee heard the Alouette's Artouste 3 engine spool up as Keegan flexed his left wrist on the collective. The helo descended to about twenty feet above the ground and skirted the mine perimeter, low and fast.

Lee was back working the radio. "Grunt One to Grunt Five."

Foyte's gravelly voice was a welcome sound. "Five here, Boss."

"Gunny, bring your guys up here right now. I'm sending one of my guys to block the northern exit while Chris is checking the shootdown."

"On the way, Major. Ah, who's down? Over."

Lee shook his head in disgust. *All that screaming on the radio. Foyte doesn't know what's happened.* "Ah, Marsh took a missile, Gunny. That's all we know right now."

"Roger." Foyte, the old pro, would adjust as necessary.

"Grunt One to Two, over."

"Two here, go." Wallender came back promptly, crisply.

"Josh, take your truck around to the west and block the road a klick or so north of the far exit. Stop anybody coming out, any way you can."

"Affirm." The word was barely out before Wallender's truck moved off the scraped road onto the hard-packed earth, headed for the left side of the perimeter.

Lee turned back to his immediate problem: two trucks facing a prepared defense. Parked in the open, no more than fifty meters from the fence, they offered tempting targets to the automatic weapons just inside the wire. He turned to Bosco and Breezy in the bed behind him. "The fact they haven't fired at us tells me the missile shot might be unauthorized. Whatever happens inside the mine is secondary right now so I'm not going to force the issue. But we're not going head to head against two belt-fed weapons. We'll move to the southwest corner where the eastern MG can't engage us."

Breezy shifted his HK. "Gotcha, Boss."

Langevin was back in the cab, a querulous look on his face. "Steve, do you want me to see if I can talk to them? Like you said, they haven't shot at us. Maybe they'll stand down and let us in."

"Negative, Bernie. Not now. I need to know their intentions before we stick our necks in there."

———

Chris Nissen's truck lurched to a stop thirty meters from the wrecked Alouette. He deployed three of his Chadians between the crash site and the northern road, then led the others toward the helo. With a professional eye, he noted that the French designed a damn good machine. The fuel cell had survived the impact, though hydraulic fluid and seeping kerosene were spreading liquid flames across the area.

A Chadian brought a fire extinguisher from the truck. "Get in there," Nissen directed the man to the largest fire. "Hose that down. We gotta get them out!"

Peering into the smoke and flames, Nissen sought any sign of movement. He could not see through the smoke-stained glass.

It was taking too long.

Nissen dashed back to the truck, seized an ax from the toolbox, and raced to the helo again. *Shoulda thought of this before*. He ignored the noxious fumes from the smoke and stepped uncomfortably close to the fire. With a gloved hand he grasped the hatch and pulled the handle. The door opened less than two inches. Nissen realized that the airframe had buckled, holding the door closed.

Behind him and on either side, men were shoveling dirt onto the flames or scooping rocky earth with bare hands. Nissen was a large, well-built man, and his powerful, overhand blows took effect. He knocked out the Plexiglas window, then began hacking away aluminum around the door latch. He was making progress when the wind shifted, blowing even more smoke at him. He turned his head, retching in the thick, cloying fumes, and stepped back.

Someone seized the ax from him and resumed cutting. It was Corporal Nassour Yodoyman: smaller and lighter than the American, but equally committed. *He has friends in there*, Nissen realized. *Like me*.

Nissen heard shouting behind him. He turned to see the three guards waving and gesturing. Moments later a Mercedes truck hauling a semi trailer raced past, headed north.

———

Etienne Stevin earnestly wished for a radio. Things had happened so quickly that he had no time to consult with Hurtubise. Actually, "consult" was an exaggeration. Stevin was a capable soldier but he was no leader. Given a task, he inevitably carried it out. But now, thrown onto his own resources, he dipped into his command psyche and came up empty.

A former Legionnaire ran up to Stevin, clearly upset at the unexpected events. "My God, what happened, Etienne? Who fired that rocket?"

Stevin glared at the inquisitor, who had asked a rational series of questions. "There's no time for that, you *hybride*." He shoved the man with both hands. "Get back to your position!"

Emile Giroud was younger than the Belgian, less experienced but lacking awe for most of his elders. He ignored the order and pointed to the southeast. "The Americans, Etienne! They're still out there. The men want to know . . ."

"I said get back! Right now!"

The two mercenaries locked eyes, both men's faces flushed with anger and tension. Stevin broke the deadlock by invoking Hurtubise's name. "Marcel said we hold until the trucks are gone. And that's what we do!"

"Are you blind? Look around you, Etienne! Look around! Deladier left in the first truck and Marcel followed him in the jeep. There's nobody to drive the second truck, and it isn't even fully loaded!"

The younger man awaited a response, then realized there would be none. He smelled the liquor on Stevin's breath, saw the wild determination in his eyes. *Legio pro patria.* Stevin turned and shouted to anyone within earshot. "*Est maintenant l'heure de faire le camerone.*" With that, he paced toward the south gate.

A South African member of Groupe FGN approached Giroud. "What in the hell is Stevin ranting about?"

Giroud made a circular motion with one hand beside his head. "He's drunk or crazy. Or both. He says, 'Now is the time to make Camerone!' "

"What's that mean?"

"It's the Legion's big holiday. Mexico in 1863. They celebrate it every April thirtieth."

"What happened?" asked the Boer.

"Sixty-five Legionnaires fought two thousand Mexicans. They killed three hundred before they were overpowered."

"Well, I don't believe in last stands. I believe in living to fight another day."

Giroud motioned over his shoulder. "Go tell him that, *mon vieux.*"

The fire was contained. Nissen and Corporal Yodoyman pulled the remains of the cabin door off its mangled hinges and tossed it aside. They heard a low, soft moan from inside the ruined cabin—the first welcome sign since the crash some fifteen minutes before.

Yodoyman leaned into the cabin, reaching to grasp the nearest soldier. "Be careful!" Nissen warned. "We can't move them right away."

He forced himself past the Chadian NCO and leaned as far inside as possible. "Marsh! Mr. Marsh! Can you hear me?" He realized that he did not know Marsh's given name.

No reply came from the front of the helo. The Alouette had pitched violently downward, crashing nose first.

Someone moved in the rear of the compartment. Another pain-wracked sound came from the interior.

Nissen weighed the options: survival of some troops versus accomplishment of the mission. He was glad it was not his responsibility. He decided to make the call.

———

Stevin cast a glance at the north gate, which had been closed following Hurtubise's departure. He counted it good. *Marcel is on his way. Now we cover his withdrawal.*

He stalked to the southwesterly perimeter wire and rested his rifle atop the sandbag parapet. He was feeling buoyant, almost giddy. *This is the day!*

Stevin turned to the hired guns around him. "Listen, you wretches. Catteau, Constantin, and Leonhart. They were the last of thirteen Belgians at Camerone. Their blood runs in my veins!" He pounded the top sandbag, exclaiming, "From this place I retreat not one step."

He propped both elbows on the sandbags and aimed his rifle toward the nearest truck. Taking up the slack, he fired one round fifteen meters in front of the vehicle.

Giroud caught up with Stevin and grabbed for his FA-MAS. "You idiot! You want to get us all killed?"

Stevin shoved the interloper back with a powerful forearm blow. "I command here! Can't you see what I'm doing? I'm keeping them out while Marcel escapes with the convoy."

"Convoy? What convoy? What are you talking about?"

Etienne Stevin had no time to explain the situation. This fool had no idea of Groupe FGN's similarity to Captain Danjou's company, protecting an arms shipment in Mexico nearly 150 years before. It was all part of the Legion's tradition: the same then as now.

The Belgian turned back toward the truck and fired another warning round, closer this time.

Giroud grasped the rifle with both hands. The struggle lasted four seconds before Stevin connected with a crushing right to the Frenchman's cheek. Giroud reeled, dazed and hurt.

Stevin shot him twice in the chest. Then he returned to his harassing fire.

———

Resting his HK-21 atop the cab of Lee's truck, Breezy bit down the urge to open fire. He was not a machine gunner by profession, but he knew the tools of his trade and was confident that he could solve the problem from where he sat. Eyeballing the distance to the perimeter fence, he made it seventy to eighty meters.

Bernard Langevin was crouched behind the front tire, wielding a handheld loudspeaker. He was a bit more exposed than Breezy would have liked, but with a bumper, engine block, and thick tire providing cover, it seemed a decent place to be, considering the circumstances. He raised the bullhorn and called again. "*Nous sommes des amis. Tenez votre feu!*"

A few more rounds snapped through the still morning air, impacting the hard ground around the truck. "That's still harassing fire," Lee shouted. He wanted to ensure that nobody got excited—especially the Chadians, who were exhibiting marked restlessness.

Lee turned to Bosco, who had taken over the radio in the cab. "This can go on indefinitely. All the time, the yellow cake is getting farther away."

"We could go after 'em, Major. It doesn't matter what these guys do here, does it? I mean, like, the mine's not goin' anywhere."

"I know, I know. It's really Mr. Langevin's call. If he . . ."

"Grunt Four to Grunt One. Over!"

Bosco picked up the microphone. "Grunt One Bravo here."

Nissen's voice came sharp and clear. "Give me the actual, over."

Bosco leaned toward Lee, extending the mike at the end of its cord. The timing could hardly have been worse. Another rifle shot from the perimeter ricocheted off the hard earth and struck Bosco's forearm. He yelped in surprise and pain, dropped the mike, and shouted, "Geez! I'm hit!" He followed that exclamation with some fervent Ranger blasphemy.

Lee scooped up the mike, pressed the button, and said, "Chris, stand by one. We're taking fire." He dropped the mike and turned toward Bosco, who was lying on his side, below the dash, grasping his injured arm with the opposite hand. Lee saw blood seeping between the operator's fingers.

"Breezy! Bosco's hit! Take out that guy!"

Breezy leaned into the German gun, focused his gray eyes on the front sight, held low left, and pressed the trigger for one second. In that tick of time, the HK spat out twelve rounds.

Mark Brezyinski was not much on literature. But having read *For Whom the Bell Tolls* in high school, he appreciated Hemingway's phrase: the slick, slippery recoil of a bipoded weapon. Atop his rocky tor, with Franco's soldiers closing in, Robert Jordan would have given his Republican soul for an HK-21 in place of the Lewis Gun that Gary Cooper wielded in the movie.

That Bergman gal was a real babe, but even more so in Casablanca.

Brezyinski rode the recoil impulse to its height, then forced the sights back down through the target as he released the trigger.

The first round hit the sandbags supporting Etienne Stevin's firing position. The next four climbed the improvised parapet, and the next three took him off the top row. The others spattered the wooden platform behind him. Stevin fell to the ground, rolled 270 degrees, and twitched to a stop on his left side. He gasped for air and spat up hot blood, staring at the Saharan sand.

Somewhere far off, beyond a ghostly horizon, he saw a figure in an antique uniform—white kepi, blue jacket, and red trousers—striding toward him to the strains of *La Marseillaise*. He was every bit a soldier: head erect, shoulders back, arms swinging purposefully.

The ethereal figure extended a wooden hand toward the fallen Legionnaire as *Capitaine* Jean Danjou beckoned him home.

––––––––––

Keegan was not sure that he heard correctly. "Say again, Steve."

Twelve miles to the south, Steve Lee did a fast three-count. He wanted to keep his voice as well as his temper under control. "Terry, I say again. Return to the crash site. We need an immediate dustoff. *Over.*"

"Ah, copy . . . Grunt." Keegan knew what must be driving Lee's order. With the Libyan frontier only a few miles ahead, and no effective way of stopping the yellow cake shipment, Lee had finally decided on behalf of the survivors. Eddie Marsh—or at least some of his crew— required air evac to Bardai and the Air Force medics. He could cut an hour or more off the transit time by truck. The golden hour that paramedics talked about.

When Keegan turned the Alouette away from its pursuit, he saw the semi rig speeding north, if anything faster than ever.

––––––––––

Trailing by several kilometers, Marcel Hurtubise watched the helicopter receding in his mirror. He grinned for the first time that day.

PART

III

LIBYA

48

SSI OFFICES

"We just heard from Steve Lee," Leopole said.

Marshall Wilmont took his half-spectacles off the bridge of his nose. "Well?"

Leopole made a point of waving the e-mail. "You want the good news or the bad news first?"

"C'mon, Frank . . ." SSI's chief operating officer seldom had time for banter.

The former Marine inhaled, then let his breath out. "Okay. We lost a helo. The bad guys had man-pack SAMs and shot down Marsh's aircraft. He's critical and three of the Chadians are dead."

"My God. What . . ."

"And the Frenchies got away with a truckload of yellow cake."

Wilmont was on his feet before he knew it. "Don't play freaking games with me, Frank! What in hell's the *good* news?"

The director of foreign operations slid the printout across the desk. "The good news is that they only got away with part of the load."

Wilmont almost seemed to deflate as he sagged back into his chair. "Tell me," he croaked.

"Long story short: Steve decided to move in at dawn because he didn't want his troops running around, maybe shooting at each other in the dark. That was a mistake, seen in hindsight. It gave the mercs enough time to load one trailer and part of another. They drove out the back as our guys approached the front. Steve had a blocking force astride the road leading to the border, but when the helo was shot down, Nissen made a command decision and went to the site. He probably saved Marsh's life and maybe a couple of others. But . . ."

"That left the way open for the yellow cake."

"Affirm." Leopole leaned forward, elbows on the polished desk. "I think Steve did the right thing, though. He was having Keegan tail the truck, keeping out of missile range, but he didn't have the muscle to stop it. So Steve recalled him as a med-evac. Keegan took Marsh and the other survivors back to the airfield where there was proper medical care."

Wilmont emitted a noncommittal "Ummm." Then he asked, "What about the mine? Did they secure it?"

"Yeah. There was a little trouble after the shootdown. One or two of the FGN guys went spastic and started shooting at our people so they killed them. Nobody else got hurt."

"So we don't know where the yellow cake is?"

Leopole shook his head. "I doubt that even Qadhafi knows."

"Come on," Wilmont said. "We need to see Mike and Omar."

SSI OFFICES

It was a small meeting: Derringer, Wilmont, Mohammed, Carmichael, and Leopold. The SSI brain trust.

"First things first," Derringer began. "I talked to Ryan O'Connor yesterday. He confirmed that State wants our training team to finish its contract in Chad. But I think we need to make some adjustments."

Leopole's brow furrowed. "Sir, are you going to pull Steve? I . . ."

"No, Frank. I think we've all been in Steve's shoes once or twice. He had to make some decisions based on incomplete information. I certainly don't fault him for that."

Leopole and Carmichael exchanged glances. If Derringer didn't catch it, Mohammed did. He could read their minds. *They don't want Lee to feel any worse than he probably already does.*

"Very well," Derringer continued. "Sandy and Frank, operations is your ballpark. What do you recommend?"

Carmichael's blue eyes fixed on her employer. "Sir, you mentioned some adjustments. I think any recommendations we make would depend on those."

"Oh, yes. Quite right." Derringer's practiced fingers performed a paradiddle cadence, as they often did when he was distracted. "Well, all I meant is that if we're going to pursue the yellow cake, we'll probably have to pull some people out of Chad."

Wilmont picked up some radiations from his sometime golf partner's emotional antennae. "Mike, you didn't mention the uranium shipment. Does State really want us to stay on it?"

SSI's CEO nodded slowly. "I think so. O'Connor is running it up the ladder, but since we're already involved and we have some assets in the area, we're likely to get a go-ahead pretty soon."

"Sir," Carmichael intoned, her voice low and earnest. "I'd think that sooner is better. That's why . . ."

"Yes, Sandy, I know. It takes me back to what we were saying about your recommendations. If we keep the team there for training, who can we put on another team to track down the yellow cake?"

She flipped through her folder. "Well, sir, obviously we want to keep our people there with language ability. That's Johnson, Nissen, and Wallender. I'm keeping a running tab with Jack Peters and Matt Finch. They're best equipped to find some more French or Arabic speakers for us."

Derringer nodded decisively. "Very well, put them on it."

Mohammed glanced at Marshall Wilmont. If he resented the retired admiral taking over the operating end of things, he did not show it.

Leopole had a thought. "Admiral, I'd like to pull Bosco and Breezy, ah, Boscombe and Brezyinski, from the training team. They're about the best door-kickers we have. Their talents would be better used on an operational mission."

Derringer remembered to check visually with Wilmont, who shrugged. Carmichael said, "Concur, Admiral." Then she asked, "What about Martha?"

No one spoke for a long moment.

49

SABHA PROVINCE, LIBYA

The heat was everywhere around them, like the heavy, dry air. Hurtubise called a midday stop and parked his Range Rover in the lee of Deladier's trailer. The four men dismounted—two from each vehicle—and conferred in the shade, such as it was.

"My motor is running a temperature," Hurtubise began. "I think we'll wait until later in the day to continue. Maybe we'll wait until night."

Alfonso Rivera, Deladier's driver, knew about working in extreme heat from his days in the Spanish Legion. "As long as we have water for the radiators we should be all right," he said. "Aren't we due in Misratah in a couple of days?"

Hurtubise waved a dismissive hand. "We have some time to spare. The ship won't be ready for a while. Cell communication is erratic out here in the desert, and I cannot always reach our contacts. But I'd rather be late than early. We don't want to have this cargo sitting around very long before loading on board. Somebody might get suspicious."

After long hours on the road, with delays for bureaucratic procedures and haggling over fuel, Deladier was growing impatient. However, he knew that Groupe FNG's Chadian government contacts had greased the skids—and some palms—to ease the journey. But other problems remained. "Marcel, we left in such a hurry. What in hell are we going to do for money? And passports?" Felix Moungar had arranged things at the border but there were intermediate stops as well.

Hurtubise gave a grim smile. "Don't you ever learn, my lad? I never go anywhere without at least one passport and a thousand dollars on me." He let the sentiment sink in, then continued. "Don't worry. We'll have new papers and cash at Birak."

Alfonso cocked his head. "You're sure of that?"

Hurtubise took a step toward him. "Yes, I'm sure! Look, just because we left in a hurry doesn't mean I haven't done all the planning. Understand?"

The young Spaniard looked upward, shielding his face against the Saharan sun. His meaning was implicit: *The heat gets to everybody*.

"Sure, Marcel. I understand."

N'DJAMENA
SSI COMPOUND

Steve Lee waited until Mark Brezyinski and Jason Boscombe had finished putting their gear away. It didn't take long, since most of the equipment used on the mine raid officially belonged to the Chadian Army.

"I'd like to see you guys in private," Lee said.

Bosco and Breezy exchanged quick looks. Breezy had the quicker tongue. "Something wrong, sir?"

Lee chuckled softly. "You know, you remind me of a guy I knew in the Army. He was an excellent warrant officer but he was always in trouble with his CO in Vietnam. Nickel and dime stuff. Then one day his XO tapped him on the shoulder and said, 'Fred, the CO wants to talk to you.' Fred asked, 'What did I do *now*?'

"The exec said, 'Well, I think they're going to give you the Medal of Honor.'"

Bosco's eyes widened. "Wow. Like, we're gonna . . ."

"No, Mr. Boscombe. You are not receiving a medal. But something better."

Breezy perked up. "Boy, that means money. What's the job, Boss?"

Lee winked as he closed the door.

"You're right. I heard from Frank Leopole. Most of us are staying here to finish the training contract, but he's putting together a team to go after the yellow cake that got away. It means working down and dirty and it'll likely be dangerous."

Breezy straightened visibly. With a straight face he declared, "Sir, danger is my middle name."

"I thought it was Casimir," Bosco deadpanned.

"Libya?" Breezy asked.

"No, no," Lee exclaimed. "Maybe Beirut, biggest port in the eastern Med. But it could be almost anywhere in the region. We won't know until there's better intel."

"Well, if they load the cake on a ship in Libya, why go to Lebanon? Why not just sail right to Iran?"

Lee nodded in deference to Breezy's acumen. "Good question, Mark. The answer is, we don't know. It's possible they'll drive a thousand miles or more and load at a Red Sea port in Sudan or even Ethiopia."

Bosco ran the options in his gambler's mind. "Major, wouldn't it make more sense to fly the stuff? I mean, just a couple of big planeloads should do it, and that'd be a whole lot faster."

Lee agreed. "Yes, it would. But there's complications having to do with international flights. So Arlington thinks that the cake will go by sea." He hunched his shoulders. "If the Frenchies and Iranians do fly it, we're out of the picture."

"So what do we do, sir?" Breezy began unloading a G3 magazine, returning the cartridges to a box on the worktable.

"All you guys have to do is tell me if you're interested. Frank wants you on the action team, and of course the combat bonus applies."

"Who'd we be working with?" Bosco asked.

"I don't know yet, but I'd think that Jeff Malten will be involved. SEALs know how to take down a ship."

Breezy went to work on a stick of gum. "Jeff did good in Pakistan. I'd go to war with him again."

Bosco nodded. "Me, too."

"All right," Lee replied. "You two continue working with Gunny Foyte but we'll start easing you out of training work. Carmichael and Leopole are leaning on their talent scouts to find other instructors, preferably with some language background. I'll get back to you on your rotation schedule."

Bosco and Breezy exchanged ritual knuckle taps. In their arcane world, it meant, "Get some" and "Me, too."

Steve Lee turned down the corridor from the small armory and looked into the cubicle that served as SSI's office. He found the person he sought.

"Hey there."

Whitney looked up from some paperwork. "Hey yourself, Maje. How you?"

"I'm just precious," Lee quipped.

"I knowed *that*, honey." She gave him the Aunt Jemima grin again.

Lee sat in the vacant chair. "Martha, I wanted you to hear from me before somebody else. Headquarters is calling you home. You'll be leaving in a couple of days, no more than three."

She nodded slowly. "Okay."

He cocked his head. "You don't seem surprised. Or disappointed."

"Naw, I'm not. After the operation went down, there wasn't much else for me to do. I been helpin' Gunny with *le Français*, you know?"

The West Pointer could not stifle a laugh. "Yeah, I know. If there's such as thing as Redneck French, I guess he's fluent."

She was all spunk and vinegar again. "Ain't that the truth? Wait'll I tell Sandy and Frank about the way he pronounces *chemin de fer*, let alone *la pièce de résistance* or *la boulangerie*!"

A pause settled over them. They both squirmed in embarrassment. At length Lee said, "Martha, you've done a good job here. I just . . ."

"I know, Steve. I know." She touched his hand. "It's just that I keep thinking, maybe I could've handled things a little . . . different. You know?"

Lee dropped his gaze to the cluttered desktop. When he looked up, he said, "Sure. All of us could always do things differently. But we don't. We only get one chance to do anything the first time. If you're thinking that you could've saved that French gal . . ."

"Gabrielle." Whitney pronounced the name in a low, husky whisper. "Gabrielle Tixier."

"Martha, she was in way over her head. She should've walked away from that bastard years ago." He stood up, eager to end the conversation.

She looked up at him. "Get him for me, Steve. And for her."

"Martha, it's out of my hands. But Arlington is putting together a covert team right now. They'll get him. You know they will."

"I'm counting on that, Maje. I truly am."

50

STATE DEPARTMENT
WASHINGTON, D.C.

Ryan O'Connor met the SSI delegation at the door of the undersecretary's office. For someone as attuned to Beltway nuances as Mike Derringer, it was as perceptible as a ten-knot wind on the face. *Something unusual is coming our way.* He thought he knew what it was.

O'Connor was unusually businesslike, almost brusque. He showed Derringer and Wilmont to their seats, offered the perfunctory coffee, and for a change, he got directly to the point. "Gentlemen. This meeting will remain off the record for reasons that are obvious. But I'm confirming that State wants you to proceed with your Chad mission. And I do not mean just the training segment. That will continue, not only to meet the obligation, but to provide some cover for the more immediate operation."

"So you want us to go after the yellow cake," Derringer said.

"Just so. You will have the full support of State and DoD intelligence assets, as well as other, ah, sources. Please understand that we may not be able to reveal those to you, but be assured that we will not pass along anything that we do not consider reliable."

Derringer asked, "What if we get contradictory info?"

The diplomat shrugged. "We'll try to filter and deconflict, but as always, it's up to the men in the field to act as they think best."

Bat guano, Derringer thought. *If anything goes south, SSI will hold the bag. But them's the risks.*

Wilmont shifted in his chair. Generally he held back, absorbing information and scribbling occasional notes, but now he spoke up. "Ryan, excuse me for asking what might seem an obtuse question. But if we're chasing the cake, which seems headed for Iran, obviously it's going by sea. Why not send the SEALs after it?"

O'Connor regarded the overweight executive with a perceptible, disapproving frown. "Well, the usual reason, Marshal. Deniability. As you say, the operation will almost certainly take place at sea, and likely in international waters. The United States Government does not condone piracy, let alone participate in such things."

Wilmont nodded vigorously. "Yeah, yeah. I understand that. But we just don't have the assets—the gear—for something like this. And we can't get it fast enough to meet the schedule."

"Oh, I think you can trust me on that score. You'll have maximum support across the board: intelligence, technical, whatever you need. If there's ever an audit of the operation—extremely unlikely, by the way—the investigators will find that all the equipment was declared surplus months before SSI ever saw it."

Derringer pulled an envelope from his Brooks Brothers suit coat. "Ryan, I brought a list of equipment needs and some operational concerns. This is for our liaison officer—whoever that might be."

O'Connor scooped up the paper but did not bother looking at it. "Right. I'll give it to the case officer and he'll get back to you today. He's arranging logistics right now. But you have the keys to the kingdom on this one, Admiral. Speed boats, a couple of leased ships, communications, even unmarked helicopters if you need them."

The SSI men looked at each other. Without a word, they rose in unison. "Right," Derringer said. "We'll get going. Ah, do we communicate with you or with the case officer from now on?"

O'Connor stood behind his desk. "Preferably through Grover Hinds, but if you need me, call anytime, day or night." He paused for emphasis. "This is off the record, of course, but I'm in constant contact with the secretary. If you need any logjams broken, she'll see to it personally."

Wilmont raised his eyebrows. "Well, that's about as much as we could ever want. Thanks, Ryan."

"Just get the job done, gentlemen. There's too much riding on this one."

51

MISRATAH, LIBYA

Paul Deladier sipped his tea and regarded Marcel Hurtubise across the outdoor table. Looking around the square, Deladier could not help comparing the elegant surroundings to his truck-bound existence over the past three days.

"I never knew there were such places in Libya," he declared. "This is wonderful! Modern facilities, an oasis, a view of the ocean. It's like a Hollywood movie set."

Hurtubise hefted his own cup. "Enjoy it while you can, *mon ami*. We will not be here long."

Deladier cocked his head. "Oh? I thought our work was finished when we delivered the shipment."

"Well, that depends." Marcel squinted against the glare—he seldom wore sunglasses—and laid down his cup. He would have enjoyed a good Mosel at the moment, but Libyan sensibilities had to be respected. For a Mediterranean seaport town, the local regulations seemed onerous. Female tourists had to wear long skirts, and bare arms were prohibited.

"What I mean, Paul, is that *I* may not be here long. The client wants extra security, so I have decided to go with the product, and the ship will leave in a few days. If you would like to come . . ."

Deladier sat back, pondering a response.

"What is it?" Marcel asked.

"Well, it's just that I . . . had not expected to do more. After all, we barely got out of Chad in time." He tugged at his new shirt. "I don't even have a suitcase for travel!" He laughed aloud, hoping that it did not sound forced. But driving a semi truck and trailer twelve hundred kilometers across the Sahara had not been an experience he cared to repeat.

Hurtubise looked at his colleague and felt a queasy twinge. *Something is not quite right. Be careful—take your time.* He made a point of swiveling his head, as if enjoying the view. Certainly Misratah had something to offer: the seventh-century caravan stop had evolved into a modern, comfortable city. The steel and textile industries had brought wealth to the place the Romans called Thubactis. Tree-lined avenues met ancient, narrow streets where Turkish architecture mixed with European. Yes, a young man might enjoy himself in such a place—for a while. "You are right, Paul. I have seen worse places. And so have you!"

Before Hurtubise could continue, Deladier asked, "When did you decide to take the ship? We didn't discuss that before."

"Just yesterday. I meant to tell you, but you were out most of the day." He forced a knowing grin. "Did you find some agreeable company in this Great Socialist People's Libyan Arab Republic?"

Deladier saw a chance and took it. "Actually, I met two agreeable ladies. Italian sisters. We did not discuss politics, but maybe tonight. Their ship sails tomorrow."

Hurtubise nodded his close-cropped head. "Well then, after you kiss them good-bye, maybe you'll consider an ocean voyage yourself. I'm going to need some good men for security."

"Mmmm. Does it pay a bonus?"

"Yes, half in advance, the rest on arrival."

Deladier leaned close enough to whisper. "Arrive where?"

Marcel arched an eyebrow. "You know where."

52

SSI OFFICES

It was a rare event: a full-scale meeting of SSI's operations staff. As officer in charge of all the firm's fieldwork, Sandra Carmichael chaired the meeting with Frank Leopole beside her.

Carmichael stood to emphasize the importance of the event. "We will come to order." She modulated her voice with West Point precision, emphasizing every word.

"The purpose of this meeting is to make some important decisions, rapidly." She reached for the console on the table and turned down the lights in the room. With deft motions she brought the PowerPoint display onto the screen.

"All right. We're operating on partial information that gets older by the hour, but since we have to start somewhere, we'll start here." She traced her laser pointer along the Libyan coast. "We have reason to believe that the yellow cake that was taken from Chad will be sent by sea to Iran."

Sandra Carmichael could be unusually attractive when she wanted— but Lieutenant Colonel Carmichael, U.S. Army (Retired), kept a brisk, almost brusque demeanor. Those who knew her recognized the signs and paid strict attention.

"Since State and DoD have given us approval to pursue the product, we're laying contingency plans. Libya is obviously off-limits— there's just no way we can operate there. But that opens a couple of options. I've asked Frank to examine them for us since our foreign ops department is most involved."

Leopole rose to his feet. "Okay, let's look at the geography." He returned to the map of Africa. "The quickest route obviously is through the Suez Canal down the Red Sea and around Oman via the Arabian Sea, then into the Persian Gulf. Call it three thousand miles or so. But look at the choke points." He ticked them off: "Suez, the entrance to the Gulf, and finally the Strait of Hormuz. The smugglers can read a map: they know that they could be intercepted anywhere along that route.

"Now, look at the other way. Yes, it's about four times longer to sail around the whole damn continent, but once past Gibraltar it's wide open spaces with an enormous amount of room for maneuver. Until they hit the Oman coast, they're practically home free. And even then, they don't have to go all the way to Bandar Abbas. There's two smaller ports on the Makran coast." He traced the southern shore of Iran, in Baluchistan.

"Sounds like you're betting on the longer route," Wilmont said.

Leopole shook his head. "No, sir. We can't afford to put all our eggs in either basket. We're going to need two teams and hope that nothing goes wrong with either one. But my gut tells me the cake will take a slow boat to Iran. After all, there's no big rush. Even if it takes six weeks, the Iranians have time to get ready."

Derringer was scanning the map like a chess master examining the board, anticipating his next moves. "Where do we base our people to intercept either route?"

"Sir, I'm thinking Cairo for the Med with Morocco as an alternate. Down in the Gulf, probably Oman, assuming that can be arranged. Our liaison at State seems to think it'll be no biggie."

"Why not keep them at sea aboard the leased ships? They'd be more flexible that way, and a lot less likely to be spotted."

Leopole knew where Derringer was coming from. The admiral's experience included pre-positioning ships at Diego Garcia in the Indian Ocean. "That's certainly a possibility, sir. We'll examine that as an option." He looked at Carmichael, who took over again. The usual cheerleader enthusiasm was absent from her voice.

"Gentlemen, this mission will succeed or fail largely on the basis of intelligence. We have Dave Dare working on it already. Frankly, I have more confidence in him and his mysterious sources than I do State and DoD and CIA and NSA and the rest of the alphabet. But we're establishing a cell within the working group to coordinate all information and provide it directly to our teams. There will be an absolute minimum of middle-level filter. If our teams want raw data, they'll get raw data and draw their own conclusions."

Joe Wolf, in charge of SSI domestic operations, sat in the back of the room. Without a direct hand in the operation, he was present as an observer but he had a thought. "Sandy, it seems that any Iranian nuke program is aimed at Israel sooner or later. What about their sources?"

Carmichael rolled her big blue eyes. "Joe, I think most of us who have ever worked with the Israelis have enormous respect for them, but we don't trust them beyond arm's reach. It's a one-way street: we give them satellite imagery and all kinds of intel, not to mention a *whole* lot of money, and we don't get much back. They let us know what they want us to know if it suits them. There are always hidden agendas with any intelligence organization, but that goes double for Israel.

"Now, in answer to your question: yes, we'll gladly accept any information. But it'll probably come via State, and that's another filter that could just get in the way. So you see why we're relying on our own sources as much as possible."

"What about Alex Cohen? Isn't he dialed in?"

Carmichael looked at Leopole. They exchanged knowing glances before the former Marine stood again. "Alex is a valuable asset. After all, he has dual citizenship and has served in the Israeli Army. I can say that he's been working on this situation in the Middle East as well as Africa, and he'll probably be on one of the teams. Other than that . . . we'll see what develops."

Derringer seldom got involved in operational details but SSI was planning for a rare naval operation and the salt water was stirring inside him. "We need SEAL expertise for this job."

"Yes, and we've got it," Leopole replied. "I expect that Vic Pope will lead the first team and Jeff Malten the second."

"Are they inbound?"

"Ah, Admiral, I talked to Jeff today. He should be here tomorrow. We're still trying to contact Vic. It's awfully short notice."

Derringer nodded slowly. "Very well. But who else? We'll certainly need more than two men from the teams."

Leopole raised a hand toward Matthew Finch. "Personnel is Matt's domain."

Finch raised partway from his seat. "Sir, we have three other SEALs in the files. I've talked to Dave La Rue and he's interested. The other two are out of touch but my assistant is concentrating on getting hold of them today."

Derringer shifted in his padded chair and looked at Wilmont. "Marsh, I've said for months now that we need more SEALs or Force Recon. There may not be enough time to teach some of our snake eaters how to debark from a Zodiac or take down a ship at sea."

The chief operating officer cleared his throat. It was rare for Derringer to raise business matters in an operations meeting. "No argument, Mike. But this is the first maritime op we've had in, what? Must be a couple of years."

Derringer rubbed his chin, staring at the map on the wall. "The thing that worries me, assuming we find the yellow cake, is leadership. Basically, it's down to two men, and while I'm sure Malten's a good man, he has no command experience. That means if we can't get Pope, we're in deep trouble." He looked up at Wilmont again. "We need more depth in the organization."

The COO gave an ironic grin. "All it takes is money. Think the board will kick loose some discretionary funds?"

"I'll damn well find out." Derringer looked back to Leopole. "Frank, is there any way we could tap some Brits on short notice?"

The foreign ops director looked surprised. "You mean former Special Boat Service?"

"Yes, Royal Marine Commandos."

Leopole scratched his crew-cut head. "That's a good idea, Admiral. I'll huddle with Jeff right after this meeting and see what turns up."

"Very well," Derringer replied. "Let's not waste any time, people. The clock is running."

53

SSI OFFICES

Sandy Carmichael poked her blond head into Leopole's cubicle. "Like some coffee, Frank?" She winked at him.

As Leopole liked to say, he was smarter than the average Marine. He took the hint and said, "Sure, I'd love some."

"I have a special blend in my office." She walked down the hall, waited for her colleague, and closed the door behind him. When she reached for the coffeepot, Leopole raised a hand. "No thanks. I changed my mind." He grinned.

Carmichael leaned on her desk. "Frank, according to the admiral, State says that we have the point on this job, and we probably do. But I just don't believe that we're the only team. I mean, if I were running a job this important, I sure wouldn't rely on one shot. I'd have at least one more team on tap, maybe two. That means another PMC, which I doubt, or active-duty guys."

"SEALs," he replied.

"You betcha." The south was back in her mouth.

"Well, I agree with you, Sandy. But I don't see any point in stewing about it. After all, if we miss the boat—so to speak—we'll be irrelevant. At that point I have to believe that somebody will move in."

"But in any case we're short of maritime operators. So tell me about Pope. I only met him once or twice and I've never dealt with him since I took the operations job."

Leopold inhaled, thought a moment, and began. "Single, never married far as I know. Late thirties. Apparently he considered becoming a priest back home in Jacksonville but he went for the SEALs instead."

Carmichael smacked her forehead. "Pope! I can just imagine. You know, 'Is Pope Catholic?' I guess he takes some ribbing over that."

"Not much," Leopole laughed. "He's one tough cookie, though it takes some people a while to figure that out. They see that baby face and shaved head and think he's some kind of wimp. They finally get the point when they look up at him from the floor."

"So why'd he get out?"

"His team had a mission in South America a few years ago. I don't know the details, but it tanked pretty bad. I only heard him mention it once: six guys went in and Pope carried the other survivor out. He got an unpublished Silver Star, for whatever that's worth. If I had to guess, I'd say he got out because he had survivor's guilt. Maybe still does."

Carmichael thought for a moment. "Well, it couldn't be too bad if he's still working in the operational world."

"He's a lot like Steve Lee. Really likes the work, especially the leadership aspects. He's a very good rifleman and he's into martial arts. *Ninjutsu* and some Israeli discipline."

"*Krav Maga?*" she asked.

"Hell, I don't know. Anyway, as you'd expect, Pope is a tremendous swimmer. His idea of a good way to start the day is to jump out of an airplane ten miles at sea and swim ashore before breakfast."

Carmichael absorbed that information. Then she asked, "Is Pope available? We need him immediately."

"I left a message on his machine and sent an e-mail. We should hear something soon."

"So you think he'll go?"

"I'd bet the ranch on it. And it's not just the action, Sandy. Pope takes his religion seriously. He and Terry Keegan really got into a pretty loud philosophical argument a while back. You know Terry was molested by a priest and left the faith as a teenager?"

She said, "Yeah, I know."

"Well, Vic says that's no reason to write off the Church of Rome. Anyway, Vic sees a spiritual aspect to the war on terror: Christianity against Islam. It's not the sort of thing we'd ever publicize, but I tell you what: I've never known anybody as motivated as he is."

54

MISRATAH, LIBYA

Deladier had shaved and showered, changing into slacks and a polo shirt with blazer. "Don't wait up for me," he said with a grin.

Hurtubise waved nonchalantly from the bed. He had a notepad and two pencils, obviously absorbed in another planning session. "I'll leave the light on, in case you're back before dawn."

The younger man ran a hand through his thick, dark brown hair and made a point of checking his wallet. He had turned one quarter of his paycheck into cash: more than enough for an extended stay in the city. "Oh, I'll be back. After all, how long does it take to lay two sisters?"

Marcel conjured up a male-bonding smile. "Kiss them for me."

"Of course! Twice each." Deladier turned to go.

"Paul."

"Yes?"

"What are their names?"

Deladier felt an ephemeral spike of fright. He recovered quickly: "Ah, Francesca and . . . Elena. Why?"

Hurtubise picked up his pad again. "I just like to know who's getting my stand-in kisses, that's all." He grinned again. "Have fun."

"Always, my friend. Always."

Forty-five seconds after the door closed, Hurtubise picked up the phone and dialed another room number. The occupant answered on the second ring. "Alfonso? Yes, he just left. Have our friends tail him from the lobby until he returns."

SSI OFFICES

"What do we want to call this mission?" Wilmont asked the SSI brain trust.

Derringer drummed his fingers in the rudimental patterns of his youth. Lieutenant General Thomas Varlowe, sitting in as an ex-officio, scrawled "USMA '66" on his notepad.

Omar Mohammed said, "Why not Prometheus?"

Derringer considered himself well read, but ancient mythology was not high on his list. "Well, I suppose so . . ."

"Consider this," Mohammed said. "Prometheus was no fool, but he attempted the impossible. He tried to deceive Zeus, who knows all and sees all, by staging a false sacrifice. Then Prometheus stole fire from Zeus and gave it to mortals on earth. Therefore, Zeus did not merely punish Prometheus: he punished the entire world for the offense that Prometheus committed."

"Well, the comparisons are pretty obvious, considering the Iranian situation. All right, it's the Prometheus Project."

George Ferraro had been awaiting the chance to discuss finances. *It's always like this*, he mused. *The company's involved in serious business, but most of the directors feel queasy about talking money.* He cleared his throat. "Ah, gentlemen, if I may . . ."

Derringer nodded. "Yes, of course, George."

"Thank you, Admiral." He turned his head, looking at each person in the room. "You know, as chief financial officer it's my responsibility to look after SSI's cash flow. I realize that we're all concerned with the national security implications of this . . . Prometheus . . . project, but since things happened in Chad we're looking at serious cost escalation. I mean, something approaching an order of magnitude."

Wilmont, as chief operating officer, appreciated Ferraro's background as a leading bean counter with Naval Systems Command. "George, I don't think anybody here disagrees with you. Certainly I do not. But you must realize that there's just no time for the usual contractual process." He grinned at the standing joke: "The U.S. Government buys slow-drying ink that doesn't blot for 180 days."

"Yeah, I understand that, Marsh. All I'm saying is that we've been focused on getting the job done, and really all we have from State and DoD is barely a handshake commitment to reimburse us for our upfront costs. That doesn't even begin to address the standard fees for personnel, equipment, and routine things like consultation."

Derringer leaned forward, fixing the younger man with his gaze. "George, please don't take this the wrong way. I realize that you're doing your job, and you've always been conscientious about it. But when I started this firm, it was not with the sole intention of making money. I saw things that needed doing because various agencies of our government were not doing them. That's what SSI is all about. If we have to dip into our reserves to meet expenses for a while, I'm prepared to do that."

Ferraro bit down the frustration he felt rising inside him. *I've got the heart of a sailor and the soul of a banker,* he told himself. "Admiral, as you say, I'm just doing my job on behalf of the firm. Our reserves are adequate at present—not ample, but adequate. I can juggle some accounts for a while, but unless we get a major transfusion in the next couple of months, we're going to be looking at red ink in seven digits. I mean, ships cost a hell of a lot of money, even when you lease them!"

Wilmont sought to placate the senior VP. "Mike and I had a face-to-face with O'Connor at State. He anticipated our concern and said flat out that we'll have everything we need, some of it gratis. His operating group is starting a set of books to show any auditors that whatever goodies we get from the Navy or elsewhere were already written off as surplus." He tapped the tabletop. "Believe me, George, we're covered."

Ferraro grinned sardonically. "Trust me: I'm from the government and I'm here to help."

"Well, there you go," Derringer interjected. "The government is by far our largest client. It's always come through before, but also consider this: Uncle Sugar keeps coming back to SSI because we deliver. If we declined an important contract because some of our accounts receivable were slow, we'd be out of business before long."

The CFO ceded the argument by raising his hands, palms up. "All right, gentlemen. I understand, that's the nature of the PMC business. I'd just like somebody to explain why I always seem to read about all these contractors being extravagantly overpaid, but it's never Strategic Solutions."

56

MISRATAH, LIBYA

Marcel Hurtubise strode along the Qasr Ahmad waterfront, seeking a particular vessel. He glanced seaward, noting the Yugoslavian-built breakwater, and took in the maritime air. It might have been restful had he been interested in resting. But he was on business. Sometimes he wondered if he knew how to rest anymore.

He found what he was looking for. With no indication to the contrary, he strode up the gangway and asked for the captain. The seaman— a Turk by the look of him—nodded brusquely and disappeared through a hatch. Moments later it opened again.

"Welcome aboard," the captain said in accented French. "I have been waiting for you." He shook Hurtubise by the hand with more vigor than custom allowed, grinning widely at the passenger. *He damn well should smile*, Hurtubise thought. *With what he's being paid.*

"*Merci, mon capitaine,*" the mercenary replied. He studied the skipper of M/V *Tarabulus Pride*, reserving judgment for the moment. Hurtubise saw a short, swarthy Libyan of indeterminate age with a face featuring a prominent nose, weathered skin, and yellowed teeth.

In turn, Captain Abu Zikri saw a reserved, fortyish Frenchman who spoke passable Arabic but whose eyes seldom stopped moving. The grip was firm, brisk, and devoid of warmth. In a word, businesslike.

"Would you like to settle in right away?" Zikri asked.

"No, I'll just look around. My men and I will stay ashore for another day or so. But we will be here every day to make . . . arrangements."

"*Très bien*," the skipper replied. "Meanwhile, permit me to show you my pride and joy."

Zikri motioned expansively as he walked, literally taking Hurtubise from stem to stern. "She's not as pretty as she once was," the Arab began, "but she's fully serviceable. Oh, I admit, she could use some paint, but most women do, too, don't you think?"

Hurtubise made a noncommittal response, preferring to evaluate the ship's layout. He began visualizing how he would board the vessel in order to capture her, then worked backward to arrive at a defense.

Zikri seemed not to notice. Striding the deck, he became expansive. "Eighty-eight meters long, thirteen meters beam. She draws six and a half meters at thirty-one hundred tons. The engines are recently overhauled, and we can make twelve knots if we have to . . ."

"How many in the crew?"

"Ah, eighteen good seamen, tried and true. Mostly Arabic, a couple of Greeks. Their papers are all in order, I assure you. But depending on the length of our voyage, I may need as many as twenty-five. You know, rough weather, long watches. That sort of thing."

"Of course," Hurtubise replied. *And the more money for you, my Arab friend, as if the crew will see much of it.*

Marcel Hurtubise never had much interest in things nautical, but he knew what to look for. Though much of the vessel was unkempt, he was pleased to see that the engineering spaces were clean. It spoke well of Captain Zikri's priorities. The Frenchman nodded to himself, a gesture that his host noticed. "You approve, *Monsieur* Hurtubise?"

"*Oui, mon capitaine. J'approuve.*"

The seaman beamed. Thus encouraged, he said, "Perhaps you would like to take some refreshment in my cabin. Some tea or . . . something else." He winked broadly.

So, my Arab friend, you are not among the devout. Hurtubise filed that information for future reference. "Thank you, no. I must meet some associates. But I will return tomorrow. I hope the loading can proceed on schedule."

"*Naturellement, monsieur. Naturellement.*"

57

ARLINGTON, VIRGINIA

Frank Leopole entered the Rock Fish Bistro on Wilson Boulevard, scanned the crowd. He was late, which was unusual.

Martha Whitney had been early, which also was unusual.

Sandy Carmichael and Colonel David Main were into their first round of margaritas while Whitney worked on her second green tea. "No more alcohol for me, sugar," she declared. "I had enough in Chad to last me for years." She did not bother to elaborate upon her conspicuous consumption with Gabrielle Tixier. Carmichael and Main looked at each other across their salt-rimmed glasses—the West Point classmates knew Whitney as a conventional Baptist who tolerated demon rum but seldom indulged in it.

"There's Frank," Carmichael exclaimed. She waved, caught his attention, and made room for him at the table.

"Anybody else coming?" Leopole asked.

"I don't think so," Whitney replied. "We done been here for ever so long." She winked at him.

"Yeah, sorry I'm late. I had to wait for the latest from Dave Dare."

Main, who provided DoD liaison for the firm, showed his interest.

"You know, I keep hearing about this Dare guy. But apparently nobody ever sees him."

"He da Phantom. Ain't nobody never see'd him 'less it be da admiral."

Carmichael almost spilled her margarita. "Honestly, Martha, sometimes I wonder what your normal speaking voice is like."

Another broad wink. "Keeps 'em guessing, honey."

Main pressed the subject. "Well, is it true? Only Admiral Derringer knows Dare?"

This time Carmichael locked eyes with Leopole. Dare's face and true identity were a corporate secret. "Oh, I'm sure somebody besides the admiral has seen him face-to-face. He has some researchers who follow his leads, but really there's no need for the rest of us to deal with him directly." She wrinkled her nose at Leopole, who ignored the hint. They had both spoken with David Dare in person, twice each. Carmichael even knew his actual given name.

"Well then, how do you know how much credibility to give his information?"

"Results," Leopole said. "I've never known him to be wrong on a major point. If he's uncertain about something important, usually he'll just tell you he doesn't know."

Carmichael leaned across the table toward Leopole. "Did he come up with anything yet?"

The former Marine shook his head. "Nothing definite. He's working on the shipping angle but said it'll be a little while. Actually, I think he probably has a lead or two but doesn't want to tell us anything until he's sure."

Sandy leaned back, brushing her shoulder against Main's. Since he was not in uniform, he could drop the military decorum. Though touching Main's hand, she regarded Leopole for a moment. She felt no special attraction to him, nor would she permit an office romance, but she wished he would let her introduce him to one or two of her girlfriends. *Not a bad-looking guy, even with the scar on his neck.* As far as she knew, he had never married.

Whitney broke the silence. "So, Frank. How're things doing in . . . Africa?" She raised an eyebrow.

Leopole looked around. The dining area was crowded and suitably noisy. He felt free to speak in a conversational tone. "Since you left Chad, Steve's team is wrapping up the training contract. Terry Keegan traveled to Germany with Eddie Marsh. The admiral got Marsh admitted to Ramstein, by the way. Since he's ex-Army, there wasn't much problem. Terry said he's still bedridden but he should recover his health. Whether he ever flies again . . ."

"Is Terry coming home, then?"

Leopold shook his head. "No, he went back to Cairo. He's putting together a jet freighter and crew in case we have to fly one of our teams someplace on short notice."

"That makes sense," Whitney replied. "So what about the yellow cake operation?"

"It's now under government and U.N. supervision, for whatever that's worth. The French PMC was ordered out of the country, but I don't know if there's going to be any prosecution. Steve says three or four embassies are involved, and basically everybody wants it to go away, so it probably will."

Whitney was building a head of steam. She set down her tea harder than intended, spilling some on the tablecloth. "But damn it, Frank! They shot down a helo." Her voice hiked two octaves. "They killed a couple of Chadian soldiers and nearly killed that Marsh boy."

Leopole made a quick motion of his fingers to his lips. "Martha, it's pretty clear that only one or two of the French security people were directly involved, and the one who fired the missile was killed. The main thing is, the leader and a couple of his aides got away. That's our priority. That and the cake."

Martha Whitney brushed the liquid off the cloth. "Well, honey, all I can say is, if it was up to me, that Marcel bastard would be *my* priority."

MISRATAH, LIBYA

Hurtubise walked up to Deladier, who was unloading a box of documents that the end users would require.

"Paul?"

Deladier turned at the sound of his name. As he swiveled his head, he heard a loud crack. A searing pain stabbed the back of his left knee. He sagged to the floor, reaching inside his jacket.

Before Deladier could pull his own Makarov, Hurtubise fired again. Once, twice. One round went slightly wide, grazing the right forearm. The other broke the radius. Deladier registered the fact that Marcel wielded the pistol with easy familiarity, shooting one-handed.

Deladier looked into the muzzle. He visualized the chamber containing 95 grains of copper-plated extinction.

"*Pourquoi?*" Hurtubise asked.

"You know why. Just end it."

The muzzle lowered several centimeters and the next round punched through Deladier's left sleeve. The pain forced a short, sharp bark from him.

Hurtubise regarded his colleague through dull, heavy-lidded eyes. "I have eight rounds left. How many shall I use, Paul?"

Deladier's mind raced, treading the precipice between outrage and resignation. He was aware that his breathing had quickened; his throat was raspy dry. He thought of the afternoon in the desert where the rival PMC men were dispatched. Gabrielle had related the incident in clinical detail. Marcel had said, "Some men choose to die on their feet, but most will lick your boots for five more minutes of life."

The next round went into the floor, a hand's width from Deladier's crotch. "Well?" Hurtubise used both hands now, obviously concerned with accuracy. "It wasn't just money, was it?"

Deladier shook his head. "Gabby."

"I thought so." Hurtubise was eerily calm. Had he not resigned himself to dying this hour, Deladier realized that he would feel bone-deep fear. But Marcel Hurtubise had time to give Paul Deladier. Man as god.

"When did you first screw her?"

"I never did. Never."

"I don't believe you, Paul."

"Screw you, Marcel!"

"Then why did you betray me?" Hurtubise's voice raised an octave, atypically agitated.

"I didn't betray you, you bastard! I told them where the load was embarked and what ship. It had nothing to do with you! The job was done! I didn't know you had decided to go along!"

Hurtubise shook his head, as if avoiding a bothersome insect. He absorbed Deladier's words, realized their validity, then focused again. "What's that got to do with Gabrielle?"

"She wanted to leave you but she had nothing, no money, nowhere to go. And she knew she would never be free of you."

"She loved me!"

"You're such a fool, Marcel. She tolerated you!"

Hurtubise aimed a fast, hard kick at Deladier's ruined knee. The blow connected and Deladier screamed from the bottom of his lungs.

"You were going to run off with her." He kicked again. "Weren't you?"

Deladier inhaled deeply, feeling again the dry rot building inside him. He could scent the fear now, seeping out through his pores and running down his face. In an ephemeral revelation, he grasped his revenge against his slayer.

"Yes, she wanted to be with me." *Spend the rest of your life thinking about* that, *you bastard.*

Hurtubise's well-oiled risk assessment machine crunched the information and spat out the conclusion. "Then you were going to kill me! That's the only way it could happen!"

Paul Deladier forced himself to smile. "That's what she wanted, Marcel. Only I told her I wouldn't do it."

Another kick. "*Menteur!* Nothing but lies!"

Deladier bit down the pain. "Then why are you still alive? If I was going to kill you, I'd have done it by now."

Hurtubise leaned forward, his face flushed with anger. "You think I'm stupid? You're stalling for time!"

"Oh, you idiot! Gabby's gone and I've already been paid. So have you! We both got acknowledgment of the deposits from Geneva, didn't we?"

Marcel Hurtubise almost reeled from the emotional shock of realization. He knew at once that Paul's logic was unassailable.

Deladier was speaking again, but Hurtubise's mind was somewhere else. He looked down at the crippled man. "What did you say?"

Propping himself on his good arm, Deladier replied, "Albert. I said Albert Rumel."

"What about him?" The voice was flat, petulant.

"He's the ex-Legionnaire you killed. You thought that he betrayed you, too. But he hadn't. And neither did I."

"Then who did you see the other night? It wasn't any Italian sisters."

Deladier managed a crooked grin. "So you had me followed." He nodded in comprehension. "Not that it matters, but I told my contact the ship's name. That's all." The crippled man bit down a moan. *How much longer?*

"Who is he?" Hurtubise demanded. "Who owns him?"

"I don't know his politics, Marcel. Only the color of his money."

Hurtubise stepped back, inhaling deeply and glancing around. Deladier knew what he was thinking. *He's just realized he made a terrible mistake, but he can't let me live because after what he's done, I'll find him again.*

Deladier closed his eyes three seconds before Hurtubise emptied the magazine.

59

LITTLE CREEK, VIRGINIA

The saltwater spray was invigorating. It hit the men full in the face as the fifteen-foot Zodiac thumped and lurched through the choppy water. At the stern of the Combat Rubber Raiding Craft, a forty-horsepower outboard propelled the inflatable boat at nearly thirteen knots.

Master Chief Carlos Bitow looked forward from amidships, assessing the rookies' performance. He had worked the SSI men up by stages, getting them progressively accustomed to the bucking, spume-tossed ride in the rubberized craft. Most were former Army pukes—a term he applied literally, considering that two had succumbed to seasickness—but at least they gamely stuck it out.

Seated amid the trainees, Bitow employed his basso profundo voice to shout criticism mixed with occasional encouragement. "Keep your balance, damn it!" He nudged the closest security operator. Hollering over the outboard's shrill whine, he called, "Stay low! Don't upset the center of gravity!"

Glancing aft, the master chief signaled the SEAL petty officer to cut the throttle. The Johnson motor subsided to a steady putt-putting and the CRRC crested a small wave, riding the tide onto the beach.

"All ashore that's goin' ashore," Bitow announced. The SSI men gratefully debarked, clambering over the side and tromping through the surf. One man, a hefty former Ranger named Pace, dropped to his hands and knees. He dry heaved a couple of times, having emptied his stomach a half hour before.

Bitow stood beside the craft, immune to the wet and cold. He wore swim trunks, boots, a floatation device, and a cap that once was green. Now it was a salt-faded shade of its former self. "Where do you think you're going?"

The SSI men immediately realized that Master Chief Bitow dealt in rhetorical questions. None required an answer, though frequently he insisted on one.

"Come back here and pick up this boat! Nobody's happy until I'm happy, and I ain't happy until my boat is happy." He pointed an accusing finger at the Zodiac. "Does this look like a happy boat to you?"

The eight trainees obligingly sloshed back to the offending Zodiac, four men to a side. They made a valiant effort to hoist its 320 pounds, but its bulk defeated them. Finally they dragged the thing to the high tide mark and let it sulk there under Carlos Bitow's perpetual glare.

Jeffrey Malten gave the daddy SEAL a knowing grin. "Well, Master Chief. Nobody drowned. Better luck next time."

As the petty officer led the men off to some hot chow, Bitow allowed himself to smile. "Actually, they did okay. Not great but okay." He regarded his former partner from Team Two. "You seem to remember what to do with a CRRC."

"Like riding a bicycle, Carlos. It's kind of nice to be back in the saddle, you know?"

"Well, in that case why'd you leave? Hell, you coulda made chief by now."

Malten elbowed Bitow's arm. "C'mon, Chief. Don't kid a kidder. We've both known guys who spent ten years eligible for their crow and never sewed it on. The Navy's still screwed up the promotion system and probably never will fix it."

Bitow conceded the point but refused to vocalize it. Instead he said, "So how do you like it on the outside? Growing your hair, staying home, listening to rock 'n' roll music that bad-mouths your country?"

The younger man adopted a relaxed stance, tipping his cap back on his head. "Well, I'll tell you. I miss some of the guys. Hell, once in a great while I might even miss *you*. But to be honest, no. I like working when I want to, getting paid obscene amounts of money, and actually getting to do the job. Not many false alerts, and . . . well, I finally got some trigger time."

Bitow knew when to shut up. "Really?" He arched an eyebrow.

Malten was tempted to tell his former superior about SSI's Pandora Project and the hunt for a radical Islamic cell in Pakistan and Afghanistan. But his professionalism stayed his tongue. Instead, he merely said, "Gotta love that Benelli entry gun."

"So what's this job about? Must be pretty damn important to take a bunch of door-kickers who don't know port from starboard."

Malten bit his lip, musing how much to tell the operator. "Chief, all I can say is that it's a hurry-up job involving maritime ops, and we don't have enough guys from the teams to fill out a boat crew. That's why Admiral Derringer leaned on the command here: to get some basic experience. Once we deploy we hope to do more mission-specific training. The only other thing I can tell you is . . . Vic Pope is involved."

Bitow's eyes widened. "No shit! Now there's an officer I'd like to work with again."

Malten saw his chance; he swung at it. "Put in your papers and you probably can. We're looking for a few good . . . SEALs."

The master chief's hazel eyes bored into Malten's. "Uh, how much did you say you get paid?"

MISRATAH, LIBYA

Marcel Hurtubise was in the business of prediction. He had become a competent forecaster of potentially unpleasant events, and the fact that he remained alive was testament to his ability in that arcane art.

Now he transferred his skill from the land to the sea.

In the *Tarabulus Pride*'s chart house, Hurtubise huddled with Abu Yusuf Zikri, pondering the many options before them. Both were concerned with avoiding the worst that could befall them while hoping to manage things so that they met with the best.

"You are sure you do not want to go via the canal?" Zikri asked. "It is much shorter and therefore faster."

The mercenary nodded decisively. "Yes. We are liable to be boarded and searched at Suez, and we could easily be intercepted in the Red Sea." On the map he tapped the northwest coast of Africa. "Once past Gibraltar, we would have all that room to maneuver, and we could change our schedule as needed."

Zikri stared at the map. At length he exhaled, blowing tobacco breath on his new associate. "It is all the same to me, *mon ami*. Our employers pay me by the day. Actually, by the nautical mile, and I do not object to receiving four times the pay for the same destination."

Hurtubise suppressed the wry grin he felt building at the corners of his mouth. The same pay rate applied to him. Considering that his future employment was uncertain with Groupe FGN, let alone the French government, it would do no harm to add to his lifetime nest egg in Geneva.

"All right," Hurtubise concluded. "We will take the long way around. Now, what protective measures do you recommend?"

"Well, you have your guards. What else do we need?"

"No, no. The men I bring are mainly to protect the cargo. But we are not sailors. What measures can be taken to prevent us from being over-taken by another ship?"

Zikri rubbed his chin and fingered his bushy mustache. "Well, the best protection against pirates is a convoy. You know, two or more ships sailing together. But that is not an option for us, unless our Iranian friends wish to lease more vessels."

Hurtubise leaned toward the Libyan. "Captain, I am not worried about pirates. As I understand it, most piracy these days occurs in Asia. But we could have visitors from places like Paris or Washington. Or Tel Aviv. And they would be well equipped. They might bring helicopters."

"Helicopters! Oh, no, you worry too much. There is no room to land a helicopter on this ship."

After a slow three count, the Frenchman kept an even tone to his voice. "Captain, they do not need to land. They can hover a few meters overhead and lower commandos on ropes. With two aircraft they could have a dozen men on deck in a matter of seconds."

"Well then, your men would just have to fight them off. Besides, how would they know about this ship? You said that security is perfect."

"I said no such thing, Captain Zikri. I said that security is as perfect as we can make it. But there is always the possibility of a leak. A careless word, one greedy man. We can take nothing for granted."

Zikri massaged his chin again, chewing his mustache. After a mo-ment he said, "We can do certain things. We can change course from time to time; we can slow down during the day or the night. We can put into port to refuel more often. And we can have anti-pirate watches. Or anti-Zionist watches, as you might say."

"Extra lookouts, day and night?"

The captain nodded. "Certainly. But it takes more men, especially at night. And that means more cost. I do not know if our clients will support such things."

"Oh, I think they will. Considering what they are already spending, and what's at stake, a few more men will be a small expense."

Zikri accepted the logic of that argument. "I will make some calls."

"Please do, Captain. As soon as possible."

SSI OFFICES

"Victor Pope to see you, Colonel."

Frank Leopole did not bother to respond to the receptionist's intercom message. He strode to the front of the building and greeted the former SEAL.

They exchanged strong-man grips—an agreed-upon tie, Navy one, Marines one.

"Good to see you, Vic."

Pope feigned astonishment. "Go on, Colonel. When was a jarhead ever glad to see a squid?"

Leopole was ready for that one. "When the liberty boat's headed for shore, of course."

"Speaking of boats, what's this I hear about Jeff Malten? Building boat teams from the waterline up?"

"We don't have any time to spare, Vic. The admiral arranged for a crash course in boat handling and deep-water survival down at Little Creek. The team we've assembled so far will be there a couple more days."

Pope nodded in approval. "Who're they working with?"

"A Master Chief Bitow. You know him?"

"Know of him," Pope replied with an informed smile. "I think he'll take good care of them."

"Okay, let's get you briefed." Lieutenant Colonel Frank Leopole and Lieutenant Commander Victor Pope adjourned to Lieutenant Colonel Sandra Carmichael's office. Without preliminaries, she laid out the situation.

"Vic, as you probably have guessed, this is a priority job. Here's the short version: we have a training team in Chad under Steve Lee and Dan Foyte. They were doing all right until word got out about a plan to smuggle yellow cake out of the country via Libya. Destination probably Iran."

Pope's face, ordinarily frozen in a mask of self-control, registered the implications. His blue eyes reflected as much light as his bald head.

"So," Carmichael continued, "State tasked our counterinsurgency training team with seizing the yellow cake. But they got there a little late and there was some shooting. One of the helos was shot down and our pilot was badly injured. Half of the yellow cake got away, driven to the Libyan border."

Pope leaned against the desk, hands clasped before him. "So now we're going to chase down the ship before it reaches an Iranian port."

"Right," Leopole interjected. "But this is pretty much a hail Mary play, Vic. We have to deploy both teams without knowing the ship's identity or its route. We're planning on sending your team to the Med and Jeff's to cover the Suez route. If we get hard intel that the shipment goes one way or the other, we may be able to commit both teams but right now we can't count on it. We're also getting a Brit named Pascoe: Special Boat Service."

Pope shifted his gaze between the former Marine and the former Army officer. "Okay. I'm in."

"Glad to have you aboard," Leopole said. Carmichael merely smiled.

"I wouldn't miss it, Frank. Not for anything." He looked at both officers, then strode toward the door. "I'll get started on requirements right away."

As Pope left, Carmichael looked at her counterpart. "Did you notice anything unusual?"

Leopole shook his head. "What do you mean?"

"Well, he never even asked about the money. Pretty unusual for somebody in our business."

"Pope's not about money, Sandy. He's about doing the Lord's work. He believes in setting things right."

Carmichael allowed the drawl back in her voice. "You know, I was raised a Baptist. Southern Baptist, actually. When I heard folks talk about doing the Lord's work, I learned to start looking for the collection plate to pass by." The corners of her mouth curled slightly. "I guess it's different with some Catholics."

Leopole's mouth did not curl. "Sandy, when they declare Vic Pope KIA, they'll find a pistol with the slide locked back in one hand and a rosary in the other."

He paused for a moment, then added, "You know, it takes all kinds to float a boat like ours. Most of our guys are operators like Bosco and Breezy: 'hey-dude' types who like the guns and gear and enjoy the down time. Farther up the ladder are the dedicated pros like Gunny Foyte and Steve Lee. Then there's a few like Vic Pope: true believers. Frankly, some of those make me a little nervous."

"How's that?"

"To them, this is more than a profession. It's more like . . . a calling. That's how Vic Pope sees the war on terror. Christianity and Western civilization against Islamo-fascism. I'm not saying he's a fanatic or anything, but he might bear watching at times."

Her forehead furrowed. "My gosh, Frank. If we can't trust him, how can we justify putting him in command?"

"Oh, I trust him. Absolutely. I'm just a little worried that when we finish this job, he may not know when to stop."

———

"How do you take down a ship?"

Victor Pope stood before a three-view drawing of a typical merchant vessel, with interior layout depicted in dotted lines.

"With a submarine?" Breezy looked around, appreciating the laughter to his flippant response.

Pope decided to ignore the former paratrooper. The SEAL veteran had read each man's SSI file, and clearly Mark Brezyinski was a qualified operator. But the California surfer persona that Breezy projected did not sit well with an intense, focused leader like Victor Matthew Pope.

"There're two approaches to a ship at sea," Pope explained. "By small craft and by helicopter. The advantages and disadvantages are obvious. Helos are fast but they're noisy, they can't surprise anybody who's half awake. On the other hand, boats like a Zodiac can approach pretty quietly, especially with a muffled engine, and avoid visual detection depending on the approach angle. It's best done at night, which of course is when the ship's crew expects an attack."

Pope used a red marker on the white board displaying the schematic. "I like to think of a ship as a moving bridge." He gave the audience his teacher's look again. "How do you take a bridge?"

"BOTH ENDS AT ONCE," the class chanted. Everybody present had attended the same schools.

"Correct. But most ships have an elevated platform." He tapped the marker against the bridge and pilothouse. "From here, the duty watch can see forward past the bow. As soon as anybody pops up over the railing, they're going to be spotted. So, what we do is . . ."

He marked an X on each side, just behind the bridge. ". . . come aboard from port and starboard at the same time. If there's enough operators, we come over the stern as well."

Bosco raised a hand. "But what about the lookouts? I mean, don't they have guys walking guard around the deck?"

"Sure they do. Or at least we have to assume so." He looked to his naval special warfare colleague. "Mr. Malten?"

Malten stood up in the front row and turned to face the others. "We used to run this scenario until we could do it in our sleep. Same thing applied whether the ship was in port or under way. In fact, it also applied to offshore oil platforms and the like. Depending what you see when you first scan over the deck edge, either you neutralize anybody there or let him go, if he's a rover. Then you get at least three men on deck immediately. They face forward and aft, covering the others while they get aboard. The third man looks up: there's always structure above you. If there's no opposition, you have a foothold and then you can start maneuvering. If it comes to a fight, at least you have some support right away."

Pope nodded his bald head in approval. "A-plus, right out of the manual." He turned to the audience again. "Any questions so far?"

Pace, who was decidedly unenthusiastic about recreational boating, raised a hand. "When you say you neutralize a guard, what's the preference?"

"We'll have suppressed SMGs and pistols. We might take a couple of rifles, but essentially a ship is a building several stories high. That applies inside as well as outside. You'll be fighting your way upward or downward as much as fore and aft, so it's usually close quarters. Now, in this particular case, we have to assume the guards will be armed and they'll shoot on sight. At least that's what I'm told, based on what happened in Chad. But even a head shot might prompt a reflex action that fires a warning shot. So if we can take out somebody without shooting, that's preferred. We'll have Tasers, flex cuffs, and gags. However, if you jump somebody and he's putting up a real fight, just pitch him overboard. He can yell all he wants but he won't be heard from a moving ship.

"Details: we don't want to get aboard and then have somebody notice wet footprints on deck. Because we'll board from the CRRCs, your feet should be dry but in case they're not, take them off and go in your socks. Tie your shoes together and take them with you."

He stood with hands on his hips, consciously exuding an air of confidence. He would seldom admit it, but he learned the trait in parochial school, long before reporting to Coronado Amphibious Base.

Green raised a hand. "Commander, what happens once we have the ship? I don't know about the other guys, but I can't run a rowboat."

"We only need a small crew: enough qualified people to run the ship while the real crew is being held. Admiral Derringer is arranging that. And we'll have a nuclear expert, Mr. Langevin, to handle the yellow cake. He's with the team in the Middle East right now." He scanned the room from front to back. "Anything else?"

When there was no response, Pope started walking to the door. "Let's get going, gentlemen. Time's our enemy right now."

WASHINGTON NAVY YARD

SS *Bruno Gaido* was nearly three decades older than any of the SSI operators who boarded her at Pier Two that morning. But the World War II Victory Ship had some lessons to impart.

Victor Pope stood on the foredeck, noting that some of the visitors interested in historic ships cast envious glances his way. Other vessels such as the decommissioned destroyer *Barry* were open for viewing, but retired Rear Admiral Michael Derringer had made a couple of calls and got his team exclusive access for two days.

"We're going to practice interior tactics during the day," Pope explained to his team. "After hours we'll haul out the Zodiacs and work on boarding. That's just as well, because in the real world we'll probably operate at night anyway."

The former SEAL began pacing, organizing his thoughts. He already had the lesson plans in mind, but he wanted to keep the training sessions logical, focused. "Let's go inside," he said.

Pope led the dozen men to the mess area, which offered the best prospects for a classroom. Once the former SEALs, Marines, Rangers, and police alumni were settled, he got right to work.

"Any of you who've never been aboard a ship can see why we're not taking any long guns. We're in tight quarters anywhere we go, so we'll be using SMGs and pistols. Eye and ear protection are mandatory. Believe me: you cap off a round inside a steel compartment and you'll be hearing bells for hours. That's an advantage we'll probably have over the opposition.

"Now, because it's so tight in here, weapon retention is a major concern. I brought dummy weapons for us to practice with: Glocks and MP-5s. All of you know about moving to corners: don't lead with your muzzle." He nodded to Phil Green, an erstwhile artilleryman who had become a motorcycle patrolman. Officer Green had written a record number of citations until some of his customers complained to the department. They objected to his custom-made ticket book, featuring a rearranged bumper sticker proclaiming, "Die, yuppie scum."

Green held a red plastic Glock close to his chest, muzzle parallel to the deck. In one fluid movement, Pope grabbed the dummy weapon with both hands and shoved it upward. As Green retreated, Pope pressed forward, keeping the muzzle beneath Green's chin.

"You can see he's purely defensive," Pope explained. "I control the gun, and he can't fight me off because he needs both hands on it. But I can use one hand to poke his eyes or smack his ear. Eventually I'm going to own his pistol."

At a signal from Pope, Green returned to the head of the room, now holding the Glock in a low ready position, angled forty-five degrees downward. When Pope made a grab for the pistol, he got one hand on it but Green stepped back three paces, pulling his assailant off balance.

"You see what's happened?" Pope asked. "He still has control. I can force the gun down somewhat, but it's still pointed at my legs. He can light me up, and after the first couple of rounds I'm going to let go."

Don Pace said, "If I'm a real smart crook, I can force the slide out of battery."

"Well, you'd have to be one really cool customer," Pope replied. "But how long can you keep the slide back? If Mr. Green gets in battery for less than one second, I'm toast."

A former SWAT cop named Bob Ashcroft raised a hand. "Are we going to have suppressors on our guns? If we are, the HKs will be about as long as an M4 carbine."

"Good point," Pope replied. "I'd recommend putting the cans on the MP-5s when we're on deck, since that might buy us a little time when we need it most. Once we're inside, I'd lead with unsilenced guns and keep a few suppressed as backups once the shooting starts. Sort of have it both ways. But ear protection is still important, since the bad guys probably won't have suppressors."

Pope glanced at his briefing notes. "We'll practice these retention drills and get used to working corners together. Then we'll move to the vertical plane, with decks and ladders."

Pace wrinkled his brow. "Ladders?"

"Okay," Pope said. "For you landlubbers, pay attention." He stomped his right foot twice. "This is not the floor, it's the deck." He tapped the wall behind him. "That's a bulkhead." Pointing upward, he said, "That's the overhead. There's no ceiling on a ship. Same applies to ladders—what you call stairs. And by the way: we're not in a 'room' with a 'corridor' outside. This is a compartment adjoining a passageway. Got it?"

"Yessir," Pace mumbled, obviously unconvinced.

"And another thing," Pope added. "We probably won't know the physical layout of our target until we get aboard, but it may have watertight doors. That means knee-knockers." He walked to the compartment entrance and kicked the lower lip of the hatchway, elevated above the deck to contain water. "If you spend much time aboard ship, eventually you'll skin your shins on these contraptions. If you're doing a tactical Michael Jackson, moon walking backward while covering your team from behind, you can trip over one of these things real easy. So I recommend single-footing it." He demonstrated by backing several steps, leading with his right foot each time.

Ashcroft shook his head. "Man, oh, man, that's a lot of really basic stuff to absorb in a short time."

"You're right. That's why we're getting started here, and we'll keep at it as long as we can. If our target vessel takes the western route around Africa, we'll have a lot more time for training."

"What about communications?" Green asked.

"We have some off the rack gear that should work but I'm still looking into that. One of the SSI directors is a major stockholder in an electronics outfit that has a new tactical headset. It's a combination radio and hearing protector. If it works, that's just what we need. I'm supposed to have a sample in a day or so."

He looked around the room. "No more questions for now? All right. Gentlemen, if you'll follow me through the hatch, down the passageway, and up the second ladder, we'll try not to get lost."

63

Bosco and Breezy were making the most of the down time.

Clad in garish swim trunks that screamed "American tourist," the two operators occupied their recliners in a strategically advantageous position. Few of the resort's patrons could enter the pool area without passing within fifteen yards of the athletic young men.

Breezy was growing tired of the routine. Their fourth day at the Mediterranean Hotel had produced another confirmed date and one probable, but they were not there entirely for R&R. "I thought we'd hear from our contact by now," the erstwhile paratrooper declared.

Bosco shrugged. "Don't matter to me, dude. The guys in Arlington know where to find us. If this Cohen guy can't be reached, we might as well enjoy ourselves, you know?"

As a string bikini wiggled past, Bosco lowered his Oakley shades off the bridge of his nose for a better view of the owner's derriere. He shook his head in appreciation of the human female's gluteus maximus. "Mmm . . . mmm. Dude, we came to the right candy store."

Breezy did not bother to look up. "Man, you know that half these babes don't even show up when they say they will."

The Ranger's ingrained confidence and sense of mission were both bulletproof. "Yeah, but half of them *do*." The latter sentiment was accompanied by a male-bonding *click-click* sound of the tongue.

Breezy finally looked at his friend from four feet distance. "Man, I can see it from here. You're approaching a state of physical and mental exhaustion."

"Like that's a bad thing?"

While Bosco was absorbing that response, his friend hit upon a fresh thought. "Hey, I gotta go shopping this afternoon. You want me to pick up anything for you?"

"Shopping? For what? Souvenirs?"

"Condoms, dude. Condoms."

Bosco returned to his supine position. "Man, you live your life between your legs."

"Like that's a bad thing?"

"Well," the former paratrooper replied, "there's more to life than sex."

Breezy knew when he had his partner's goat. "Of course there is. There's violence, too. They go together, sorta like the yin and yang of the universe. Like, you know, the duality of nature."

Bosco sat bolt upright. "The duality of nature! Brezyinski, where the hell did you ever hear a phrase like that? You sure didn't read it."

"Hell, man, I dunno. I heard it somewhere."

"But you don't know what it means."

Two Alitalia flight attendants walked past, chattering in delightfully melodic voices. Both Americans interrupted their philosophical discourse to track the young women for several meters.

At length Breezy said, "Of course I know what it means."

"What?" Bosco was still distracted. He was seriously serious about slender, raven brunettes.

The Ranger tagged the paratrooper with the back of one hand. "We were talking about the duality of nature. You know, like, sex and violence."

Bosco was focused again. "Are you trying to tell me that you like war as much as sex?"

"Well, I don't know. I mean, I've never been to a real war. That's why I got out. But what I'm saying is, if I had to choose between sex every day and combat every day, I don't know what I'd take."

Bosco regarded his friend, as if seeing him for the first time. "Well, for one thing, if you got shot at every day of your life, eventually you'd be KIA."

Breezy unzipped a knowing grin. "Sex can kill you, too."

"So you're trying to tell me that you enjoy sex as much as killing people. That's pretty far out, dude."

"No, not exactly. I'm saying that I really like shooting people who shoot at *me*. It doesn't matter if they're killed or not. C'mon, man, you know what I'm saying. You wouldn't be here if you didn't."

"Look," Bosco said. "Yeah, sometimes I enjoy the rush of double tapping some guy who's trying to kill me. But that's not why I stay with SSI. I'd do the same work for the same pay if I never had to shoot."

"So it's the gear more than the job."

"Well, yeah, pretty much. I mean, I still get paid really well to do what I like: parachuting, rappelling, stuff like that. But it's a lot better than the Army because I do it on my terms, and I can walk away almost anytime I want. With the money I'm saving, it's a no-brainer."

"Excuse me," a voice intruded.

The Americans looked up from their recliners. They saw a thirtyish, obviously fit young man who spoke almost unaccented English.

"Are you Mr. Boscombe and Mr. Brezyinski?" the man asked.

Bosco raised his sunglasses, better to inspect the stranger. "You Mr. Cohen?"

"Alex Cohen. Frank Leopole sent me. We need to talk."

64

MISRATAH, LIBYA

A crewman of *Tarabulus Pride* approached Hurtubise, who was compiling notes in his two-bunk cabin. "*Monsieur,* a man to see you. He is on the pier."

The mercenary secured his papers, stuck the Makarov in his waistband, and pulled on a jacket. Making his way to the starboard gangway, he saw a familiar face. "René, *mon vieux.*" Hurtubise strode down the plank and embraced the former Legionnaire. After much back slapping he exclaimed, "Your timing is good. I was beginning to wonder about my sources."

René Pinsard grinned broadly. "I did not get your message until last night, and I could not reach you on board your mighty ship." Pinsard tilted his head toward the cargo vessel.

"Oh, I'm spending most nights aboard now. My other three men alternate so they can get more rest. I never knew that ships were so damned noisy."

Pinsard's hazel eyes focused on his former Legion comrade. "You do look tired. But now that *Caporal* Pinsard is here, your problems are over!"

Hurtubise tried not to appear too skeptical. "My personnel prob-lems or my equipment problems?"

"Both, of course!" Pinsard reached a tanned hand into his shirt pocket and produced a list. "There's the inventory of what you wanted and what we can provide. As you will see, eight men instead of twelve, but they're reliable. I have worked with them all. Two or three even have some nautical experience."

"And the hardware?"

As if on cue, a van drove down the pier and stopped a few meters away. The sign on the side proclaimed that it belonged to a maritime provisioning firm. "Everything you wanted, Marcel. And I mean every-thing."

"RPGs?"

"RPG-7s. Four launchers with ten rounds apiece. I could have got some 18s, but they cost more. Speaking of which . . ."

Hurtubise knew where his friend was leading. "That is not a prob-lem, *mon ami*. Everything in cash, as agreed. My, ah, financiers are quite generous in that regard."

He returned to the list that Pinsard had provided. "Hmmm . . . gas masks, good. Small arms and ammunition, heavy machine guns, very good. Oh, maybe not enough body armor for everybody."

"Enough for you and me." Pinsard smiled.

Hurtubise appreciated the man's humor—and priorities. "What about motion detectors?"

"I have some but we should talk to your captain. I am not sure that they will work on a ship. I mean, they should work, but too well. All that rolling, and water coming over the deck." He shrugged. "I would not count on them being very useful. Too many false alarms."

Hurtubise pocketed the list and looked at the van. "All right, let's get everything loaded. I want to leave tomorrow or the next day."

65

Derringer and Carmichael huddled with Leopole for an update on the deployed teams.

The former Marine officer began, "Jeff Malten is taking the SEAL cadre to Israel. He'll arrive today and meet Bosco and Breezy, who've been there a few days. Jeff's coordinating with Alex Cohen on intel and he'll be our go-to guy when we learn about the ship. If the yellow cake heads east, we know it's Suez and Jeff's team will follow. If we learn the ship's headed west, that means Gibraltar and the long way around."

"There could be false leads," Carmichael said. "You know, disinformation."

"Affirm. We expect that. But between Dave Dare's shop and what we get from State and elsewhere, we should be able to shake things out."

"Okay, then," Sandy replied. "Let's hope it's Gibraltar. That'll give us a big breather."

At length, Derringer spoke up. "You know, one thing really bothers me. About the intelligence, that is. Yes, we're getting reports from Dave and State and DoD, but we don't know how independent the sources are."

"How's that, Admiral?" Leopole asked.

"Dave and his spooks are good at what they do—really good. But without access to the raw data, we could be relying on just one or two actual sources. You know the routine: A tells B; B tells C; C tells A. It looks like three reports, but actually it's one."

Leopole's forehead wrinkled. "Admiral, we already talked about sources. Dare's working group is supposed to get raw data when we request it. That's how the operation was set up."

"Yes, but I talked to Dave this morning. That's one reason I wanted to meet with both of you. So far, he's got nothing more than what we see from government sources. He said that worries him, because usually he can get inside the loop in a matter of days and at least conclude whether data is original or filtered. So far, he thinks most reports come via Israel."

Carmichael set down her coffee cup. "Well, things happened so fast that we didn't have much time to establish a more thorough network. But you're right: we don't know if the intel so far is raw or not. It could be doctored."

"That's what I'm saying," Derringer said.

Leopole rubbed his crew cut. "Well, we need to let our operators know that."

"Yes, but it'll need some delicate handling. Alex is in the loop and . . ."

"My God," Leopole exclaimed. "You're saying he might be the reason . . ."

"We have to consider it."

Carmichael resisted the impulse to bite one of her manicured nails. "Sir, maybe we're overlooking an obvious source."

"Yes?" Derringer replied.

"Well, Iran."

The two males exchanged wide-eyed looks.

"Sure," Carmichael continued. "If I understand it, all our information so far comes from our own sources but maybe it's all from the Israelis. Well, you know them. They'll share what's in their interest to share and not much more. But if we could tap into one or two Iranian sources, that'd tend to confirm or deny what we've heard so far."

Leopole raised his hands, palms up. "Sandy, that's a primo consideration. But presumably anything originating in Iran would come to us via NSA or the CIA or State or whatever."

"Yes, Frank. But we don't know. That's why it's so important to see raw data, and Dave Dare is saying he can't break it out. I'm just wondering who else we can call on."

Leopole slapped his knee. "Under our noses."

"What?"

"Omar."

Derringer grinned. "Get him."

HAIFA, ISRAEL

"Hey, there's Jeff!"

Breezy turned at Bosco's exclamation and glimpsed Jeff Malten walking through the hotel lobby.

Bosco could not help himself. "Hey, we're a circus act!" The ex-Army men extended their arms like Joan Rivers, clapping their hands and balancing imaginary balls on their noses. "Arf arf! We're trained SEALs!"

Malten looked at his Navy friend. "Some things you can always count on in a changing world." He shook hands with his colleagues and introduced his partner. "Bosco, Breezy, this is Scott Pfizer. He's another trained SEAL."

Breezy allowed himself to grin. "Trained? Does that mean you balance balls on your nose or do you do water tricks?"

Pfizer was short, muscular, and businesslike. "Well, I'd say that I do tricks. By the way, how far can *you* swim under water?"

"Depends on what I see," Breezy quipped. "But I met this Greek gal the other night and she could hold her breath longer than—"

Bosco interrupted his friend's reverie with an elbow to the ribs. "Jeff, what's the rest of the team look like?"

Malten swiveled his head. "I think we'd better talk in one of the rooms. This Cohen guy was supposed to make reservations for us."

"Yeah, we met him. He seems to have things organized. C'mon, we can talk in our room until he gets back."

Following Brezyinski down the corridor, Malten asked, "Where'd he go?"

"Damn if I know. He comes and goes all the time, like he's the only one involved but there has to be other people. Maybe the Israelis just like to keep their contacts to a minimum."

In their room, Bosco helped himself to the refrigerator and offered drinks to the others. Malten passed while Pfizer accepted a ginger ale. Dropping Breezy's wet trunks on the floor, Malten occupied the chair and organized his thoughts. "Are you guys in contact with Arlington?"

Bosco sipped his beer and nodded. "We check e-mail at least twice a day. We have a phone card but we're not supposed to use it if we don't have to."

"Well, then you're probably pretty much up-to-date. Vic Pope is running the other team, and he'll take the ship if it goes the long way around. I'm getting another SEAL and four other guys to start, with maybe a couple more besides. It's real loosy-goosy, but I guess it has to be until we know more. If the ship goes via Suez, we'll get the nod."

"So we'll have, what? Eight or maybe ten guys?"

"Yeah, I think so. Frank wanted to load what he's calling our East Team with most of our SEALs because we won't have as much time to prepare as Pope's team. Our job is to get you guys aboard the ship. After that, it's pretty much interior tactics."

"Fine," said Breezy. "But what then? I mean, like, what do we do once we own the boat?"

Malten shrugged. "That's still up in the air. I guess part of it depends on what Cohen turns up."

Bosco asked, "So what do you know about Cohen?"

"Just what Frank and Sandy told me. Dual citizenship, apparently a lot of experience with the Israelis, though I don't know details. He's worked with SSI before. What'd he tell you?"

"Well, he's lined up a ship for us to use. He wants a twenty-knot speed and big enough to carry a couple of Zodiacs. He said it needs to be foreign registry, which I guess means anything but Israeli."

Malten glanced at Pfizer. The younger SEAL said, "That's not a big deal. Ships change registry now and then, and they can fly a flag of convenience."

Bosco gave him a blank stare. "Flag of convenience?"

"It's a tax dodge. Panama is a real small country, but I think it registers more ships than anyplace else. There are even countries without coastlines that register ships because the fees are so low."

"You mean, like, Nebraska could register ships?"

Pfizer chuckled aloud. "Well, I don't know about that, but I've seen merchant vessels with Mongolian registry."

"You gotta be shitting me," Bosco exclaimed.

"No lie, GI."

The operators heard four sharp raps on the door. Breezy looked through the peephole and said, "It's Cohen." He admitted the Israeli-American and introduced the new arrivals.

Alexander Cohen quickly surveyed the team but showed no interest in the individuals' opinions. Instead, he took charge of the assembly and exercised his home-court advantage. "I know that none of you have been to Israel before, but that doesn't matter too much. We won't be here very long because I just have confirmed that our target is docked in Misratah. It will probably sail in the next two days or so."

"Where the hell's Misratah?" Bosco asked. He resented Cohen's attitude and could tell that most of the others shared his impression.

"Oh, that's in Libya." His tone seemed to imply *Of course*.

Jeff Malten was not prepared to accept much on faith. "What's the source of that information?"

Cohen raised his hands, palms up. "I cannot discuss sources, Mr. Malten. I'm sure that you understand the need for security."

"No, actually, Mr. Cohen, I don't. Especially when it's our necks. I think we're entitled to know something about the information we're acting on." He made a point of looking around. "I think we all do."

"Damn straight," Breezy said.

Bosco added a Ranger "Hoo-ah."

Pfizer, sensitive to his status as the new guy, merely returned Cohen's gaze.

"Another thing as long as we're discussing priorities," Malten added. "As far as I know, I'm leading this team. That's what Colonel Leopole told me when Scott and I left Washington yesterday, and I don't think anything's changed since then. If I'm wrong, now's the time to hear it. From him."

Cohen's brown eyes took a gunslinger squint at the former SEAL; a gaze of respectful resentment. At length Cohen said, "That is my information as well, Mr. Malten. But since this is my country and since I am arranging our equipment and shipping, I believe that SSI grants me control over the preparations. Once the operation begins, of course you are in charge."

Malten's brain registered the phrase *My country*. He could not resist making his point. "Well, maybe that's the difference between us. These guys and me, we're Americans. That's our country. I understand that you have dual citizenship . . ." He allowed the sentiment to dangle in the thickening air.

Alexander Cohen was unaccustomed to having his loyalty questioned by Americans or Israelis. He bit off the response he felt building in his throat and, controlling his voice, replied, "I was born in America of Israeli parents. Considering what that ship is carrying to Iran, I think we both have cause for concern, don't you?"

Jeffrey Malten nodded, then pressed his point. "So how do you know what ship we're after?"

Cohen decided on a middle course. "The ship is called *Tarabulus Pride*. It's Libyan registry, about three thousand tons. Apparently it's loaded and ready to sail. We don't know why it hasn't left yet, but maybe the French security firm wants to get more men. They must know we'll be tracking the shipment."

Malten was unwilling to concede the intelligence argument. "Okay, that helps. But how do you know all this?"

Cohen folded his arms. "Mr. Malten, for now I can just say that we are confident of the information. I can ask for permission to share that with you, but it will take some time. And I do not think we have much time."

"All right, I'll trust you to do that. Now, what about our own ship and equipment?"

Cohen sat at the writing desk and laid down a notepad. "Our ship is leased for one month, which should be plenty of time if the yellow cake goes via Suez. It's fully fueled and manned. We have three Zodiacs, weapons, radios, and boarding equipment. Here's the list. Let me know if you need more."

Malten looked at Pfizer with raised eyebrows. "Well, that's a lot of gear in a short time. Mr. Cohen, I don't . . ."

The Israeli smiled. "As long as we're arguing so well, make it Alex."

"Okay, I'm Jeff." Malten looked at the list again. "Ah, right now I don't know if we'll have enough men for three boats. But it's good to have a spare."

Cohen leaned back, hands behind his head. "Nothing's too good for our American friends."

SSI OFFICES

Mike Derringer was a well-known workaholic: he arrived early each weekday and often spent part of a weekend at the office. Today was no different. He checked the coffeepot, noticed that Peggy Springer already had turned it on, and not for the tenth time admired her efficiency.

He turned on his office computer to check overnight e-mail and found the usual clutter of messages: reminders, jokes, reunion notices, occasional obituaries. SSI's computer support division had installed a powerful firewall in all the company's machines, and Derringer—certainly no prude—gladly did without the Internet's marketing pollution: penis enlargement, enhanced sexual performance, and teenage Asian sluts. Occasionally Karen assured him that, at age sixty-seven, he needed neither of the first two, but she would personally see to organ reduction if he ever dabbled in the third.

He believed her.

Quickly working his way through the list, making frequent use of the Delete button, Derringer saw a message from a sender called "Double Dare." Derringer opened the message.

Admiral: Our boat left late yesterday PM, probable heading 270. More to follow. DD.

Derringer swiveled in his chair, punched the intercom, and buzzed Wilmont's office. There was no response, nor did the admiral expect one at 0745. *Marsh is more an 0900 kinda guy,* the admiral thought. In descending order down the ladder, he buzzed Sandra Carmichael and Frank Leopole.

"Leopole here."

"Frank. I'm glad you're in. Our bird has flown the coop."

"Be right there, sir."

"Ah, have you seen Sandy?"

"Negative. I think she's still inbound."

"Very well. Hustle up here and I'll try her cell phone."

Derringer checked his Rolodex—he still trusted electrons just so far—and punched in the number.

"This is Sandra Carmichael."

"Sandy, Mike."

"Yes, sir."

"What's your ETA?"

"Ah, I'm still on Sixty-six, approaching the Twenty-nine exit. Call it one-five mikes. Less if this idiot ahead of me moves over."

Derringer visualized the geography. Carmichael's Nissan would exit onto the Lee Highway, take Danville Street south across Wilson Boulevard to Clarendon, and proceed east toward Courthouse Road. "Very well. Come straight to my office. Frank and I are working the latest intel."

"You heard from Dave?"

"That is affirm."

"Gotcha, sir." The line went dead.

Leopole walked directly into the office without bothering to knock. "What've we got, Admiral?"

"Just a preliminary report from Dave Dare. He says the ship left yesterday afternoon or evening, probably westbound. That's all we have for now."

"Then Jeff Malten's team is . . ."

"Way out of position in Israel. Yes, I know. I understand that Pope's people are set to fly out today."

"Yessir." The foreign ops director stood for a moment, rubbing his chin and wishing he could dispense with his tie. "Admiral, we could try repositioning Malten but I think maybe we . . ."

"Concur." Derringer allowed himself to laugh. "Frank, if we keep this up much longer, we're going to be telepathic. It took me about eight years before I could do that with Karen."

Leopole laughed politely, then loosened his tie and unbuttoned his collar. "Looks like a long day, sir. But if I read you, we still don't know for certain that Dare's report is complete enough to act on. I mean, yes, the ship could've left, but until we know that it's definitely headed west, we could end up chasing our own tail."

"Concur again. But get on the horn and see if you can talk to Malten. Or Cohen might be a better prospect. Just call it a warning order: prepare to fly to Morocco, but also be ready to execute the Suez option."

"Well, Terry Keegan's back in Cairo with a leased cargo plane and crew. That's one of the better contingencies we arranged. He should be able to get to Haifa on pretty short notice."

"Yes, we should let him know as well." Derringer looked at the ship's clock on his wall. "Call it 0800 here—about 1500 there. I'll try that call myself. Report back here when you're done and we'll huddle with Sandy."

Minutes later, Carmichael entered the office. She dropped her purse in a chair and waited while Derringer got off the phone. "Sandy, good morning. Sit down and I'll fill you in."

"Thanks, Admiral. I take it that we're talking to Jeff Malten this morning?"

"Frank's doing that. I just talked to Terry Keegan in Cairo. He says he could be gear-up for Haifa with less than an hour's notice, though the air traffic regs are more bureaucratic in the Hindu-Muslim part of the world. He's going to talk to our embassy and see if they can get him a short-notice waiver."

Carmichael's blond hair bobbed as she nodded. Then she said, "Admiral, the thing that worries me is intelligence. Not that I doubt Dave Dare, but I just don't think we can launch two teams without more confirmation."

"I agree. In fact, Frank and I already discussed that. Sandy, I know it's below your usual responsibility, but could you coordinate all our intel sources until we know something positive? Dave's working group will have its hands full."

She stood, straightened her skirt, and said, "I'm on it." She turned to go, then stopped. "Oh, I meant to ask: anything from Omar about some Iranian contacts?"

"Just that he's working it. Actually, I wouldn't expect too much,

Sandy. At least not anytime soon. After all, he's been out of the country over thirty-five years. He said he still has some relatives there, but I don't think they're connected. If he turns up something, it'll be among the expatriate community."

"Okay. I'll get to work, Admiral."

Watching the retired Army O-5 walk out, Derringer admired the view. *Best legs on any light colonel I ever saw.*

MEDITERRANEAN SEA

The acrid oxyacetylene scent lingered in the ship's relative wind, but Hurtubise ignored the odor and the sparks. Striding from port to starboard, he supervised installation of machine gun mounts on the *Tarabulus Pride*'s guardrail while René Pinsard and some of his associates degreased the weapons and laid out belted ammunition.

Abu Yusuk Zikri appeared from forward of the superstructure. Hurtubise already recognized the captain's ambivalence to the modifications, but it mattered little. The Libyan skipper appreciated prompt payment far more than any concerns about quasi-legal alterations to his ship.

"You are nearly finished?" Zikri asked, the hope obvious in his voice.

Pinsard's welder finished fusing the vertical pipe to the rail, completing the crude weapon mount. Then he snuffed out his torch, turned off the regulator. He raised his visor and nodded to Hurtubise. Then he pulled off his gloves and prepared to move the portable equipment.

"Back here, yes. Now we'll add two more mounts ahead of the pilot-house."

"Oh," Zikri replied, noncommittal as ever. "Is that necessary?"

Hurtubise gave a sly grin. "I hope not."

"Ahem. Yes, I see your point." He returned the smile, minus the enthusiasm. "Ah, *monsieur*, could we speak? In private?"

"Of course." He walked farther aft, away from Pinsard's men.

Though clear of the others, Zikri still spoke in a low voice. "I have received a confidential message from our . . . benefactors. I thought you should see it immediately."

Hurtubise accepted the message form and read it twice. Then he raised his eyes to Zikri's. "Who else has seen this?"

"Only the radio operator and me."

"Is the operator trustworthy?"

"*Monsieur*, he is my second cousin. We grew up together."

But can he be trusted? The Frenchman decided against repeating the question aloud. "All right. Just make sure he does not discuss any messages with anyone else, not even my men."

Zikri nodded animatedly. "He already knows that."

"What about the others?"

"Which others?"

"You have other radio operators, don't you? Your cousin, he does not remain on duty twenty-four hours."

"Oh. Well, anything but routine traffic always comes to me or the first officer, day or night. But my second operator is reliable. His mother's mother's family is still in Palestine. They hate the Jews."

Hurtubise thought for a moment, sorting priorities. "I want to talk to each of your operators, with you present. I want them to know that Pinsard or I are to be told of any such messages, no matter what time of day or night." He lanced the captain with a predator's stare. "No exceptions."

"As you wish, *monsieur*."

Hurtubise dismissed the captain with a curt nod. Then he rejoined Pinsard's men.

"René."

The mercenary looked up from his work. He had just hefted a pintle-mounted MAG-58 onto one of the welded stanchions. It swiveled reasonably well. With a word to one of the armorers, he joined his former comrade.

"Yes, Marcel?"

Hurtubise handed him the message without comment. When Pinsard finished reading, the concern was visible on his face. "How did they know?"

"I can guess." *Paul, you bastard. I was right to kill you. And I was wrong to regret it.* "But that doesn't matter. Right now, I think we have to assume that we'll be intercepted rather than consider it a possibility."

"What's the source of this information? It doesn't say."

"It doesn't have to. I know who's involved, and the authenticator is valid. If the source says the Americans and Israelis know we've sailed, that's the end of it."

Pinsard returned the paper, folded his arms, and regarded his friend. "You think it'll be the Americans or the Jews?"

Hurtubise arched an eyebrow. "*Qui sait?* Maybe both. Anyway, we made the right choice by avoiding Suez. Too much chance of being boarded for routine inspection. This way, the captain says we can alter our course and speed, maybe give them the slip. For a while, anyway."

Pinsard looked outboard, scanning the Middle Sea. "There's a lot of ships out here. It will not be easy finding us among so many others."

"No, it won't be easy. But they will find us. I feel it, here!" He punched himself in the solar plexus.

Pinsard unzipped a confident smile. "Then we'll just have to give them a warm reception."

"The best kind, *mon ami*. The best kind."

69

"REACH ZERO THREE HEAVY"

The C-5B Galaxy climbed away from Dover Air Force Base, Delaware, propelled by forty-one thousand pounds of thrust. At the controls was the newest aircraft commander in the wing, flying her first trip in the left seat. Captain Debra McClintock turned the steering bug on the autopilot console to refine the outbound heading. "Next stop, Azores," she told her copilot. The blond first lieutenant, a former cheerleader called Barbie, gave a thumbs-up. She received no end of kidding about her fiancé, a captain named Ken.

In the passenger deck farther aft, the SSI team settled down to make use of the ensuing several hours. Though the compartment held seventy-three seats, the operators kept to themselves, carried on the passenger list as retirees flying space available to Europe. The cargo manifest made no mention of their Zodiacs nor the shipping crates containing interesting items common to the spec-ops trade. They wore standard-issue nomex flight suits to blend in as much as possible.

Phil Green leaned back, hands behind his head. "I gotta hand it to the admiral and his guys. I mean, coordinating two teams five thousand miles or more from D.C. takes some doing. Let alone getting us on this plane."

Don Pace looked around. "Yeah. How'd they arrange this, anyway?"

Pope knew the background. "There's two hooks they can hang this on: joint airborne and transportability training, or a special assignment airlift mission. I don't know exactly how the blue suits will log this, but I'd guess SAAM since we're not actually military. But the fact that they're delivering spare parts and some people to Spain and Italy provides decent cover."

"What's it matter?" asked Pace. "I mean, we're all working for Uncle Sugar, aren't we?"

The former SEAL looked around, satisfying himself that the adjoining seats were empty. "Right now it doesn't matter at all. But if this thing tanks, and Congress starts investigating, then it could matter a lot."

"Politics," Green said.

"You got it." He shrugged. "That's how it is with government."

"I'm an anarchist," the erstwhile cop declared. "When my great-great-grandfather got off the boat from England, he asked, 'Is there a government in this country?' When they told him there was, he said, 'I'm against it!'"

Pope felt himself warming to Green. The onetime motorcycle patrolman came across as cynically flippant, but when he rucked up, he put on his game face and remained focused until the gear was stowed. Pace, on the other hand, was perennially laid-back. He appeared unflappable, possessing a street cop's visceral disdain of front-office types. Pope knew that Green had shot for blood, and the fact that both had been SWAT instructors lent credibility in the SEAL's opinion.

"Now, everybody gather 'round." Pope waited for the other team members to close in for the impromptu briefing.

"A lot can go wrong just getting the full team together," he began. "The admiral has to coordinate not just our schedule with the ship in Rota, but getting approval for Keegan to fly Malten's team there in time to meet us. Then we have to move our gear as well as his to the ship, get everything and everybody aboard, and be ready to deploy."

"Isn't Cohen handling some of that?" Green asked.

"I suppose he is, at least the Israeli end. But I don't want to dwell on that: there's not much we can do about it, and we have to proceed based on a unified operation plan."

"I understand there was some sort of argument about who's calling the shots. With Cohen, I mean."

Pope cocked his head. "Where'd you hear that?"

"I heard Leopole and Carmichael in the coffee room."

"Well, you know almost as much as I do. Frank told me the same thing, but he said there's been a phone call and it's thrashed out. Cohen has authority feet dry; Jeff takes the conn when they're feet wet."

"How does that work with getting their ship?"

"I don't know, other than they already have a fast one lined up. But Jeff's a good head. He doesn't let his ego get in the way."

Green's blue eyes sparkled in the cabin lighting. "Gosh, how'd he ever get to be a SEAL?"

70

M/V *TARABULUS PRIDE*

"Captain, what can we expect at Gibraltar?" Hurtubise had informed himself of the basics of maritime traffic control but there had been no time for details. He had to trust Zikri on matters of seamanship.

The Libyan skipper looked forward, visualizing the exit to the Atlantic, somewhere beyond the mist and haze. He turned to a map on the chart table. "We are here," he said, tapping a position opposite Bizerte. "About four hundred miles out of Misratah, day before yesterday."

Hurtubise shook his head. "What is that in kilometers?"

Zikri rubbed his stubbled chin. "Ohhh . . . maybe seven hundred." He grinned at the landlubber. "There are nautical miles and statute miles. We do not bother with statute—that's for the Americans.

"Anyway, we are making a little over ten knots—say, eighteen kilometers per hour. At that rate we reach Gibraltar in about ninety hours. When we approach the eastern end of the strait, we contact traffic control. Most ships identify themselves, but the international convention permits corporate security." He grinned broadly. "Very considerate, yes? We file a discreet report that avoids public announcement. After that, we monitor Tarifa Radio for traffic information. As long as we stay in one of the shipping lanes, there should be no problem."

Hurtubise viewed the map with practiced eyes, noting the geographic geometry. "Are there other ways to track us?"

"Well, there is satellite coverage that helps with traffic control. I think about two hundred ships pass the strait every day. It can get very crowded: the narrows are only eight miles wide." He looked at the Frenchman. "Twelve kilometers."

"How good is the satellite coverage?"

Surprise registered on Zikri's face. "You mean for identification?"

"Yes."

"Well, I do not know for certain. But I doubt that a ship could be identified beyond its length and maybe its beam. That is, width. Certainly not by name."

"*Mon capitaine*, do not be so casual about the Americans with their statutory miles. They have satellites that can show a golf ball."

The Arab shrugged. "Maybe so. But I believe it is a very great problem to position a satellite to cover a moving object, like a ship. Besides, how could they pick us out of hundreds of other vessels in a given area?"

"Maybe they can't. But I want to take no unnecessary chances. Once we are past Gibraltar, I want the crew to start repainting."

"Well, yes, we can do that. Not the entire ship, as I explained before. But we can use a different color on the upper works, and change the name on the stern." Tikri regarded his colleague. "We will need your men to do the work as fast as possible."

"Of course. They're not here for a sea cruise."

PART

IV

THE ATLANTIC

M/V *DON CARLOS*

Cadiz Bay slid astern as the leased cargo ship departed the Spanish coast. Standing on the stern with some of his team as Rota Naval Station faded into the distance, Victor Pope said, "Hard to believe we left Dover barely thirty hours ago."

Phil Green massaged the back of his neck. "Hard to believe I've gone that long without sleep. Whoever said that people can sleep on airplanes?"

"You'd be surprised where people can sleep. I've seen guys curl up on coral rocks and drop off in thirty seconds. And we weren't on the C-5 even ten hours, including the Azores. Besides, the pilot was a nine and the copilot was at least a seven."

"Like they'd ever give me the time of day. You know, all my life, my problems have involved women: both because I had one and because I didn't." The ex-cop glanced around. "Well, I'll say this: whoever arranged for this boat had his priorities right. Nice bunks and the kitchen smelled good."

Pope gave his erstwhile Army colleague a sideways glance. "I don't know about the kitchen, but I think they're shelling crab in the galley."

Green responded with an exaggerated shrug. "Brrr . . . I get nervous when I hear about ships and galleys. You know, like in *Ben Hur.* 'Row well and live.' "

Don Pace ambled up, slightly unsteady on his feet. "I couldn't sleep downstairs. Too much noise from the motor."

The former SEAL realized that he was being set up. He ignored the landlubbers' studied ignorance and returned his gaze to shore. To no one in particular he declared, "We could be at sea for a week or more. Maybe a lot more. We'll have to get used to this sort of life."

Geoffrey Pascoe strode to the stern on experienced legs. Pope had only met him hours previously, but the former Royal Marine Commando took to a ship's motion in marked contrast to most of the Americans. He spoke in terse, clipped tones. "Commander, I understand you want to see me."

"Yes, thank you, Geoff. We don't stand on rank here."

"As you wish. Sir." The Brit gave an icy smile.

"I want to get acquainted while we have time," Pope said. "I'm certainly glad to have you aboard. Especially on such short notice."

"Well, apparently your Admiral Derringer and I have a few mutual acquaintances. I've only been out barely a fortnight—was planning to get married. But when a couple of chaps in trench coats bought me a drink and waved a lot of money in my face, I found myself on the way to Heathrow with a ticket to Spain." He shook his head in wonderment. "I still don't think that Leslie believes I plan to return."

"You were in M Squadron?"

"Yes . . . *sí* . . . ah, yes. Two years."

"Right up our alley," Pope replied. He noticed querulous expressions on some of the Americans. "M Squadron, Special Boat Service, is the Royal Marines' maritime counterterror unit."

Pascoe asked, "Commander . . ." He grinned self-consciously. "Sorry about that. Old habits, you know. Ah, what do you think about this setup?"

"It's a good ship. I wish we could've got our gear loaded faster, but I think SSI did a really good job coordinating everything. Not just the air transport, but having the trucks ready to move us from the air station to the pier. I halfway expected that we'd land and find nobody waiting for us."

"No," Pascoe replied. "I mean the captain and the crew. Here we are, going to sea for who knows how long with these guys, and we don't really know anything about them."

"Spooks," Pace declared. "I can always tell."

Pope nodded his bald head, which somehow seemed immune to sunburn. "Not a doubt in my military mind. But that's okay. I've worked with the company before. The Langley types may be screwed up six ways to breakfast, but the operators I've known are almost always good guys. I think these guys will tell us what we need to know."

"Don't ask, don't tell," Pace responded.

Pope pointed abaft the bridge. "They should know plenty. Look at those antennae. VHF, UHF, and satellite. This ship is wired."

He stretched his muscular arms and flexed his shoulders. "Well, we're far enough out now. I'll go talk to the captain and see about arranging a training schedule."

Jeff Malten joined the group, squeezing his grip strengthener with his left hand. "Vic, I just came past the bridge. Cohen's talking to the skipper right now."

Pope gave the junior SEAL a suspicious look. "Do you think they know each other?"

"Damned if I know. Why?"

"Just a thought. They both work this part of the world, and I wouldn't be surprised if they're both company men, if you know what I mean."

Malten thought for a moment, quickening the squeezes of his left hand. "Well, I still don't know the details, but he had a twenty-knot ship ready for us to take from Haifa if we needed it. How many door-kickers have that kind of pull?"

Pope dismissed the subject: he preferred to focus on the future. "As long as we have some slack time, we can put it to good use. Especially boat handling."

Geoff Pascoe knew an opportunity when he saw one. He leveled a gaze at the ex-cop. "You'll love it, Pace. Nobody throws up more than two or three times in a Zodiac. After that, it's just the dry heaves." He smiled broadly.

Pace gave an exaggerated gulp. "Uh, when're we gonna do that training?"

Pope kept a straight face. "As often as possible. In fact, I'm going to check with the captain to see when we can put some Zodiacs over the side."

In the pilothouse, Pope found Cohen just leaving. They exchanged brief greetings before the SEAL stepped inside. "Captain? Do you have a minute?"

The skipper turned toward the American. "Oh, sure." It came out "Chur." Captain Gerritt Maas spoke a vaguely accented English that shifted between western and northern Europe. That was small wonder, since he spoke Dutch, French, Spanish, and Norwegian, and could produce convincing proof that three of them were his native tongue.

"Sir, I'd like to discuss some details with you. We got under way so fast that we didn't have time to get acquainted."

"Vell, ve verk for de same people," Maas replied. His eyes said as much as his voice. "Besites, ve haf plenty of time now." He gestured with his pipe. "Seferal days at sea, maybe efen veeks."

Pope decided to talk shop before moving to more delicate subjects. "Tell me about this ship. What can she do?"

"*Don Carlos*, she can do almost anything. At ninety-four hundred gross registered, she can make seventeen knots. We have bow thrusters so we can dock without tugs. She's 128 meters by 20.5 in the beam. She draws ten to eleven meters."

"How long can you maintain seventeen knots?"

Maas smiled broadly. "As long as fuel lasts."

Pope eyed his colleague. "Skipper, who really owns this vessel?"

A light illuminated in the skipper's hazel eyes. He inclined his head, as if studying a specimen in a bottle, then said, "Consolidated Industrial Affiliates, out of Amsterdam." After a pause he added, "I can show you the papers."

"You're kidding, right?"

"My dear commander, do you think it implausible that Certain Important Associates would have no sense of humor?"

Pope almost allowed himself to smile. "Actually, yes, I do."

Maas sucked his pipe and muttered a noncommittal, "Ummm."

The American judged the European to be ten to twelve years older than himself—enough to justify some deference. "Sir, I'd like to confirm the, ah, command relationship. I mean, among you, me, and Mr. Cohen."

The skipper blew an aromatic smoke ring. "Easy enough, I think. I command this ship, you command the commandos, Cohen provides the information. That's how SSI wants it, yes?"

"Yes, sir. That's my understanding. But I don't know anything about the communications setup. Command and control, we call it. If you or I need some additional information—more details about the operation—I don't think we should have to go through Cohen for everything."

Maas's eyes narrowed as he studied the former SEAL. "So you don't trust him."

"Well, I . . ."

"Neither do I."

"Sir?"

"He's Israeli, yes?"

Pope nodded. "Israeli-American. Dual citizenship."

"You work with him before?"

"No. But he's a regular SSI employee."

Maas grinned. "Admiral Derringer, good man. I've known him for years now. Don't see him so often, of course, but I trust him." He motioned with the pipe again. "This one, Cohen. I think he's a good one, too. Competent, I mean. But . . . where is his loyalty? Maybe more in Tel Aviv than Washington."

Pope was surprised to find himself feeling defensive about Alexander Cohen. "Captain, it seems to me that we have to trust each other. Considering what's at stake—the shipment headed for Iran—we're all . . . in the same boat, should I say?"

Maas chuckled and slapped Pope's arm. "Good one, boy!" He cackled again.

"Well, Captain, as I was saying, I need to know about the communications setup. I understand that we receive intelligence through Cohen, but that doesn't mean we're limited to asking our own sources for other information." He thought for a moment. "Besides, what if something happens to Cohen? There has to be a contingency—a backup."

The skipper nodded decisively. "There is. But for now, come with me. I'll show you the radio shack and you can talk to the operators."

"I saw your antenna layout. I guess you can talk to SSI and anybody else you need to."

"Commander Pope, we can talk to the man in the moon."

M/V *TARABULUS PRIDE*

"We need to talk," Zikri said.

Hurtubise laid down the FA-MAS he was cleaning and wiped his hands on a stained cloth. The two men walked to the portside rail where they could be alone.

"What is it?" Hurtubise asked.

"My second radio operator, Shatwan. Since we are making no more calls than necessary, he has much time on his hands."

"Yes?"

"Last night he entered the radio shack earlier than he was scheduled. He noticed Aujali transmitting by key, which is most unusual. When Shatwan asked what was happening, Aujali appeared a little flustered. He said that he was communicating with an amateur operator in Rabat."

The Frenchman rubbed his perennially stubbled chin. He focused on the horizon for a long moment, then turned to the captain. "Didn't you tell the operators that no messages would be sent without approval from you or me?"

"Yes. You were going to tell them yourself, but I think you were called to inspect something."

"The machine-gun mounts. Yes, I remember now."

Zikri spread his hands. "In any case, I thought you should be told."

"What did Aujali send in that message?"

"We do not know. He said it was innocent enough: asking for news reports from Palestine."

Hurtubise folded his arms and leaned forward. "Do you believe him?"

"I have not questioned him. I thought it best to tell you first."

The mercenary nodded slowly. "You did right." He thought for a moment. "What do you know about him? Not what he told you: I mean, what do you *really* know?"

"Well, I have his papers as a seaman and radioman. I suppose they could be forged, but he has sailed with me before. I have never had reason to doubt him."

"You said he has relatives in Israel?"

"That's right. His grandmother's family. They have tried to emigrate but the Jews always prevent it."

Hurtubise chewed his lip, as if physically masticating the information. *Why would the Israelis want to keep an old woman from rejoining her family?* "And Shatwan said he was communicating about events in Palestine?"

"Correct."

"You trust Shatwan completely?"

"As I said before, we grew up together. He is a younger cousin."

Hurtubise gave an ironic smile. "Captain, my brother-in-law once tried to put a knife in my back. I trusted him up to that moment, too."

The Arab's eyes widened. "I do not suppose he tried that again."

The wolf's smile reappeared. "He did not try anything again."

Zikri thought better of asking details. Instead, he said, "Well, *monsieur*, Salih Shatwan and I are as close as brothers. I cannot add anything to that."

Hurtubise turned and paced several steps. At length he returned and faced the captain. "Do you have a way of monitoring all broadcasts without the sender knowing?"

"Not that I know of. I would have to discuss it with Salih. But I think that we could be monitored from another ship with knowledge of the suitable frequencies." He looked more closely at the Frenchman. "You think that Aujali will continue transmitting?"

"I think that he might. And I would be very interested to know what he's really saying to his friend in Morocco. If it is Morocco."

Zikri shifted his weight in response to the ship's movement. *Tarabulus Pride* was approaching Gibraltar, where the current increased in the narrows. "We will be within easy range of Rabat for the next few days, and communication is easier with nighttime atmospherics. I can talk to Aujali and tell him to stop all communications, or we can see about arranging some discreet monitoring. But that will take time."

Hurtubise thought for a long moment. Then he said, "All right, tell Aujali to stop all unauthorized communication. But I want to talk to Shatwan right away. I'll have him contact some friends of mine to see what they can find out about this Palestinian family."

Zikri's face betrayed his reaction. "You can get such information?"

"Yes, given time."

The seaman nodded. "Time is one thing we have in quantity."

"I hope so, but I have learned not to take it for granted. I see your crew has started repainting part of the superstructure. Some of my men can help."

"Well, that would speed things along." Zikri gave an ironic smile. "Assuming it is not beneath their dignity as men of war."

Hurtubise leaned forward. "Captain, I will tell you something. It is not beneath *my* dignity to deceive my enemies. So my men will do whatever possible to cause doubt or confusion among those who pursue us. Whether the men's dignity is scratched"—he made a deprecating gesture—"it will be repaired as soon as they are paid."

The captain made an exaggerated bow. "*Monsieur*, I salute your sense of priorities."

72

Strategic Solutions did not have a facility that anyone would recognize as a "situation room." But the company boardroom often was strewn with easels and maps for reference to far-flung operations, and such was the case at the moment.

Frank Leopole had taped a map of the Mediterranean and northwestern Africa to a cork board appropriated for that purpose. He referred to the colored pins depicting *Don Carlos*'s known location and *Tarabulus Pride*'s estimated position. "Our guys are in a good position to intercept the target vessel when it clears Gibraltar. That should be sometime today."

Sandy Carmichael looked at the map. She pointed a polished fingernail. "Cadiz to Tangier must be—what? Only fifty miles or so?"

"Less, I think. The trouble will be sorting out the *Tarabulus* from all the other ships in the area. Pope seems to think that could take a couple of days or more."

"Really? Why's that? Don't they have photos?"

The operations chief nodded. "Yeah. Cohen's contacts got digital images in Misratah and e-mailed them to him. But there's just a lot of shipping in that area, Sandy. Somebody said a couple hundred a day. And Alex thinks the Libyans might change the *Tarabulus*'s appearance. New name, false flag, maybe even false structures. Sort of like the Q ships in World War I."

She cocked her head. "Q ships?"

"They were armed vessels disguised as merchantmen. A U-boat would see a lone ship, surface and close in to gun range to save torpedoes. Then the Q ship would drop its facade and blast the sub."

"What's the Q stand for?"

"Nobody knows," a familiar voice said. Carmichael and Leopole turned to see Derringer in the door. He was almost smiling. "I checked Wikipedia and a couple of other sites a while back. It's still a mystery after all this time," he added.

Carmichael looked back at the map. "Well, I still don't understand how our team is going to ID the target ship. It's like we said before: we're relying on Alex Cohen and we don't know much about his sources."

Derringer walked to the board and took in the situation. "I'm not too worried yet. I know our skipper, Gerritt Maas. I met him during a NATO tour, and he's tops. I wasn't surprised when I learned he was working for the company."

"But, Admiral, if the captain has to rely on Cohen for all his intel, we're no better off, are we?"

"Sandy, I don't think that Gerritt would limit himself to one source, especially on a major operation like this. I've avoided bothering him other than to say we'll lend any help we can provide. But trust me: with his knowledge and contacts, if Cohen falls through, Captain Maas will have a Plan Bravo and a Charlie as well."

Carmichael folded her arms, obviously unconvinced. "I'd feel better if we knew more about the intel on this op. If Dave Dare can't turn up something, you know it's deep."

Derringer flipped the North Atlantic with a forefinger. "It's a big ocean, Sandy. We should have lots of time."

M/V *DON CARLOS*

Pope stood before the combined teams, jotting notes on a white board in the crew galley. He wore khaki Navy swim trunks, a sleeveless sweater, and Nikes. The space was empty except for the SSI operators. Chatter abated as the audience caught his serious demeanor.

"All right, people, listen up. I want to go over the contingencies that I've drafted with the captain. Like any special op, this is one has low prospects for total success but I think we stand a good chance of achieving the primary goal, which is intercepting the yellow cake."

He turned to the list he had penned on the board. "Best case: we achieve surprise, take the ship without casualties, and put our prize crew aboard. They sail it to a neutral port, depending on where the intercept is made, and we disappear. We could be back home in less than seventy-two hours." He checkmarked the first item.

"More likely: we get aboard, meet resistance, and shoot our way to the bridge and engine room. After some time, we own the ship, evacuate our casualties, and come on home." He crossed off that item.

"Case three: we get aboard but there's a standoff. We can't get to the critical areas but the opposition can't push us off. At that point I'd probably put an EOD guy over the side to disable the screw. The ship goes dead in the water, this vessel comes to 'render assistance' "—he etched quote marks in midair—"and rigs a tow. At that point the bad guys probably would surrender. If for some reason they scuttle, we step off and come home. Mr. Langevin would take charge of the salvage operation, assuming there is one." Another check mark.

"Case four: we can't get aboard or can't gain a foothold. That's a tough one, guys. We don't know for sure what's aboard, but Mr. Cohen's sources seem to think they have automatic weapons and some kind of explosives."

Several of the operators turned toward Cohen, seated in the middle of the group. He remained expressionless, looking straight ahead.

"Getting off the ship, under fire, means losses. There's just no way around it. We'd probably have to leave the critical cases, and as much as that galls any of us, that's how it has to be. There's no point losing men who may have to come back and try again."

"Sir." Breezy raised his hand.

"Yes, Brezyinski."

"I have some medic training. I'd be willing to stay with any WIAs."

Pope scratched his bald head. He noticed some other men looking at the former Ranger. "Well, that's very generous of you. We'll just have to leave that decision until it happens."

Pope returned to the board. "Now, at that point we still might have a card to play. If it's apparent that we can't board or stay on deck, I'll call or signal one of the boat crews. They'll try to place charges around the rudder or near the screw before we leave. It's a low-percentage shot but it's still an option." Another check mark.

"Case five: actually, from our view it's better than case four. We're spotted inbound, take fire, and cannot close the target. At that point we break off and come back here."

"What then?" Malten asked.

"I don't know right now, Jeff. I suspect that one of the DDs or frigates in the area would take overt action rather than let the yellow cake get away."

"That's illegal, isn't it? High seas and all that."

Pope's heavy-lidded eyes seemed to light up. "To paraphrase Chairman Mao, 'Legality grows from the barrel of a gun.'"

Bosco could not suppress his enthusiasm. "Break out the jolly roger, Cap'n. Show 'em our true colors." Obviously his arm wound from Chad wasn't hindering him.

Breezy adopted a Wallace Beery scowl. "Arrr, matey, arrr . . ."

Pope resumed speaking. "For now, let's say we get aboard. Once we have more than a couple of men on deck, we're pretty much committed. A retrograde movement off a ship is a losing proposition."

He picked up a timer used to detonate explosives. It resembled a miniature cooking timer, variable to sixty seconds. "We'll have breaching charges to blow the hinges off any dogged hatches. Each team has an EOD tech, but I want each of you familiar with these gadgets. Remember: mainly we want control of the bridge and the engine room. If the bad guys are holed up somewhere else, we can probably just contain them. Get them out later.

"Now, we have a minimum crew to put aboard once we control the ship. At that time the *Don Carlos* will come alongside, transfer the 'prize crew,' and proceed, assuming there's no engineering casualty."

"What kind of casualty?" Pace asked.

"Engineering. If the engine is damaged or the rudder's jammed, something like that. In which case we'll have to rig a tow—slow going but it can be done. At that point, depending on where we are, we'll make for a neutral port. With a U.S. Navy warship escort."

Tom Pfizer, a former SEAL, was impressed. He asked, "How'd you arrange that, sir?"

"I didn't. The admiral did. There's two frigates available: the *Woodul* in the Med and the *Powell* off Gibraltar. I understand that the *Millikin* might be rounding the cape sometime this month, too. Additionally, there are two frigates that could be detached from an exercise with Spain—*Greenberg* and *Helfers*."

"Wouldn't it be easier just to have one ship tail us?"

"Yeah, but that could draw attention. And if we actually chase the yellow cake all the way around the Horn of Africa, that ship probably will need to fuel somewhere."

Pope surveyed his audience once more: an assembly of serious, focused young men who belonged to the same guild, having paid mostly the same dues to gain membership. The only exceptions were Bosco and Breezy, typically laughing and scratching. "All right," Pope concluded. "If there's nothing else for now, we'll break it off. Continue checking gear, especially the Zodiacs. Boat captains, take over." He nodded toward Jeff Malten, Tom Pfizer, and Geoff Pascoe.

As Malten started to leave, Pope beckoned him aside. "Jeff, I'd like your take on Bosco and Breezy: I can't always tell them apart. They seem to feed off each other."

Malten laughed. "I had the same trouble in Pakistan. Bosco's about two inches taller, otherwise they're interchangeable Army pukes to me."

"This afternoon I saw them clowning in the galley. They're taken to wearing kerchiefs on their heads and one of them got an earring from someplace. Next thing you know, they'll have a peg leg and a parrot on one shoulder."

"Yeah," Malten said, chuckling. "They've started saying things like 'Avast!' and 'Aye, Cap'n,' and saluting with two fingers. Breezy even got the lyrics to 'Fifteen Men on a Dead Man's Chest.' I think they've seen too many pirate movies."

"They act like frat boys," Pope said. "Frankly, it makes me a little nervous. I'm thinking of putting them on two of the M-60s."

Malten's eyebrows raised. "I know they come across as juvenile delinquents sometimes. But don't sell them short: they're real serious after the kickoff."

Pope glanced down while rubbing his bald head. "Well, I admit it surprised me when Breezy volunteered as a stay-behind medic. He may be some kind of surfer dude, but he doesn't strike me as a grandstander."

"He's not. Like I said, I worked with both of them on the last op in Pakistan and Afghanistan. They're solid when we're in contact."

"You mean when there's lead in the air?"

Malten kept a straight face. He rendered a two-finger salute and uttered a throaty, "Aye, Cap'n."

"Now don't *you* start that!" Pope made a shooing motion. "See to your boat, Mr. Malten."

"Aye, Cap'n."

73

M/V *TARABULUS PRIDE*

Hurtubise motioned to Zikri in the galley. They went to a far table and sat down. "We need to have a more definite plan if we are intercepted."

The captain said, "I thought you would fight off any attempt to board."

"That depends on the attacker. If we are hailed by a warship, we do not have many options, do we?"

"Well, no. Other than surrender, there are only two choices: fight or scuttle. If we fight, we lose. If we scuttle, we lose. From my view, it would be far better to stop and let them search. There is a chance they might not find all the yellow cake."

"But you said we were unlikely to be stopped by a warship," the Frenchman reminded him.

"Yes, that's right. We are exercising legitimate right of passage. Where possible, I will keep within the territorial limits of each country we pass. The Americans have no authority there—even less than in the open sea."

Hurtubise bit his lip in concentration. "Very well, then. We are most likely to be intercepted by an American or Israeli commercial ship, with naval commandos." He paused, considering the likelihood. "We have a good chance of beating them off, but they may chase us."

Zikri gave an indifferent shrug. "They can chase us all they like. As long as we are in international waters, and they cannot actually stop us, all they can do is follow."

"Well, what could they do to stop us?"

"If they cannot put a boarding party on deck?"

Hurtubise nodded.

"Maybe they would try to disable our rudder or propeller, but to do that they have to get very close. They must have no deck guns or heavy weapons. Maybe if they have rocket launchers . . ."

"No, they cannot get that close. Our machine guns and RPGs would rip their speedboats apart." Hurtubise thought for a moment. "What else could they do?"

"I cannot think of anything else. Unless . . . well, maybe they would ram us."

"With their own ship?" Hurtubise asked.

Zikri's eyes went to the vinyl tabletop, then back to the Frenchman's. "It is possible. But that is no guarantee they could stop us. They might only dent some plates."

"Could they disable your steering by collision?"

Zikri did not like the direction the conversation was turning, but he tried to remain objective. "Perhaps. But it is unlikely. You see, our stern overhangs the rudder and propeller. They would have to ram us very hard from just the right angle to have a chance. And I would be maneuvering to avoid them."

"So that could go on for a long time?"

"Yes, yes."

Hurtubise tapped the table in a momentary pique. Finally he said, "If they get that close to us, I could turn my RPGs on them. I doubt that they have anything comparable, and after we put a few grenades on their bridge, they will have to respect us. That should keep them at least a hundred meters away."

"Would your grenades be effective against a ship?"

"They cannot sink a ship. But the warheads are powerful enough to penetrate a tank's armor. So . . . ordinary steel plate?" He snapped his fingers with a surprisingly loud *pop*.

"But they could still follow us indefinitely."

"Then we are back to where we began," Hurtubise replied. "As you said before, let them follow us to Iran if they like."

Before Zikri could reply, Hurtubise pursued another subject. "With so many men repainting the ship, we are starting to look different already. Now, what identity have you found for us?"

The captain touched the side of his nose in an exaggerated gesture of confidentiality. "We have many flags to fly. But the blue and white paint fits Greece so I have decided on a new name. *Star of Hellas.*"

"Is there such a ship?"

"Yes and no. That is the beauty of the name. There was such a vessel a few years ago, but apparently she was sold for scrap. However, that name still appears on some registries. Anybody who checks closely will learn the facts, but it will take time. Meanwhile, I have a man over the stern, painting the new name right now."

"Greece," Hurtubise mused. "I have been there only twice. I didn't much care for ouzo."

Zikri leaned against the back of his chair, adopting a relaxed posture. "Well, *mon ami*, whatever you like to drink, I suggest that you finish it before we get to Iran. You will find my Shia friends far less tolerant than I am."

M/V *DON CARLOS*

Pope finished the briefing and set down his marker. He folded his brawny arms and looked around the room. Fifteen operators stared back at him. He decided not to comment on Breezy's and Bosco's attire: both wore pirate-style kerchiefs on their heads. Bosco even had an improvised eye patch. Green grinned; Pace yawned.

"There's not much else to say," Pope stated. "I'm certainly not going to give you guys a pep talk. In the first place, you don't need it, and in the second place, you'd resent the hell out of it. But I do want to say just a bit about how I feel about this mission."

He glanced at the deck, then looked up again. "I think we're engaged in a battle for Western civilization. No, I don't think it's going to be settled tonight. This is a long-term commitment, probably for generations. After all, the Crusades lasted two hundred years and the Moors occupied Spain for about eight hundred. I see myself as one man among other men—you guys. Whatever happens to me tonight, there's no place I'd rather be and nothing else I'd rather be doing.

"That's enough oration. Now, let's ruck up and get going."

———

Gerritt Maas spoke with Pope, Malten, and Cohen on the bridge. Tapping the Feruni color radar display, the skipper pointed out nearby ships. "You should not have much trouble identifying the target. These two are well to the south and not in your intercept area." He noted another blip nearby. "This big one is a supertanker, at least one hundred thousand tons. Depending on whether it maintains course, you might use it to cover your approach to *Tarabulus*."

The captain touched the display to indicate another large vessel. "This is probably a container ship. If you match its speed for a while, you might get within one or two miles before you break out of the radar coverage of the tanker." He looked at Pope. "That's up to you, of course. I will monitor your frequency the full time."

Alex Cohen added, "I'll be in the radio room the full time. If I hear anything unusual, I'll pass the word to you immediately."

Don Carlos's executive officer stood behind the operators. "Captain, we also have light signals in case radio communication fails."

"Yes, yes," Maas responded. "I am glad you reminded us, Carl." He looked at Pope and Malten again. "I think our main concern will be finding anyone overboard or a lost Zodiac. We will flash a Morse Code DC. You do the same."

"Delta Charlie," Malten replied. "Dah-dit-dit, dah-dit-dah-dit?"

The Dutchman smiled around his pipe stem. "I don't know! I haven't used Morse since I was a cadet."

Then he turned somber. "Good luck, gentlemen. And good hunting."

M/V *TARABULUS PRIDE*

"There's a quarter moon," Zikri said. "I think they would prefer a dark night."

"That's what I would choose," Hurtubise agreed. "But we don't know their schedule. They may want to take us closer to friendly ports around Gibraltar."

"Well, no matter. I set the duty watch already. With some of my men as lookouts as well as yours, we should be all right."

The mercenary hefted a night-vision device. "We cannot count on radar picking up their boats very far away. So I gave my men some extra night vision." He raised the commercial product, a three-power NZT-35 monocular.

"How good is that?"

"This? It's supposed to be good to something over a hundred meters. It's waterproof besides. But the trouble with the old Soviet devices is that you never know how much tube life is left. Any of them could quit on you at any time—probably when you need it most."

The Frenchman hefted another model. "This model with third-generation technology is good to three hundred meters." He almost laughed. "It costs about thirteen dollars per meter."

Zikri had thought out his steaming plan for the night. "I can continue zigzagging as you wish. Or we can do random direction changes. Either way, it will not be very easy for small craft to track us. They can't see very much, riding so low."

"Well, all we need is some warning. We can put up a barrage of flares and use the machine guns and RPGs. Once we open fire, nobody's going to keep coming in a rubber boat. It would be suicide. We're on a much more stable platform than they are."

The Libyan leaned back against the plotting table. "What do you want to do after we repel their attack? Surely they won't try the boats again."

"At that point, they probably will back off, at least for a while. Unless they have a plan that Cochon and I have not considered, they will either let us go or they will turn to the Navy."

"I agree," Zikri said. "And we can enter almost any port and wait out their warships if we have to."

Hurtubise turned to the map. "What do you recommend?"

"Oh, almost anywhere once we're south of Western Sahara. It's still occupied by Morocco, yes?"

"Correct. That means it's probably friendly to America."

"Well then," the seaman continued, "just look at the options. Senegal, Gambia, Guinea, Sierra Leone. Considering the diplomatic situation, Liberia and Nigeria and Ghana may not be such good choices, but after that we have the Côte d'Ivoire and Benin. On and on down the continent."

Hurtubise gave an exaggerated sigh. "This is turning into a very long trip."

"Cheer up, my friend. A long sea cruise is good for your health!"

M/V *DON CARLOS*

"Where's Pope?" Pfizer asked. "We're ready to go."

Malten thought he knew, but kept the information to himself. "Uh, I think he's with the captain. I'll go check."

The team leader trotted down the passageway to the berthing area and undogged a hatch. He peeked inside the compartment and found what he suspected.

Victor Pope was kneeling beside his bunk, rosary in hand. Malten was struck by the seeming incongruity: a muscular, bald young man in his late thirties, bedecked with tactical gear, his submachine gun resting beside him. Malten withdrew a few steps around the corner but could hear Pope's low baritone reciting the ancient words.

"Ave Maria, gratia plena, Dominus tecum. Benedicta tu in mulieribus, et benedictus fructus ventris tui, Iesus. Sancta Maria, Mater Dei, ora pro nobis peccatoribus, nunc, et in hora mortis nostrae. Amen."

He still uses Latin, Malten realized. *None of the modern recitation for him.*

After a few seconds of silence, Malten risked another peek. He saw Pope cross himself, kiss the crucifix, and tuck it inside his shirt.

Malten backed up several steps and rapped loudly on the hatch. "Vic? You in here?"

Pope stepped through the hatchway. "I was just taking a minute for myself."

"I hope you said one for me." The younger operator kept any levity from his voice.

Pope cocked his head slightly. "You're allowed to pray for yourself, Jeff."

"Don't need to," Malten replied. His tone now was flippant. He tapped Pope's vest with the back of his hand. "I got you, babe."

"Let's rock," Pope said.

"Let's roll."

———

In the dim light of the bridge, the screens glowed according to their purpose. Mostly green for data; color radar for navigation and weather. Awaiting a last-minute position report to confirm the target's position for the raiders, Maas paced until Cohen arrived.

The SSI operative stepped onto the bridge. "Captain, we got it. I just received confirmation."

Maas turned to face Cohen. "Well?"

Cohen was momentarily taken aback. He had not expected jubilation, but he did anticipate some degree of enthusiasm. "Same speed and course as before. And it's definite now. They've finished repainting most of the superstructure and the stack, and they changed the name." He held out a message form with the information penciled in block letters.

The captain accepted the paper, read it twice, and set it down. "I will stay here until our people return. You can tell them the news."

Cohen looked at the Dutch seaman. The man's eyes were mostly concealed in shadow amid the subdued lighting. Cohen realized that reflection on the windows could detract from visibility, but for a man who had spent much of his life in the desert, the shipboard ambience was cavelike, eerie. "What's the matter, Captain?"

"The same thing as before, Mr. Cohen. You are forcing me to send four small craft in harm's way based only on your information, which you refuse to explain to me or to them." He paused, wondering if the younger man could be moved by such sentiment. When he drew no response, he continued. "I do not like the arrangement any more now than before. Less, in fact."

Cohen shifted his feet, less from the ship's motion than from resentment at being challenged again. "Why less?"

Maas inclined his head toward the Zodiacs on deck. "Because in a few minutes those boys are going on a mission that could turn sour. That's why."

"Captain, if the information is wrong, that's my fault, not yours. Our operators know that. They accept it. But my sources are too sensitive to risk, so there's no option but to continue as planned."

Sources. Plural. Does he really have more than one? While Maas was formulating a reply, Cohen turned and walked off the bridge.

Don Carlos continued on course through the dark.

75

"Frank, we just got an encrypted e-mail from Alex Cohen. Pope and Malten's teams are going in right now." Sandy Carmichael's southern accent smoothed over the emotional ridges she felt.

Leopole looked at the wall clock. "They're near the Canaries? It's 2135 here; plus four is 0135 there. Did he say when they'll board?"

"No. Just that the boats are in the water. I'd imagine they're several miles out."

Omar Mohammed, ordinarily the soul of composure, was sharing the watch. He surprised his two colleagues by biting the nail of his ring finger. "I wonder who else he's told."

"What's that?" Carmichael asked.

The elegant Iranian caught himself and dropped his hand to the table. "I am just wondering out loud, Sandra. I am sorry, but I just do not trust Cohen yet. Oh, I don't mean he would send our people into unnecessary danger. Nothing like that. But he may be communicating with Tel Aviv and who knows who else."

Carmichael pulled out a chair and sat down. "Well, he's certainly not telling State or DoD. This whole thing is about deniability."

"Yeah," Leopold said. "I guess we don't need to call O'Connor or anybody else until we know what happens."

Carmichael gave him a tight grin. "Small favors, Frank. That's up to the admiral or Marsh Wilmont."

Several laden moments ticked by. Finally Leopold spoke. "Damn. I feel like Ike on D-Day."

Mohammed eyed him. "The waiting?"

Leopole nodded. "Once you've pushed the button, all you can do is wait for the machine to go to work. I think we've built a pretty damn good machine. But there's always some cog waiting out there to foul it up."

76

AFRICAN COAST

The four combat raiding craft sped away from *Don Carlos* on a southerly heading. As Pope plotted the relative positions of his ship and the target, he would maintain 190 true for nine miles. Presumably there would be no return trip, since the plan called for Maas to rendezvous with *Tarabulus Pride* once she was secured.

Meanwhile, Maas planned to keep *Don Carlos* to seaward of *Tarabulus*, lest she veer westward and try to lose her pursuers in the expanse of the North Atlantic.

In the lead Zodiac, Pope kept a constant watch on the other three craft, conned by Jeff Malten, Tom Pfizer, and Geoffrey Pascoe, late of Her Majesty's Special Boat Service.

Pope could think of nothing else to be done. Now he was focused on the unfolding mission. He turned to the former Force Recon Marine at the stern of the CRRC and motioned slightly to port. He wanted to compensate for the southwesterly Canary Current that predominated off the Moroccan coast.

M/V *DON CARLOS*

"There's the first one," Maas said, pointing out the blip on the radar screen. "And there's the others."

Alex Cohen took in the display, noting the transponder codes indicating each Zodiac. "It sure simplifies things on a dark night," he offered.

"Umm." Maas did not enjoy conversing with the Israeli-American. But they were both professionals, accustomed to putting aside personal opinions in favor of accomplishing a mission.

Cohen sought a way to ease the tension between them. He had to admit that he would feel much the same as Maas if their roles were reversed. "Which is the target, Captain?"

"Same as before," Maas said. Immediately he regretted his choice of words. Cohen could not be expected to keep a changing radar picture in his head after leaving the bridge to see the raiders on their way. The skipper touched an image almost straight ahead, just inside the ten-mile circle. "It's keeping course and speed. Our boys should overtake her in about ten minutes."

"How well can they see a Zodiac on a night like this?"

Maas shot a sideways glance at the SSI man. He recognized the question for what it was: a peace offering of sorts.

"Same as we can, Mr. Cohen. With the naked eye, maybe a hundred meters or so if the boats stay out of the reflected moonlight. But Pope thinks they'll have night vision. Depending on how good—two or three hundred meters."

"That makes it hard to take them by surprise."

"It certainly does."

AFRICAN COAST

Idling in the waves, compensating for the Zodiac's motion, Malten glassed the merchantman off the port bow. His five-power night-vision binoculars provided a green glimpse of the nocturnal world. He turned toward Pope in the nearest rubber craft. "Looks like part of the name is *Hellas*. Hard to tell about the flag. I guess it'd be Greek."

"Well, that's the info Cohen gave us. I still think the only way he could know that is from somebody on board. Mossad must've bribed somebody."

"I just hope he stays bribed," Malten replied.

Pope nodded and pulled his balaclava over his face. Green did not know Pope well enough to insult him about possible shine off his bald head, but Malten recognized that was exactly why the leader wore the trademark commando garment. Pope gave the signal and the boats deployed as briefed: one off each quarter, one astern, and one farther astern as backup.

Bouncing through the water, taking salt spray that spattered on their goggles and roughened their lips, the operators kept their focus on the objective. From 250 meters out, they tried to discern whether anybody was visible on deck. It was no good—the rough, tossing motion of the Zodiacs precluded a clear picture of the objective.

The coxswains opened the throttles and four outboard motors whined.

M/V *TARABULUS PRIDE*

René Pinsard had never fought a battle at sea. For that matter, neither had anyone else aboard, but the mercenary did not object to the prospect. He accepted Zikri and Hurtubise's assessment that an interception was likely in the more confined waters between the Canaries and the Moroccan coast, and therefore stationed himself in the most favorable position. He stood beside the stern machine-gun mount overlooking the stern, night-vision device in hand.

The gunner, a man of indeterminate age and French-Algerian extraction, stifled a yawn. He stamped his feet as if to keep warm, though the night air was almost pleasant. "Three more hours," he said, ruefully acknowledging that he had drawn the longest watch of the night.

"Suit yourself," Pinsard replied. "I'm going to stay here until after dawn. They won't try to attack in daylight."

"Speedboat to starboard!"

The call came from somewhere forward. Immediately, hired guns and hired sailors crowded the rail, looking to seaward. As practiced, a quiet alarm sped through the ship, sending men to their stations.

Hurtubise found Pinsard looking to port.

"Situation," the leader demanded.

"There's a small boat out there maybe two hundred meters, slowly pulling ahead of us," Pinsard explained. "I think it's a diversion. It makes more sense for an attack from this side, so they're not silhouetted."

Hurtubise looked toward Africa and slapped his friend on the back. "I agree. They'll blend into the shore." He paused long enough to admire the professionalism of the intruders, then moved to deal with them.

"There! Two boats behind us!"

A Libyan sailor, augmenting Hurtubise's shooters, spotted unnatural dark shapes near the wake. Shapes that did not belong there. One of the Frenchmen picked up a flare gun but Hurtubise stayed his arm. "Not yet."

"But, Marcel, they're almost close enough . . ."

"Not yet!" Hurtubise raised his voice in a calculated combination of authority and anger.

Pinsard lowered his Russian night goggles and called over his shoulder. "Marcel! There's one out there on my side. Maybe 150 meters."

Hurtubise visualized the geometry of the developing situation. In military terms, a multi-axis attack calculated to split his defenses. He suspected that at the last moment two or more of the boats would converge on one point and try to gain local superiority.

It was what he would do.

AFRICAN COAST

It was time for a command decision.

Pacing the ship to port, Victor Pope ran a last-minute communications check. "Flipper One is up. Check and go."

"Two. Clear to go."

"Three. Looks good, Boss."

"Four. Go."

Satisfied that his boat captains saw no sign of danger, Pope accepted their assessment. Keeping the tension out of his voice, he said, "Stand by. Stand by. Execute!"

Pope, Malten, and Pascoe turned their CRRCs toward the target.

78

M/V *TARABULUS PRIDE*

On the bridge, Captain Abu Yusuf Zikri paced from port to starboard and back again. Acutely aware that he could not see what was happening behind him, he had to rely on cryptic, often unintelligible calls from Hurtubise and his European hirelings.

"All ahead full," he ordered the engine room. Though he had no chance of escaping the Zodiacs, at least he could prolong their approach and thereby render them more vulnerable.

The Libyan noticed the helmsman and navigator watching him closely—more than he liked. *I am behaving like a nervous woman*, he realized. He stopped pacing and adopted as dignified a demeanor as he could manage. Ordinarily he would open up on the international emergency frequency and request help before he was boarded. But under the circumstances, being found hauling contraband uranium ore to Iran did not seem a career-enhancing option.

He placed his trust in Marcel Hurtubise and his gunmen.

Overlooking the stern, Hurtubise and Pinsard deployed their men to repel boarders. In frustration, Pinsard shook his NVG. "This damned thing is no damned good! It's whiting out!" In frustration he tossed it overboard.

"Too many tube hours," Hurtubise commented calmly. He handed his commercial optic to Pinsard, who scanned to port. "There they are! Three coming this way."

"Let me see," Hurtubise said.

Activating the device, Hurtubise took in the situation, then set it down. "We can ignore the boat to starboard. The threat is here."

He turned toward the stern machine gunner. "Prepare to fire." The French-Algerian mercenary tugged the MAG-58's charging handle twice.

Hurtubise looked around. Two RPG shooters were nearby. Almost with disgust in his voice, Hurtubise nudged Pinsard and pointed to the men. *"Merde!"* Pinsard exclaimed. Shoving two automatic riflemen farther forward, he screamed, "You imbeciles! Get the hell out of the way of the RPGs!" One or both would have been seared the instant the rocket-propelled grenades were fired.

Meanwhile, Hurtubise had taken the flare gun from one of his men. Holding the pistol overhead, he began a countdown. "When you see them, fire!"

———

Fifty meters out, Victor Pope realized that he was holding his breath. There was very little illumination on the ship's stern—only the required navigation lights. He took that as a good sign.

Then the world turned garish-white as a parachute flare erupted overhead.

In the second boat, Jeff Malten thought that his heart skipped a beat. "We've been made!" Without awaiting orders, he directed his coxswain to reverse course.

Automatic weapons fire erupted from the port quarter of *Tarabulus Pride*. None of the initial volleys were on target, but many were close. The water was spumed with geysers as bullets impacted around the Zodiacs.

Two smoke trails leapt outward from the ship. Both struck the waves within meters of the lead boat. "Christ! They've got RPGs!" Victor Pope did not even realize that he had just committed blasphemy.

Pope's boat and Pascoe's were closest to the ship. Men in the bows returned fire with their MP-5s, more for morale than for effect, as the Zodiacs swerved to escape the fusillade.

By then, Hurtubise had reloaded and launched another parachute flare. The sea was turned into a black-and-white film: garish overhead lights burning with phosphorescent intensity, clashing starkly with the dark waves while red tracer rounds scythed the sea.

Before Pascoe's boat could get out of the way, the shipboard gunner got a quick sight picture and fired. Once the tracers entered the Zodiac, the shooter held the trigger down.

Three men were hit: Pace was knocked overboard almost before anyone noticed. One operator took a grazing round to a leg. But another man, a former Ranger named Peter Chadburn, took two rounds through the torso. His body armor was not proof against armor-piercing ammo. Green dropped his weapon and began removing the man's gear, trying to render first aid. In the jostling, water-swept craft, it was almost impossible.

In Pope's boat, Bosco and Breezy returned fire as the CRRC sped away. Each emptied his magazine, reloaded, and stared at each other, wide-eyed and gasping for breath.

79

M/V *DON CARLOS*

"What in hell happened?" Cohen asked.

From the cryptic chatter on the tactical circuit, Cohen had a decent idea of what had gone wrong. But he needed more information before sending the bad news to Arlington.

Victor Pope unslung his MP-5 and handed it to Breezy. Then he stalked up to the Israeli and prodded him with a gloved finger. "I think I'm the one to ask that question, Cohen. They were ready for us and we lost people! Now you tell *me* what the hell happened."

Cohen stood his ground, glaring at Pope. "Nothing went out from this ship except the e-mail to SSI that the op was under way. It was sent in the company's encryption program so there was no breach." He inhaled, exhaled, and willed himself to stare down the former SEAL. He modulated his voice, aware of the slight tremor.

"Come on, Vic. I need to send the preliminary report."

"You can talk to somebody else. I'm going back to look for Pace."

Cohen raised a placating hand. "Vic, come on. Just give me the basics. Of course you can look for him. Hell, I'll go with you. But I need to confirm what I heard. One dead, one missing, and one wounded."

A terse nod of the bald head. "Correct."

Jeff Malten overheard the dispute while supervising the retrieval of two Zodiacs. He was tempted to let Pope continue arguing with Cohen but thought better of it. "Vic, I don't know how long Pfizer can keep searching. Do you want to refuel your boat? Pascoe's needs serious repairs, probably more than we can do, and my motor took a round."

Pope thought for a moment. At length he said, "All right. Jeff, you take mine. Tell Tom that you'll relieve him, but work out a search pattern that doesn't duplicate his area."

"Will do. Oh. What shall we do with Chadburn's body?"

"Uh . . . take him to the freezer, I guess. I'll confirm that when I talk to the captain."

Malten disappeared forward, where Pascoe's shot-up CRRC was hauled aboard.

Pope tugged off his gloves and began unbuckling his gear. As he brushed past Cohen he croaked, "You come with me."

SSI OFFICES

Sandy Carmichael delivered the news.

"We just heard from Vic Pope. Here's the text, quote: 'CRRC attack 0220 local failed. One KIA, one WIA, one MIA. Regrouping. Unodir will attempt later today. Require highest priority msg to DDs this area deliver at least two 7.62 miniguns this ship. Send op-immediate. Advise soonest.' "

Marshall Wilmont asked, "What's 'unodir'?"

Leopole almost grinned. "Unless otherwise directed. It means he's taking the responsibility and doesn't want to hear 'no' from us."

Wilmont still seemed perplexed. "So what do we do?"

"We wake up the secretary of the Navy," Mohammed interjected.

Derringer spoke up. "To hell with him. We'll wake up SecDef. In fact, let me do it." He strode toward his office.

Leopole checked the clock again. "That was barely an hour ago. But I doubt they'll be able to try again before dawn, which means at least twenty-four hours more." He looked at Carmichael. "With the ship alerted now, it's going to be even harder than before."

Carmichael sat down and braced her chin on her hands. Her voice was barely a whisper. "I wonder who's dead."

M/V *TARABULUS PRIDE*

"We've beaten them!" René Pinsard's volubility bubbled to the surface of his normal sangfroid. "They won't dare try it again."

Hurtubise made one more scan of the dark ocean, then set down his NVD. "Not tonight, I wouldn't think. But we will take nothing for granted. Keep at least half the men on watch until dawn."

"All right. As you wish, Marcel." Pinsard's tone was plain: he considered the crisis at an end.

The mercenary chief leaned against a bulkhead and rubbed his chin. It was stubbled, as usual. Sometimes he thought he might grow a beard, but that required trimming and grooming. Easier just to shave whenever he felt like it.

He looked closely at Pinsard. "Think, René. Put yourself in their place. What would you do now?"

Pinsard pondered for a long moment. At length he said, "The only option I can think of would involve helicopters, and apparently they do not have any."

"Very well. Suppose they get helicopters. How would you deal with them?"

The younger man patted a MAG-58 on its improvised mount. "Automatic weapons will keep them away. Too bad we do not have any SAMs, but we could not anticipate everything." He paused, then added, "But we still have some RPGs."

Hurtubise nodded. "Keep two teams on alert, and keep all the guns manned. It's still a long damned way to Iran." He straightened himself and began walking forward.

"Where are you going?" Pinsard called out.

Hurtubise stopped and turned briefly. "I am going to ask some very pointed questions."

M/V *DON CARLOS*

"Flipper One, this is Four. Over."

"That's him!" Pope exclaimed. On the bridge, standing beside Maas, he pressed his hand against his headset. "Four, One here. Go."

Pfizer's voice came back, subdued and tentative. "Ah, be advised. We recovered the, uh, item. Over."

Even on the dimly lit deck, Cohen could see Pope's eyes close and his lips move. *He's praying.*

"One here. RTB, Four."

"Roger that." Pfizer went off the air with chilling finality.

Cohen asked, "My God, how'd they find him in the dark?"

"Our PFDs have strobe lights on them. They're water-activated."

The SSI men and Maas were still consulting when the last Zodiac pulled alongside. Looking down from the glass-enclosed bridge, Pope felt a dreadful sense of responsibility. Without a word, he walked through the access and headed amidships, where Pfizer was holding position at the accommodation ladder.

When the former SEAL arrived, Phil Green was helping move Don Pace's body on a wire litter. It was not easy: it took four men to carry the load. Pope placed a hand on Green's shoulder. "You can take him to the freezer, Phil. I'll be there as soon as I can."

Malten knew Pope's meaning. *He's going to say a prayer over him.*

When the litter bearers set down their burden, Green said, "I'll take it from here."

Bosco knelt beside the ex-cop. "I'll be glad to help."

Green shook his head. "No. He's my friend."

When he rose, Bosco gave his colleague a squeeze on the arm. *We're not really friends yet but we got shot at together. That means a lot.*

As Bosco stepped through the access, Green turned his head. "Hey."

"Yeah?"

"Tell Pope, whatever's going down, I'm in."

Bosco silently nodded, then closed the door behind him.

M/V *TARABULUS PRIDE*

"How did they find us?" Hurtubise demanded.

Zikri almost rocked back on his heels. "I do not know, *monsieur*. But we . . ."

"They had to have a source on this ship. It's the only way I can imagine they picked us out of all the ships in this part of the ocean."

"I agree," the Libyan replied. "We should talk to Aujali again."

"Where is he?"

"He came off duty about ninety minutes ago. He must be in his cabin or maybe the galley."

"Come on," Hurtubise said. "And bring your cousin."

Four minutes later, Nuri Aujali landed on his face in a vacant compartment. Shatwan dogged the hatch and leaned against it, arms folded. Zikri stood over the prostrate radioman, ready to translate Hurtubise's pointed questions while René Pinsard applied physical motivation to reply promptly and accurately.

Aujali screamed in pain, yammering in a high, fast voice.

"What's he say?" Hurtubise demanded. His Arabic had its limits.

Zikri turned to the Frenchman, obviously uncomfortable with the process but unwilling to interfere. "He says, he does not know why you abuse him."

"Tell him this is an object lesson. We will do far worse if he does not tell us what we want to know."

The captain translated, immediately gaining a pained, gasping consent from the suspect. "Yes, he will answer. He says the Zionists forced him to do it."

Hurtubise shook his head in mild confusion. "To do what? I have not even asked him anything."

Aujali choked out something incomprehensible. "The pain," Zikri explained. "Your man, he . . ."

Hurtubise tapped Pinsard on the shoulder. The younger mercenary released the victim and stood up. With one hand Aujali massaged his ears, reddened where Pinsard had applied hard, twisting pressure. His other hand was impaired by a broken finger. The ex-Legionnaire was disgusted: he had suffered worse for much longer in routine training exercises.

After more back and forthing, Zikri summarized. "His mother's mother's family have tried for years to leave Israel and join him in exile. They are always denied. He says the Jews keep promising to let them leave after each job he does for them. This time, two were given exit visas with a promise that the others would be released when we reach port."

Hurtubise nodded to himself. *So that explains it.* "The Jews have been blackmailing him. I wonder how many others there are."

Zikri shrugged eloquently.

The Frenchman squatted by the young man, speaking English. "You are a radioman. You understand me?"

Aujali nodded. "Yes. Some English . . ."

"How did you communicate with the Americans?"

The seaman raised himself to a sitting position on the deck. "Not with the Americans. With an Israeli."

"Who is he?"

"I do not know. He only goes by a code name."

Hurtubise's right hand snaked out, hard and fast. He slapped Aujali twice, once on each cheek. "You want to deal with René again? Tell me everything when I ask a question!"

Aujali's dark eyes betrayed all his emotions. For a man of Marcel Hurtubise's vast experience, they were easily read. Fear and anger. Basic psychology. *Anger is fear expressing itself.*

"Jacob. Only Jacob."

"Good. Very good. Now, how long have you been in contact with him? What did you tell him?"

Aujali's Arabic pride overcame some of the fear. He looked up at Zikri. "I want some water, Captain."

Zikri motioned to Shatwan, who retrieved a bottle and handed it to his colleague. Before he opened it, Aujali glanced at Pinsard, then began speaking. "I was approached by a Frenchman in Masratah. He called himself Remy LeClerc. He said he worked with Jacob and gave me the frequencies and schedule."

As Aujali sipped some water, Hurtubise's eyes narrowed. *Paul, you bastard! Working both sides of the fence!* "Describe him."

"A young man, about my age. Sandy hair, built like a wrestler."

Hurtubise looked at Pinsard. "That was Deladier. You met him in Marseille, I think."

Pinsard absorbed that information with typical aplomb. "I don't suppose I will meet him again."

"Not this side of hell."

Hurtubise rose to his feet, regarding the radioman. "We will keep this one for a while. He might be useful later on." He nodded to Shatwan, who escorted the younger man from the compartment.

Zikri finally found his voice. "What do you intend for Aujali?"

Hurtubise's eyes were shark-dull. "Do not ask stupid questions."

SSI OFFICES

They held a death watch in Arlington, Virginia.

None of the SSI officers wanted to leave without knowing which of their associates had been killed. It was nearly midnight when the next e-mail was received. "It's from Vic Pope," Leopole explained. "He must've bypassed Cohen."

"Well?" Sandy Carmichael's tone was unusual: curt, insistent.

"Don Pace is dead. They found his body."

"So that's Chadburn and Pace killed. What about Verdugo?"

"Apparently he's going to recover but he's out of action." Leopold dropped the printout on the table before Carmichael. The gesture said, *Read it yourself*.

Omar Mohammed understood the tension but wanted to defuse a potential eruption. While he admired Sandra Carmichael more than most women he had ever known, she had an Alabama country girl's feistiness. "We should let Matt Finch know. Personnel is his responsibility."

Nobody in the room knew any of the casualties well, but everyone felt a sense of responsibility. Finally, Carmichael said, "I think it'll keep 'til morning." She looked up at Leopole, who nodded agreement.

Marshall Wilmont fidgeted in his seat. He felt somehow out of place among operators and planners, even though everyone else in the room rated below him on the organizational chart. "You know, Sandy, the admiral usually contacts next of kin himself."

"Yeah, I know." She turned toward to door, as if expecting Derringer to appear. "I wonder if he's woken the SecDef yet."

M/V *TARABULUS PRIDE*

"Look at this," Zikri said.

Hurtubise looked over the Libyan's shoulder. "What is it?"

The navigation radar gave a God's eye view of the area south of the Canary Islands, operating on the ten-mile scale. Zikri fingered a blip astern of *Tarabulus Pride*. "This one has been trailing us all day. I have been watching it since dawn. Twice I sped up and slowed down, but it never varies more than two or three knots faster than we are making."

"You think it's our Jewish friends?"

Zikri gave a grunt. "*Monsieur* Hurtubise, you know that I have no Jewish friends. Or Americans. But yes, I think so. Otherwise they would have passed us, like many other ships."

"Well, what can they do? Ram us?"

"I think they would have done so by now. But then what? As you say, they are probably not going to try their rubber boats again. So we watch them. And wait."

"I have one-third my men on guard all the time. Until the Jews try something else, there is little for us to do. Now I am going back to sleep. But call me if there's any change."

Hurtubise descended the ladder from the bridge and went aft. He wanted to talk before he slept.

"René," he called to his deputy.

Pinsard was sunning himself with his feet up. Officially he was supervising the lookouts. "Yes?"

Hurtubise knelt by the reclining Frenchman. "The explosives you brought aboard—where is it stored?"

"Semtex in the aft storage locker. Caps and detonators in my compartment. Why?"

"I may want to place some quantities in the engine room and else-where down below. See me when you come off duty."

Pinsard cocked an eye at the older man. "Marcel, are you thinking of scuttling this rust bucket?"

"I am just thinking, René. But keep it to yourself."

M/V *DON CARLOS*

Pope sat down next to Maas and said, "I want to see how this ship compares to theirs."

"Well, that's not difficult. I can tell you right away that we are bigger and faster. Let me see . . ." Maas turned to his computer console and accessed a commercial shipping Web site. "*Tarabulus Pride*, right?"

"Yes."

Maas put on his glasses and his fingers flicked across the keyboard, then he hit Enter. The data and a photo appeared on the screen. "Yes, Greek construction, thirty-four hundred gross registered tons, twelve to thirteen knots. We are nearly three times her tonnage and four to five knots faster."

He raised his spectacles. "What do you have in mind?"

"Assuming she maintains ten knots, how long would it take to overtake her?"

"Oh . . . several hours. But if she sees us—and she will—she could go to full speed and prolong the chase." He paused. "Although . . ."

"Yes?"

Maas looked at the screen again. "She's rated at 12.5 knots but that's probably absolute top speed. I doubt that she can hold it indefinitely, whereas we can make fifteen all day long. Seventeen maximum."

The captain looked at Pope again, scanning for a hint on the SEAL's impassive face. "To repeat, Commander. What do you have in mind?"

Pope ignored the question. "Let's assume her mast is fifty feet above the waterline. How far is the radar horizon to us?"

Maas applied his dexterous fingers to the keyboard again. In seconds he said, "Fifteen to seventeen miles, depending on her height versus ours. That's mast height—superstructure is less, of course."

"All right," Pope replied. "Let's say she sees us hull down and identifies us. She goes to full speed at fifteen miles. With our overtake, that's about four hours to catch up."

"Correct. Commander . . ."

"Captain, could you match your speed to hers and hold position if she was maneuvering?"

"Hold how close? One hundred meters or so, probably no problem. I have an excellent helm."

"I'm thinking more like five meters or less."

Maas stood up and faced the SSI man. "Mr. Pope, what in the hell are you thinking of doing?"

M/V *TARABULUS PRIDE*

Marcel Hurtubise and René Pinsard huddled in the latter's berthing area. He pulled a box of detonators from beneath the bunk and slid them across the deck. "There you go. These are time delay. The others are command detonation."

"These will do."

"Marcel, you didn't say what you plan to do. If we're boarded, are you going to . . ."

"If we're boarded, we've probably lost," Hurtubise interrupted. "We cannot hold this ship against a determined assault if they get enough men on deck."

"No, but how would they do that? We already showed them they can't surprise us."

"Just the same, I'm planning for contingencies. I will rig some surprises for our uninvited guests. Enough to buy us some time to take action—or get away."

Pinsard wanted to ask for details, but a few years of working with

Marcel Hurtubise had proven useful in delineating certain barriers. Professional matters: almost unlimited. Personal matters: proceed at one's own risk. The present subject seemed to tread the hazy boundary between the two. "How would we get away?"

Hurtubise gave a wry grin. "The enemy may provide that for us, *mon vieux*. I would not object to hijacking one of their boats. Would you?"

"Not if that's the only way out."

Hurtubise slapped his partner on one knee. "There's always a way out, René. If you do enough thinking beforehand." He winked at the younger man, then added, "Just don't say anything to the captain. Or anyone else."

On the way out, humming loudly enough to be heard, Hurtubise exuded an air of mysterious confidence. It would be distressing to sacrifice a good lad like René, but if things turned sour, it would not be the first time that Marcel Hurtubise had faced that choice.

84

M/V *DON CARLOS*

The Sikorsky SH-60B of HSL-44 normally answered to its squadron call sign—"Magnum"—but for this operation its identity was intentionally generic. As arranged on a discreet UHF channel two hours before, the VHF transmissions would be short and cryptic.

Maas's senior watch stander was on the bridge when the Mayport-based sub hunter made its approach. "Charlie Delta, this is U.S. Navy helicopter. I am approaching your starboard quarter. Where do you want your supplies? Over."

The merchant officer glanced rearward, saw nothing, but sensed the geometry of the situation. He keyed his mike. "Ah, Navy helicopter, we are ready on the bow. Over."

Two mike clicks acknowledged the instruction. Moments later the gray Sea Hawk hove into view off the starboard beam and settled into a thirty-foot hover over the bow. The crew chief winched down three rectangular metal containers that the deckhands hauled in. Fighting the rotor wash, they disconnected the load and set each container aside. The helo then delivered a smaller box that was easier to handle.

Jeff Malten supervised the operation and quickly inspected the contents of each container. Satisfied, he stood up and waved to the HSL-44 Swamp Fox's detachment commander. The helo pilot nodded, added power, pulled pitch, and motored away.

Malten led the way into the vessel's superstructure where other SSI operators were waiting. "Are we set?" Pope asked.

"Affirmative. Three '60s and about a thousand rounds of linked ammo."

"Okay. Get 'em ready. We need to function test every one and then work out the best way to mount them."

Malten nodded, then asked, "Who do you want for shooters?"

"Whoever's the most experienced. I'll leave that to you. But keep our naval people for the boarding party."

Malten eyed his senior colleague. "Wish we had night sights. It'd be a lot quicker target acquisition."

"There's nothing we can do about that, Jeff. Besides, I think the muzzle flash will white out the NVGs. We'll just have to establish fire superiority from the start."

"Well, yeah. But if we don't, there's no way we can get aboard."

Pope slapped his friend's arm. "That's why we get the big bucks."

85

M/V *DON CARLOS*

Victor Pope made a final tour of the ship's exterior. Gerritt Maas's men had been up most of the night, fashioning mounts for the M-60s, and Jeff Malten was still supervising the test firing. They met aft of the bridge.

"How's it going?" Pope asked.

"Well, we had to headspace that one gun. Those idiots on that destroyer hadn't even bothered to do that. Obviously they hadn't tested it."

"Beggars can't be choosers, and we're the beggars."

Malten shifted his weight against the transport's roll. He was hardly aware of his movement. "Well, Admiral Derringer must've been kneeling on a pretty thick carpet. I didn't really think we'd get the guns this soon."

Pope merely nodded. Then he said, "We have thirteen healthy operators but we need at least three on the guns. I don't like trying to take down a ship with just ten guys."

"Hey, I was going to tell you. One of the crew saw what we were doing and took an interest. He even helped us degrease the '60 that hadn't been fired. Turns out that he was a Marine E-3. Think we can use him?"

"Well, yeah. I mean, is he any good?"

Malten smiled. "He had a pretty good pattern around the empty can we tossed overboard. And he doesn't lean on the trigger too much."

Pope thought for a few heartbeats. "Does he know what's likely to happen?"

"Yeah. I told him everything. The bad guys have belt-fed weapons and RPGs, and any M-60 is gonna be a priority target. But he said he spent Desert Storm afloat off Kuwait and figures this is his chance to make up."

"Well, okay. I'll talk to him. What's his name?"

"Ritter. Goes by Tex."

"Figures. Texans are like that."

Malten laughed again. "That's what I thought. But he's from Vermont."

Pope leaned against the bulkhead, arms folded. "Okay. That gives us eleven operators, unless another crewman can help."

"I talked to Dr. Faith. He says that Verdugo can stand up as long as he doesn't have to move."

"That's what Esteban said when I checked on him, but he didn't mention doing any shooting."

"Might be worth checking out," Malten offered. "We can see how he does with the gun and the mount to hold on to. That would make a dozen door-kickers."

"Let's do it." Pope turned to go, then stopped. "Oh, one other thing, Jeff. Tell the gunners that if possible, they need to stagger their firing. We don't have a lot of ammo, and there won't be any A-gunners to reload for them. I don't want everybody running dry at the same time."

Malten nodded. Then, eyeing his superior, he asked, "Vic, what's your plan? Can we take a ship with only two full boats?"

"Actually, Jeff, I'm not planning on using the boats."

Malten muttered, "Whiskey Tango Foxtrot?"

Pope turned and walked away from the workers. "Here's what I have in mind."

M/V *TARABULUS PRIDE*

Hurtubise gawked at the nine-thousand-ton ship pounding alongside, looking as big as a small mountain. Zikri watched out the starboard side of the bridge, gauging the intruder's interval. Abruptly the bigger vessel's bow swung to port.

"My God!" Hurtubise shouted. "They're going to ram!"

The Libyan captain braced himself, then said, "Maybe not."

"What? What do you mean?"

"*Monsieur*, I think they intend to grapple."

Hurtubise took six fast heartbeats to absorb the implications. Then he spun on his heel and shouted down to Pinsard. "RPGs up here. Now!"

Before Pinsard could respond, Hurtubise was on the opposite side. "Man the machine guns! Starboard fore and aft but keep one amidships to port."

René Pinsard gave his superior a wry grin. "You're sounding very nautical this morning, *mon vieux*." Then he was gone.

M/V *DON CARLOS*

From the bridge, Gerritt Maas judged the closure nicely. He ensured that his ship established a three-knot overtake, anticipating his rival's likely move. "Steady as you go," he told the helmsman. "Wait for it . . . wait . . ."

Tarabulus Pride began veering to port, away from her assailant. Her thirty-four hundred tons answered the helm more quickly than the larger Spanish flagged vessel, but with the speed differential she could not escape.

Phil Green manned the center gun, watching for likely targets. When armed men appeared on the target vessel's superstructure, he called, "Fire!" At the same time he drew a bead on two men abaft the bridge and pressed the trigger. He walked his rounds across the targets, holding slightly low to offset the ship's rolling movement.

Several yards on either side of him, Verdugo and Ritter also opened fire. Glass shattered as 7.62 mm rounds punched their way across the superstructure. Green, mindful of Malten's caution against everyone shooting at once, held his fire when his targets went down.

M/V *TARABULUS PRIDE*

Hurtubise flung himself on the deck as incoming rounds snap-cracked overhead and ricochets pinged off the bulkheads. Zikri kept low, turning bug-eyed to the Frenchman, mouthing words that were inaudible.

An RPG gunner appeared at the port access. Hurtubise gestured in anger and frustration. "Their bridge! Shoot their bridge, you idiot!"

The shooter possessed a wealth of Middle East experience but none at sea prior to the Zodiac assault. Now he low-crawled to the aft access, raised himself to a kneeling position, and looked behind him. The blast zone was clear so he placed his sight reticle on the offending ship's bridge and pressed the trigger.

The back blast nearly destroyed the hearing of everyone on the bridge. Hurtubise, knowing what was coming, had clapped his hands over his ears, but the high decibels in the confined space were incredible. The shooter screamed in pain and collapsed backward. Hurtubise handed him another rocket and yelled, "Reload!"

M/V *DON CARLOS*

"Incoming!"

Maas did not recognize the voice of whomever screamed the warning, but he saw the rocket-propelled grenade's smoky ignition. With everyone else on the bridge, he dived to the deck and awaited the impact. It came with a loud, authoritative *smack*, punching through the near windows and exiting beyond.

"What happened?" asked the watch officer.

"Too close," Maas muttered. "We're too close for it to arm!" He giggled in giddy gratitude. He scrambled to his feet.

"Now!" Maas shouted. "Move to contact!"

With the helm over to port, *Don Carlos* cut across the remaining twenty yards of seawater and slid hull to hull. The impact sounded worse than it was: screeching steel plates protesting in a high, ringing sensation.

M/V *TARABULUS PRIDE*

Hurtubise realized that something was missing. Outgoing gunfire.

He crouched below the level of the bridge windows and stepped over the prostrate RPG man. Risking a look outside, he saw only one MAG-58 in action. The gunner was firing intermittently, alternately triggering ill-sighted bursts and ducking the retaliatory fire from the larger ship. With a fright, he realized, *They have fire superiority.*

"René!" he shouted. "René, get some gunners going."

There was no answer.

Reluctantly, Marcel Hurtubise decided that he had to take action himself. He assumed almost a sprinter's posture, bracing hands and feet on the deck, inhaled, and shot out of the bridge, headed for the nearest MAG.

Abruptly, Pinsard appeared. He shoved the body of the previous gunner aside, grasped the weapon, and swiveled it toward the nearest American shooter. He pressed the trigger as two swaths of M-60 fire intersected him at belt level. The results were a vivid crimson gout sprayed across the steel structure.

Hurtubise reeled in shock and surprise. Sprayed with his friend's blood, he shrieked in a microsecond of outraged panic.

Then he was in control of himself. He went prone again and rolled away from the gun position. Back inside the bridge, he yelled to Zikri. "We cannot win this way! You have to get away from them!"

The Libyan raised his hands in frustration. "Are you crazy? How can we? They are faster!"

Hurtubise's mind raced. He sorted through every option that occurred to him, and came up with only one that might work.

"Stop your engine! They'll shoot ahead."

Abu Yusuf Zikri knew that would only afford a temporary respite, even if it worked. But he also knew this was not the time to explain basic seamanship to a gun-wielding French mercenary. He gave the order.

M/V *DON CARLOS*

On the superstructure, the three gunners had run out of targets. Green and Verdugo had cut down the last opponent—a brave man, no doubt, but a foolish one. Green glanced to his left to acknowledge Verdugo's contribution. Then he glanced to his right and gasped at the sight.

The volunteer gunner was slumped on the deck, motionless beneath his M-60. Green suppressed the urge to go to him, but the hard-won fire superiority had to be maintained. Green shouted as loudly as he ever had.

"Medic!"

Green turned back to business. With Verdugo on the aft gun, he took turns peppering the enemy's bridge and any portholes or hatches that might afford an RPG gunner a likely shot.

Victor Pope appeared beside Green. "All clear?" he asked.

"Yessir." He looked to his right again. Dr. Faith was bending over Ritter. "How is he?"

"I don't know, Phil. The crew will take him inside, but I gotta go."

Green nodded impassively. "Good luck, Boss."

M/V *TARABULUS PRIDE*

Hurtubise sensed what was coming.

He heard Zikri give additional orders in high, rapid Arabic, and sensed the engine change pitch three decks beneath his feet. But as the ship decelerated, the Frenchman realized that the Zionist vessel's greater length would temporarily negate the speed differential. It would take a minute or more to force the other ship into an overshoot, and surely the hostile captain would compensate.

Hurtubise tapped Zikri on the shoulder. "I'm going below to organize the defense. I'll send two men up here to guard you!" Without awaiting a reply, he was gone on a far different mission.

M/V *DON CARLOS*

"Away all boarders!"

Riding rail to rail, the two ships were mere feet apart as Maas kept *Don Carlos* almost within arm's length of *Tarabulus Pride*. Victor Pope said a silent prayer, then was the first to leap across the narrow gap, feeling eerily vulnerable as he seemed to dangle suspended in space. He knew that Green and Verdugo would hose down anyone who threatened the boarders, but SEALs were conditioned to operate by stealth rather than *coup de main*.

M/V *TARABULUS PRIDE*

Pope hit the hostile deck, slumped to his knees, and instantly brought his MP-5 to the ready position. Other operators alit on either side of him. He glimpsed the two juvenile delinquents and almost laughed aloud. Both still had piratical bandanas on their heads, and Breezy, the young fool, clenched a Randall fighting knife between his teeth.

Looking around, Pope was satisfied that his men were deploying as briefed: pairs guarding the approaches fore and aft, two more maintaining a watch on the superstructure above them. Only then did he perceive that *Don Carlos* seemed to be accelerating ahead when actually *Tarabulus* was sliding astern.

Automatic fire erupted behind him. Green and Verdugo were shooting into the superstructure behind the bridge. Apparently some hostiles were trying to repel boarders.

Pope led his stern team around the aft end of the superstructure, treating the ship's exterior corners as they would a building. Visually slicing the geometric pie, they moved with the fluid precision of experienced operators, surveying each segment of deck and bulkhead as it became visible. Their timing was good: within seconds, three armed men appeared on deck, obviously hoping to take the boarders from behind. A quick exchange of gunfire produced no casualties but forced the defenders back inside.

Pope leaned down toward Breezy. "Keep them bottled up here. We'll have MG support from the ship on the other side, so don't go forward over here."

Breezy nodded in acknowledgment, gloved hands supporting his MP-5 while kneeling at the corner. Bosco stood behind him, providing double coverage. He felt almost giddy. "Shiver me timbers, matey, we made it!"

M/V *DON CARLOS*

Gerritt Maas realized that the relative motion of the two ships was changing. It took a few seconds to recognize what was occurring, but he quickly compensated.

"All stop. Back two-thirds." He did not wait for the situation to stabilize. Knowing that Pope's team needed the fire support of the M-60s, he kept the helm into the hostile vessel, feeling the hulls contact intermittently.

He picked up the mike on the tactical radio and hailed Pope. "Flipper from Dutchman, over."

Seconds passed with no reply. Maas pressed the button again. "Flipper, this is Dutchman."

". . . man, Flipper here."

"Victor, they're backing down but I can probably match them. Over."

"Ah, roger, Dutchman. Just keep abeam so our guns cover the deck. Over."

Feeling unaccustomed excitement, Maas lapsed into his native accent. "Chur ting. Ah, you going to Point Alfa or Bravo?"

"Alfa. Watch for us. Out."

Looking across the several meters separating them, Maas saw Pope lead the first assault team up the ladder toward the bridge.

M/V *TARABULUS PRIDE*

Pope paused just below the top of the ladder, his weapon poised to engage any threat that peered over the lip of the platform. He waited what seemed a long minute—actually it was less than ten seconds—before he heard Maas's exec on the tactical net. "Flipper, it looks clear from here." The officer spoke unaccented English—rare for a seafarer from Maine.

Nice to have somebody watching over your shoulder, Pope thought—a friendly observer with a better view of the top of the world you were about to enter half blind. Those last three feet could be critical.

Victor Pope believed in leading from the front. It was not always the best choice, because it put the commander at the point of contact, and when the action began, inevitably made him a shooter more than a leader. But it was his way and the others accepted it.

Pope made a lobbing gesture with his left hand. Behind and below him, two operators pulled the pins on concussion grenades and tossed them over their leader's head. One short, one long.

The black and yellow cylinders rolled toward the bridge and exploded with stunning effect. Before the sound had abated, Pope was up the last steps and lateralled right, giving his team room to maneuver past him.

Automatic fire spurted from inside the bridge as somebody hosed a long, searching burst from an AK. An SSI man went down, cursing loudly with a round through his calf. Another Mark 3 sailed through the open access and its eight-ounce charge detonated, blowing out much of the remaining glass.

Pfizer and his partner were instantly through the access, their suppressed MP-5s clattering in short, precise bursts. Three and four rounds. Two more bursts, then silence.

"Clear!"

"Clear!"

Pope signaled the other operators to watch fore and aft while he entered the bridge. Two men were sprawled in positions that can only be assumed by people who are dead. Three others were flat on the deck, one bleeding from the nose and ears.

Everybody's hands and feet were tied with flex cuffs, including the two corpses. Pope glanced at the dead men, noting that both had been killed by multiple head shots. Pfizer saw the look, knew its meaning, and said, "They got body armor, Boss."

Pope stepped outside, standing on the starboard wing of the bridge. He waved and saw Maas return the gesture. Pope saw him turn and speak to two crewmen.

Back inside, Pope knelt beside the oldest man on the deck. "Where is Marcel Hurtubise?"

The man, obviously an Arab, shook his head, sucking in air. *He's still stunned*, Pope realized. He waited a moment, then asked, "Are you the captain?"

Abu Yusuf Zikri shook his head again. "No. Captain gone."

Your mother eats pork, Pope thought. "Where is Hurtubise?"

The Libyan closed his eyes, as if willing the apparition to vanish. Then he felt something sharply uncomfortable in his left nostril. When he looked, he realized that the American had a three-inch knife pressed inside the nasal cavity, and the blade was slowly rising. Soft flesh parted and blood began to flow.

"Below! He is below!"

"Where's the captain?" More upward pressure.

"Me! I am captain!"

"Name?"

Tikri began to cry. He sucked in more oxygen, inhaling some blood at the same time. Choking and panting, he managed to get the syllables out. "Tikri. Abu Yusuf Tikri."

The knife disappeared and the pain abated.

One of the operators was behind Pope. "Boss, the bridge crew is here."

Pope turned to see the men whom Maas had recruited to conn the ship. He stood up. "All right, let's drag these people out of here and let these gentlemen get to work."

M/V *DON CARLOS*

Maas heard, "Dutchman, Flipper. Point Alfa secure. Proceeding to Bravo."

The captain knew that the SSI men were about to enter the belly of the beast, descending toward the engine room. He acknowledged Pope's call, then signaled the new bridge watch on *Tarabulus Pride*. Both vessels resumed course at a reduced ten knots.

Satisfied that things were temporarily under control, Maas turned to his other colleagues. "Gentlemen, you may stand by until we hear from Pope. I do not think you should go aboard until the ship is fully in our control."

Alex Cohen nodded, indicating neither dissension nor enthusiasm. Bernard Langevin said, "There's no hurry, Captain. The yellow cake isn't going anywhere."

M/V *TARABULUS PRIDE*

Pope quickly briefed his team on deck amidships. His assets were being diluted, having to leave guards on the bridge and the stern. He ran the numbers: one casualty plus four security men topside and two manning M-60s on *Don Carlos* left nine to go belowdecks, including himself.

"All right," he began. "Two and three-man stacks, everybody going down and aft to avoid confusion. We'll leave two men to guard the passageways forward in case some tangos are up forward. Remember, they have body armor and hearing protection, so don't take chances. Clear any suspicious compartments with flash-bangs, and if you have to shoot, double tap above the eyebrows.

"Second: look for booby traps. If you find an undogged hatch, push it open before you enter. Better that way than step into an IED. If it's dogged, Malten and Pfizer will blow the hinges.

"Third: Jeff's team will start here. My team will enter from the other side. Wait for my call so we all go in together.

"Everybody clear?"

There were no questions, nor did Pope expect any. "Okay. Pfizer, Pascoe, Collier, and Jacobs. On me."

Pope led his team aft, around the stern where Bosco and Breezy still guarded the deck portside. Approaching the corner, Pope called, "Boscombe, Breezy, you copy?"

"Read you, Boss." It was Bosco.

"We're coming around your end. You guys take the point and move forward of the access while we enter. I'll leave one man inside while we head below."

"Gotcha."

Moments later, Bosco felt Pope's hand on his shoulder. Without fur-

ther words, Bosco and Breezy advanced side by side, Breezy's eyes following his HK's muzzle that swept the upper deck. Once past the
hatch, they stopped while Pope prepared to enter. He spoke into his lip
mike.

"Jeff, we're ready on this side."

Malten replied from the other side. "On your mark."

"Okay, I'm testing the hatch. The handle's not moving."

"Same here, Boss."

"Prepare to blow it." He looked over his shoulder. "Tom, you're on."

Pope stood aside while Pfizer quickly attached plastique to the access door's hinges and handle. He linked the three charges with primer
cord and inserted an adjustable one-minute detonator. "Fifteen seconds?"

Pope nodded. Then he called, "Jeff, set your detonator for one-five
seconds. Start on my mark."

"Ready, Vic."

"Ready, ready, go!"

Malten twisted the dial one-quarter of a rotation. "Fire in the hole."

Bosco and Breezy did a reverse moon walk, muzzles elevated, while
Pope's team retreated to a safe distance. The Composition Four charges
detonated in a rolling, metallic eruption that left Pope's hatch dangling
at an awkward angle. While the team stacked behind him, he peeked inside and saw Malten's men entering over their flattened door, scanning
left and right.

"Clear!" Malten shouted.

"Cover us," Pope replied. He wedged himself through the opening
and the others followed. "Jacobs, you stand by here. Give a shout if you
see something."

Malten looked at his superior. "Well, Boss, they know we're here
now."

"Roger that." Pope adjusted his protective goggles and took position
behind Pascoe. Checking visually with Malten, he said, "See you guys on
the next level."

———————

"They're coming," Rivera said. The explosions two decks above could
only mean one thing.

"Of course they are," Hurtubise replied. Considering what was
about to happen, he remained unusually calm. Especially since he was
not accustomed to working with explosives.

"How much longer?" the Spaniard asked.

"Maybe ten minutes. Just keep them out of here until I signal. Leave Georges and Felix here to guard the entrance."

Alfonso Rivera was a competent young man within certain limits, but shipboard tactics remained beyond the ken of his experience. Nonetheless, he hefted his AKM and climbed the ladder from the engine room to the next level, remembering to dog the hatch behind him. He wondered how he was going to hold off a dozen or more intruders with three men besides himself.

———————

Approaching the second level down, Pope's operators heard the machinery more clearly than before. Even though the SSI prize crew manned the bridge, the ship's engine remained under control of the black gang.

Malten led the starboard team, descending the narrow ladders between decks. A few yards away, on the opposite side of the hull, Pope's team kept pace. The two elements were able to maintain visual contact with one another most of the time, communicating by hand signals and occasional whispers over the tactical frequency of their headsets. Pope wanted to present the defenders with a dual-axis offense, concentrating two pairs of leading shooters against whatever the Frenchmen deployed against him.

Malten and Pope took no chances. Knowing that defenders had to be waiting on one or both of the last two levels, the operators stopped to drop flash-bangs down the ladder on each side. The second man in each team produced a Mark 84, pulled the pin, and on Pope's signal dropped the grenades down the ladders.

The SSI operators had eye and ear protection but reflexively most turned their heads. Two seconds later the stun grenades detonated with 170 decibels, a horrific sound only amplified in the confined steel spaces within the hull.

Instantly the first two men on each side were down the ladders, scanning left and right.

"Clear!"

"Clear!"

Finding nothing on the second deck, Malten and Pope advanced several steps aft to the next ladder. With compartments on either side, they took time to clear each one in turn, the last man in each team leaving the doors fully open to mark them as checked.

The teams proceeded to the next ladder. They knew that this time somebody was certainly waiting for them.

On the next level, Alfonso Rivera licked his lips. His throat was dry but he was as well prepared as possible, with body armor, gas mask, and hearing protection. He doubted that the intruders would use flash-bangs this close to the engine room, as Mark 84s could ignite fuel vapors, and nobody wanted to fight aboard a burning ship at sea. He glanced at his companions: Georges appeared calm; Felix fidgeted constantly.

From interrogating the bridge crew and one of the wounded mercenaries, the SSI men knew what to expect. Gas would be negated by the defenders' masks, and smoke would only confuse matters. In extreme close quarters, where a tenth of a second was a meaningful measure, it would be easy to confuse friends and enemies. But a straight-out attack would surely result in friendly casualties.

Pope dropped a Mark 84.

The five-inch-long object clattered down the steps and rolled along the grilled platform where the defenders stood. Instinctively, the three men turned away from the impending blast that could blind and deafen them.

Pope and Pascoe were instantly down the ladder on their respective sides. The next men in the stack were immediately behind them, deploying left and right. Pfizer tripped on the next to last step, tumbling into Collier and causing momentary confusion that could have been fatal.

"Freeze!"

"Ne pas se déplacer!"

"Drop the weapons!"

"Laisser tomber les armes!"

Rivera was closest to the intruders. Wide-eyed behind his mask, he looked down at the grenade. The detonator had been removed. He realized that he had been bluffed and dropped his Kalashnikov. Slowly he raised his hands.

A few feet farther away, the gunman called Felix had a fraction more time to react to the collision at the bottom of the steps. He raised his AKM from the low ready position, aimed at the closest opponent, and began to press the trigger.

Eight 9 mm rounds shattered the faceplate of his mask. Pope's and Pascoe's suppressed MP-5s clattered audibly from ten to twelve feet away, spilling empty brass onto the deck. Felix's body went limp as a rag doll and seemed to collapse inward upon itself.

Rivera and Georges were screaming inside their masks, waving their empty hands. "No shoot!"

"*Ne pas tirer!*"

Collier defaulted to his television youth. "Cuff 'em, Danno!"

While the survivors were secured with flex cuffs, Pope and Malten considered their next move. Only one hatchway separated them from the engine room, and as they decided how to blow their way in, the door slowly opened. A dirty gray rag appeared at the end of a hand.

"Do not shoot! We surrender."

Seconds later, Victor Pope looked into the eyes of Marcel Hurtubise.

M/V *DON CARLOS*

Gerritt Maas could hardly believe what he heard.

"I say again," Pope advised, "the ship is secure."

The captain exchanged disbelieving glances with Cohen and Langevin. "That was quick," Langevin exclaimed. "I thought sure it would take longer."

Maas puffed aggressively on his pipe, as if seeking an explanation from it. "Well, maybe they saw how things were going and did the smart thing. But I guess you gentlemen will want to see for yourself."

"Yes, sir," Cohen responded. "Can we get close enough to jump deck to deck again?"

"Yeah, it'll take a few minutes though. I think that Captain Harvey will want to lay to."

Langevin was headed for the exit when he pulled up. "Captain, what about your man? The one who was shot."

Maas removed his pipe and blew a smoke ring. "Oh, he's probably going to be okay. Dr. Faith is still with him."

M/V *TARABULUS PRIDE*

Langevin stalked up to Pope on the bridge and offered congratulations. "That was good work, Commander. Faster than I expected."

"Yeah, I'm still wondering about that, Doctor. We're searching the engine room and will look everywhere else once we get time. Right now we're still securing the prisoners and Cap'n Harvey's prize crew is learning about this ship."

"Well, they have their job and I have mine. I'd like to look at the cargo."

Pope nodded toward the bow. "Apparently the yellow cake is in the forward hold. But all the hatches are secured and it'll take a while to open them."

Malten's voice crackled over Pope's radio headset. "Vic, this is Jeff. Come back."

"Yes, Jeff. Go."

"You better come down here again."

"On the way."

"What's up?" Langevin asked.

"Something in the engineering spaces. You're welcome to come along."

———

Malten met Pope at the hatchway. The junior SEAL extended a hand with an unwelcome sight. Pope's eyes widened. "Command detonation?"

"Affirm. We're looking for more."

Pope took the Yugoslavian made device and turned it over. "How much of a charge?"

"Semtex. About twelve or fifteen pounds."

"Where was it?"

Malten turned and walked aft. "Down here, under one of the mounts."

"Where's the initiator?" Pope asked.

"Haven't found it."

Pope glanced around, noting the myriad of possible hiding places. "I'll get you more guys to search. Meanwhile, I'm going to have a word with Mr. Hurtubise."

———

In the galley where the crew and surviving mercs were held, Marcel Hurtubise saw Pope coming. Both knew what to expect.

Pope laid the detonator on the table where the Frenchman sat, hands cuffed behind him.

Hurtubise pretended to examine it. Then he looked up. "Most interesting."

Leaning forward, Pope braced himself with both hands on the table. He positioned his face eight inches from Hurtubise's. "Where are the others?"

"Whatever do you mean?"

Pope's hands shot out, grasping Hurtubise by the collar and pulling him off the bench. The American took a nylon line off his tactical vest, looped it around the prisoner's throat, and hauled him thirty feet across the deck. Other prisoners scrambled to get out of the way.

"Talk to me," Pope said. His voice was low, calm, chilling.

Hurtubise gasped for air. "I . . . cannot . . . breathe . . ."

Pope loosened the line slightly. "Well?"

"I am . . . a prisoner. You cannot . . ."

The former SEAL snugged up the line, hefted it over one shoulder, and proceeded to drag the bound man another twenty feet. Hurtubise's face was turning a bluish hue.

Pope leaned over the prostrate Frenchman. "I don't think you're in a position to tell me what I can't do!" He delivered a swift kick to the man's ribs. "I can hang you from the overhead, *monsieur*. If you die, I'm no worse off than if you don't talk." He added another hard kick for emphasis. "Well?"

Hurtubise realized that he had sustained a cracked rib. After some gasps and croaks, he managed, "One more."

"Where?"

"Behind . . . the main . . . control panel."

Pope dropped the line and walked toward the exit. He adjusted his lip mike. "Jeff, Vic here."

"Yeah. Go."

"Look behind the main control panel."

Less than one minute later Malten's voice was back. "Got it. But what about the initiator?"

"Stand by one."

Hurtubise was still on one side, gasping for breath. Pope had not loosened the nylon line more than a fraction of an inch.

"Where's the remote detonator?"

The victim gagged and coughed. "One in my cabin. The other beneath the chart table."

Pope ran a finger between the line and Hurtubise's chafed neck. Then he stood erect and called Malten again. "Jeff, I'm sending somebody to get the remotes. But keep looking." He glanced down at the exhausted mercenary. "I don't trust this bastard."

"Will do, Boss."

Pope looked around. The ship's original crew and the remaining mercenaries regarded the tall American with unblinking interest. An idea stirred inside Victor Pope's bald head.

"Bridge, this is Pope."

"Bridge, aye." It was Harvey, the British captain now conning the vessel.

"Cap'n, we're removing two explosive charges from the engineering spaces but I think there might be more. I recommend that we evacuate to *Don Carlos* until we know we're safe."

After a pause, Harvey came back. "That's prudent, Commander. But we still haven't opened the holds. I'm told that will take some time because they're welded."

"It's your call, Skipper. But we may not have much time. Over."

Harvey took a moment to ponder the situation. "Stand by, please. I'll consult with Captain Maas on the ship-to-ship frequency."

Pope looked around again. Nearly twenty captives were guarded by Bosco and Breezy, who had run out of decks to watch.

"You two," Pope said. "Start these people topside along the starboard rail. We can save some time by getting them up there now."

Bosco grinned. "Right, Boss. But, uh, what about him?" He indicated Hurtubise.

Pope looked down and registered mild surprise, as if just noticing the supine prisoner. "Him? Well, he's going to stay here." Pope wrapped the loose end of his line around a stanchion and secured it with a half hitch. "If he's lying to me, he'll ride this boat to the bottom."

Marcel Hurtubise heard the words and concentrated on the man's tone. From a lifetime of closely reading human behavior, he thought he had taken the measure of Victor Pope. But now was not the time for discourse. The Frenchman emitted a realistic gagging, choking sound.

It was not imitation.

M/V *DON CARLOS*

"Everybody back?" Langevin had not made a head count, and as chief investigator he felt responsible for the operation at this point.

"Everybody but one," Pope said.

Langevin looked around. At that moment *Don Carlos*'s sailors and the SSI men were leading the captives to a holding area. Cohen was with them—he seemed especially interested in one of Zikri's radio operators.

"Vic, are you really going to let that Frenchman go down if the ship sinks?"

Pope almost grinned. "Well, let's just say I want him to think so."

"My God," the scientist exclaimed. "If there is another charge hidden someplace, the ship could sink pretty fast. I mean, it's not very big."

Langevin lowered his voice. "Look," he began. "My area is physics, but I know one or two things about explosives. If Hurtubise is hog-tied, he can't detonate any hidden charges if even he wanted to. So what's the point?"

"My point is, Doctor, that he could've set a timer. And I don't think it would've been for very long because he wouldn't want us looking in the hold. If we get some contraband yellow cake, that can be used against him."

Langevin lowered his gaze to the deck, obviously pondering the SEAL's logic. "Okay, that makes sense. But how much longer will you wait?"

Pope looked at his watch. "It's now been about fifty minutes. I'm going to let him wait an hour-plus and then I'll go back."

"Well, okay. But I sure would like to get to that hold before something . . ."

A low, rumbling *ka-whump* interrupted the physicist. Heads swiveled toward *Tarabulus Pride*, dead in the water two hundred yards away.

"That's it!" Pope exclaimed. Ignoring Lanvegin, he called over the side. "Jeff! Fire up the Zodiac! Get me over there right now!"

M/V *TARABULUS PRIDE*

The old freighter was settling by the stern when Pope scrambled up the accommodation ladder. He dashed down to the galley and found Hurtubise still bound hand and foot.

"Ah, Commander," the Frenchman exclaimed. *"Bienvenue à bord!"*

Pope barely resisted the urge to put a boot in the man's face. "I ought to let you sink!"

"But you will not. Just as I knew you wouldn't." The smug tone in Hurtubise's voice told Pope the story. *He read me all along.*

The American leaned down, produced his knife, and held it to Hurtubise's nose. Pope wondered if the mercenary had heard of Captain Zikri's acquaintance with that same piece of tempered steel. The blade made no obvious impression on the phlegmatic saboteur, so Pope cut the flex cuff on the Frenchman's feet. Hurtubise was hauled upright and shoved toward the exit.

Descending the boarding ladder was awkward with his hands bound behind his back, but Hurtubise wasted little time getting off the doomed ship. As the Zodiac motored away, he looked back. The bow was well clear of the water now, the hull beginning to list to port. "I fear that Captain Zikri will be disappointed in me," he said. The crooked smile on his face was more than Pope could abide. He erased the superior grin with a right hook that laid the offender prone in the rubber craft.

"Watch your mouth," Pope said.

90

M/V *DON CARLOS*

A day out of Casablanca, the SSI team held a meeting to discuss options. There had been time on the way north to "interview" the former passengers and crew of M/V *Tarabulus Pride*.

Bernard Langevin scanned the interrogation reports and shook his head. "This Hurtubise is a crafty SOB, I'll say that for him. He left two fairly small charges for us to find and put the big ones where we wouldn't see them unless we inspected the hull. And there wasn't time for that."

"But why'd he bother to scuttle the ship?" Malten asked. "He still knew he'd get caught."

"Well, yes, but there's more to it," Langevin replied. "Basically, no evidence, no crime. Look, we know the ship had yellow cake aboard. But even if we had some of it, who's to say where it was headed?"

Pope was incredulous. "My God, Bernie, we *know* where it was headed."

"Sure we do. But how would we prove it? The cargo manifest didn't list it, of course, and the ports of call included three countries *except* Iran. As long as nobody talks, everybody's safe."

"How's that?"

"Well, look at it legally," Langevin replied. "Basically, we committed piracy. That's right: we seized a ship conducting rightful passage through international waters. We had no formal standing with any government— especially the United States—and that's how Washington wants it. So it's a standoff. Neither side can complain without drawing unwelcome attention on itself."

"Well I'll be dipped." Pope turned to Cohen. "Alex, what do you make of all this?"

The Israeli agent shrugged eloquently. "Near as I can tell, Bernie's right. But the main thing is that we prevented the yellow cake from reaching Iran."

"I still don't understand one thing," Pfizer said. "Why didn't they rig the ship for scuttling before? I mean, if they intended to surrender anyway, why go through all the trouble? They lost people they didn't have to."

"Good question," Langevin replied. "From what I got from their captain, he didn't know about it. My guess is that he wouldn't have allowed Hurtubise to prepare for scuttling. From his view, getting boarded and having the cargo confiscated was preferable to losing the ship, even with insurance coverage. Looks like Hurtubise just pretended to go along with the program until he saw how things shook out."

Pope asked, "So what happens to Hurtubise and his mercs?"

"That's beyond me. But I'm somewhere between a cynic and a skeptic regarding international legal matters. After all, neither the U.S., French, Libyan, or Iranian governments want this thing publicized." He wanted to add, *I'm not so sure about the Israelis.* "Besides that, who would we turn him over to? The only provable offense was in Chad, and if he goes there I guarandamntee he'll disappear in a New York minute. My guess is they'll be released."

Phil Green was still mulling over the death of Don Pace. "Excuse me, sir, but these bastards killed two of our guys. And where's the Chad Government in all this? After all, their contractor was smuggling yellow cake, and killed some troopies in Chad."

Bernard Langevin, with wider knowledge of the world than Phil Green, tried to recall a time when he shared the younger man's sense of justice. He could not.

"I guess this isn't the first time that two PMCs have shot at each other, and I don't suppose it'll be the last." Gathering his thoughts, Langevin added, "The Chadian government has lots of people. Believe me, it doesn't care about a few casualties. Not even those that SSI trained."

Green regarded the scientist with a level gaze, equal to equal. "Don't make it right, sir."

Langevin chose his reply with care. "No, it don't."

SSI OFFICES

Derringer walked into the firm's lobby, barely nodded to the receptionist and guard, and proceeded straight through the security door. SSI's
leadership was awaiting him in the boardroom.

Marshall Wilmont asked, "What's the bad news, Mike?"

Derringer set down his fedora and smoothed his thinning hair.
"What makes you think it's bad news?"

"Mike, you're a lousy poker player. I can read your face, and right
now you look like you're holding a pair of deuces."

Derringer began to pace. The others had rarely seen him so distracted; Sandy Carmichael and Frank Leopole looked at each other, concern in their eyes. Omar Mohammed remained unflappable as ever, but
he followed the CEO's circular pattern across the carpet, sensing the
nuances of posture and expression.

At length Derringer dropped anchor. Turning to face his colleagues,
he said, "O'Connor laid it out for me. We've been had. In fact, everybody
involved has been had, including DoD and State."

"What the hell do you mean?" Wilmont's tone contained more
anger than he intended.

Derringer took a seat at the head of the conference table. "You all know how we were worried about credible intelligence on this mission. Not even Dave Dare could break out the real sources. He came closer than most, apparently, because he traced what he could back to one source."

"Israel?" Carmichael already had her suspicions.

"You got it," Derringer replied. "O'Connor may be a liberal leftover of the Carter era, but he's able to tap some diplomatic sources. This is not for publication, people, but when I arrived, he was with John Shaw of the U.N. Secretariat. They knew each other at Brown."

Mohammed sat upright. "Shaw? He monitors private military contractors, doesn't he?"

"That's right. He's even less of a friend to us than Ryan O'Connor, but neither of them likes being stiffed by Tel Aviv."

Nobody asked the obvious question; everyone present knew that Derringer would fill in the blanks.

"It turns out that the Israelis were behind the yellow cake shipment. It's part of a plan to focus attention on Iran's nuke program. But State and the U.N. didn't know that at the time, otherwise they probably wouldn't have sent us after it."

Leopole's tanned hands were clenched into fists. "How do they know that, Admiral?"

"They wouldn't reveal sources, Frank, and I guess I can't blame them. But they talked freely in my presence, and there's no doubt that both State and the U.N. are sure of the facts." Derringer made a dismissive gesture with one hand. "For all I know, the leaks could be from inside Israel. Evidently there's a power play under way in their intel community, on top of arguments about what to do about Iran."

Carmichael gave Leopole a sideways glance. He nodded.

"Admiral, while you were out, we got word from Victor Pope in Casablanca. Langevin took the captured crew and French mercs ashore to hand them over to French and Libyan diplomats. Where they'll go from there we don't know. But Cohen went with the ship's radio operator, who had been feeding him information on *Tarabulus Pride*'s location and activities. Nobody's seen them since."

Derringer's face betrayed his emotion: disbelieving anger.

Leopole interjected. "There's more, and it fits with what you've said, sir. Pope and Maas both confirm that Aujali, the radioman, was an Israeli asset who'd been blackmailed into cooperating in exchange for release of some relatives in Israel. We think Cohen probably took him there to complete that part of the bargain."

"I don't understand," Derringer replied. "Why would Alex Cohen just up and disappear? He's on our payroll, for Pete's sake!"

Mohammed cleared his throat, gaining the attention of everyone in the room. "This seems to be a day of revelations, Admiral. David Dare called for you just after you left so I spoke to him. It's after the fact, but here's what he found:

"Cohen wasn't just coordinating with the Israelis; he was working with Mossad, which apparently was pulling everybody's strings. Obviously he didn't want to answer any embarrassing questions. Once Mossad learned the ship involved, they made sure that we and Hurtubise knew what each other knew. The Israelis wanted us focused on the ship, and the ship aware that we were closing in. It's a perfect game; a classic double cross to the exclusion of both parties for the satisfaction of the third party. Israel."

Derringer shook his head as if avoiding a pesky fly. "How did Dave learn that?"

"He's waiting to talk to you. Whenever you can call back."

Leopole was on his feet. "The bastards! They . . ."

Wilmont was almost never involved in operations but he recognized the anger building in the room. SSI still had potential contracts in Israel and the Middle East. "Easy, Frank. Remember, they're protecting themselves from possible nuclear attack."

People rose from their seats as their voices became shrill.

"Damn it! We lost people on this op!"

"What the hell's the matter with you?"

Derringer rapped on the table. It was one of the few times he regretted not having a gavel. "Hey! Everybody! Knock it off. We're all on the same side here."

When the voices subsided, Derringer regained control of the meeting. "Where's *Don Carlos* now? Still in Casablanca?"

"Yes, sir," Leopole replied. "Maas is awaiting orders, which he'll pass to Pope. I imagine everybody wants to come home, especially those who were in Chad."

Michael Derringer slumped visibly. He seemed burdened with a weight on his head and shoulders. Looking around the room, he said, "I haven't told you everything yet. State wants us to stay in position."

Carmichael cocked her head. "Sir, what does that mean? We keep our people there? For how long?"

Shaking his head, Derringer said, "I don't know, Sandy. But I'm allowed to tell you that something's brewing in Iran."

M/V *DON CARLOS*

With little to occupy them in port, Gerritt Maas and Victor Pope had
taken to walking the ship twice a day. Maas had been to Casablanca previously, but the city's exotic reputation held little interest for the former
SEAL. He preferred to exercise, walk, and talk.

The Dutch skipper tapped his pipe bowl and regarded the Ameri-
can. Maas finally felt comfortable enough to ask a personal question.
"Victor, I understand that you considered becoming a priest before the
Navy."

Pope thought, *He's been talking to Derringer.* "That's right."

"Could I ask why you changed your mind?"

"Oh, there's a couple of reasons. Even after the Second Vatican
Council I was willing to consider the priesthood, but eventually it just
wasn't the same church anymore."

"When was the Vatican Council?"

"It sat from 1962 to '65. John XXIII and Paul VI."

"My God. You couldn't have been born yet!"

Pope laughed. "Well, there were other reasons. In my early twenties
I thought about spending the rest of my life celibate, and it just wasn't

for me." He gave a rare grin. "Besides, neither the Jesuits nor Bene-
dictines issue firearms."

They continued walking aft, momentarily content to pace in silence. Then Maas said, "Sometimes the occupation finds the man. Like
me. I grew up in a farming family—had no interest in the sea until a
friend's father took me sailing."

Pope nodded quietly. Approaching the stern, he said, "I always enjoyed athletics, competition, and shooting. The SEALs seemed the
biggest challenge. But sometimes . . ."

"Yes?"

"Well, sometimes I wish I could just do the job, you know? Without the responsibility. Sometimes I wish I could just be like . . . them."
He gestured toward Bosco and Breezy, sitting on a tarp spread on the
fantail.

The two friends were still practicing their pirate routine while
cleaning the M-60s. According to one's perspective, either they had perfected the act beyond all reasoning, or it still needed a great deal of
work.

Bosco set aside a spare barrel, cocked a squinty eye at his partner,
and pitched his voice into a low, gravelly octave somewhere between
Wally Beery and Yosemite Sam. "Aye, matey, when we took the *Tarabulus*, the decks ran red!"

In a poor Johnny Depp imitation, Breezy replied, "Avast! You're the
second best pirate I ever saw."

"Second best? Why's that?"

Breezy explained, "You need a peg leg and a parrot named Carl
Bob."

"Well, matey, next time we're ashore for grog, we can go shopping
at a pet store. But by Davy Jones's locker, I'm keeping both me legs."

At that clue, the friends broke into something resembling a song:

"Fifteen men on a dead man's chest.
Yo ho ho and a bottle of rum!
Drink and the devil had done for the rest!
Yo ho ho and a bottle of rum!
The mate was fixed by the bosun's pike,
The bosun brained with a marlinspike
And cooky's throat was marked belike,
It had been gripped by fingers ten;

And there they lay, all good dead men
Like break o'day in a boozing ken.
Yo ho ho and a bottle of rum!"

Unseen by the latter-day buccaneers, Victor Pope regarded the happy youngsters and envied their buoyant emotions. He knew that the mood would not last long.